FERRY DOWN

By Brian Callison

A Flock of Ships
A Plague of Sailors
The Dawn Attack
A Web of Salvage
Trapp's War
A Ship is Dying
A Frenzy of Merchantmen
The Judas Ship
Trapp's Peace
The Auriga Madness
The Sextant
Spearfish
The Bone Collectors
A Thunder of Crude
Trapp and World War Three
The Trojan Hearse
Crocodile Trapp
Ferry Down

FERRY DOWN

BRIAN CALLISON

HarperCollins*Publishers*

HarperCollins*Publishers*
77-85 Fulham Palace Road,
Hammersmith, London W6 8JB

Published by HarperCollins*Publishers* 1998
1 3 5 7 9 8 6 4 2

A catalogue record for this book
is available from the British Library

ISBN 0 00 223806 3

Set in Meridien by Rowland Phototypesetting Ltd,
Bury St Edmunds, Suffolk

Printed and bound in Great Britain by
Caledonian International Book Manufacturing Ltd, Glasgow

AUTHOR'S NOTE

Early in the morning of 7 April 1990, the 12,000-ton Bahamian-registered ro-ro ferry *Scandinavian Star* caught fire in position 58° 34' N 10° 43' E, while on a scheduled service passage between Oslo, Norway, and Frederikshavn in Denmark. She had sailed with a crew complement of ninety-nine, drawn from nine different nationalities, and 383 passengers.

In the ensuing holocaust, 156 passengers and two crew members perished, most from the effects of smoke inhalation. The cause of the fire was found to be arson. While a few individuals made efforts to save life at considerable risk to their own, the crew made little organized attempt either to inhibit the fire's spread, or to evacuate passengers from smoke-affected areas. Even when the ship was abandoned, uncertainty still prevailed as to whether or not anyone remained aboard.

During the previous month the ferry had arrived in Europe from the USA, where she had been providing day cruises out of Miami. There she was transferred into new ownership, and a new crew hired. Many of them had poor, and in some cases no, knowledge of English, the ship's working language. On the night of the disaster voyage only nine of the *Scandinavian Star*'s crew had sailed with the vessel under her former management and were familiar with her: the rest were unacquainted with the ship. Although carrying the necessary safety certificates required under national and international law to carry up to 1,052 passengers on the trade in which she engaged, certain flaws in the ship's design, maintenance, manning and operating procedures were later found to exist.

While drawing, for some matters of fact, on passages from the Norwegian official report on the circumstances leading to the loss of the *Scandinavian Star*, the novel that follows is not, in any other respect, the story of that ill-fated ship. Most certainly it does not, and is in no way intended to, portray any individual involved in that tragic voyage. Neither does it attempt to account for, or imply any explanation for, the apparent shortcomings of those managers and ship's staff who were held to be responsible, at least in part, for the flawed preparation of the vessel, nor for the actions – or perhaps more properly, the omissions – of some crew members during the disaster itself.

It is the story of an entirely fictional roll-on roll-off passenger ferry of a type becoming ever more rare in northern European waters. Soon, thanks to long-awaited maritime safety legislation approved by the European Council of Ministers, the last of them will be gone.

. . . or gone, at least, from northern European waters.

Certain nations in other parts of the world have still to ratify international proposals specifically intended to improve the safety of through-deck ferries, which were first tabled in 1990.

In order to speculate with any semblance of realism on how disaster might strike a long-haul ferry inadequately managed and inappropriately crewed, I felt it important first to observe how vessels operated by a company pre-eminent in the passenger-ship industry maintain the stringent safety standards of which they can be justly proud.

In that context I am grateful for the support and technical assistance afforded me in the writing of this novel by P&O North Sea Ferries, and, in particular, to the captains and crew members of the MV *Norsea*.

I understand, now, why ferry transport can quite properly be regarded as being one of the safest means of travel.

Brian Callison 1998

CATACLYSM

'Sailormen 'ave their faults,' said the night-watchman,
frankly.
'I'm not denying it. I used to 'ave myself when I was at
sea.'

W.W. JACOBS (1863–1943)

When Second Officer Delucci registered an audible alert and turned
to see a red light blinking on the bridge fire warning panel, he was
sceptical.

The light indicated that someone had triggered a manual alarm
in way of cabins 312 to 320 on C deck, starboard side. Either
that, or a fault had developed in the system, a not inconceivable
alternative in a near-thirty-year-old ship, and Delucci's scepticism
was justified.

The Captain's night orders were unambiguous. The officer of
the watch was to call him the instant any situation gave rise for
concern. The instruction is both traditional and prudent.

An equally prudent move on the part of the watchkeeper is to
take a moment to reappraise such initial concern before grabbing
too hastily and too habitually for the hotline. Delucci had learned
to follow that course of action from occasionally acrimonious
experience. It helps you hang on to your job, for a start. Which
was why, at seventeen minutes past two in the morning, with
the Old Man snatching a much-needed respite before docking in
Sweden in a few hours' time, Second Officer Delucci's reluctance
to rouse him only to be judged to have overreacted was understandable. And particularly in view of the part of ship from which
the alert appeared to be emanating.

C deck, far below the bridge and situated just above her waterline, was largely taken up by the roll-on roll-off ferry *Orion Ven-*

1

turer's car deck, a vast internal hangar extending almost her entire 148-metre length. Although entry to the echoing steel cavern was expressly prohibited to all but authorized crew members when at sea, corridors running either side of it afforded drivers access to their vehicles on arrival and departure. That restriction on movement throughout C deck didn't, in itself, cause Delucci to question the alarm's veracity. Those same corridors also served a single row of economy class cabins situated to port and starboard of the vessel, and so might normally have been expected to experience passenger or steward activity at any time during the passage.

And after all: critical events do have to originate somewhere, and be discovered by someone. It was simply that the fire monitor, intended to facilitate an informed response by the bridge watch to any emergency, appeared to be behaving illogically in defining the whereabouts of that hypothetical someone who might just have chanced upon flame . . . or even flood?

Delucci found himself drawn into a moment of masochistic digression at that unthinkable prospect. But find yourself up to your knees in water in a ship – especially a ro-ro ferry – and you're likely to hit the first panic button to hand without reading the label on it.

. . . anyway, the board pinpointed the warning as having been activated by a manual alarm positioned in the aftermost section of the vessel. Even more specifically, by an alarm positioned in the short length of starboard service corridor running between cabins C312 and C320 . . . it was an irony not entirely lost on Delucci that the dilemma causing his indecision at two-something-o'clock in the middle of the night was actually being generated by a system expressly designed to *encourage* prompt decision-making on his part.

But, so far as he was aware, those particular cabins, still awaiting refurbishment, had been left unallocated on this, the *Venturer*'s maiden UK–Scandinavia service under her new owners. No stewards would be working C deck, that was for sure – the ship was operating at minimal manning levels in order to undercut the established ferry companies running the North Sea routes. It also seemed highly unlikely that any passenger would have found cause to explore an unoccupied and pretty spartan area at the expense of the other on-board distractions available . . . which only left the duty night-watchman on his rounds as the possible harbinger of doom. But *he* carried a walkie-talkie and would have radioed confirmation of any emergency to the bridge in addition to triggering a local alert.

. . . but the red light indicating a fire or other crisis in way of empty starboard cabins C312 to C320 was indisputably on. Which, pursuing logic full circle, meant that either the hypothetical someone who shouldn't be down there in the first place had nevertheless pressed an alarm button . . . or that the lamp, an intellectually moronic light bulb, all said and done, was in fact faulty and merely 'crying wolf'?

And ever present in the young officer's deliberations was an awareness that ship's captains do tend to display a predilection towards unjust accusation of the well intentioned innocent. Especially when called at two-whatever in the morning just to fix a bloody fuse!

Delucci chewed his lip uncertainly, frowned, then cancelled out the alert. The little red light blinked off and the cabinet, schematically displaying the arrangement of all nine decks of the combined passenger and vehicle ferry *Orion Venturer*, reverted to passive status. Not one of the 56 manual alarms fitted throughout the ship afforded so much as a retrospective flicker.

The Second Officer continued to stare at it for a full thirty seconds, willing it to make up its mind so he could start to panic if it came on again. But it didn't.

Through the darkness he sensed the anxious scrutiny of the duty Quartermaster, the only other watchkeeper on the bridge. A careful officer aware of the grave responsibility he bore, Delucci had instructed the helmsman to stand close by the wheel despite the fact that they were currently running on auto-pilot. Just in case. Delucci had known autosteering systems to fail. Usually at critical moments in close quarter situations, in faithful observance of Sod's Law.

Usually because of a glitch in their electronics?

The Quartermaster was Spanish, Delucci was American. Mike Delucci had been with the ship on her previous charter – for over a year, in fact, while she was still running day cruises out of Florida

– but, because of their Indonesia-based owner's decision to press the ferry into North Sea service earlier than scheduled, the rating hadn't served aboard the 12,000 ton *Orion Venturer* for more than a week.

Judging by what he'd seen of the rest of the crowd hurriedly scraped together by the crewing agency in Hamburg, the man's command of English was probably limited to basic nautical, Delucci reflected morosely. The only communication they'd shared so far had been his repeating commands like *Port ten degrees*, *Steer two thuree oh* and *Steady as she goes*.

'You see walkie-talkie, Quartermaster?' he urged experimentally.

The helmsman, eerily underlit by the shaded green light from the compass binnacle, indicated the binocular box beside the starboard wheelhouse door. Delucci grabbed the handset from it and hit the pressel switch while moving out to the wing, gazing anxiously around a bleak horizon only faintly discernible as a ragged, grey-cold slot between the black sea and the low cloud ceiling.

It was hardly the thought uppermost in his mind, but he couldn't help appreciating, even at this ungodly time of the morning, that the ship was still alive with sound. The thrum of the rain-laden headwind orchestrated by taut-secured signal halyards; the steady putter of gases exhausting from the streamlined funnel rising high and far behind him; the crashing protest of seas fracturing and whirlpooling out from the *Venturer*'s waterline far below the bridge to fade excitedly astern – all the auditory justifications for Delucci's having pursued a career as a sailor. He accepted the somewhat less than romantic beat emanating from the Ocean Runner Night Club abaft the navigating officers' quarters on the boat deck as representing the penance you invited when standing middle watch aboard a night ferry . . .

That – and hitting something similarly ship-shaped at the best part of twenty knots if a guy got so preoccupied with querying little red lights on a board that he forgot to keep a sharp goddamned *look*-out!

Delucci's visual confirmed the radar check he'd completed a few minutes before. A cluster of fishing lights well astern on the starboard quarter: the rain-diffused halo of a cruise ship or another ferry hull-down to the north, and the solitary white stern light of a small vessel maybe four miles ahead on the port bow, making a course roughly similar to their own. The western entrance to the Skaggerak appeared comfortingly traffic free. At least collision avoidance wasn't detracting from Second Officer Delucci's priorities.

He nuzzled the walkie-talkie. 'Fire patrol . . . bridge. You read?'

Surprisingly the response was immediate. And in mother-tongue English. Kind of.

'Conroy . . .'oose that then?'

Delucci felt uncharacteristically relieved that Able Seaman Conroy, one of the few Brit deck ratings aboard, was duty night-watchman. He'd never felt such warmth towards the man on previous occasions when they'd . . . well, *clashed* was the only way to describe trying to give an order to AB Conroy, a sea lawyer if there ever was one. But at least the guy could communicate.

'OOW! State your location?'

There was a moment's silence while Conroy worked up a plausible lie, then decided to come clean on the basis of his contractual rights.

'Crew mess. I'm on me break. Watch orders says I'm entit . . .'

'How long since you patrolled C deck starboard side aft?'

''Bout ten, fifteen minutes ago . . . sir.'

Meaning forty, forty-five probably. As night-watchman Conroy was permitted a pretty free hand in setting his own patrol schedules. The counter to his abusing such privilege was that the AB carried a clock device to record the time of insertion of some forty keys placed at various locations on his round. Delucci made a mental note to check Conroy's last print-out. Later.

'I got a manual fire warning in way of cabins three-twenty-odds starboard side. Get along there fast and check it out.'

'I'm supposed to 'ave . . .'

'Do it, Conroy. *Now!*'

'*Señor Mate!*'

The shout from the wheelhouse didn't need interpretation. Even as Delucci swung to race back inside he heard the chilling warble of the audible alarm repeating itself. The same red light was blinking on the board again – still located starboard side aft on C deck . . .

. . . but now another light had come on. Right next to it!

5

Second Officer Delucci snarled 'Awwww, *Jesus*!' and lunged for the direct line to the Captain's cabin.

On the bulkhead above and behind the green-faced helmsman the hands of the wheelhouse clock moved to 0220.

Neither man realized it yet, but three minutes of the passenger and vehicle ferry *Orion Venturer*'s fast-closing survival window had already elapsed.

Conroy faced a fair old haul ahead of him. The crew messroom where he'd been nursing a mug of tea when he got the summons from Delucci was situated amidships on A deck, the lowest deck of the *Orion Venturer* and far below her waterline. Down there only the ship's double bottom, a space above her keel barely the height of a stooping man which contained tanks of oil fuel, ballast and fresh water, separated Able Seaman Conroy and his mug of tea from the fish of the Norwegian sea which swam below him.

But Conroy, who'd spent his life as a merchant seaman living in the oddest and most inhospitable parts of ships, gave no thought to the precarious barriers that existed as much to keep the cargo dry as to keep him from drowning. He was discomfited only at being ordered to retrace the patrol route he'd just completed . . . well – completed within the last hour or so . . . by climbing back up two decks and trailing aft along corridors which got longer every time he bloody walked them – just to appease some 'ardly-wet-behind-the-ears mate's anxiety over a suspect flash on a probably corroded electrical board.

It took him four vital minutes to make that return journey. Give him his due, Able Seaman Conroy had seen what fire could do to ships and didn't hang around longer than it took to drain his mug. On the other hand, he didn't exactly push himself either. It would have saved a precious minute if he had run aft, but seamen don't run aboard ships unless in the direst of straits – and besides, a cynical lack of faith in the abilities of marine engineers to maintain electrical gadgets properly, combined with Able Seaman Conroy's having inhaled fifty-plus duty free cigarettes a day for the past thirty-odd years, all conspired to restrict the pedantic night-watchman's passage to a purposeful amble.

Not that those sixty squandered seconds were to matter, as things turned out. Not in the end.

To be fair to Conroy, Second Officer Delucci didn't call him again during that period to advise of the further warnings flashing up on the bridge board, and so add impetus to his mission.

But the initial scepticism of Mike Delucci, seven decks above AB Conroy, had by then given way to anxiety verging on panic, and he'd been too preoccupied with calling the ferry's Master, as well as alerting her Chief Officer and Chief Engineer and – in between – trying to decide whether or not he, as a lowly Second Mate, had the guts to take it on himself to sound the *Orion Venturer*'s general alarm before any one of his seniors arrived panting on the bridge to take the crucial decision for him. A decision which, Delucci estimated, could cause upwards of five hundred people to assemble at the four emergency muster stations – even worse, turn up on the boat deck itself – in their pyjamas in the middle of a bitterly cold night in the middle of the Skagerrak at a point not quite equidistant between Denmark and goddamn Norway!

. . . not that 2/O Delucci's nightmare scenario would have come to pass, as it happened. Only some two hundred-odd people were statistically likely to have headed immediately for their muster stations in the various lounges, or played it ultra safe and gone directly to the *Orion Venturer*'s boat deck in their nightclothes always supposing they'd read the statutory safety notices on their cabin doors, had been given colour-coded boarding cards to help make sense of them, which they hadn't, on this trip – and knew where, or what, a muster station or even a boat deck was, anyway.

But then, Delucci wasn't aware that the history of previous ship-board emergencies suggests that, initially, some forty-six per cent of passengers – with or without boarding cards – remain in their cabins despite hearing any kind of alarm: just awaiting instructions from the crew.

Always supposing the crew are, themselves, familiar with the ship. And well enough trained to know what instructions to give in the first place?

*　　*　　*

Conroy finally arrived at the self-closing door separating fire containment zone 2 amidships from fire zone 1 aft at twenty-four minutes past two in the morning, some seven minutes after the first alarm had indicated itself to the bridge. The reluctant Able Seaman had reached a peak of disgruntlement by then, having just remembered he'd left his walkie-talkie in the crew mess and, the way *his* luck was shaping that night, the bloody internal phones would probably turn out as reliable as the rest of the soddin' ship's electrics. An' that could mean he might even have to trail all the way up to purser's reception on E deck to report all clear to the brid . . . ?

Conroy hauled the door open with an irritable yank . . . and then, quite simply, froze. Stood rooted to the deck, gaping horror-stricken down the length of the corridor serving cabins 312 to 320 starboard side aft while feeling the hair on the back of his tanned-leather neck beginning to crawl as if brushed by the bleach-boned fingers of some long drowned sailorman.

An understandable reaction, even for a seafaring man as phlegmatic and unimaginative as he.

Considering Able Seaman Conroy had just become privy to the kind of wide-awake nightmare no man should ever be called upon to experience.

DEPARTURE

The Committee is in no doubt that ... [the owners] should have been able to see that safe operation was not being given priority when it put a ship for so many passengers and with such an untrained crew into service within so short a time.

Norwegian Official Report, NOR 1991: 1E
The *Scandinavian Star* Disaster of 7 April 1990

Townsend Car Ferries Ltd internal memorandum, 18 August 1986

There seems to be a general tendency of satisfaction if the ship has sailed two or three minutes early. Where a full load is present, then every effort has to be made to sail the ship 15 minutes earlier ... I expect to read from now onwards, particularly where FE8 is concerned, that the ship left 15 minutes early ... put pressure on the first officer if you don't think he is moving fast enough ... let's put the record straight, sailing late from Zeebrugge isn't on. It's 15 minutes early for us

Report on loss of mv *Herald of Free Enterprise*
UK Court No. 8074 Formal Investigation

CHAPTER ONE

I am about to take my last voyage, a great leap in the
dark.

Last words. THOMAS HOBBES (1588–1697)

Carlsson never intended to destroy the *Orion Venturer*.

No more than Carlsson, being barely thirty years old when it happened, had planned to die prematurely. Not to die in the manner he did. And certainly not aboard a ro-ro ferry on a rain-swept night on an unsettlingly alien sea. Particularly as Sven Carlsson had never harboured any inclination towards being a sailor in the first place, and actually drove an intercontinental refrigerated truck for a living although he'd always felt destined for much greater things.

But then, neither did Carlsson mean to kill so many – indeed, not any – of his fellow travellers at much the same time as himself. All Carlsson had figured on doing, as he released the brakes of his giant Scania rig with a hiss of compressed air and began to ease forward onto the vehicle loading ramp, was to somehow draw attention to his qualities – elevate himself above the crowd – and, as a result, hopefully open the kind of doors that could lead to a more rewarding future than the doors of a lorry cab.

But fame isn't easy to achieve, as Carlsson had reluctantly come to recognize. Not without qualifications. Not the kind of fame that makes people sit up and take notice of you . . . other than by doing something pretty special, of course. He'd given that premise considerable thought over thousands of kilometres of solitary driving during the past few months. A close observer might even have considered him obsessed with the concept, but he wasn't. Carlsson had simply been mulling over his options. He could, for instance, go for making it big as a pop star or a football demi-god or . . . or

10

a leading TV personality, say? Trouble was he didn't have the right connections. Or any talent to speak of. Just a burning ambition to be special.

Until, roughly three thousand kilometres back down the road, Carlsson hit upon his big idea. All he needed to do was to become celebrated as a national – maybe even an international hero! Now heroes didn't need qualifications, did they? Didn't even need talent, come to that. A person didn't exactly have to make it as a brain surgeon or a prime minister first to qualify as a hero. Just a run of publicity following the event, to prise open the grateful hand of opportunity.

Carlsson had got quite excited at that point. It was a cracker of an inspiration – a fast lane to fame. All he'd had to figure from then on was how, exactly, he could overcome the one last hurdle blocking his strategy for self advancement. Like how he might go about becoming a hero. The snag, Carlsson grudgingly conceded as he'd worked on the problem, was that being a hero isn't exactly a vocation a guy can elect to pursue. Heroes tend to be produced out of crisis, whereas crises, by definition, are never pre-planned.

. . . or they aren't under normal circumstances, anyway.

Not unless you possess a mind as disturbed, as divorced from reality, as the mind of Sven Carlsson had become by the time he lined up his reefer truck on the approach to the vehicle deck of the passenger ferry *Orion Venturer*.

Grace Miles felt pleasantly reassured when Michael first swung their Volvo estate into the loading dock and she found she had to crane her neck to view the upper decks of the ferry in the dawn light. It seemed so much bigger, so much more substantial than she'd feared.

There was something else about the vessel that afforded her an even more welcome sense of security, and that was the manner in which the vehicles due for shipment were being taken aboard. A simple observation; one that calls for some understanding of Grace's earlier misgivings to properly appreciate its significance, but one that was nevertheless proving of great comfort considering that for weeks now, ever since they'd booked their Swedish Drive-

As-You-Please holiday with the brand new ferry company, her apprehension at the prospect of making a surface crossing of the North Sea had steadily grown.

She'd never expected to feel such unease. Some travellers' phobias feed on a fear of aircraft, trains, long-haul coaches . . . in past years Grace had travelled by all of those even more unnatural methods with equanimity – hardly given a thought to the minimal risk involved – which was why it had seemed so perverse, once the die had been cast and her mind concentrated by anticipation, to discover that the looming possibility of seaborne disaster could still, apparently, prove capable of fuelling the darker side of her imagination.

Not that Grace had lost all sense of proportion, even then. She'd always known about the *Titanic*, for instance – everybody knew about her. And the *Lusitania*. All those poor people, hundreds of them, carried down to the bottom of the cold black ocean by a single act of war. Equally, she'd never related either drama to her family's sailing aboard the *Orion Venturer*, being perfectly aware that the likelihood of striking an iceberg in the North Sea is as remote as the prospect of being torpedoed by an eighty-year-old U-boat.

But apprehension refuses to be thwarted by logic, which explained why, despite the enduring fame accorded those tragic vessels, two more recently lamented names would come to dominate her twilight anxieties. *The Herald of Free Enterprise* and the . . . the *Estonia*, wasn't it?

Somehow the random, exquisitely cruel nature of those catastrophes had generated a very real disquiet within Grace Miles. Had succeeded in overwhelming the protective psychological barrier she'd always previously managed to erect between her loved ones and their exposure, however statistically improbable, to threat when venturing beyond the garden gate . . . until Michael had come home with the ferry tickets one day, and the almost forgotten media coverage of what could happen to ordinary families just like hers had surfaced with a rush, to make such fragile denial impossible to sustain.

They'd both been roll-on roll-off ferries which had foundered on what should have been routine, uneventful passages. The appalling television images of the semi-submerged *Herald* lying on her side were what had particularly kept Grace awake at night, replaying them over and over in her mind's eye although she'd never once mentioned her concern to Michael. She'd just got on with planning and packing and arranging to leave Button in kennels for the fortnight they'd be away; and smiled tolerantly when seven-year-old William had demanded she bought him a yellow sou'wester for the voyage like proper sailors wore, while reassuring a concerned Lucy, aged all of four, that Teddy *wouldn't* develop a sore tummy like Aunt Rachel claimed she'd had when she went on a boat once.

Ironic, really. All that secret anxiety, only to come face to face with the object of her paranoia and find it patently ill-founded. Because all the lorries and coaches and caravan trailers were entering the cavernous maw of the vessel's car deck through its *rear* end – or its stern, she supposed she should call it, what with it being a ship? All clattering cautiously up the ramp like animals entering the Ark, only one by tentative one in this case – and, while Grace had never quite grasped the technical details of why those previous ferries had been lost, she did know that some sort of malfunction of their *bow* doors had been responsible. That the front ends of both ships had proved their common weakness.

Ahead of them the last commercial vehicle – the white Scania articulated lorry with Swedish licence plates – gunned up the ramp trailing a spurt of diesel fumes, and rumbled into the belly of the whale. A uniformed crewman wearing a white hard hat, a fluorescent orange waistcoat with SECOND OFFICER stencilled across it, and carrying a walkie-talkie radio beckoned them to approach next.

Michael said dryly, 'Now we know how Jonah must have felt,' and engaged first gear.

'I'm hungry, Mummy,' Lucy announced. 'And so's Teddy.'

'Too bad, 'cause they make you eat biscuits with *worms* in 'em when you're on a ship,' William told her cruelly. 'They'll make you sick. Probably put Teddy in *hospital*!'

'Teddy likes worms,' his sister informed him, unimpressed. 'I gave him one las' week and he ate it all up.'

It was proving a morning of revelation for Grace. Now she'd

even discovered why she'd had to dunk Teddy's head in hot soapy water before he got shoved in the car ready for his Scandinavian holiday.

'Worms? What's he on about – worms?' Michael muttered as the front end of the car bumped up then rode over the hinged steel plate marking the start of the ramp. The cavernous inside of the whale stretched ahead. It seemed comfortingly vast to Grace, punctuated by rows and rows of overhead strip lighting and big red signs warning RÖKING FÖRBJUDEN – NO SMOKING. The Swedish refrigerated truck slowly led the way through the car deck towards a mass of vehicles already parked at the far end, the grumble of its now throttled-back engine reverberating hollowly within the scratched, white-painted steel walls of the whale's carcass.

'I think he means weevils,' she smiled, actually beginning to relish this new travel experience. 'He's been reading about the old sailing ships.'

It was just as well for Grace Miles' peace of mind that her knowledge of passenger shipping losses was sketchy, restricted largely to those which have managed to maintain a high profile in the history books.

On Saturday 31 January 1953, a British Railways car ferry foundered in the Irish Sea some nine miles east of Donaghadee, County Down, with the loss of 133 lives.

The *Princess Victoria* sank after massive waves smashed open her stern loading doors.

CHAPTER TWO

'What's the water in French, sir?'
'*L'eau*,' replied Nicholas.
'Ah!' said Mr Lillywick, shaking his head mournfully. 'I
thought as much. Lo, eh? I don't think anything of that
language – nothing at all.'

CHARLES DICKENS (1812–1870)

'At least you c'n speak English half decent for a feller black as the
ace o' spades, I'll grant you that, Cookie,' Able Seaman Conroy
generously conceded as he leaned, arms akimbo and one foot
planted with seamanlike insouciance on the boat deck lower rail,
observing with idle interest the pre-dawn activity on the loading
dock far below. 'Not like the rest o' yer foreigner mates in the
caterin' department.'

'P'raps that's 'cause I'm third-generation Scouse and them's
mostly Portugees and Eyeties, wack.' Assistant Crew Mess Cook
Henry Manley offered, straight-faced helpful. 'Me Gran and Pa
come over to Liverpool from Trinidad after the war . . . along with
the first bananas?'

But Assistant Cook Manley had long learned to recognize, and
get along with, a fascist bastard when he sailed with one. While,
give the grizzled old matelot his due, AB Conroy didn't claim to
be single-minded in his prejudice. Since joining the *Orion Venturer*
he'd displayed equal and amiable bias against policemen and passengers; bishops; children; Merchant Navy officers; the whole of
the Royal Navy; ship's engineers – especially engineer officers . . .
especially Royal Navy engineer bloody officers – the government;
shipowners, dog owners, property owners, Scotsmen, Welshmen,
rabbits . . .

15

Henry had never quite figured why Conroy was so against rabbits.

'Yeah? Well, you got to expect all kinds in ro-ros nowadays, even blokes from the Pool. I mean she's flag o' convenience, i'n't she?' Conroy jerked his head to indicate the Bahamian ensign hanging rain-sodden limp over the taffrail, happy to bite the hand currently feeding him. 'Multi-national crew, exploitation management. Cheap labour we are, mate.'

Henry thought about that a moment while chalking up another convoy of prejudices to Conroy's tally. Sure the pay was lousy. So what was new? Ever since he'd gone to sea crewing had been a hirer's market, particularly for the fly-by-night companies dipping into an international pool of unemployed officers and ratings and not always questioning their certificates of competency too closely. And he was a cook, not a sea lawyer. He didn't know and didn't particularly care whether being registered in Nassau categorized the *Orion Venturer* as a tax-efficient vehicle sailing under the ensign of a state where, to attract hard currency investment, maritime legislation tends to be, well . . . more open to interpretation in accommodating the financial interests of shipowners?

You took things as you found 'em in Henry's book. Either signed where the crewing agents marked the cross, or watched her sail with some other chef from Turkey or Russia or one of the Third World countries filling your berth for half the wages a west European needs to feed his family on.

And, while he'd never signed aboard a passenger ferry before, the *Venturer* seemed okay. Big. Bit old, maybe, but obviously still qualifying for all the safety and survey certificates needed to satisfy the maritime inspectorates either side of the North Sea. Smartly turned out, too, if you didn't explore the shabbier parts of her. More of a cruise ship than an overnight ro-ro. Wasn't as if she was flagged out to one of the *really* slack FOC regulatory havens – Panama, Monrovia, Liberia . . . Real floating palace far as Henry Manley was concerned, whose previous sea time had been logged in cargo ships, an' some of *them* pretty iffy. Apart from anything else, her scheduled sailings out of the UK meant he stood a chance of getting home odd times during turnaround. See a lot more of Emma and the kids than he'd ever managed to before.

Not that he took issue with his somewhat disparaging new ship-mate, Conroy, regarding the frustrations of tryin' to communicate on board. Henry worked in the crew mess. He'd heard the buzz around the tables . . . when he'd been able to interpret what some of 'em were saying, that was. Seemed the more sea-experienced hands – not that there appeared to be that many aboard the *Orion Venturer* and no doubt Conroy would express a view on that particular aspect, give him time – it seemed there was a general feeling that the crewing agency had bitten off more than they could swallow in the time the owners had allowed them.

Hiring over a hundred crew members from scratch, ranging from pastry chefs and peelers through croupiers and duty free shop assistants – many of whom, Manley himself had been a bit taken aback to discover, had come straight from the hotel industry and never even worked a ship before – to electricians, motormen and deck ratings, and all at short notice, must have provided a mega headache for the Hamburg personnel agency. Hard enough to identify immediate availability, never mind fulfil the fine print of the Bahamian legislative requirements for safe crewing which, in the job spec Henry had barely been given sight of, appeared to include the applicants possessing *a satisfactory knowledge of English*.

What Henry Manley did not know, because he *was* a cook and not an international maritime lawyer, was that such linguistic accomplishment is not an absolute requirement of the Bahamian Merchant Shipping Act. Section 77 of Part III contains a clause which an old-fashioned cynic like Able Seaman Conroy might just have considered, well . . . open to interpretation, so to speak, by any unscrupulous shipowner. Broadly it adds, ' . . . *or that adequate arrangements should exist on board for transmitting orders in a language of which individual crew members do have sufficient knowledge.*'

Work that one out, Henry. How a seaman officer, one who isn't too fluent in Ning-po-dialect Chinese, or Sumatran or Croat or Azerbaijani, makes his orders understood to often ill-educated hands at abandon ship stations in the middle of a crypt-black night in a force ten with a list on her and green seas slopping into the vehicle deck.

By sign language?

The bottom line was that nine mother tongues actually competed for audience in the crew messes of the *Orion Venturer* when she sailed on that first North Sea service. According to Assistant Purser Everard – who was involved in on-board personnel management and could display an aversion towards FOC multi-national manning roughly equivalent to Conroy's when his mouth ran away with him and no one from Head Office was listening – give some thirty per cent of the crowd a shout in the ship's official language and they woul'n't know whether you was inviting them to a barbecue on the sun deck or orderin' them to abandon bloody ship!

It seemed – according to Assistant Purser Everard – that the *Orion Venturer*'s deck officers were either British or American, although Captain Halvorsen was himself Norwegian: largely on account, it was spitefully rumoured, of his holding pilotage credentials for both the Oslo Fjord and the approaches to Gothenburg, which promised to save the owners significant bucks through not having to pay out hefty pilotage fees each trip.

The Chief Engineer, Bracamontes, who, like Mike Delucci the Second Mate and a few other key personnel, had stayed with the ship following her Florida service, was New York Colombian. The rest of her engineer officers were either Brit, Danish or Swede, while the black gang . . . Assistant Mess Cook Manley, whose Gran and Pa hailed from Trinidad, hadn't been able to help smiling a bit wryly at that still-cherished throwback to the days of coal-fired boilers . . . the engine room motormen were most of them either South American or Filipino.

As for the rest – according to Assistant Purser Everard – his own Purser's department offered a mix of Scowegian and Brit, which was okay. The catering department, on the other hand, was largely composed of Portuguese stewards and Italian galley staff – there were only a few fluent English speakers between the lot of them, and that assumed Henry to be one of the few according to Conroy's somewhat grudging standards. The carpenter was a Greek Cypriot; his assistant a Turk. They couldn't be expected to chat much even if they *had* been able to understand each other. The deckies also appeared to be of Mediterranean origin in the main, though there was no denying the Bosun, Pascal, a Spaniard from Santander, could not only speak fluent English but commanded a vocabulary of internationally understood epithets that would have earned him stunned respect even in the foc'sle of a 1920s tramp flying the Red Duster.

And finally there was Able Seaman Conroy. Sort of dinosaur Anglo-Saxon. The *Orion Venturer*'s lone but vociferous champion of a sea-trading age long gone. A perversity on Conroy's part, really – considering it had been those same British shipowners who, in their time, had written the definitive textbook on how to exploit sailormen.

'You know we even gotta . . . got an *Australian* aboard?' the self-same Able Seaman Conroy appealed morosely, appalled at the very idea.

'The Eck-teck – Ed the electronics officer?' Manley defended. '*He* speaks English. He has to. He doubles as our radio operator.'

'Not proper English, though. Not the kind what *I* learned to speak,' Conroy persisted without even a trace of irony. He flicked his exhausted cigarette butt outboard into the rain. They both watched it fade until lost in the flotsam-fouled water trapped between *Venturer*'s slab side and the time-scarred face of the dock.

'She won't be run proper, Cookie. Not like a British ship, mark my words. Notice how we 'aven't even had a crew boat or fire drill since the new faces joined? Though I'll guarantee there's one entered in the log book to keep the Marine Safety Agency blood-hounds 'appy.'

Henry yawned. He'd been working since 0430, frying up break-fast for the crew. One thing British about this ship, he thought proprietarily. She might be registered in an exotic island paradise. She might be owned by Far East shadow Chinecmen or whoever. Half her crew might come from sun-washed shores an' warmer climes – but they still got fed a cholesterolly lethal all-round English start to the working day.

'Had your breakfast yet?' he asked, fishing for a compliment.

'Don't believe in breakfas',' Conroy dismissed airily. 'Just picked at the odd bit o' bacon, rissoles – couple of eggs. Sausisgis. Black puddin'. Scoop o' beans . . . one o' them Yankee flapjack things an' a few fried potatoes. Can't stand blokes 'oo stuffs themselves first thing in the morning.'

The diet-conscious AB turned away from the rail with a last dark glance at the ensign. 'You see if somethin' goes pear-shaped, mate.

Then try sortin' the men from the boys in a real emergency.'

. . . or the women from the girls? Nearly one in five of the ferry's complement was female, but Conroy hadn't quite made it into the twentieth century yet. Seemed he was still struggling to come to terms with the nineteenth.

Henry shrugged solemnly, trying to look as if he was giving the prediction due weight while remaining cheerfully unperturbed. He considered himself a simple, uncomplicated soul who put great store in simple, uncomplicated logic. Didn't this being the *Venturer's* first service on her new run mean complacency hadn't had a chance to take root, especially at command level? Wouldn't the navigating officers in particular be on their toes? So, considering most marine accidents are caused by human error on the bridge, didn't that make it virtually inconceivable anything untoward could happen? And a bit further down the line, once they'd got a couple of trips under their belts, the whole crowd would've shaken down, got to know the ropes.

Biggest crisis Henry could visualize occurring over the next few days was letting Conroy shoot his mouth off to the passengers. Five minutes with him and they'd be demanding a fast boat ashore and a ticket refund before they reached the fairway buoy – then none of the *Orion Venturer's* girls and boys would have a job.

It never struck Henry that, once upon a time, another ship – and British to boot – run by officers who, considering the admiring eyes of the world were upon them should have had every reason not to feel complacent, had nevertheless gone down on *her* maiden voyage. Rushed to embrace disaster by steaming full ahead through an ice field in fog thick as a whaleman's jumper! Probably with all the paperwork certifying how safe and unsinkable she was still filed, nice and neat, in the Old Man's safe aboard the RMS *Titanic*.

But then, neither did it occur to Crew Mess Cook Manley, looking down on the roof of the big white Scania truck as it disappeared from sight, roaring up and into the *Orion Venturer's* car deck while causing the ferry to dip fractionally lower in the water, that the deprecatory Conroy might just have been, well . . . right?

Unconsciously voicing the sixth sense of a man who'd spent all his life in ships?

CHAPTER THREE

No man will be a sailor who has contrivance enough to get himself into a jail; for being in a ship is being in a jail, with the chance of being drowned. A man in a jail has more room, better food, and commonly better company.
SAMUEL JOHNSON (1709–1784)

Herr Neugebauer travelled in ladies' underwear.

He didn't sell it. He wore it. Discreetly of course, underneath a rather dapper Italian-cut business suit. He was actually a consultant in hydraulic engineering by profession.

Given privileged knowledge, one might have been tempted to conclude – not from his being a hydraulic engineer sporting Italian suits so much as from his affinity for satin lingerie – that passenger Neugebauer was a tad eccentric. But that would have been an overly simplistic assessment and one which quite underestimated the true depths of the outwardly reticent and considerate little man.

Because Herr Neugebauer was actually mad as a hatter. He just covered it up well. Every bit as well as he covered his skin-hugging flirtation with feminine lacy things and – some two years previously – had covered Frau Neugebauer with one and a half metric tonnes of meticulously laid concrete under the patio of their small suburban house in Dortmund.

He'd made sure she was dead first, of course. Strangled her with the flex from the reading lamp on her side of the bed before cutting her throat in the bath. Then left her in it for a week before looking out his shovel and the cement, just to make absolutely certain. It would have been quite improper, an inexcusable breach of marital faith in Neugebauer's view, to have planted his good lady while there'd been the remotest chance of her still being alive and capable

21

of suffering. The fact that Trudi, after thirty-three years of wedded harmony, had betrayed him by succumbing to the temptation to explore his special private drawer – and then indulged herself further by launching into a quite immoderate tirade of hurtful derision – hadn't diminished by one jot the concern he'd felt for her obvious distress on first feeling the cord tighten around her neck.

... none of which had anything whatsoever to do with Herr Neugebauer's travelling to Gothenburg as a single occupant booked into cabin E318 starboard side aft on E deck. In fact, as he boarded by the skywalk linking the passenger terminal to the *Orion Venturer*'s spacious reception area, he wasn't even thinking of Trudi: with or without her concrete suit. He was actually more engrossed in noting, with professional approbation, the gangway's complex system of hydraulics which enabled a significantly weighty body of people to walk through a precisely positioned tunnel elevated some twelve metres above dock level.

Certainly it was unlikely that anything so dramatic as a request from Interpol to clap him in irons, ready for uplifting on arrival in Gothenburg, would be received by the *Orion Venturer*'s radio operator, as had happened in the case of Doctor Hawley Harvey Crippen and his mistress Ethel Le Neve in 1910: the first fugitives from justice to be apprehended on the high seas through the medium of a wireless telegraphic transmission. The Dortmund CID had long pegged Frau Trudi as yet another missing person after interviewing the bespectacled Herr Neugebauer and deciding there was nothing weird enough about the guy to justify calling in a local plant hire firm.

For that matter it was statistically unlikely that anything out of the ordinary would happen to passenger Neugebauer en route. Not in the North Sea on a relatively calm night, during a passage only lasting some twenty-four hours.

In fact Herr Neugebauer's somewhat unconventional approach to extracting the best from life is only worthy of recording in that it tends to endorse the view of the lugubrious Able Seaman Conroy.

That you gotter expect all kinds o' people in a ro-ro ferry.

*　　*　　*

22

In October 1944, US Admiral Sprague's invasion group of light escort carriers and painfully slow troop transports was heading to reinforce Douglas MacArthur's tenuous bridgehead on the Mindanao and Leyte beaches.

The Imperial Japanese Navy, in the form of an incomparably stronger task force of four battleships, seven cruisers and twelve destroyers commanded by Admiral Kurita, was steaming to intercept, and prevent them from doing just that. The future course of the Pacific war hung in the balance.

When, at dawn on the 25th, battle was joined, the American escort screen nearest to the enemy included an eggshell-fragile destroyer, the USS *Thompson*.

When, after a desperate three-hour action east of Samar Island, the *Thompson* was finally overwhelmed and sunk, eighteen-year-old Machinist's Mate Second Class Charles Periera was closed up to his battle station in her after engine room.

Over half a century later, Charlie Periera gripped his wife's hand as the echoing claustrophobia of the *Orion Venturer*'s car deck embraced their tour party's Speedliner luxury coach. He did so with uncharacteristic tension. It was the first time he'd boarded a ship since they'd hauled him out of the Gulf of Leyte, his left leg almost severed at the knee.

'You okay, honey?' Margrite asked, a mite concerned.

He turned to gaze at her. Even in the stark shadow cast by the deckhead lights she was beautiful. Forty-nine years wed and she was still the most beautiful creature had ever come into his life.

'Yeah,' ex-US Navy MM 2/c Periera said. Then turned back to the window while everyone else on the bus was easing age-stiffened backs and fumbling with gnarled hands to retrieve luggage from overhead lockers. The Brit authorities had been pretty good: let them drive through passport control at the vehicle check-in rather than climb all them stairs to the overhead boarding ramp from the terminal. It had been a long drive through the night to get here for the dawn sailing, and they were all getting on a bit now: all the once-young guys from the *Thompson* who'd survived the intervening years long enough to club together for probably their final reunion – kind of an *it's Thursday, it must be London, England*, whistle-stop tour of Europe. Except they did London yes-

23

terday ... tomorrow was Friday, so it had to be Gothenburg, Sweden.

A hundred and eighty-six of their former shipmates hadn't been permitted the chance to even try for it. To veteran Charlie Periera they would always stay young. Still boys. Still down there, asleep under the Leyte waters.

Their Captain had stayed with them. Commander Edward B. Daryl. Full-blooded Cherokee Indian and one formidable navy man. On commissioning the *Thompson* less than a year previously, he'd told MM 2/c Periera and the rest of his new crew straight: *This is going to be a fighting ship. I intend to go in harm's way. Anyone doesn't want to go along had better get off right now!*

And by God, he did. Took the *Thompson* – took all of them right into the jaws of the Japanese tiger. Outgunned and outranged, she drew fire from the heavy cruiser *Kumano*, set on decimating the escort carrier *Gambier Bay*. Absorbed three hits in twenty minutes before she'd closed enough to fire a shot in return ... Cap Daryl steered for the last burst. Classic tactic in the tradition of John Paul Jones. Tricked the enemy rangefinders clear out of guessing time, with the *Thompson* shuddering and reeling under the blows that did get through. Guys screaming, parts of ship – parts of *men* exploding ... gyro compass a whirligig, the bridge afire, steering gear shot to hell and operated by handraulic ... and then their own 5-inch turrets opening fire – no, *returning* fire, godammit! Two hundred rounds, ten torpedoes outgoing into the Rising Sun before the waters closed over the USS *Thompson*'s riddled hull.

Charlie just sat there remembering, staring out at the bracers of the ferry's car deck. A fault in one of the overheads was causing it to flicker intermittently. Reflections on cold metal ... flame-flicker on steel bulkheads. Fire consuming a dying warship's aft machinery room. Decks buckling, beginning to tilt, convert to bulkheads – Jesus she's *going*, guys ... *still* nobody leaves their post. The order finally comes down the pipe – *Abandoooon SHIP!*

MM 2/c Marcora from Saratoga: nineteen years young that morning. Challenging black eyes that could pull a dame before you'd even eased off your bar stool. Won eighteen bucks shooting craps to celebrate before they went into action – now Marcora's crucified but still alive, spread-eagled where the blast has hurled him against the only watertight door offering escape, with his long-lashed eyes wide open in shock and his mouth still working and the big star-fish spokes of the wheel-lock protruding clear through his chest . . .

Zach Goss, Machinist's Mate First Class, burned red raw down one side his face, clawing at Marcora like he's side of pig in a Chicago abattoir. Marcora starts to whimper, blood gouts from his trauma-slack mouth. Goss hollering, 'Help get this bastard off, Periera – grab his arms . . . *haul*!' Marcora arches, screams, comes off in two pieces – an' *still* the Birthday Kid's making animal sounds.

Goss plants a heel on the feebly writhing Marcora to steady himself. Spins the bloodied wheel . . . yanks the heavy bulkhead door ajar – but now, Dear Jesus, the *sea's coming*! The ship gives an almighty shudder, leans over crazy. Somethin's given way forerard. The machinery space flooding and rumbling with flash-fires racing across the surface oil. Somewhere behind them in that charnel pit there's guys – messmates, buddies, screaming for help . . . Goss squirms through the door, eyes bulging. MM 2/c Periera follows – but suddenly the green-black blood-red sea's catching up with them, roaring and gouting like a constantly expanding critter spewed from the abyss!

'Shut the door, dog it down . . . we ain't gonna make it topside elsewhys!' Goss is hollering.

Periera sees him then – the Lieutenant. Engineer Lieutenant (jg) O'Kane. Good officer, twenty-two going on forty wisdom-wise. Looked out for the guys; earned himself a lot of respect . . . now he's wading thigh deep, still grit-eyed determined, towards them, the spume whirlpooling to drag him back; khaki shirt shrapnel-ribboned and smoke obscene, left hand supporting a bloodied stump where the other used to be . . .

Nine feet . . . Eight! The part of MM 2/c Marcora that was whimpering flops over face down, drifts away spread-eagled and slowly revolving. Marcora is quiet now. The Lieutenant lets his own stump swing free. Lunges for the door.

Five feet, four . . . ! O'Kane's eyes lock on to Periera's. There's a plea there, a prayer of anguish'll stay with Charlie Periera the rest of his life.

25

'*Wait*, Goss! Hold fast f'r the Looten . . . !'

Goss slams the watertight door.

And spins the wheel . . .

'Honey?' There's real concern in her voice now. 'You *certain* you're okay, honey?'

'Sure, Margie pet. Sure am,' Charlie says again, frowning at the steel walls of the ferry and praying to God none of the others sense the dread he still carries with him, of being entombed in a sinking ship. He should never have come. Knows he's going to have to sweat out this night at sea. Fifty-plus years on and he still wonders if, some day, the Lieutenant won't surface from the black spewing waters of old Charlie Periera's recurring nightmares to claim his due.

'Hey, sailor, the wake-up chow line calls. You better get off your butt or you ain't *never* gonna make it topside elsewhys.'

He's heard that phrase before. He ain't never forgot it. Periera blinks aloft through rheumy eyes. The burns on the face grinning challengingly down at him from the aisle are still faintly discernible. Apart from the fact he's seventyish, bald and run to fat now, ex-Machinist's Mate First Class Goss hasn't changed that much. He's still loud. Still pushy. Never did warm to him, and still don't.

As he levers himself erect, Charlie's leg aches a bit where they'd pinned the bone, sewed the flesh, then handed him his Purple Heart. But they never recognized the most grievous injury from the *Thompson*'s sinking had been to the inside of his head.

Pretty clear Zach didn't carry no problems with him. No guilt. Even got himself promoted petty officer grade later. Went back to the war a Navy hero. And maybe he wus. Maybe they both were.

Except one time.

CHAPTER FOUR

With regard to safety functions, the Committee does not consider that it was justifiable to sail with a crew consisting of so many persons with a poor command of English. The [ship's] emergency plan was in English, and since no fire and abandon ship drills had been held, many of the crew were unable to make themselves familiar with the emergency plan.

Norwegian Official Report, NOR 1991: 1E
The *Scandinavian Star* Disaster of 7 April 1990

McCulloch was uneasy. He was also exhausted and overstressed.

Soon as Second Officer Delucci had relieved him from supervising the activity on the car deck, he'd snatched a quick breakfast then hurried straight up to the Mate's office and thrown himself into tackling the long-overdue jigsaw of revising the emergency plan.

Overseeing the vehicle loading should have been *his* job, dammit! His first trip as Chief Officer and instead of doing what he should've been doing he was frigging about up here in his poky office below the bridge, pushing paper around. Cargo stowage is the Mate's routine responsibility in any ship, whether she's a bulker, container, crude oil carrier or just a drive on-drive off garage-cum-hotel like the *Venturer* – but this wasn't normal routine, this was pressure. And under pressure something has to give.

Which was why Mike Delucci, being the most experienced Second Mate out of the three bridge watch-keeping seconds they carried, had drawn the short straw as McCulloch's stand-in down below. The young American shouldn't even have been working this time of the morning – his would be the twelve to four bridge duty on passage to Gothenburg, meaning the afternoon and middle

27

watches. Take out his rest period and it was predictable that they'd have a tired man up there tonight, alone but for one rating as lookout, driving the ship during the hours when concentration is at its lowest ebb anyway.

But they were all pressured. All tired. All running short of time to complete what should have been pre-planned and signed off weeks ago.

This emergency plan, for instance. Two hours to sailing and Chief Officer Stewart McCulloch was still trying to solve the problem of who would do what and where, and who would give the orders should some crisis overtake the *Orion Venturer* – a task made harder by the fact that he, despite being an experienced long-haul ro-ro officer, had never been called upon to prepare an emergency plan before. He'd accepted as a matter of course, when serving his own time as a watch-keeping second mate with occasional spells as relief Chief Officer with one of the long-established British ferry companies, that such crucial safety measures had long been in place. Under those pre-eminent owners, as with all big passenger operators sailing out of UK waters, the crew's responses to emergencies were continually being reappraised and refined: rehearsed and counter-rehearsed as part of a process of evolution considered vital to the safety of their passengers and ships.

. . . whereas this was winging it with a vengeance. This was make-do and mend, an' just hope to God nothing goes wrong, Mister, before you get the chance to fix it!

The only plus was that he hadn't had to begin his task at square one. It wasn't as if no emergency plan existed. There was one, and a good one, drawn up and rehearsed in drills long before the *Venturer* transferred to her role as an overnight ferry on European international service. A plan so sound that, after consultation between Captain Halvorsen and the owner's representatives, it had been decided to retain that tried and tested blueprint, modifying it only where necessary – apart from which, it looked good . . . well, it looked good on paper, anyway. Impressive enough to satisfy the scrutiny of most port state control surveyors already faced with a mountain of safety certificates and documents to inspect.

Sheer pragmatism had also played a part in making the decision. Nearly everyone aboard had been working fourteen, sixteen hours a day for the past fortnight in order to prepare the ship for her new task – longer for those like Delucci and Chief Engineer Braca-montes, who'd brought her across the Atlantic even while the internal modifications were being carried out. That work had involved the enlargement of the reception area on E deck, the conversion of some former casino areas to tax- and duty-free shops and, because her overnight accommodation had been largely unused and neglected for years, the refurbishment of the majority of passenger cabins, particularly those economy class spaces situ-ated lower in the ship.

Add to that the fact that the crew, particularly catering staff and stewards, had been turning up in dribs and drabs from whichever airport the hiring agents had flown them into – some blinking owlishly on arriving at the head of the gangway while staring round as if wondering which side was port and which was star-board, and whether forward meant the pointed end?

Add to that McCulloch's own personal responsibilities as safety officer, in addition to being the *Orion Venturer*'s executive officer, to familiarize himself with the ship and her various systems. To oversee not only the work in progress but simultaneously to draw up deck crew watchbills and a vehicle distribution plan for this first voyage; liaise with the engineers on the condition of fire alarms, fire extinguishers, smoke-diving equipment, the car deck sprinkler system . . . inspect lifejacket stowages, boats and rafts, escape route signing, emergency planning . . .

The emergency plan!

Chief Officer McCulloch glanced anxiously at the bulkhead clock and reached for the folder. It was this complex reappraisal above all which was so far proving the straw to break his figurative back – although he was damned if he'd concede as much to the Captain. The young Mate was already deeply troubled by his relationship with the ferry's Norwegian master . . . if such an extravagant term as 'relationship' could be used to describe what little interaction the disconcertingly remote Halvorsen encouraged between them.

McCulloch massaged his eyes. *Lord*, he was tired. Maybe it was that which was causing him to become paranoid? Maybe, being new to the way a single ship fleet operated, he'd expected too much in the way of support from management – certainly Captain

Halvorsen must be aware that his workload was above and beyond the norm – but he didn't think so. Most of the *Orion Venturer*'s officers had given way to outbursts of resentment, complaining openly they weren't happy with the Old Man's increasing indifference to their problems. Frustration as much as anything . . . a few weeks ago he'd been a powerhouse. Progress meetings, encouragement, a shipmaster acutely aware of the need for a co-ordinated approach to the business of preparing for service.

Since then they'd all seen a subtle change in Captain Halvorsen. He'd become ever more remote. Now, dammit, you couldn't get through to the man. Even when you did run across him in the ship he came over as cold and introspective. Didn't shout, didn't criticize: was invariably civil in a distant sort of way – and didn't do a damn thing to help take the strain!

Like by offering his vastly more experienced input to help crack the inconsistencies in this all-too-crucial emergency plan. At the end of the day, as with every other factor relating to the safety of a ship and its complement, it is the Master's – not the Mate's – ultimate responsibility to ensure that adequate provision exists to meet the unexpected.

But a thirty-seven-year-old, newly appointed Chief Officer doesn't exactly further his career by pointing that out to a Captain who'd gained his first certificate of competence before he was born.

. . . wearily he yanked the top off his pen with an urgent *plop*.

Fortunately it *was* a well-structured plan. Even the harassed McCulloch could cling to that consolation. A minutely detailed counter to every form of hazard that might potentially assail the *Orion Venturer*, assigning each crew member, according to his or her qualifications, to an emergency response group. Each response group, commanded by a specialist officer, would assemble at a predetermined point on hearing the alarm sounded from the bridge. They would then be further briefed on the nature and location of the crisis by orders given over the ferry's public address system or through personal walkie-talkie radios.

At that stage – according to the plan – fire, evacuation, casualty search and damage control teams would be targeted to the seat of the emergency. Other groups were nominated for duties ranging from ensuring the continued running of the ship to readying all boats and rafts for launching. From securing and making safe deep-frying and cooking ranges to passenger control and reassurance. The plan even made provision for such fine detail as the retrieval and custody of documents and valuables. It really was a splendid plan.

And McCulloch had done his level best to ensure its promulgation. Copies of the plan overview, the lifecraft launching plan and the evacuation plan had been distributed throughout all crew messes and sleeping accommodation by Bosun Pascal. In order that these plans should be readily accessible to external services coming to the aid of the ship, copies enclosed in protective coverings had also been posted on the after mooring deck, by the entrances to the reception area and throughout the car deck. Each crew cabin had been furnished with a pamphlet condensing the procedures, and further emphasizing the importance of acquiring close familiarity with them.

No question, it really was a jolly good plan – yet McCulloch was still unhappy with it. Or rather, worried sick would have been a more accurate description, considering he was acutely aware that the *Orion Venturer*'s crisis strategy contained at least two major shortcomings, either of which could prove fatal to its practical application.

The first flaw was largely outside his immediate control, although no doubt Able Seaman Conroy would have been quick to draw a parallel with his own sardonic view of the problems which can arise from multi-national manning. Much to McCulloch's dismay he'd discovered that the owners, always careful with the dollars, had only provided copies of the plan printed in English. It shouldn't have needed a genius to recognize that such a penny-pinching oversight meant – to a cabin steward who, until a few weeks back had been working a local *taberna* down Alicante's Playa del Postiguet, or a seaman rating whose last berth had been aboard a Greek tanker in which English wasn't exactly conversation medium *numero uno* . . . that, until a full-scale rehearsal could be held for the *Venturer*'s current complement, all the safety posters, all the emergency instructions so assiduously distributed by Bosun

31

Pascal promised to prove about as intelligible as if he had given each of them a copy of a Gideon Bible from a London hotel room.

Considerably less useful for some. The way things turned out.

The second, infinitely more serious shortfall in the plan, and the one which was causing McCulloch his greatest anxiety, arose from the fact that, as with every grand design, its key had to lie in its implementation. No point in having a plan unless everyone knows their part in it. And the thinking behind the plan had certainly provided for that element of pre-organization as well.

In concept, each crew member was allotted a unique number in the hierarchy of combating disaster. The plan called it their *emr number* – designating a place for everyone, and everyone in their place from the Captain down to the most junior messboy. An eminently sensible system . . . look up your name on the notice board, find your emr number, and tally it against a second list detailing where you go, who you report to, and what task you perform should things get a bit iffy.

McCulloch's problem lay in the fact that the original strategy had been drawn up by her previous management while the *Orion Venturer* was still operating day casino cruises out of Port Canaveral. Voyages to Nowhere, they called them: in effect steaming in circles in international waters to frustrate the US gaming laws. On that deployment her usually well-heeled passengers had been pampered in true American style. To ensure that was the case she'd carried 230-odd crew members.

Yet when she prepared to sail across the North Sea to Sweden under her new lean, mean, cost-cutting regime as a ro-ro cargo-passenger ferry, her complement had been cut by over fifty per cent. Still adequate to comply with the international minimum safe manning standards demanded by the Bahamian maritime authorities, as well as by both the United Kingdom and the Scandinavian flag states, but nevertheless reduced by enough to throw the fundamentally crucial emr numbers game into complete disarray.

Particularly as McCulloch, pressured to attend to all his other duties in a fraction of the time any truly safety-conscious and less revenue-hungry owners would have allowed, simply hadn't been afforded the opportunity to complete his down-scaling of the plan sitting in his *immediate action* tray.

Like taking into account the gaps in it created by the *Orion Venturer*'s vastly reduced crew. Which entailed figuring precisely how, in the admittedly unlikely event of a problem arising on this first leg of their first voyage, 104 people – including a pianist, a disc jockey, two croupiers and three shop assistants, none of whom had ever been to sea before – were going to perform the functions originally envisaged for a complement of 236.

A riddle he hadn't quite managed to solve so far. The key emr lists still lay on his desk with more white space than names set against the task groupings . . . not to mention those names that had two emr numbers provisionally scribbled against them because he'd had difficulty in identifying precisely who, among the crowd, actually held fire training or first aid credentials. Or even certificates of competency in the handling of boats and rafts, despite the crewing agencies' assurance that they'd hired more than enough to satisfy the statutory requirements for a minimum of 48 qualified lifeboat men or women demanded by the *Orion Venturer*'s passenger ship safety certificate.

. . . as well as enough to conform with the *International Convention on Standards of Training, Certification and Watchkeeping for Seafarers (STCW), Chapter VI, Regulation VI/1* . . . and with the *Convention on the Safety of Life at Sea (SOLAS), as amended by the Protocol of 1978: Chapter II, Regulation 10, subsections III an' bloody four . . . !*

Chief Officer McCulloch rested his head in his hands and permitted himself a moment of wry reflection. A Scot born and bred in the port of Leith, he'd gone to sea aged sixteen. Like most, he had a passing familiarity with Burns. *The best laid schemes o' mice an' mon gang aft a-gley.*

In a nutshell, Rabbie: in a nutshell. Nae wonder they ca' you the Scottish Bard.

A splendid emergency response plan, Mister McCulloch. So long as you discount the fact that very few aboard know where they fit into it. And that some won't even be able to read it. With or without a bloody number!

CHAPTER FIVE

All the physicians and authors in the world could not give a clear account of his madness. He is mad in patches, full of lucid intervals.

MIGUEL DE CERVANTES (1547–1616)

Sven Carlsson jumped down before turning to yank his overnight bag from the high cab of the Scania traction unit. Not too keen on seagoing as such, the bustle and urgency proclaiming a ro-ro's sailing still gave him a buzz each time. Same with this one. The hum of ship's generators filling a vehicle deck ringing with metallic echoes. Chains dragging and clanking over steel; the hiss of air brakes being applied; voices shouting above the grumble of engines.

He hung around long enough to satisfy himself that the ferry crew were indeed securing his employer's expensive rig to the ringbolts set into the deck in what he considered a seamanlike manner, then, as soon as they'd properly wedged the wheels to prevent the mammoth truck taking charge should the ferry meet heavy weather on passage, picked his way behind a still nervously manoeuvring private car to the steel sliding exit door over to starboard, signed: ALL CABINS – BOARDING CARD HOLDERS ONLY.

Jealous of his roots, he thought they might at least have posted the signs in the Nordic languages as well, considering this was a new line out to grab a slice of Scandinavia's North Sea traffic action. Lucky his English was passable – he had picked it up during his temporary role as a trucker – but then he was a pretty exceptional guy. Not every Swede or Dane aboard would be so qualified.

Come to that, there was a lot they could have done to sharpen up the image. First impression of the vehicle deck, and therefore of the ship to those passengers taking their wheels abroad with them, was that it was shabby. An exercise in hastily retouched paint, applied without a lot of preparation.

Carlsson felt pleased at having identified that flaw in marketing philosophy. Play his cards right, the shipping company itself might well recognize him as a mover and shaker. Hurry to grab him for themselves before the offers flooded in.

Talking of cards – no one had offered him a boarding card at the loading dock check-in. The berth number printed on his ticket was the only indicator he had of where he would sleep that night and he wasn't too comfortable with that. He'd logged a lot of sea miles aboard overnight ferries. In most a colour-coded boarding card had been issued to each passenger, intended to help facilitate the smooth handling of any emergency on passage – and it almost certainly *would* on this particular trip, in view of what he had in mind.

And to be scrupulously fair to Carlsson, the last thing he wanted to do was initiate a full-scale panic: maybe cause elderly folk, kids, even people with disabilities to mill around not knowing precisely where to go or how to get there when the whistle blew. He wasn't inconsiderate. Just because you got motivation to move up in the world don't mean you should disregard those less privileged, less enterprising than you.

Though wouldn't being thrust into public prominence mean he'd *have* to accept some inconvenience to others as being the downside of fame, irrespective of how caring he was? Had he chosen to become a pop star or a Swedish cabinet minister as his route to the top, he'd've caused problems with crowd control as well. Maybe, once he was acknowledged as a hero, he could push for starting some kind of socially responsible fund – even let them use his name. Somethin' like the . . . like . . . yeah – something like The Sven Carlsson Charitable Foundation for the Underpriv . . .

An open padlock hung from a welded hasp on the sliding steel fire door from the car deck. The padlock suggested an intention to secure it on voyage once everyone was out. The door itself led into a long, fairly narrow alleyway running fore and aft, with a row of cabins ranged along its outboard side. On the obverse of the once white-painted door was stencilled:

35

EMERGENCY EXIT
Crew Only
KEEP DOOR CLOSED

Bloody English again: an eccentric language at the best of times. For instance, did the sign *really* intend to imply this was an emergency exit for the crew only? The grubby frame, the door's pattern of oily palm prints and the fact its colour had long faded to sad-yellow matt made it even more curious that someone should recently have considered it necessary to add, in large red letters:

SALIDA DE EMERGENCIA

Spanish? Italian? Portugee . . . ? An' why? Not many of them around the North Sea, and those that were could usually be seen hoovering the bottom clean of good Scandinavian fish stocks . . . or maybe the ferry had been running down the Med previously?

Carlsson stole a quick glance either way along the corridor. A family carrying cases were walking uncertainly towards him from the exit further aft. Two young kids with their parents. He'd noticed them disgorging from the GB-plated Volvo that boarded after him, notably because the mother had revealed nice legs as she'd swung them out of the car. Almost as shapely as a Stockholm woman's. The couple looked harassed, as if they'd been driving all night. Now the little girl was trailing a disconsolate-looking teddy bear while the boy was wearing what looked for all the world like . . . well, like a yellow sou'wester?

Not only the Brit language was eccentric.

The adults nodded thanks as he leaned back against the door to allow them to pass while, at the same time, removing the padlock and slipping it into his pocket. Chances were there wouldn't be any spares to hand. He didn't *have* to sneak back to the truck later but, if he could, fine. It would make things easier.

More people began to materialize from the vehicle deck, many frowning between their tickets and the arrowed directional signs denoting cabin numbers and decks. The signs were yellow, blue, green and red, and beside each sign was a stylised logo showing a ship's lifeboat. That tallied with his understanding of where individual boarding cards came in – check its colour and you knew exactly which route to follow to your emergency muster station.

. . . if they'd *given* you a boarding card.

It wasn't like he was a neurotic or anything. Hung up on signs and colours and stuff. It was more a case of preparing his homework in anticipation of his new role. Man, would he sharpen these guys up: hammer some organization into the system when *he* began working for the company . . .

More passengers began appearing in the corridor. Americans this time: the voices and the clothes and the blue rinses told him that much. A group of sunset citizens from one of the tour coaches. He decided it wasn't smart to be seen hanging around. Play it cool. Carlsson's eyes took in a lot of the ferry's geography as he mingled with the stragglers to work his way up one deck to his cabin.

By the time he got there he'd become a very satisfied potential executive. A number of doors to the cabins at car deck level had been left standing ajar. From the corner of his eye he'd noted paint tins and dust sheets in some: lengths of timber and sanitary fittings in others . . . obviously that lower section of the ship was still undergoing refurbishment and would be unoccupied during this trip. It was as if God was greenlighting his future. Giving him all the support he could have asked for.

The first thing he did was get out his best jeans and a spotless white T-shirt: lay them on the berth ready for tonight. He'd shave after he'd breakfasted: maybe even shave again later. Looking sharp could prove critical. The public were entitled to expect their heroes to look the part. Companies positively demanded that their top executives projected an image.

. . . less than two hours before the *Orion Venturer* was due to sail, the increasingly disturbed mind of passenger Sven Carlsson had begun to accelerate towards meltdown. Programme itself to the firm conviction that his transition from denim to business suit was already a matter of fact.

That the only thing left for him to do now was trigger the process.

CHAPTER SIX

The fact that other Masters operated the same defective system does not relieve [the Captain] of his personal responsibility for taking his ship to sea in an unsafe condition. In doing so he was seriously negligent in the discharge of his duties.

Report on loss of mv *Herald of Free Enterprise*
UK Court No. 8074 Formal Investigation

The Captain was facing a dilemma.

To sail, or not to sail.

Which was an extraordinary conflict for a man whose energies should have been focused on his first voyage in command of the *Orion Venturer*.

Even more odd considering he had every reason to believe she was a good and stout ship. By all accounts her winter repositioning voyage across the Atlantic under her previous master had, once again, proved her an excellent sea boat. Fast enough to maintain tight schedules, manoeuvrable in close situations. Constructed with a welded steel hull in the early seventies under the supervision of the French classification society Bureau Veritas, she'd undergone all the strict periodic surveys required of her by the Bahamian authorities in addition to the rigid quarterly inspections visited by the US Coastguard on every vessel carrying passengers from ports in the United States. Although built to conform with international rules agreed forty years previously, making her elderly by European ferry industry standards, the *Orion Venturer* could still boast the ultimate maritime accolade of being classed *+100 A1 Passenger/ Ro-ro Cargo/Ferry, LMC* in *Lloyd's Register of Shipping*.

And, as her newly appointed master, Jorgen Truls Halvorsen, the third son of a poor fisherman from Tromsø, held custody of all the documentation to prove it – every scrap of official paper that a ship requires under maritime law to warrant her suitable for sea-going service. In his cabin safe were certificates ranging from the *Venturer's International Load Line Certificate* to her *Certificate of Safe Manning*. From her MARPOL Certificate stating that she did indeed conform with the International Requirements for the Prevention of Pollution at Sea, to her certificate certifying she was permitted to carry a maximum of one thousand, one hundred and eighteen passengers in regular traffic between the United Kingdom and those Scandinavian countries she was about to serve.

It so happened that, because the whole of C and the port side of D decks cabin space was still under refurbishment and the main holiday season hadn't yet begun, on this first voyage she would only be carrying just over five hundred.

Which was just as well. Particularly in view of what happ . . . ?

. . . but to pursue that unhappy vein would be to digress from the reason why, less than an hour before his command was due to slip the umbilical cords securing her to land, 59-year-old Captain Halvorsen still found himself torn by indecision as to whether or not he should even take the *Orion Venturer* out beyond the breakwater.

The answer, in part, was because he sens . . . no, rather deeper than that – he *feared* she was unsafe, whatever her certificates certified. Or at least, that she concealed the potential to prove so. A bit like the gut feeling expressed by the morose Able Seaman Conroy really, in that the Captain was unable to attribute his unease to any single, apparent fault of the vessel. His was more an experienced seaman's awareness that many pre-departure tasks still remained undone: largely operational and mostly minor when considered in isolation but which – collectively and under certain circumstances – could be foreseen as creating a significant hazard. It followed, therefore, that until those discrepancies were rectified his ship was not ready to go to sea.

To harbour instinctive doubt about the safety of his vessel before a voyage is no unique situation for a ship's master to be faced with. It never has been, and probably never will be. Today and every day, ships still sail with a question mark hanging over their fitness even to survive the passage to their next port – particularly ships registered in certain countries which pay only lip service to the concept of regulation . . . particularly ships already of that ilk which trade between certain *other* countries where the regulatory inspectors themselves can become stricken blind by a terrible disease: one usually transmitted from captain to official by the exchange of bank notes under a desk.

Fortunately such a malady is not endemic in western Europe and seldom, if ever, afflicts the maritime safety officers of Flag States bordering the North Sea. Halvorsen, an honourable man, would not have contemplated such an alternative in any case.

No. The Captain's options, like those faced by many before him, were both simple and stark. Either he packed his suitcase and walked off his vessel that minute, declaring himself unwilling to compromise his professional integrity by placing a single human life at risk – or did nothing. Took no action which could, well . . . rock the boat, so to speak.

Or did nothing until he received the pre-sailing report from Chief Officer McCulloch, anyway, confirming that all vehicles were aboard and secured; that the Assistant Bosun was about to close the stern loading doors; and that the ferry was otherwise ready to go to harbour stations. Whereupon he could decide to live, or die, with his apprehensions and his passengers: shrug into his number one reefer jacket with the brass buttons and the four gold rings of abandoned responsibility on its cuffs; place his oak-leafed uniform cap at a reassuringly jaunty angle on his head – and climb the short stairway to the bridge to begin the *Orion Venturer*'s departure checks.

. . . it was having to make that choice which was turning the bile in the stomach of Jorgen Truls Halvorsen to acid as every tick of the clock brought his personal point of no return ever closer. Had made him ill, in fact. Undermined both the physical and mental resilience of a man already debilitated by the strains of his profession, because commanding any large ro-ro passenger ferry is a stressful occupation even in the best-regulated vessels.

The Captain could have saved a lot of agonizing had he been honest with himself from the start. Faced the unpalatable fact that all of us become prey to the insecurity of ageing. If he'd only been able to bring himself to such self-critical introspection, then he

40

would have long recognized he'd never seriously weighed his first and most challenging option: that of conscience. Not even when it had become worryingly clear that the ship could not be got ready on schedule despite the pressures applied by remote corporate financiers concerned more with the interests of investors than of seamen.

At least then he might have come to accept, without the mounting stress caused by continual soul-searching, that he would sail the *Orion Venturer* despite his reservations. Take the alternative of moral compromise because he was fifty-nine and approaching the twilight of his career, and had become desperate to cling to what was left of the only way of life he'd known.

The spectre of retirement terrified Jorgen Halvorsen – retire to what? He'd long severed his roots ashore. His wife had died in a car accident over a decade before. They'd never been blessed with children. He'd already experienced the imagined loss of self-respect, the sense of redundancy forced on him after years of diligent service when his former Norwegian operators bowed to commercial pressures to cut back their ferry fleet, although – by the grace of God allied to his willingness to work, even for a pittance – he'd been fortunate in that instance. He'd succeeded against the odds in acquiring another command in an industry where there are ten . . . twenty times more unemployed captains than ships on the seven seas.

Unfortunately there are also three . . . four times as many ship owners without principle as there are companies of repute who, because they do place the genuine concerns of their shipmasters above profit, can fly their house flags with pride. The already insecure Captain Halvorsen soon began to learn he'd fallen in with the former. His very first request – to accelerate the signing of a full crew – had been met with barely concealed outrage despite his arguing that the measure was essential, not only to ease the pressure on his skeleton staff struggling to cope with preparation but, most crucially, in order that all hands about to sail in the *Orion Venturer* were afforded time to familiarize themselves with a ship new to them.

Such profligacy would add thousands of dollars to the payroll before their investment began to earn a cent, his owners had reprimanded, wounded to the core of their balance sheet. Such a tendency towards frivolous expenditure was not what they expected of their masters . . . the implication had been clear. If Halvorsen felt unable to keep within the budgetary limitations imposed on him, was not prepared to lean on his heads of department, cut a few corners to ensure the *Orion Venturer* was made ready in time to meet her inaugural service date no matter what – then they would find another, more co-operative master who would.

It was at that point that the first fractures began to appear in Jorgen Halvorsen's resolve. When compromise took precedence over conscience. He began to avoid holding planning discussions with his senior officers and simply issued targets instead. And – because he was a gentle man at heart who, unlike his owners, knew that you can push an already tired crew too far – when he found those targets were proving unattainable, he simply said, 'Do your best. We're all under pressure.'

As when, for instance, Chief Bracamontes had complained that only enough time had been allowed to strip and clear eighty per cent of the car deck sprinkler heads of rust before his junior engineers had been harassed into moving to their next scheduled task of freeing and greasing recalcitrant fire hydrants . . . or as many as possible before being forced to hurry on to test the first, second, maybe even the third of the ten motorized lifeboat engines which should all have been overhauled before sailing.

Like when the *Venturer*'s Australian Electronics Technical Officer and Radio Operator, the irreverent Ed Talbot, shrugged laconically on being flatly refused permission to extend the coverage of the emergency alarms. 'Suit yourself, Cap'n. Tell you what. Ask the owners whether they rather I put paper ear trumpets or prayer mats in some of the outside cabins. Up around E deck the panic bells wouldn't wake a dozing pussy cat!'

He sympathized particularly with the problems which arose in the cut-to-the-bone deck department headed by Chief Officer McCulloch. The Captain, also a seaman officer, fully appreciated his young First Mate's dilemma.

McCulloch, having sacrificed the structured but slower career path open to most junior officers with premier passenger lines in order to gain a third gold stripe sooner, had suddenly found himself in thrall to a previously alien safety culture. Instructed to concentrate on priorities more cosmetic than sea-prudent, he'd been forced to assign the *Orion Venturer*'s predominantly Spanish ratings to painting when they should have been checking out cables and running gear. To stowing away a detritus of timber and painting equipment left by ship-fitters now safely ashore, instead of greasing and overhauling lifeboat falls.

McCulloch, unwilling to be seen as failing and so trying desperately to make do, should have been monitored more closely. Halvorsen was guiltily aware that the Mate needed discreet support – was having difficulties with revising the emergency plan, for instance – but had done nothing to help.

A psychologist – any perceptive observer – would have understood why not. Previously a responsible seaman, the Captain, disillusioned and mentally drained to find himself so compliant in enforcing economies against his instinctive judgement, had become prey to overstress. And overstress, in the case of Jorgen Truls Halvorsen, had evinced itself in clinical depression. In his embracing a withdrawn, head-in-the-sand attitude to his continuing problems.

It was a condition which would kill him.

It would also play a significant part in killing his ship.

Had the Captain only been thirty-nine years old, or even forty-nine, with the fire to have taken a firmer stand against those shadow men who paid his derisory salary with cheques drawn on a bank in Ujung Pandang – the first of which had already required re-presentation before finally being honoured – he would still have been prudent to weigh the likely cost of taking such an altruistic step as to court dismissal. Certainly he would have been wise to harbour little illusion about his chances of ever being offered another seagoing appointment, never mind another command this side of a Liberia-flagged ferry running out of Haiti.

. . . which couldn't happen anyway, now. Not if the whole truth ever came out.

Because there was a further, and even more compelling, reason for Captain Halvorsen to sail the *Orion Venturer* out into the North

Sea on that rainy day without drawing attention any more closely than necessary to his secret anxieties. Particularly as the British Marine Safety Agency, acutely sensitive to lessons learned from the loss of the ro-ro *Herald of Free Enterprise*, had already proved uncomfortably assiduous in ensuring the letter of the law was observed before granting him authorization to sail from a UK port.

Or as assiduous as their own limited resources permitted. Government regulating bodies are every bit as constrained as ship operators by manpower and fiscal limits. They too have targets to meet regarding the number of ships they must inspect while they are in harbour. The regulations allow for that function to be restricted to satisfying themselves that the vessel's certificates are valid, and that all statutory safety drills have indeed been held and entered in her official log. Only if they have 'clear' grounds for believing the visited ship does not 'substantially' meet the requirements of the relevant safety conventions, are they bound to subject the vessel to a closer, more detailed inspection.

It was during one such official scrutiny that Captain Halvorsen had effectively passed his personal point of no return – and invited his stress level to soar into the red. He did so the moment he presented the *Orion Venturer*'s log book for examination, declaring it was a true record of recent actions taken aboard his ship in full conformity with maritime law. One part of that law, *SOLAS Chapter III, Regulation 25* states: *On passenger ships, an abandon ship drill and fire drill shall take place weekly.*

No such drills had taken place since the *Orion Venturer* had cleared American waters some weeks before. Just one boat hastily lowered part way to the water by a handful of crewmen, then retrieved just as quickly. There had never been an appropriate time for a more comprehensive exercise, in Halvorsen's hard-pressed view. To authorize a full-scale emergency rehearsal for such a new and still incomplete crew would have squandered a whole day more profitably spent in such revenue-enhancing tasks as cleaning and polishing the bars and restaurant, setting up the gaming areas, stocking the duty-free shops . . .

The company's operations superintendent, an executive with roots more in marketing and PR than the seabed, had laconically endorsed his decision.

'What the hell, Cap'n: it's just a scribble on a page and who needs all the red tape? Passengers don't care if a steward knows squat about which end of a lifeboat's which – but they'll sure kick up shit if their cabin ain't ready. You and me: it's our job to sell the sizzle, not the steak, huh?'

. . . that was the real reason why Jorgen Truls Halvorsen could risk doing nothing further to rock his particular boat. Why he would wait, constantly questioning whether it was worth having a command to cling to any longer, until it was time to put his hat on rather less jauntily than before, and climb to the bridge where, for a few infinitely precious years longer, he might hope to regard himself as a God among men with fewer rings.

The Captain would try to forget that, by having knowingly made a false entry in the log, he had committed an offence which, were it to be exposed at this late stage, even with the bulk of her passengers and vehicle cargo on board, would invite a detention order to be immediately placed upon the *Orion Venturer* and so prevent her from sailing, as well as lead to his own certain ruin.

During the next twenty-odd hours he wouldn't allow himself even to *think* on the consequence of such action, should the inconceivable occur.

Or at least, he wouldn't – until the moment when it actually did.

CHAPTER SEVEN

The control functions exercised by the classification soci-
eties and by the Bahamian nautical inspectors are concerned to a very small extent with the crew's operational
abilities and abilities in an emergency . . . [yet] . . . there
is no question that ship's crews vary in quality. Their
degree of competency is often not as high as it should be
. . . [in particular] . . . replacing a large proportion of the
crew may have a considerable negative effect on the stan-
dard of safety on board, especially since it takes time
for the new crew to become familiar with the ship, the
operation and function of the safety equipment, etc.

Norwegian Official Report, NOR 1991: 1E
The *Scandinavian Star* Disaster of 7 April 1990

At sixteen, Pantry Rating Filippo Lucchetti was the youngest crew
person on board the *Orion Venturer*.

He was listed in the harassed Chief Officer McCulloch's stop-gap
emergency plan not only as nineteen years old, but as being in
possession of both firefighting and sea survival qualifications as
well as of a Certificate of Competency issued by the Italian Ministero della Marina Mercantile stating that he was fully proficient in
the handling of lifeboats and liferafts.

The snag was that Pantry Rating Filippo Lucchetti had never
been in a lifeboat in his life. Hadn't even stood on the deck of a
ship, for that matter.

In fact the one professional qualification that young Filippo *could*
lay claim to wasn't actually listed in his discharge book. Not that
the oversight mattered. It would have held little relevance to his
ability to take charge of a survival craft full of terrified and seasick
passengers in a force ten gale in the middle of every seaman's
nightmare.

Because Pantry Rating Lucchetti was actually what is known in the Neapolitan Mafia as a *Picciotto di Onore* – a Lad of Honour. He had earned himself that title because, when only twelve years old, he had killed two men. He'd done so because he knew no better, having been raised in the foetid Mergellina port area where the Camorra controls the souls of all too many of its residents through fear, and corrupts the minds of the young.

When an urchin such as Filippo, a kid of no significance from the gutters, volunteers to become a servant of the *Famiglia* he is first expected to prove himself. No money changes hands, only a gun and a test target – in his case two foot soldiers of the rival Nuova Camorra Organizzata then attempting to seize control of the local crime scene: drugs, prostitution, intimidation, extortion . . .

The child Lucchetti came of age – qualified as a *Picciotto di Onore* in a frantic chatter of automatic pistol shots and a hysteria of screaming from the other patrons of the pavement trattoria where his nominee victims were sipping quality Lavazza coffee. The measure of Filippo's success was reflected by the welter of blood and brain tissue fouling the white stucco wall behind their over-turned seats a moment later.

All in all it suggested that Filippo Lucchetti was a hard little bastard. And that was certainly true – you have to be hard on the streets of Mergellina or Frattamagore if your parents are uncaring and you want to eat – but it isn't the only quality you need to rise above your own disadvantage to get yourself sent to Chicago, or even Rome, to live in a fine apartment and ride in a stretch limo and cut deals for the Mob.

Which largely explained why, since that day, instead of being encouraged to feel a perverse pride at being apprenticed to his Godfather, Filippo had been driven to becoming more and more cynical about his lot. Some said he was too intelligent to suit his local, middle-management *mafioso* – too sharp altogether for the long-term comfort of those above him, whom he showed promise of eventually displacing. So they deliberately kept him to the per-iphery of evil and withheld the commendation so necessary to his advancement through the hierarchy of the Mafia.

For four years he'd played an increasingly subservient role as a look-out, a petty crack dealer, a low-grade *contrabbandista* . . . until he began to realize there had to be more to life than ducking and weaving each time a Squadra Mobile patrol hove into sight. The by then sixteen-year-old wannabe hoodlum's crunch had finally come when, one day, he was called before his lieutenant.

'You have been chosen for a great honour,' the Lieutenant had said with the smile of a wolf. 'You, Filippo Lucchetti, have been selected to become a *Picciotto di Sgarroe.*'

Young Lucchetti knew then that he was finished, although he didn't really appreciate the politics of why. He merely assumed he had not been seen as assiduous enough in his criminality. Either way, to receive the accolade of becoming a *Picciotto di Sgarroe* is hardly an upwardly mobile career move – it is an order to take yourself to the Carabinieri and confess to a crime you did not commit, and duly serve the true perpetrator's time for it as your tithe to the *Famiglia.* Effectively, to take the rap for the anti-social indiscretions of a more senior *camorristo* in order that he may continue in the lifestyle to which he has become accustomed.

. . . which does not include waking up in a stinking cell in the maximum security *supercarcere* at Nuoro on the island of Sardinia every day for the next fifteen to twenty years. It is you who will be doing that. And – if you're *really* as thick as the sauce on a good *bolognese* – boasting all the while of the exceptional qualities you possess which earned you such a bizarre privilege.

Filippo was fortunate. To attempt to leave the Mafia, to insult them by refusing such a remarkable honour, promises to be even more hazardous than qualifying to join it. A positively downwardly mobile career move, in fact, as a result of which you are likely to be installed under the dehydrating tufa soil of the Cimitero Monumentale on the Via Santa Maria del Riposo minus your ears, tongue and genitalia.

But Filippo, still having access to dealer's stock, knew a man who needed cocaine, who knew a man who needed heroin who, in turn, knew a man who not only needed every buzz his shaking hand could inject, but who also possessed a seafarer's discharge book among other negotiable assets. It turned out he'd acquired the precious papers from a drunken Italian youth off one of the big cruise ships before the police arrived to fish the late messboy's corpse from the dockside waters into which he had – well . . . fallen?

As the *Orion Venturer* made ready for sailing, the most junior member of her complement was a dark-haired lad willingly applying himself to the honest endeavour of scraping, then stacking dishes on the crockery-wash conveyor in the sweatbox of her utilities galley: a humid compartment deep in the ship and only marginally less claustrophobic than the cells of Nuoro's *supercarcere*.

A happy ending, and one with an uplifting moral. The Sinner That Repenteth. The urchin from the gutter who, despite having killed two men, had nevertheless come to appreciate that becoming a good guy offered the best way to salvation.

It was ironic, then, that Pantry Rating Filippo Lucchetti should have opted to steer the one path of righteousness already shaping to prove the most downwardly mobile career move of his life.

Marianne Nørgaard was enormously proud of her Junior Purser's uniform with the single thin gold stripe on its traditional white ground.

She'd worked hard for it, having spent six years in Danish-flagged ferries since leaving school: first as a bar assistant, then cabin stewardess and, ultimately, cabin supervisor on services running from Ålborg and Frederikshavn across to Sweden. She'd always wanted to follow a career at sea. Her greatest ambition was to become Chief Purser of a cruise ship.

When she'd been contacted by the Hamburg crewing agency and offered the opportunity of transferring, not only to a long-haul North Sea ferry but, even better, as a junior officer, she'd hardly been able to contain her euphoria. Admittedly the pay scale they'd offered was disappointing. She'd earn less wearing her smart uniform aboard the Bahamian-registered *Orion Venturer* than she did when making up berths and sterilizing toilets under Scandinavian rates of pay, but, more importantly, it represented a further step up the ladder.

It did involve one slightly disquieting condition of service. She hadn't been directly employed by those who owned the *Venturer* – in fact she wasn't entirely sure of who they actually were. Instead she'd been signed by the agency to a fifteen-week contract with no certainty of continuance. She'd felt a bit disappointed at that, although she realized it reflected the shape of seagoing employment to come.

From a small fleet owner's point of view, such a perfectly proper arrangement holds considerable attraction: especially to cruise and long-haul ferry operators where the Purser's catering and on-board services represent by far the largest and most transient department, comprising some sixty per cent of a passenger vessel's total complement. Crewing agencies, with their comprehensive personnel databases, ease the difficulties of replacing staff who move on or fail to measure up. Neither is the shipowner required to continue paying salaries to personnel on leave: a somewhat more questionable advantage affording them a commercial edge over competitors who believe that, by retaining and rotating long-service crews familiar with their ships, they are underwriting a safety premium for their passengers.

. . . while if, perish the thought, the agency's client also happens to be a ship operator prepared to exploit the system – then wouldn't a little contractual insecurity in a hirer's market tend to encourage smaller complements to work harder for lower pay over longer hours?

But Marianne, who, as though to prove the point had only been given five days to settle in aboard the *Orion Venturer* before sailing and very little information, never mind training in her duties, didn't have time to reflect too deeply on that. Now she was immersed in the pre-departure bustle filling the wide reception area around her post at – ironically – the ferry's information desk.

Passengers were still arriving hesitantly through the skywalk, frowning at the cabin direction signs until strategically positioned stewards interpreted their tickets and gave directions – or frowned equally uncertainly at cabin allocations which they themselves hadn't yet had time to become acquainted with . . . a system which had come as a further unexpected departure from usual ship routine to Nørgaard. Most ferries she'd served in previously had issued colour-coded boarding cards.

The apparent anomaly caused her a moment's anxiety. Had she missed something crucial in the ship's organization? If not, then how would the passengers be advised of their muster stations in the event of an incident occurring on passage?

50

Junior Purser Marianne Nørgaard, an experienced seafarer, held all valid sea survival, boat and lifecraft handling certificates required of her by the provisions of the Danish Shipping Act, *Sønæringsloven SNL*. She knew of the existence of the *Orion Venturer*'s emergency plan – had even considered it important enough to study in her all-too-short watches below – but, as nobody had yet allocated Marianne an emr number and there were no crew lists posted anyway, she hadn't so far been able to discover where she fitted into it.

. . . she determined to ask as soon as one of the more senior pursers became free. But that wouldn't be for some time.

As the queue at her desk lengthened, asking everything from where baby changing facilities were located to could they book a window table for dinner, Marianne dismissed the concern as being secondary to more immediately pressing duties, and absorbed herself once more with the activity on the reception deck.

In the main area some travellers, already installed, ostentatiously fingered cabin keys while scrutinizing the Ship's Amenities notice board. Others passed through more briskly, intent on exploring the ferry. A group of youngsters studied the all-night rolling programme of feature films showing in the cinema on F deck above. A queue had formed at the Bureau de Change window where Assistant Purser Everard dispensed Swedish krona and welcoming banter in equal measure.

A small boy wearing a yellow sou'wester broke away from his parents who'd just appeared from the direction of the car deck.

'Please can you tell me what time the captain keel-hauls people?' the awful child asked with atavistic relish.

'I don't think he's going to on this trip,' she smiled. 'None of the sailors have been naughty enough.'

The disappointed sou'wester was retrieved by an embarrassed father. 'Sorry! He's been reading a book . . .'

Assistant Purser Everard grinned. A bit too patronizingly.

'Welcome to the Giddy Galleon, sweetheart. Think you can work out what you're going to say when some old dear asks whether we anchor at night or just tie up to a sandbank?'

Marianne frowned.

'But won't that depend on how deep the water is when it does get too dark for the Captain to see, Mister Everard?'

She smiled sweetly, enjoying Everard's momentary discomfiture.

. . . though there were other members, particularly of the *Orion Venturer's* hotel services department, who might have considered that question seriously.

E deck cabins steward Pinheiro Cardoso, for instance. Who, this time last week, had been a waiter in Lisbon's Hotel Supremo on the Avenida Duque de Loule . . . *he* might just have been tempted to give the matter tentative thought, rather than be rushed into giving an instant answer.

But that was largely because, like Pantry Rating and somewhat superfluously qualified *Picciotto di Onore* Filippo Luchetti, Cardoso had never been aboard a ship before. In fact he'd already begun to feel a little queasy as he fussed anxiously from cabin to cabin in his neatly pressed white jacket, even though the ferry hadn't yet begun to single up on her mooring lines for leaving.

It had all been the fault of his close . . . well, not to put too fine a point on it – his *very* close friend, Jorge Guimães, who'd been a *sous chef* in the same hotel before the manager bulleted him on account of his propensity for smiling rather too welcomingly at newly arrived guests.

Particularly at newly arrived single guests.

Particularly at newly arrived single *gentlemen* guests . . .

Anyway, it seemed the abruptly unemployed Jorge, driven by fascist management in a time of pre-season recession to earn himself a few escudos through the only other skill he possessed, had been cruising down . . . well, he'd occasioned to strike up a temporary, albeit unreservedly intimate relationship with an elderly and rather naive chap who just happened to work in the Direcção Geral de Marinha over on the Praça do Comercio.

The next morning but one he'd turned over in bed to face Pinheiro, propped his head on one exquisitely tanned arm, and said, 'Fancy working on a *barco grande*, Pinny?'

'Oh, *sim*? And how d'you plan to fix that, *Senhor* Sleazebag?' Pinheiro had retorted somewhat waspishly. But then, he was still overwrought with jealousy and everything ... and besides, the last sailor he'd met had told him he'd need an official Portuguese seafarer's licence to escape the poorly paid grind of Lisbon hotel service.

'I could get these photos developed, Pet ... ?' Jorge had suggested.

Jorge Guimãres was now Assistant Pastry Chef in the *Orion Venturer*'s kitchens, under strict caution not to smile at *anybody* ...

Give him his due, Pinheiro Cardoso had never professed to the crewing agency that he could either speak or understand English – or no more than to claim to be able to advise haltingly on a menu, or take a room service order. And while his expeditiously acquired seafarer's papers implied by definition that he'd received some form of basic sea safety training, he'd certainly never claimed to be qualified to take charge of anything so utterly alien as a ship's *boat*.

In fact, in the two exhausting days he'd been aboard Pinheiro had even found problems in deciphering, from the illustrated card on the back of his cabin door, exactly how to go about putting his *own* lifejacket on – never mind assist some distraught passenger scrabbling halfway up a tilting wall to avoid the water coming through their window.

Tomorrow he planned to grab a minute or two of quality time. Expand his knowledge of nautical technicalities. Tomorrow he firmly resolved to find out where the *Orion Venturer*'s lifejackets were kept!

... all in all, Pinheiro Cardoso's curriculum vitae suggested that, while he could well prove absolutely indispensable in taking orders from his fellow survivors in his raft for a short order *Ervilhas à Portuguesa*, or a plateful of deep-fried *Rissois* on the run, he wouldn't be of much bloody help in ensuring they lived a moment longer than the state of the ship, the sea, and the fickle disposition of Fate decreed.

He'd still got the job. But then, like shipmasters, safety inspectors and managers under pressure from owners, the staffs of crewing agencies also have targets to meet.

At two-seventeen tomorrow morning, when Second Officer Delucci is first alerted to a manual alarm triggered in way of supposedly vacant starboard cabins C312 to C320, Steward Pinheiro Cardoso will be the only crew member on night duty in the after section of the *Orion Venturer*'s E deck.

The first occupied sleeping area directly above the source of that warning.

Junior Third Engineer Stamper is yet another middle watchkeeper fated to be caught in the frame at the moment when 2/O Delucci's entire night shows promise of being ruined, and it will slowly begin to dawn on Cabins Night Steward Cardoso that he should have asked earlier where the lifejackets were stowed.

Admittedly, in Bert Stamper's case, that latter concern will prove rather more moot considering he'll be right down in the bottom of the ship – in the engine room control room – when it happens. And anyway, Bert already knows where his lifejacket is. Assuming he won't reach the personal preserver lying in his cabin, it's whichever one he fancies that's left over by the time he gets topside, out of the 1500-odd stored either in lockers to port and starboard of the survival craft embarkation deck – deck G, eight stairways up – or even higher, in chests on the funnel deck . . . *nine* levels above him.

There are no lifejackets kept in the *Orion Venturer*'s engine room. Lifejackets are bulky. They restrict the agility of movement on which survival may depend. Many ship's engineers would forgo donning one while still enclosed in what promises to become a revolving steel coffin. They can all too easily become snagged on pipework, escape hatches, the hook-like dogs of watertight doors . . .

Not that Stamper felt any sense of premonition as sailing time approached. Being only twenty-six, he hadn't accumulated the sea time of men like the Captain and Able Seaman Conroy who'd developed a gut feeling for these things.

No, Third Engineer Stamper was more preoccupied right then in trying to explain to Motorman Teofisto Garilao, in words of one syllable, precisely how he wanted the indefatigably amiable little Filipino to go about the business of stripping down number two oily-water separator ready for the Chief Engineer's inspection. It was a routine task which, had the planned maintenance schedule drawn up by Chief Bracamontes on the voyage from Florida been adhered to, should have been completed last week.

Stamper, like Second Officer Delucci, currently supervising the last of the loading into the car deck, shouldn't even have been working. He too should have been relaxing in preparation for his four-hour afternoon sea watch commencing at noon.

But a lot of essential jobs had been allowed to slip. Far from having been completed last week, they hadn't even been completed now, with hardly an hour to go before main engine start-up. Elementary tasks like stripping the rest of the car deck sprinkler heads; checking out the remaining lifeboat engines, the fire hydrants . . . word in the engineering department was the Chief had finally blown his stack with the Old Man – told Halvorsen straight that they, the owners, better approve some shoreside goddam help when they docked in Gothenburg because he wasn't prepared to tolerate any further slippage in his boys maintaining the fundamental goddam mechanicals that kept the goddam ship moving through the goddam *water*!

'Start slacking off the nuts diametrically *opposite* each other – like on either side of the flange, see? Not just as they bloody come,' he repeated wearily. 'You're a qualified motorman.'

He thought about that a minute. 'Leastways you're a *Philippine*-qualified . . .'

'Bebbies, Turd Engines Officer?'

Stamper looked up blankly. The little brown man was proffering a photograph, presumably just arrived in the agent's mail pack. It showed eight or nine children surrounding a pretty woman, all smiling shyly into camera.

'Bebbies. Wuff,' Teofisto elaborated proudly. 'Ate bebbies. You see?'

Bert dragged the back of a grimy hand across his brow. According to Assistant Purser Everard, an authority on the language difficulties which existed aboard the *Orion Venturer*, forty-four per cent of Philippine households spoke English. He had to go and pull a guy as his watch assistant who was Daddy to one of the fifty-six per cent of families that bloody didn't!

Even when he was capable of concentration, Motorman Garilao

couldn't comprehend the spoken Anglo-Saxon word. Not even at its most simple, most courteous level. The sort British seamen have employed to communicate their wishes in all corners of the globe throughout history.

'Nice. Very nice, pal. Your old lady looks proper tasty. Now . . . get yer bum scratcher round that fucking spanner – *savvy*?'

Jerónimo Solbes Madariaga loved to dance.

He wore his jet hair drawn tight back in a oiled ponytail. His eyes were points of Toledo steel set in black velvet. His sensual, never-quite-smooth-shaven features were as refined and as cruelly handsome as those of Torquemada. He liked his jeans high-waisted and tight as a snake's skin, his denim jackets short. When ashore he walked . . . no, he *stalked* with arms straight by his side, fingertips extended, head arrogantly aloof, black fedora tipped dramatically forward over one eye. He nurtured the *Pasión Gitana* – the passion of a true Cordoba gypsy in his heart, and fire in every square centimetre of his high-heeled suede boots hammered with metal studs in the style of his great contemporary dance hero, the legendary Joaquín Cortés.

Jerónimo Solbes Madariaga was, throughout every fibre of his being, a flamenco dancer.

Unfortunately he wasn't a very good flamenco dancer.

. . . which largely accounted for his also being one of the nine deck ratings aboard the *Orion Venturer*, and why, instead of delighting yet another packed house with a tattoo of stamps and handclaps as he clattered towards the climax of his set-piece *Ferruca Andalucia*, Able Seaman Madariaga was sweating to negotiate one of several trolley-loads of unwieldy equipment through the starboard after fire door leading from the car deck. It represented a further task which should have been completed long before sailing: clearing the exhaust-hazed hangar of the remaining items of shipwrights' gear which had accumulated around those temporary workshops first set up to facilitate the ro-ro's refurbishment during her transatlantic repositioning.

But it appeared that, during his recent walkabout, the surveyor from the Marine Safety Agency had taken one look at some of the

56

particularly hazardous equipment left lying by the ship fitters, and shaken his head firmly.

'No way,' he'd said, albeit choosing a slightly more diplomatic form of words as befitted a Man from the Ministry. 'No way are you sailing with *that* bonfire waiting to happen on the car deck, Captain. With or without passengers!'

Another threat of delay. Another pressure ... the system, already near to breaking point, had ground unhappily into gear.

'I would be obliged if you would give priority to having the vehicle deck cleared before sailing, Mister McCulloch,' Halvorsen, frostily courteous even when angered, had instructed his Chief Officer before retreating to his lofty refuge to worry about the boat drills he'd signed for in the log.

'See the bloody stuff's stowed out of the way in double quick time, Mike,' the Mate had delegated wearily before dashing back up top to worry about his emergency plan in the hour or so he had left.

'Get it shifted *now*, Bosun,' Second Officer Delucci had ordered before hastening to check out the vehicle dispositions forrard.

'You, Madariaga – grab hold o' Atienza and Valverde. You got till harbour stations to make it soddin' vanish!' Bosun Pascal had growled ill-temperedly before disappearing in the Second Mate's wake.

'Yeah? And just where, exactly, d'you expect me to put *that* lot in the hour we got left, Bose?' the disgruntled Madariaga had yell ... well, had called respectfully after him. But not even an already-frustrated *bailador tradicional* fired by the *Pasión Gitana* yelled at Bosun Pascal, an uncouth man who lacked not only the sensitivity of the *artistico* but also happened to be built like a brick deckhouse.

Not without a field gun for back-up, he didn't.

... not even when he'd got no one else left to delegate to.

So, after listening in aggrieved silence to his chief's throwaway suggestion of one place of stowage, while promptly dismissing it on the grounds that to follow such anatomical instruction would unquestionably inhibit him from dancing the flamenco so good ever thereafter, the Able Seaman had hissed a discreetly contemptuous '*Hijo de bruto!*' before falling back on using his initiative.

A bad mistake. While Jerónimo Solbes Madariaga may have looked like Torquemada, he couldn't think like Torquemada. In fact, although well qualified as a seaman and holding all the necessary certificates, Madariaga's capacity to display reasoned initiative was equalled only by the ineptitude of his footwork.

. . . twenty minutes and two precariously balanced trolley-dolly loads later, Second Officer Delucci had chanced to hurry by on his way back to the stern ramp, where vehicles were still gunning up and into the Ark. He noticed the starboard after fire door into the accommodation was open, and frowned.

'Where exactly *are* you guys putting those things?' he'd queried uneasily.

One of the ratings, the sullen one who looked like Torquemada, virtually spat something which indisputably referred to the Bosun. The other two simply looked blank. Delucci hesitated, stole an anxious glance at his watch, then shrugged . . . what the hell. Pascal seemed a sound PO. Knew what he was doing.

'Just make damned sure they're tight secured – plenty lashings, *oui*? *Comprenez vous*?'

2/O Delucci couldn't figure why, this time, all three deckies looked mystified. But then, neither did he realize that, by forfeiting his responsibility to press for an answer, he had just colluded in the total breakdown of a chain of supervision intended to protect a floating village like the *Orion Venturer*.

Had, in fact, unwittingly sanctioned the addition of yet another potent ingredient to the alchemy for disaster already brewing aboard the still-slumbering ferry.

CHAPTER EIGHT

We mortals cross the ocean of this world,
Each in his average cabin of a life.
                    ROBERT BROWNING (1812–1889)

Grace Miles thought the cabin they'd been directed to by a white jacketed steward on ... E deck, was it? ... was very nice. Four up-and-down bunk beds, each with its individual curtain for privacy, and vertical ladders to climb into the top ones. A washbasin with mirror over hung on one wall. A small en suite compartment smelling of fresh paint offered a spotlessly clean shower and toilet.

The bedlinen was crisp and neatly tucked in; hand towels and a tartan travel rug placed neatly at the foot of each bunk, though she didn't think they'd need the rugs. It was too warm in the cabin despite the steady hiss of ventilation from an adjustable blower above the door.

It did feel a little more claustrophobic than she would have liked, what with it being an inside cabin as the brochure had called it, and so not having a window. But then, ease of movement wasn't exactly made easier by the children trying to squeeze past to explore everything.

'You two sit on that berth until we get organized,' Michael ordered sourly. He was sweating slightly and looked flushed, having carted the suitcase along a hundred miles of corridor and up two flights of stairs. 'Where d'you want this?'

'Under a bed,' Grace said. 'They won't need their pyjamas until tonight, and their toilet things are in the squashy bag.'

'Sailors don't wash,' seven-year-old William decreed with authority. 'They only get half a cup of water a day an' they have to *drink* that to stay alive.'

'There's sea water,' Grace suggested, anxious to keep the peace.

'If you drink sea water you go mad,' her offspring retorted enthusiastically. 'Your tongue goes furry-black and your eyes pop out an' you jump over the side and get ate by sharks.'

'I meant for washing in, darling.'

'You shouldn't have given him that bloody book,' Michael muttered.

'William doesn't wash anyway, Mummy – not unless you're there to make him!' Lucy grassed. '*And* he jus' runs his toothbrush under the tap so's when you feel it after, you think he's cleaned his teeths.'

'D'you remember when we used to go on holiday on our own?' Michael asked wistfully.

A steward materialized at the still-open door, tapping the frame discreetly to attract attention. A small man smiling out of a sun-tanned face.

'*Bom dia!* I am Pinheiro . . . *Senhor a Senhora* Meeles?'

'Miles.'

'*Sim* – Meeles! There is special brakefass sitting for the leetle ones serving now, *sim*? In the *autoserviço* – the service for yourself – on main deck eff?'

'Cafeteria on deck F. We'll take them up now. Thank you,' Grace smiled back.

'In the tomorrow's morning when we arrive . . . you wish tea? *Café*?'

'Coffee, please. For both of us.'

'The childs, they would like juice of *laranja*?'

'Rum,' William specified.

'Orange juice would be fine, thanks.'

When the steward had gone Michael frowned uncertainly. 'You reckon this *is* the Swedish ferry we're on? We won't find ourselves arriving in Santander or Cadiz or somewhere?'

'I think he's Portuguese.'

'All right – Lisbon, then?'

'No point in *being* onna ship if I can't have rum,' William grumbled and punched Teddy on his already shapeless nose. Lucy, tired out with being awake most of the night while they were driving down, started to cry.

Grace Miles began to feel completely at home aboard the *Orion Venturer*.

On the same deck – E deck, three decks above sea level – but slightly further aft than the Miles lay the starboard outer cabins booked by the veterans of the *Thompson*. They rated as de luxe two-berth, offering what the brochure euphemistically described as 'sea views'. In reality that meant peering through an armour-glazed porthole less than the diameter of a slim woman's hips and attempting to eyeball the horizon through an encrustation of salt from the *Venturer*'s earlier transatlantic repositioning voyage.

Still, the committee decided the *Thompsons* had travelled steerage class more'n enough back in World War II and, this being their swansong sea duty-wise, only the best was good enough. Well, not quite the best. There were a few first class cabins forward with serious luxury – satellite TV, trouser presses, complimentary toiletries and bathrobes, even rectangular windows you could see through – but we're talking retired people here. Guys who'd raised family, spent their best years behind store counters or tool lathes, in auto spray booths or on hog farms. Few of them were rich; most of 'em had struggled to survive the brave new world they'd fought for, and half their buddies had died for.

And they'd negotiated a good deal from the ship company, which had helped stretch the dollar rate. Seemed they'd crossed the Pond just in time to benefit from the start of a fare war . . . some Pacific Rim outfit taking on the established North Sea operators, they'd been told. The tour agents hyping the *Orion Venturer* packages had sure joined battle with all incentives blazing. Block discounts, upgrades – the Admiral Kuritas of the economy travel task force was the joke among the *Thompsons*.

De luxe two-berth for the economy four-berth regular fare had been the deal. And de luxe double was okay on a ship this size, with or without bathrobes. Hell, *better* than okay – real style. Officer country and off limits for most of them last time they crewed a can together.

Even so, Lieutenant Junior Grade O'Kane would have taken a first class flat, Periera thought, blinking at the gaunt old man facing him from the mirror over the de luxe faucets. Engineer Lootenant (jg) O'Kane US Navy wouldn't have felt pushed to trim a few bucks extra off of the premium. Mister O'Kane had got himself a future to look forward to. Big city material. Potential Wall Street man. It had showed plain in his breeding: the way he spoke with the guys. Authority without arrogance. The kind of officer you called *sir* without thinking. *Harvard Class of '41*, the scuttlebutt had whispered. Would have finished up a banker, corporate lawyer . . . maybe even a high flyin' stockbroker playing them futures markets.

But retired now, of course. Like most all of them. White haired and distinguished in the Lieutenant's case, mind you – not like him, Charlie Periera, and fat ol' Zach Goss who'd both been enlisted men from the wrong side of the tracks without no pedigree, and showed it by the toil lines on their faces. One glance at Mister O'Kane would have been enough to tell he'd raised a family of educated gentlemen and class ladies by now. Would've had grand-children – might even have brung them along to take in Europe. Meet the guys that survived. Meet the steel-jacket bluejackets . . . the Pacific Fleet musketeers who took on the Japanese Tiger in an eggshell, and prevailed. The heroes of the USS *Thompson*.

All for one and one for . . .

'Honey?' This time there was real anxiety in Margrite's voice. 'Charlie honey – you ain't . . . you ain't *crying*, are you?'

Ex-MM 2/c Periera blinked hard before he swivelled on his good leg. She'd been laying out her dress with the magnolia print, ready for the special dinner they'd all planned in the Nordic Restaurant topside later. Now she was frowning over with such an expression of . . . it wasn't sympathy, was it?

'Crying?' Charlie protested, putting on his grumpy look. 'What makes you think I'm so baby as to cry, woman?'

When she hobbled from the berth he could tell the pain wus getting to her. It didn't make no difference. When she put her arms around him and brushed her soft silver hair against his cheek, he could still smell those magnolias clear as if they'd been growin' in a pot. Sweet *Jesus* but he loved her.

'I think I'm going to enjoy being on a boat with my sailor hero,' Margrite whispered, clinging tight.

Charlie Periera began to feel frightened all over again then. What if the Lieutenant was really smart? Didn't come for him at all on this, his final sea duty?

What if he come and took Margrite instead . . . ?

Five hundred and seventeen passengers were settling in aboard the reassuring bulk of the 12,000-ton *Orion Venturer* as she made final preparations to sail on that rain-spattered British spring morning. Many of them had travelled overnight to make the dawn departure, content to suffer a little inconvenience in the knowledge that they'd at least arrive fresh after a good night's sleep, with the whole of tomorrow ahead of them filled with Swedish promise. Come to that, on a twenty-four hour passage the options are fairly restricted. Particularly if you're a parent.

In that case it's either up at crack-sparrow and hope to share a snatched forty winks between you and your child-watchkeeping spouse while the ferry's *en voyage*, or sail at a conveniently later time only to arrive when the kids have been bouncing around the cabin most of the previous night anyway, and burned themselves out with excitement and should be in bed, while you've still got to find and check in to your hotel, or even have to drive into the small hours on usually unfamiliar roads to wherever you planned to stop over when you were a lot more optimistic and a lot less frazzled.

If, on the other hand, you're an adult without small hyperactive encumbrances, then you probably don't care. You've got all day to replenish your sleep reserves in anticipation of the on-board evening diversions. You can doze through a feature in the ship's compact cinema on F deck. Unwind in the Admiral's Lounge overlooking the after decks; sip strong Norwegian-style coffee and watch the world go by. Browse the twinkling, perfumed treasure trove displayed in the ferry's two duty-free shops. You can play the slot machines in the games area beside reception until the Golden Casino opens for a more serious flutter later. You might care to nurse a tankard of bitter in Ye Olde English Tavern until the beat from the after-dinner-'til-you-drop Ocean Runner Night Club begins to draw you . . . or encourages you to stay firmly put and order yet another pint while reflecting wistfully on names like Glenn Miller, Hoagy Carmichael and Ella, and on the days when you were young and music had a tune.

Or you might just seek out a sheltered spot on deck that's screened from the North Sea wind and – like Second Officer Delucci high above you on the bridge, who's never grown complacent about his chosen career – quite simply enjoy the sensation of being in a ship at sea which, without any man-made diversion at all, can prove a quite magical experience.

You might, when you arrive aboard, be like newly wedded twenty-year-olds Gertrud and Lennart Gustafsson: still very much in love even after a whole fortnight of marriage. Their honeymoon in Britain's Lake District being over, they are now returning on this inaugural service of the *Orion Venturer* to their new house in Söder-köping, a quiet little harbour on Sweden's Göta Canal. If you *are* like the Gustafssons, then you probably won't care too much about what part of the ship you are in, or what you're going to do to pass the time on the voyage home. Not so long as you can hold hands while doing it.

The Gustafssons are among only twelve economy class passengers booked into the otherwise vacant lower level cabins on D deck. They plan to go to bed early. Or at least, retire early and get undressed. They may even sleep for an hour or two before the ferry docks.

If you're one of the fourteen pupils from the junior school in Nor-way's Østfold Region, who have just boarded for the UK–Göteborg and onward-to-Oslo elements of the *Orion Venturer's* intended tri-angular service, then you won't so much decide what you're going to do as have what you're going to do decided for you.

Because you'll be travelling under the custodianship of Miss Evensen and young student teacher Trygve Valle. Nobody in the class even knows Miss Evensen's first name. All you'll be aware of is that she's formidably large, wears her hair severely coiled, is incredibly old and is only ever referred to as *Frøken* Evenson even by her fellow staff members at your *barnescole*. Even twenty-one-year-old Teacher Valle has respectfully called her that all the time you'd been away, although she might have responded with the odd 'Trygve' on occasions.

Mind you, if you're aged just eleven and a wide-eyed member of that particular party excitedly being convoyed, in single line ahead, through an increasingly confusing maze of internal corridors to your allocated block of four-berth inside cabins on what is mysteriously referred to as *'E deck starboard aft'*, then you probably glimpsed the adventure playroom lying invitingly open as you passed. That was before Frøken Evenson shooed you onwards trailing your suitcase, which, after ten days of a schools exchange visit to Britain, is going to demand all of Mother's fortitude even to open when you get home the day after tomorrow.

If you did manage to peep into the playroom, which looked like the great hall of a bouncy castle full of safely squashy furniture inside, then you've probably already decided where *you'd* best like to spend a lot of your time – *if* Frøken Evenson will allow you to let your hair down so to speak. Which she fully intends to do because she actually loves all of you, her sticky-fingered charges, although you wouldn't appreciate that, what with you only being eleven and her having been so strict in England and everything.

Mind you, there are other things you couldn't be expected to know about Frøken Evenson, such as that she's even older than you thought – she's actually thirty-six. That she isn't so much 'large' in adult terms as Viking-voluptuous – male-fantasy-wise, at least – and that, when Frøken Evenson lets *her* hair down, it cascades from schoolmarm wreath to the small of her back in a tumble of wild golden strands . . . a grown-up discovery still faintly disbelieving student teacher Trygve Valle had made after you kids went to bed on the second night of your schools exchange visit: whereupon the kind of extra-curricular seminar most young and virile apprentice educationalists can only dream about, had taken place under the tutelage of Frøken Ev . . .

Well – of Inger, by then. Trygve had definitely felt free to call her Inger, among other intimacies.

Without even a formal 'Frøken' panted between them.

* * *

65

If, on the other hand, you make up one of the couples who have paid a little more to spoil themselves completely, and are booked into a first class cabin situated against the forward face of the accommodation on E deck – and you don't really have to be a ghost who was killed in action half a century ago to afford that; never mind have the income of a New York stockbroker or corporate lawyer, whatever bluejacket veteran Charlie Periera's thinking right now in his cabin further aft – then your name could well be plain Mr or Mrs Somerville.

In that case you'll be in your early sixties: you'll have travelled overnight by rail from Edinburgh to join the *Orion Venturer*; you'll have stolen a week's holiday from your family butcher's business, and you'll be sailing to Gothenburg partly in fulfilment of a long-promised second honeymoon but, more importantly, to visit your only daughter who is a junior lecturer in English studies at Göteborg University.

Should you, on yet another hand, be one half of the middle-aged duo currently unpacking in starboard inside double cabin E 248, then you'll tell everyone who chances to ask that you are Mr and Mrs Charles Smith – and, unless they happen to glimpse your individual passports and find you don't actually share the same married name, then they'll have no reason to disbelieve you because you do seem made for each other. You'll try not to look furtive, or anxious about what your true marital partner may suspect when you return home appearing surprisingly reinvigorated despite having spent what you'll claim was an utterly exhausting five days at the sales department conference or staying with your sister.

You might be a member of the thirty-strong male voice choir from the Welsh valleys, collectively about to achieve your greatest ambition by singing your heart out through a string of Swedish cultural engagements, commencing tomorrow evening with a performance at the beautiful concert hall in the Götaplatsen. In that case, you'll already have arranged to meet up in the Admiral's Lounge for a few beers after dinner tonight. And maybe a little song or two – eh, boyos?

If, in addition to being one of that harmonious group of Welshmen settling in on E deck, you also happen to be a baritone whose

66

name is Morgan Evans: you're married to Gwynneth, have two lovely daughters but only a single arm to hold your glass of ale with, then you could well be a former member of the British Army.

If you *are* that particular Morgan Evans, then not only will you share a harmonious bond with your fellow travellers of the choir – you'll also have something in common with yet another passenger just along the corridor. Veteran ex-US Navy Machinist's Mate Second Class Charles Periera.

Like Charlie, you will be viewing your imminent North Sea voyage in the *Orion Venturer* with mixed feelings, and for a very similar reason.

Because the last time you had been aboard a ship was when you, too, were sailing to war, albeit rather more recently in the litany of global conflicts – in your case, on 8 June 1982. On that day you were fresh faced Guardsman Evans of the 1st Battalion Welsh Guards. Your seaborne mode of transport then was a British Landing Ship (Logistics) called the *Sir Galahad*. In company with her sister LSL *Sir Tristram* she was unloading troops and supplies off a desolate place called Bluff Cove in San Carlos Water in the Falkland Islands. Wearing full battle order you were still waiting apprehensively to disembark, along with the bulk of the battalion, when five A–4BS Skyhawk strike aircraft of the Argentine V Air Brigade, led by Primer Teniente Cachon, streaked towards your ship from the Sound at wave-top height.

Time had run out on you.

At 1.15 p.m. on that grey afternoon Cachon, supported by wingmen Teniente Rinke and Alferez Carmona, released their ordnance. The *Sir Galahad* was hit by two – some said three – 500lb bombs . . . and that marked the instant in which you, trapped in a stricken ship, began to share a common experience with Charlie Periera. Fifty men died in the ensuing explosions and fire, fifty-seven more were seriously wounded . . . you, Guardsman Evans, lost your left arm, but they got you off, heloed you from the dying auxiliary's foc'sle through the black rolling smoke and the *crack* of detonating ammunition.

You'll never know it, of course, but perhaps you were luckier than old Charlie, although he's still physically whole. At least when they snatched you from your personal holocaust they didn't lift an unseen companion with you – a spectre of guilt to loom over your shoulder for the next fifty years.

. . . always supposing, that is, you can count on having fifty years of life still ahead of you, Morgan Evans. Because, while there are no Argentine Air Force Skyhawks prowling the North Sea for targets – no more than there are eighty-year-old U-boats or icebergs, as Grace Miles is sensible enough to realize – the clock has nevertheless begun to run against you for a second time.

It started to tick the moment you were reluctantly persuaded, after choir practice that night, to sail with the rest of your melodious brotherhood aboard the *Orion Venturer*.

To paraphrase the sage observation made by Able Seaman Conroy to Crew Mess Cook Henry Manley: it just goes to prove you meet all kinds o' people in a ro-ro ferry.

All of the 517 passengers settling in the big ro-ro as she prepares to sail are as unique by reason of their background as they are typical. In the main they are ordinary people about to embark upon what is an extra-ordinary but most agreeable adventure. Even if you don't recognize some aspect of their past lives as mirroring your own, then you will almost certainly know someone who could.

. . . other than that of avuncular passenger Neugebauer, perhaps. He who left his wife Eva in Dortmund – or rather under Dortmund, to be absolutely accurate – and is now about to explore, with pleasurable anticipation, the diaphanous contents of a Marks & Spencer carrier bag in the privacy of his single-occupancy cabin not too far from, and located in the same starboard corridor on E deck as, the children and their nubile mentors of the Østfold.

It is unlikely you would wish to identify yourself with – or maintain associates so bizarre as to be able to relate to – the lethally eccentric Herr Neugebauer.

Whereas you might well recognize some trait of the stubborn independence demonstrated by Antoinette Chabert, an eighty-two-years-young Belgian spinster from the province of Liège, who loves her cat Jozef. So much so, in fact, that she smuggled him into Hull from the Zeebrugge ferry three weeks before in defiance

68

of British quarantine regulations, and is now sneaking him out again to keep her company on her grand, if somewhat quaint, tour by public transport of nations bordering the North Sea.

You may, in the past, have had occasion to make the acquaintance of a kindly man not unlike Austrian-born Pastor Oskar Lütgendorf, now sailing to take up his new post as superintendent of a homeless shelter in Norway after spending four weeks at a religious retreat in Scotland agonizing over why he should suddenly have begun to question his faith. Regrettably Pastor Lütgendorf's period of reflection hasn't helped a lot – hence his reason for booking this ferry passage to Oslo rather than risk flying over the North Sea: a prospect which scared the hell . . . well, which caused him some apprehension.

The good Pastor's sojourn did, however, serve to reinforce his conviction that *Someone* had placed him on this earth for the sole purpose of helping needy people. It's just that he isn't quite sure of who that Someone is any more. Either way, being in his late fifties and – not unlike Captain Jorgen Truls Halvorsen, currently suffering his own pre-sailing crisis of conscience – having a wry appreciation of the prospects for launching on an alternative, less spiritually focused career at his time of life, he feels it prudent to continue under his former vocational umbrella while dispensing as much material help as he can. Being a pragmatist, he's resolved to keep his fingers firmly crossed behind his back on those occasions when he feels pressed to offer religious comfort beyond the bounds of his own capacity for belief.

You will hardly fail to notice Mr Kumbweza Munyenyembe from Mzuzu, Malawi, should you chance to run across him on board. He stands out from the denim and casuals so prevalent among today's travellers: a giant of a man made even more striking by his colourful caftan and woolly beret. He sports a beaded money purse hanging from his shoulder and a wide, engaging grin. Give him half a chance and he'll tell you in a rich, booming voice that he's a salesman for an African exporter of fancy goods, and you'll suspect right away that he's a very good one. He'll also invite you to call him Fred, and for that small linguistic mercy you'll be extraordinarily grateful.

You may not identify with, but you'll certainly have observed clones of, the six Japanese gentlemen with their wives, all seemingly bent on a photo-reconnaissance of Europe but who actually represent a delegation from the Nippon motor industry travelling the leisurely way to confer with executives of the Volvo factory.

You will surely feel concern to know that there are three babies under six months of age aboard.

You might feel sympathy for the fifteen-year-old Finnish girl from Jyväskylä called Heikki Niskanen, travelling with her mother, who has somehow got it into her head that there might well be four – babies aboard, that is – before the *Orion Venturer* docks in Gothenburg early tomorrow. But she has no need to worry . . . well, not about giving birth on passage anyway. She's a month adrift in her calculations and only suffering from a mild stomach upset . . . No, Heikki's biggest worry should be telling Mum who, despite having noticed her daughter's recent weight gain allied with what she presumes is normal adolescent moodiness, still doesn't even suspect that . . .

Unhappy Heikki Niskanen reads rather too many luridly romantic novels and carries the consequence of taking them too literally within her. Now she can only dream that the ferry might meet with some terrible fate tonight, and bring her peace in the arms of the sea. Whereupon all those who love her dearly will turn their faces to that storm-tossed ocean and shed tears of forgiveness.

. . . but that's only a young and frightened girl's fantasy. Heikki doesn't really mean it.

Certainly she doesn't imagine for one moment that such a terrible and Gothic solution will, before this time tomorrow, have moved towards becoming a reality.

CHAPTER NINE

The ship was cheered, the harbour cleared,
Merrily did we drop . . .
S.T. COLERIDGE (1772–1834)

The terminal skywalk retracts just before the start-up rumble of
twin 8,000 horsepower main engines causes glasses to clink gently
in the already filling bars and in the Admiral's Lounge. Hotel-
efficient servery staff dispense breakfast and professionally welcoming smiles to parents and children now converging for the first
sitting on F deck. Only a few look up as the ro-ro's Tannoy calls
a discreet *harbour stations*. Even fewer brave the biting east wind
on deck to observe the ferry's sailing. Those hardiest of souls will
see white-capped heads appear over the bridge wing to gaze critically down as the first of the already singled-up mooring lines is
cast off to splash in the water.

The forepart of the ship begins to bounce gently as the metallic
submarine clamour of the Kamewa transverse bow thrusters
chatters briefly, then dies as the foc'sle head begins to swing off
the berth.

A walkie-talkie crackles. 'Let go aft!'

'Leggo aft, sir . . . Let go the stern rope!'

Survival-suited jetty men, hunched disconsolate against the rain,
struggle briefly to ease the heavy plaited hawser over the lip of a
bollard already polished by the departing of a thousand ships before
you. A final splash, and a smoothly revolving mooring winch
begins to retrieve the dripping watersnake.

'All gone aft! Propellers clear.'

The first whorls of aerated water cream from under the counter;
flotsam pirouettes; harbour mud whirlpools in a steadily spreading
arc. Now you can detect forward movement as shoreside

installations creep bodily astern. The gap between ship and quay-
side begins to widen.

You start involuntarily – a booming cacophony fills the moisture-
laden air! Reverberates to send the malicious-eyed gulls screeching
and skying while the few bystanders shoreside raise arms in desultory salute. But this is the ro-ro's maiden sailing on her new
deployment, and someone up there on the bridge feels the event
worthy enough of recognition to afford a celebratory blast on the
deep-throated ship's whistle.

The next time you hear it will be in very different circumstances.

One hundred and four crew members. Five hundred and sixteen
travellers taking passage in their care. Six hundred and twenty
voyagers comprising seventeen nationalities, not one of whom has
previously met, or even heard of, the six hundred and twenty-first
member of their soon-to-be isolated company.

A Swedish truck driver. A seemingly amiable enough young
man with his blonde hair and engaging blue eyes and that ready,
though sometimes strangely enigmatic, smile. A responsible, go-
ahead sort of chap, you might think from casual acquaintance.
And to be fair to Sven Carlsson, he generally is.

. . . apart from the illness which has affected his reasoning. His
grand delusion.

Which even now, as the distance between ship and shore opens
inexorably, has begun to trigger the cataclysm that, in eighteen
hours and twenty minutes, will overwhelm the *Orion Venturer*.

OUTWARD BOUND

At the time of [sailing] there were a number of deficiencies in the ship and its equipment: workshops and stores had been set up on the car deck, some of the heads in the sprinkler system on the car deck were blocked with rust, pressure bottles were stored incorrectly, there was a defective fire door on the port side of the car deck, and the motorized lifeboats were generally in poor repair.

> Norwegian Official Report, NOR 1991: 1E
> The *Scandinavian Star* Disaster of 7 April 1990

They did not apply their minds to the question: What orders should be given for the safety of our ships ... From top to bottom the body corporate was infected with the disease of sloppiness.

> Report on loss of mv *Herald of Free Enterprise*
> UK Court No. 8074 Formal Investigation

CHAPTER TEN

Oh! Combien de marins, combien de capitaines qui son partis joyeux pour des courses lointaines dans ce morne horizon sont évanouis . . . *Oh! How many sailors, how many captains who have gaily set out for long voyages have vanished behind that sad horizon!*

VICTOR HUGO (1802–1885)

The mood of those on the bridge lightened perceptibly once the big ferry had crossed the bar into deep water, and set course to pass several miles clear of the Hanstholm Light on the north-west corner of Jutland.

Other than when the rule of the road calls for her to give way to other vessels, the *Orion Venturer* will remain on that heading all the way across the North Sea until she enters the sixty-mile-wide sleeve of the Skagerrak after darkness has fallen. Less than a four-hour run from there lies the finger of the Skaw and a final course alteration to take her across the Kattegat to the tortuous approaches to the port of Gothenburg.

Following the alien activity of previous weeks, the prospect of spending even twenty-four hours on passage afforded a psychological watershed for those charged with the responsibility for her safe navigation. Now they could turn their hands to seamen's things: shake down into a watchkeeping routine familiar and as old as tradition, instead of managing crises that had little to do with seafaring and everything to do with cobbling together a clean-scrubbed, healthy exterior for a ship still a little sick at heart. They could even relish the luxury of sensing the sea wind in their faces once again, should they feel inclined to step from the vast air-conditioned wheelhouse to the open wings of the bridge where rain had already begun to wash away the shoreside grime.

74

Even Captain Halvorsen, elbows propped comfortably on a window ledge as he gazed ahead over the stubby foc'sle, appeared infected with the easing of tensions brought about by leaving the fairway buoy astern.

'When I was a young second officer, I seem to remember making coffee for my captain after engines full away,' he reflected solemnly to no one in particular.

'Just a thought – would you care for a coffee, sir?' Second Officer Sandalwell, who had just come up from stand-by on the mooring deck aft to take over the eight to twelve morning watch, proposed with alacrity.

'You show promise of becoming a good officer, Mister Sandalwell,' Halvorsen predicted without the trace of a smile. 'Eventually.'

2/O Delucci frowned up from the VDU in the chart area, where he'd been entering the vehicle distribution into the ship's computerized stability programme. The final count showed that, on this maiden service, the ro-ro had loaded 73 private cars and vans; 4 tour coaches; 4 self-driven pantechnicons; 12 accompanied trailers – including a certain white Scania refrigerated artic with Swedish registration plates – and 77 unaccompanied TIR trailers. Most of the last would be unloaded in Gothenburg by specialist port tractors before being collected by power units belonging to Scandinavia-based hauliers for the last stage of their North Sea journey.

'Hey, I do believe I am detecting a brownish tinge around the tip of your nose, Ollie,' Delucci hissed *sotto voce*.

Oliver Sandalwell grinned unrepentantly, heading for the little domestic cuddy in the after end of the wheelhouse to put the kettle on. The rivalry between the *Orion Venturer*'s three watchkeeping seconds was friendly but guarded. The pyramid to sea command is broad based, but a pyramid with a sharply narrowing apex nevertheless.

'One day it's going to be me, you, or Bill Pert up for relief mate's job, pal. A bit of ingratiation – a cup of the right stuff at the right time in the right hand – could swing it my way.'

'Mine's black, no sugar,' Delucci specified, unimpressed, 'and a chocolate cookie.'

'Biscuit, you cultural minority. On British ships we call them biscuits.'

'Sure you do. Like you call gas petrol, and channel marker boowies *buoys*. Except this ain't a limejuicer, is she?'

Sandalwell hesitated, his smile fading. Two years previously his mother had insisted on accompanying his father, as was her privilege, on Dad's pre-retirement voyage in command of a 50,000-tonne ore carrier. The giant bulker had sailed into a North Atlantic depression and never reappeared.

The subsequent, almost perfunctory inquiry into her loss – not a particularly special event; most weeks a ship and crew disappears without trace somewhere in the world – revealed that, only months before his parents' last and greatest adventure together, she'd failed her periodic condition survey. Some of her longitudinals were noted as having corroded to thirty per cent of their original design strength. Immediately sold from UK ownership, she'd been 'flagged out' to sail under the Monrovian ensign without major repairs being effected. Both ship and cargo had been amply – some witnesses had cynically suggested *over* – insured.

Her crew had not.

Much the same thing will happen to the *Orion Venturer* when the new SOLAS 90 rules of construction, intended to decrease the vulnerability of through-deck ferries, eventually come into force around the Millennium . . . at least, for her and other ro-ro ferries operating in European waters north of Finisterre. Most of the rest of the world, several years later, still hasn't got round to considering, never mind ratifying, the International Maritime Organization's proposals.

But happily by the turn of the century, before being permitted to sail from a UK port the *Orion Venturer* will be required to have the ability to survive the de-stabilizing effect of shipping up to 50 cm of water on her vehicle deck in significant wave heights . . . which she can't. Chances are she'll capsize with little more than half of that – less than the depth of a seaboot – swilling around on a free surface as vast as her vehicle hangar . . . so she, and a generation of passenger ships just like her, will be sold on yet again. Moved around the globe to a less arduously regulated climate. Only the oldest and most rust-fragile death traps will finally die under the breakers' torches. The rest will merely be 'repositioned'.

Second Officer Sandalwell still found himself lying in his berth staring up at a strangely misty deckhead, wondering whether his mother had died in his father's arms, or he in hers. The sea shows little regard for chauvinistic postulation: gives no priority of gender to the order in which it slaughters its victims, although, in a straight fight against ocean exposure, women have been shown to endure marginally better than men. On the other hand, according to the Centro Internazionale Radio-Medico in Rome the sea has been observed to cherish an ethnic bias. Black persons cast adrift generally die more quickly than the white races, yellow people tend to survive longer than any.

'No, Mike, this one sure as hell isn't British,' 2/O Sandalwell said.

Quietly.

. . . so the Captain wouldn't hear him.

CHAPTER ELEVEN

The remainder of the Morning Watch
0900 hrs to noon

Cataclysm minus seventeen hours
Within minutes of clearing the buoyed channel the coast had faded
from sight, already swallowed astern by the grey North Sea mist.

It was an eerie condition, known as advection fog, into which
the *Orion Venturer* sailed on that morning: the result of relatively
warm humid air condensing into water vapour upon meeting a
cold sea surface. Happily the phenomenon tends to be geographi-
cally discriminating, confining its appearances largely to the north-
eastern shores of Britain, the Newfoundland Banks, and off parts
of Japan and the west coast of North America. Unlike its sister fog
on land, the ocean's climatological steam is able to persist even in
quite strong winds.

The ancient Vikings credited such North Sea fog with malignant
power, fearful of its clammy envelopment. Today, to the less fanciful east coast Scots it's jist a gey cauld nuisance and they call it
the *haar*. Off the north-east coast of England it's dismissed as *sea
fret* with equal petulance, particularly when observed lying low . . .
an undulating blanket blocking off an otherwise clear sky through
which the slowly moving masts of ships occasionally protrude:
skeletal, disembodied fingers pointing remonstratingly to Heaven
for affording them such inconvenience.

Other than the fog, nothing more inclement than a fresh breeze
was forecast to meet the ferry more or less head-on during that
first and, as it happened, last forenoon watch. Easterly force five
on the Beaufort Scale: promising a low swell in which the waves
could be anticipated to be little more than two metres high at most,
with only occasional rough spray blowing from the tops of their

78

white crests. Such weather conditions, and from such a direction, offered no hindrance whatsoever to the *Orion Venturer* despite the fact that the surface area of her high, sheer sides was greater than the full press of sail once carried by the fastest East Indiaman.

Equally, the outlook offered cheer to anyone predisposed towards the discomfiting affliction referred to as *mal de mer* among the most proper of ocean voyagers, sea sickness by the majority, and 'calling for Hughie' by the rough sailory who have served their apprenticeship in maritime misery either bent double over the nearest lee rail or with spinning, sweat-plastered heads stuck resolutely down toilet bowls. Just as well, really. The near-thirty-year-old *Orion Venturer* was not fitted with the ubiquitous stabilizers of later generation ferries – apart from which, the drag caused by deploying such add on flippers adds considerably to fuel consumption on a cut-price ride – and so, in a lusty beam sea, could be expected to roll like . . . well, like a mad sea cow.

Still, it augured well that on this, her longest course leg, the big ro-ro would be inclined only to adopt a gentle pitching movement and cause few pallid faces to be encountered hurriedly leaving the restaurant halfway through lunch.

Whereas the fog . . . ? Now that was another thing altogether.

Because it was curious how, at the very time when the Captain – a Viking himself, albeit one now fortified by radar, echo sounder and a satellite-tuned global positioning system – set the *Orion Venturer*'s bridge combinator . . . her remote engine and propeller pitch controls . . . to *Full Ahead* and thus finally sanctioned the countdown, hour by inexorable hour, sea mile by restless sea mile, of the part-day his ship had left to live . . . how the same North Sea *haar* which had once caused Halversen's Norse forefathers such cabalistic anxiety did, indeed, choose that moment to close around and embrace his command.

But that is an unfounded and patently melodramatic observation. There can be no question that the malign influences which ultimately combined to overwhelm her had everything to do with commercial irresponsibility compounded by human fallibility, and owed little to supernatural forces.

Can there . . . ?

In the interim the bulk of her passengers will choose to remain isolated in their own private worlds, for the passage is only expected to be a transient experience: too long to ignore, but too short to forge anything other than casual relationships with their fellow voyagers.

Other than in the case of one of their number. An inadequate young man driven by a crippled mind, who cherishes a far wider agenda.

. . . and who has never even heard of – never mind paid heed to – the warnings contained in the Nordic sagas.

Cataclysm minus sixteen hours

Following a handsome early breakfast which even the sharpest eyed executive-designate couldn't have faulted, reefer-truck driver Sven Carlsson had gone back to his cabin to shave then, just after ten a.m., had wrapped up well and risked a brisk stroll on the upper decks.

Not so much because he relished feeling the North Sea wind in his face – which he didn't, being an inveterate landlubber – as to start putting together a list of . . . well, not exactly criticisms – more profound observations on how the company might improve this particular ferry's image. Not that he was stupid, of course. He was acutely aware of the delicacy of his situation: of the need to ensure he put his suggestions discreetly. Couldn't afford to place his prospective bosses on their guard. Have them suss him as being so smart he might pose a very real threat to their own jobs were they to hire him.

Carlsson began to develop something of a proprietorial feel for the *Orion Venturer* as he walked. He also began to get a little angry about the way things had been allowed to slide. Within a matter of days the presentation of the public face of this ship could well become his responsibility . . . or would after he'd worked his notice, anyway. He didn't intend to let his current employers down, even though they hadn't shown the wit to recognize him as being management materia . . .

Concentrate, Sven, lad! Can't spend all your life a slave to conscience. Point is, the ship's plain seedy when you look past the paint. Those rails, for instance. Never been properly prepared and primed. Blisters of corrosion already flowering under that super-

80

ficial gloss. Any ordinary passenger seeing that would be bound to question how well maintained she is in the areas that really count. Maybe he should even take a look behind a few of those doors marked CREW ONLY, huh? Check out the condition of the engine room, for instance? He wasn't exactly a marine engineer, but he'd worked around trucks for long enough – he'd soon assess whether or not the chief mechanic on board was up to his jo . . . !

He ducked distastefully as a gust of rain-laden wind swept across the green-painted skid-resistant steel deck, snatching at the lifeboats cradled in their swan-necked gravity davits above him, causing frayed – unseamanlike frayed? – ends of rope to clatter and bang against orange-metal hulls. Five boats either side, and every one of them looking like they needed a good wash down at the very least . . . *Orion Venturer – Nassau – 143 persons* the stencilled legends on each proclaimed. Had to be a nice place, the Bahamas . . . sun, sand, straw hats and palm trees. Maybe the Company would send him there one day. Keep an eye on things for them . . . ? But in the meantime, well, I mean – what kind of confidence does it give a fare-paying punter to know even the lifeboats are dirty . . . ?

Carlsson made the mistake of looking down then, from the embarkation deck to the surface nearly twenty metres below him. He'd never had a head for heights. *Jesus*, but it was a long way to the water! And the malicious energy of it: the way the waves seemed to close in on the hull, clawing and atomizing against the ferry's slab sides to collapse back on themselves in recoiling frustration as she powered through the steep grey seas. Just for a moment he wondered if he shouldn't reappraise his whole strategy. Say something went wrong? Say events *did* get out of hand . . . ? Never mind the old and the very young, the halt and the lame . . . imagine the terror he himself would endure at being suspended in several tonnes of lifeboat lowering down the side of a constantly angling cliff into that maelstrom . . . ?

A movement caught his eye from further aft and the steadily disintegrating butterfly mind of Sven Carlsson immediately became diverted yet again. A man, a small man muffled fastidiously against the elements in tartan scarf and suede-collared Harris tweed overcoat – a sartorial anachronism, judged by the standards of

81

modern-day voyagers – was approaching at a determined pace: chest puffed out, elbows bent and pumping like a choo-choo train. Sven had to grin. It was like being spirited back in time. He'd read a magazine article. Once. About the age when upper-class passengers aboard great ocean liners performed laps of the boat deck as their regular morning constitutional.

Carlsson stood obligingly aside, smart as a brush, inclining his head respectfully: every inch the perfect company representative deferring to a client.

'Good morning, sir. Welcome on board.'

'*Guten Morgen!*' Herr Neugebauer panted shortly as he swept past the scruffy, anorak-huddled young man while thinking what curious people one did seem to come across on a North Sea ferry.

Already he'd caught sight, through the part-open door of one cabin, of an elderly woman feeding, of all things, a cat. Of a Portuguese steward who, judging by the sheepish way he'd emerged backwards from a linen closet with a plastic bucket draped under a towel, had been sea sick . . . *before* they'd sailed? Of a small *Englisches Kind* wearing a sou'wester – inside the ship? And of a sailor on the mooring deck, who looked like Torquemada in denim – admittedly rather sensuously tailored denim – dancing a *paso doble* all on his own and for no apparent reason . . .

The Merry Widower Neugebauer, a man perfectly prepared to concede that he harboured the odd secret of his own and so considered himself tolerant to a fault of others' eccentricities, was nevertheless becoming convinced that he might well be the only normal, well-adjusted person aboard the *Orion Venturer*.

Cataclysm minus fifteen hours

Michael had slipped into one of his moods even before they'd left their breakfast table.

By eleven that morning Grace had become uncomfortably aware that her husband's growing irritability wasn't going to subside, just as she was acutely conscious of the reason behind it, although she still found the realization difficult to accept even after eight years.

Simply put, Michael Miles resented his children.

Oh, it didn't mean he had no love for them. He did. He showed his affection regularly. Before Christmas there had been the secretive hours spent, after the kids had gone to bed, in making that doll's house for Lucy. The even greater care he'd taken in assembling a radio-controlled speedboat kit for William's last birthday . . . Grace tended to discount the further time Michael had invested in trying it out on their local pond as being more a nostalgic quest for his own lost childhood than selfless dedication to the spirit of being a Dad – especially after William's interest had waned yet he'd still been hauled off in the back of the Volvo nevertheless, protesting volubly that he 'Din't *want* to go to the rotten park with Daddy's rotten boat *again*!'

But it had become an inescapable fact that the minute William or Lucy's interests conflicted with Michael's, then his mood became sour: grudging the need to accommodate the children in any plans he wanted to make. Even the most minor inconveniences would escalate to become a source of friction between Grace and himself.

This touring holiday they'd just embarked upon? Already it was providing a typical example of the unnecessary stress Michael always seemed to instil in everything they did as a family. Unnecessary because . . . well, because children *are* children. Once you conceive them – commit yourselves to parenthood, which both she and Michael did quite intentionally – then, in Grace's view, you must expect your life to change by definition. In her case the change had been for the better. She'd gained so much extra from her babies: so much added happiness; so much previously unimagined satisfaction . . . whereas Michael had tended to react the opposite way. Been the one to evince all the symptoms of post-natal depression, if fathers can suffer such a disorder. He'd come to view William's arrival not so much as a source of joy – although he undoubtedly felt that, most times – but, more disconcertingly, as a restriction of the freedoms he'd previously known. And Lucy's appearance three years later had only helped to compound his frustration at being denied a lifestyle they both knew could never be regained.

She'd never quite forgotten Michael's comment in the maternity ward, made after his first flush of paternal reverence at examining the miracle of Baby Lucy . . . at her wondering, unfocused stare, her exquisitely formed fingers and toes, the tiny nails so fragile and so breathtaking in their miniaturization.

'Back to square bloody one, eh?' he'd muttered wryly.

Grace had cried that night, after Michael had left. If he'd known he would have been upset, too, but she'd never told him. She'd stopped telling him a lot of things over the years . . . like how unjustifiably apprehensive she'd felt about this North Sea crossing on board the *Orion Venturer*. He'd have found some way of blaming her nervousness on the children. Claimed her perceived anxiety had only been for their welfare, not her own.

Which was, of course, true. Because William and Lucy were a part of her. Grace Miles, the individual, simply wasn't Grace Miles the individual anymore. She was a mother. And a wife. Never once in seven years had she ever given a thought to the possibility of being anything other than . . . well, anything other than a mother, anyway.

Michael wasn't even consistent in his resentment. Two hours ago he'd been mild as anything when helping to mop up the mess Lucy had made, spilling her juice over the litter of the breakfast table. Now he was getting tight-lipped and distant as they tried to decide how best to spend what was threatening to become a very long day at sea.

He wanted to go and put his feet up in the cabin until lunchtime.

Grace did too. Desperately. It had been a long drive from home. But things weren't as simple as that.

'What about the children?' she asked doubtfully.

'What *about* the children?'

'They won't sleep just now. They're too excited. And anyway, they both slept while you were driving.'

'If you'd thought to snatch forty winks as well, when you had the chance, you could've looked after them for a while.'

Grace let it go. Several times she'd found herself nodding off on the way down, but she'd forced herself to stay awake to keep Michael company.

'I want to see over the boat, Daddy,' William decided unilaterally.

'Well you can't. Not just now. We'll walk round her in the afternoon.'

'They'll need to sleep in the afternoon,' Grace pointed out. 'They'll be tired out by then.'

84

'*Jesus!*' Michael appealed to the ceiling in frustration.

'Teddy's tired already. Teddy din't sleep in the car,' Lucy warned, compounding the problem. 'The lights coming the other way was in his eyes *all* the times!'

'We'll need to bath him first, darling,' Grace qualified. 'He's gone soggy with juice since his accident.'

'Okay – fine!' Michael snapped. 'Dead on my feet or not, I'll stagger round the bloody ship with Cap'n Ahab here while you go and attend to the real priorities – like washing her teddy bear!'

'Just go and put your feet up, Michael. I'll take them both along to the playroom for now,' Grace said.

Wearily.

CHAPTER TWELVE

The Afternoon Watch
Noon to 1600 hrs

Cataclysm minus fourteen hours

The first change of watch for crew not classed as day workers as, at least nominally, were most of the hotel services staff, took place at noon . . . or eight bells in the forenoon watch according to traditionalists such as Able Seaman Conroy. From then on, whether on passage or in port, the bulk of the deck and engineering departments – apart from Able Seaman Conroy, curiously enough who, being night-watchman, didn't fit into either category and wus somethin' of a law unto hisself anyroad – apart from him, the ferry's last stubborn bastion of the British red duster, the rest of them could look forward to settling into a four hours on, eight off routine other than when called for entering or leaving harbour.

. . . or that was the theory, anyway.

In practice, the majority of those scheduled to turn to for that first afternoon's twelve-to-four hadn't been permitted time to relax since long before sailing. In fact, the senior officers' ideas of service aboard the ill-prepared *Orion Venturer* seemed to be developing into more a *watch on: bloody STOP on* routine to the really disgruntled ones like Seaman Jerónimo Madariaga, a sort of younger Hispanic version of AB Conroy only rather more good-looking: albeit that Conroy was probably still a better flamenco dancer with ten pints of Guinness in him, an' the hell with the *Pasión Gitana* . . . especially to Madariaga who, having finally finished tidying away the equipment lying about the car deck, had only been allowed moments by Bosun Pascal to grab a quick shower in the crew quarters and re-twist his now somewhat dust-impregnated pony tail into a mockery of a proper gypsy *coif*, before belting off up to the bridge to relieve Quartermaster Acevedo as stand-by helmsman and lookout.

Junior Purser Marianne Nørgaard, on the other hand, continued uncomplainingly with her work in reception, as she'd done since six a.m. On the ro-ro's Watch and Station Bill she was officially allocated to the twelve-to-four rota . . . even after six hours of new-found responsibility she still enjoyed the buzz she got from succumbing to an occasional temptation to caress the thin gold stripes on her epaulettes which demonstrated she was an officer at last. The prospect of spending a further four hours dealing with passenger problems, mislaid children, stores manifests, currency exchange vouchers and Assistant Purser Jimmy Everard's self-defeating persistence in attempting to chat her up, didn't daunt her in the slightest. You don't become a Purser on a North Sea ferry if you're scared to work all hours.

Admittedly she did hope someone would notice how long she'd been on duty and allow her to stand down when the next crew change came round. She'd be tired by then, and would need some sleep before midnight came around and she was due to report back as middle watch receptionist . . . not that she expected to be all that hard pressed. Not during the small hours of the night.

But then, Junior Purser Marianne Nørgaard, a former cabin stewardess new to the *Orion Venturer* and still uneducated in the ferry's emergency procedures, felt no premonition had no conception whatsoever, of just how hard pressed she would be during that next shift of hers.

. . . the one seamen often refer to as the Graveyard Watch?

Third Engineer Stamper didn't exactly notice much change in the pace of things at midday, either. Under the eagle eye of Chief Engineer Bracamontes he was still working on stripping number two oily water separator, along with the amiably hamfisted Motorman Garilao, when eight bells came around and he became official Engineer of the Watch.

'I'll just get along to the control room then. Relieve Hellström, Chief,' he shouted gratefully above the roar of the engines while easing his back.

'You got five minutes for the hand-over, Bert,' Bracamontes, who'd been in a black mood since standby – the one for leaving Florida – growled. 'Then be back to finish lashing this pile of junk together. She don't need no one lounging with his feet on the console all afternoon, watchin' no dials . . . and tell Hellström he got less chance of saying hello to his bunk when you've relieved him than a snow cat has of catchin' varmints in Hades. I want him down on the car deck after he's grabbed chow, clearin' the rest of the sprinkler heads.'

'What about *my* lunch?' Stamper jerked his thumb at Garilao. 'And his?'

'You ain't had lunch, Stamper?'

'I ain't . . . haven't . . . even 'ad breakfast, Chief.'

'Okay. Negative five – take a whole fifteen minutes out, you guys,' the New Yorker conceded grudgingly. 'I may be gettin' soft but what the hell. Go spoil yourselves . . . do lunch as well!'

Cataclysm minus thirteen hours

By one o'clock Second Officer Delucci had begun to feel happier. In control. He'd finally been left with the bridge to himself . . . well, to himself and the Duty Quartermaster anyway, after a self-conscious hour spent willing the Old Man to go below and leave him to get on with the driving.

Halvorsen had hung on rather too long after the change although, give him his due, he'd kept discreetly out of the way while Mike and Sandalwell had run through the routine watch handover procedures . . . course and present speed – nineteen point eight knots through the water, already putting them some sixty miles off the UK coast since *Full Away*. Check the autopilot setting, check the pencilled noon position laid off by Ollie on the chart spread across the table at the after end of the wheelhouse . . .

Responsible for the *Orion Venturer*'s safe navigation during the remaining three hours of his watch, Delucci would continue to monitor and plot the progress of the ferry every twenty minutes from data provided by her global positioning system or, when possible, from physical observation – ensure his fixes coincided with the *Venturer*'s projected course line already laid off across the chart. Finally, a glance through bridge standing orders. No recent Navwarns to shipping in the area, no nasty surprises hidden in the latest Met and Weatherfax updates.

Visibility was poor, admittedly. Less than a mile. The North Sea fog still blindfolded the big ro-ro in its vaporous menace. Tense stuff. Steaming at twenty knots left you all of three minutes to take evasive action in your juggernaut before you hit whatever solid object materialized without warning from that clammy camouflage. Not that long ago, forced to rely purely on visual and sound signals, she'd have reduced to half speed . . . well, she would unless her name had been *Titanic*.

But not nowadays.

The two radars on the *Orion Venturer*'s bridge had been set on different ranges – five and thirty miles. No targets showed up on the five-mile screen at all. On the other, three big ships and a cluster of several smaller vessels, probably fishing boats, threw back echoes, but all were over seven miles off and none tracking on a collision course. The electronic flares of two oil platforms registered at twelve miles plus on the port bow . . . their radar bearings and distances tied in with the latest Admiralty chart corrections plotted before sailing.

'Just where they should be. You must've got your noon fix right, Ollie,' Delucci had commented solemnly.

'Man cannot gain promotion by coffee and subservience alone, pal,' Sandalwell retorted, smirking.

'Go grab lunch, creep,' Mike grinned. 'I have the watch.'

Around two bells the Old Man had finally stirred and turned from the window. Nearly an hour since Sandalwell had gone below, yet the *Orion Venturer*'s Master had never uttered a word.

'I'm going down. Keep a close watch, Mister Delucci,' he'd cautioned unnecessarily. 'Call me if you have any cause for anxiety.'

Delucci nodded, 'Aye, aye, sir,' and watched him go. Strange guy. Withdrawn. Kind of unapproachable. No – totally unapproachable! Was it genuine introspection, the distance the dour Norwegian maintained between himself and his officers, or was he simply a mean-spirited bastard at heart? Delucci had sailed under a few oddballs in his time but, since assuming command, Halvorsen had taken the biscuit . . . the cookie? . . . for hiding behind those four gold rings around his cuffs which dictated he controlled the privilege of striking up any idle conversations first – which, it had become quite clear, he didn't propose to do.

The truth was that Delucci was a bit scared of his Captain. The irony was that he didn't have to be. Because it was the failures Halvorsen confronted in himself that were preoccupying the Master's deliberations, not those of his officers. He wasn't – never had been – an arrogant man. Simply a compromised man, unconsciously evincing the outward symptoms of overstress.

But the harm had been done: his junior's readiness to communicate without fear of inviting an unsympathetic backlash blunted. Such understandable reticence on the part of Second Officer Delucci, himself a key watchkeeper destined to play a crucially reactive role at the first suspected indications of disaster, would prove one of many systemic weaknesses to claim unnecessary lives within the next thirteen hours.

. . . when the centuries-dormant folk fear once experienced by the Captain's forebears, of being embraced by those same undulating tendrils of the North Sea *haar*, turned to reality for the *Orion Venturer*.

Feeling uncommonly relieved at being his own man at last, Delucci took a turn around the twenty-three-metre-wide bridge deck – a space nearly wide enough, including the open wings to port and starboard, to accommodate two tennis courts laid end to end. Eventually he stopped to appraise the twin radar plots again.

Still all clear ahead. No sweat. He smiled inwardly. Which wry humorist was it who'd first commented: *a collision at sea can spoil your entire day*?

Satisfied, he turned to study the only other soul left to share this, and the middle watch tonight, with him as his stand-by helmsman. According to the crew list the man's tally was Madriga . . . or was it Madariga – or Madriaga? Spaniard anyway, like most of the Bosun's crowd. AB rated as Quartermaster. Delucci recognized him as the teed-off sailor who'd led the detail to clear the car deck earlier. Hadn't proved much of a linguist in that case. Or hadn't wanted to. Well enough turned out, although the guy looked a bit gipsyish with the seven-o'clock shadow and a pretty unkempt pony tail. Good-looking in a cruel, saturnine sort of way: a bit like Mike imagined Torquemada might have looked . . . though it was hardly likely Torquemada had worn denim down the Inquisition torture chambers. Still, the man had at least turned-to for his watch on time, even though he'd been panting a bit.

'Fancy a coffee, Quartermaster?'

'*Café . . . ? Si, señor oficial de guardia. Muchas gracias!*'

Mike waited a minute but the lookout didn't turn away from the window. Either Madria-whatever was very dumb or very smart. Trying it on. He shook his head. 'That's not the way it works, sailor. *You* make the Java: *I* keepa da watch out here, huh?'

'Ahhh . . .' The guy had the grace to look sheepish. '*Arrepentido, señor. Arrepentido.*'

Delucci watched him disappear into the cuddy before suddenly remembering he'd intended, soon as the Old Man had left them alone, to check out just where Torquemada *had* finally stowed that heavy plant from the car deck.

He hesitated, opened his mouth to call while the query was still fresh in his mind, then took another glance through the big window ahead and muttered 'Shit!' instead. In a matter of seconds the fog had closed in even further.

Urgently Delucci turned back to the short range radar, searching the screen for the minutest trace of a blip . . . feeling the first traces of unease. Now his visual reaction time must be down to around two minutes. He just hoped to Christ there weren't any small craft out there crazy enough to try passaging the North Sea without a decent radar reflector to enhance a wood or fibreglass hull's virtually non-existent electronic profile . . .

Had Second Officer Delucci pressed his still-niggling concern with Madariaga even at that late stage – as, equally, had he understood the true reason for his Captain's seeming unapproachability, and so been less fearful of reporting a red light that may or may not have been faulty on a panel – then things might have turned out rather differently. Perhaps less tragically.

... at least, they might have done for some aboard the *Orion Venturer*.

But nowhere near for all.

Many would die because of errors made thirty years before Delucci and Madariaga even joined the ro-ro. While they'd both been small children and she'd still only been a concept on a naval architect's drawing board.

Cataclysm minus twelve hours

For fifteen-year-old Finnish schoolgirl Heikki Niskanen from Jyväskylä, two o'clock that afternoon marked the beginning of a really weird experience.

The event led to her becoming a shoplifter, for a start – which is almost as hard a thing to do in the middle of the North Sea as is being a whole month out in calculating when your baby's due.

It all arose from her mother's expressed wish to go back to their cabin for a lie down after lunch. 'You should too, Heikki. You've been looking very peaky recently, you know.'

'I'm really not tired, Mum,' Heikki had protested even though she was, considering she hadn't slept properly for ages because of the worry. 'Can't I stay and have a Coke in the lounge or something. Explore a bit. Please?'

'Well, don't leave this deck level, and don't go outside, darling,' Mrs Niskanen cautioned. '... and don't go speaking to any boys, whatever you do!'

You might, Heikki brooded, watching Mum disappear while easing the now alarmingly contracting waistband of her jeans, *have jolly well told me that nine months ago!*

But she'd always been a bit of a rebel. Basically that was what had got her into her present mess in the first place. Pretty well all the heroines in the novellas she so loved to immerse herself in, had been rebels ... so how come *they* hardly ever got pregnant?

There were two shops on F deck: one selling tax-free cigarettes and drink and stuff which didn't interest Heikki – although she *had* once heard a whisper at school that sipping warm Dutch gin while sitting in a steaming hot bath could ...?

Not without some regret she dismissed that solution as being both too late and too impractical. The shower compartment in their cabin could hardly be a metre square, not having been designed to double as a maternity ward.

The second shop did, however, offer something of a perfumed treasure trove at first sight. Glass showcases tempted with scent and toiletries; cameras, clocks, watches, glittering fashion jewellery. Along one wall a counter displayed toys and paperback books, sweets, little die-cast models of the *Orion Venturer*, camera batteries and film, travel bags. Dolls . . . ?

Heikki found herself frowning at the doll-baby for ages. It wasn't particularly special: just a mass-produced pink plastic effigy swathed in a towelling nappy and contrived with artfully appealing Cupid eyes – yet there was something about it: something about the way it gazed back at her from its open display box that held her attention . . . *demanded* her attention.

At first the doll had struck her as simply being commercial cute. The kind of gift a four-year-old might love to bits for a whole day then chuck in the redundant toys box and never pay heed to again . . . until, gradually, she felt conscious of a strange preoccupation – found herself transfixed by the replica infant's eyes. Even more disconcertingly, began to detect a . . . a capacity for malevolence contained within their artificial, glassy appraisal.

The doll stared up at Heikki, emanating evil. Heikki stared down at the doll. The sensation didn't frighten her. She didn't get the feeling that the Thing was directing its malice at her personally. It was more as though the counterfeit baby was attempting to communicate. To establish a rapport with her?

It was, of course, ridiculous to attribute any such capacity to a plastic blob extruded from a machine in Taiwan. Almost as ridiculous as the idea that voyagers so fearless as the ancient Vikings could seriously have vested the North Sea *haar* with maleficent powers. But Heikki was a fanciful teenager with tummy ache and a capacity for wish-fulfilment of Gothic proportions. Her misplaced reliance on the truth of fiction had already given her cause to grasp at any straw which promised to release her from her resulting condition – and by the time someone, mistakenly or not, is expecting to deliver a baby at any hour, straws are becoming a bit thin on the ground.

The upshot was that, having once launched on such a bizarre

train of reflection, her lurid imagination needed little further persuasion to convince Heikki that some sort of paranormal bond existed between them . . . between her and that rubbery-fleshed toy.

She simply had to have it. Had to explore the precise nature of their silent communion. Trouble was, Mum hadn't left her with enough money to buy anything more than a tin of Coke. Not that that would have presented a major hurdle to her fictional – no – real! . . . well, sort of half-real – heroines. Glancing surreptitiously around, Heikki slipped the doll beneath her leather jacket and walked casually, albeit with racing heart, from the shop on F deck.

It was only after she'd found a quiet corner of the lounge, and frowned long and hard and queryingly into the doll's eyes, that Heikki finally understood why she'd been right to believe that the effigy's malice wasn't focused on her at all – because it was directed at the unborn child within her!

. . . and the only conceivable justification for such hostility had to be that the plastic was jealous!

Which marked the point when the all-too-fertile imagination of poor distraught Heikki Niskanen changed gear from the bizarre to the ultra-macabre. *If this doll is covetous of taking the place of whatever grows inside me*, she reasoned, *then isn't it offering itself up as a substitute?*

A big mistake on its part!

But then, the doll couldn't have suspected she didn't want to have a child – all said and done, how perceptive can a lump of plastic be? No more than it would have been aware that she'd recently become enrapt by the occult adventures of *Nicole of the Plantation*, which had been all about the beautiful rebellious daughter of a French colonial ensnared in the foul world of Haitian voodoo, delivered only at the last moment from a fate worse than even Heikki herself was anticipating, by the granite-jawed and quite incredibly handsome young Marine guard Tug Rockingham, stationed just down the road from the zombies' graveyard at the United States Embassy.

It became perfectly obvious to Heikki then. If she were to do something really terrible to the doll, perform some idolatrous sacrificial rite as the voodoo priests in thrall to the Tontons Macoute had in their, mercifully thwarted, attempt to gain control of Nicole's exquisitely proportioned sun-bronzed body, then the unwelcome Being she carried in hers might . . . well, might even cease to be.

I mean, stranger things have happened, haven't they? she argued, more out of desperation than conviction, *in lots of books I've read.*

Of course Heikki, pushed for time and already throttling the doll vigorously below the concealment of her lounge table, isn't aware that, if she could only be content to wait a further eleven hours and seventeen minutes, she will discover that the *Orion Venturer* itself contains, within its twelve-thousand-ton bulk, the power to make anything possible.

To make anything – or any*one* –cease to be.

Cataclysm minus eleven hours

It seemed, in Charlie Periera's view, that Zach Goss had gone out of his way to embarrass the *Thompsons* after lunch.

The group of them had been drifting through the reception lobby on their way back to their cabins – de luxe air-conditioned with windows, remember? Not like the dim-lit sweating-steel guts of a Fleet screen escort.

Anyways: Goss had been loud and as wearing as ever with his constant banter. Dammit, the portly ex-USN MM 1/c . . . Periera couldn't never let himself think of Goss as having made petty officer, never mind as no war hero . . . anyways, fat Zach hadn't let up on his puerile joshing of all an' every one of 'em since they'd climbed aboard. Not since they'd flown out of Kennedy into London, England, at the start of this pilgrimage, come to that . . . which meant, by now, that he, Charlie, was gettin' fed up with it.

A fair guess was that most of the others in the party felt the same. He could read it in the wooden expressions they began to adopt the moment Goss opened his mouth.

Zach had become even more aggravating now they were at sea, he reflected irritably as he supported Margrite's arm while she hobbled bravely past the information desk, smiling friendly at the Purser's staff in their crisp white uniform shirts, black ties and them stylish gold-on-white epaulettes . . . Charlie lost his drift for a minute at that point. Lord, she looked so good when she smiled. But then, Margrite had always been blessed with the kind of joy that lit up her whole face. Smoothed away the wrinkles and made him forget the anxiety he'd recently been feeling about the increasingly paper-thin translucence of her once peaches and cream skin . . .

It had seemed, from the moment they'd boarded the ferry, that Goss had gone overboard, so to speak, with his use of what now sounded plain silly Navy expressions. *All Ahead Full, you guys!* he'd holler from the back of the slowly moving group when they come on a hold-up in the alleyway: *Right Full Rudder, Skipper,* when you come to a turn . . . *Flank speed! Commissary bearin' two points on the starboard bow, Navigator,* when you was already heading as fast for the laden servery as an empty belly could persuade your travel-stiff legs to carry you . . .

'There's one tired expression this company hasn't heard yet, Zach,' Bob Land had called suddenly, almost conversationally, from back of the line.

Land had rated Radarman 1/c far as Charlie could remember. Been closed up in the little search shack abaft the bridge when they'd bored in on the Nip *Kumano*. Now Bob was a retired NYPD cop with a wife not so different from Margrite. Pretty . . . well, almost as pretty. Soft spoken, too; not brash like the Alabama-raised Polly Lou Goss. Funny how some women seem to pick up on the less edifying characteristics of their menfolk.

'Yeah, Bobby? So what expression's that, then?' Zack hoots back across the reception deck.

'Can it!' Land snaps coldly. 'Or, put another way – for once on this goddamned trip, keep your mouth zipped tight and *butt out, sailor!*'

Well, that was when it happened. When Zach went over the score.

He'd ground to a halt by the bulkhead next the desk: dumbfounded at first but with the burned patch on his already florid face getting redder and redder as Land's message sunk in. By then, of course, everyone else nearby was staring over at them. Except any Brits who was around . . . the Brits, from what Charlie had seen of 'em, affect to notice nothin' that ain't their business. Give the impression if you fell frothing and writhing on the deck they'd just step around you with a polite but distant *excuse me*.

Anyways, with tempers already fraying some by that stage, Polly Lou had begun to get *her* dander up, too. Clutched Zach's arm protectively, her smudge-scarlet lips already shaping to form an outraged response, when the door to the Chief Purser's office opened and a crewman, still kind of half-turned to finish his conversation with an officer inside, backed from it onto the concourse without lookin' where he was going. It hadn't been no big deal. Just a mite careless.

Trouble was the crewman, a chef of some kind judging by the white drills and the sweat rag knotted at his neck, had gone and planted his non-skid galley boot right atop of Zach's foot before he realized his error – and that signalled the moment when what should have been dismissed as a minor mishap blew into a reg'lar storm in a teacup. Inexplicably at first, it seemed that, by tryin' to apologize, all the chef was actually managing to do was add insult to Passenger Goss's injury . . . either that or, as Charlie suspected was the more likely case, to offer a provident excuse to shift the focus from Zach Goss's own public embarrassment.

Whichever way, it soon come clear that Zach's ire was being fuelled not so much by the fact that the crewman had been kinda clumsy but by the realization that he was black.

'Oh 'ell – *sorry*, mate!' Crew Mess Cook Henry Manley exclaimed solicitously while reaching out to steady Zach, who was hoppin' about clutching his paw by that time, besides hisself with rage.

Goss slapped his arm away with uncalled-for viciousness. 'Don' you lay one black hand on me, you goddam *nigra*!' he shrilled.

'Beg pardon?' Henry queried doubtfully, wondering if AB Conroy wasn't going to appear any second, deny all his prejudices, and confess the whole thing was a wind-up.

'You got it all wrong, boy. You say "Pardon, SUH!" to me,' Zach foams. 'Your place in this white man's world is to call me *SUH – Boy*!'

Well, Henry stares disbelievingly a split second longer, gets himself really pissed off by then, and ultimately decides it's worth getting bulleted back into cargo ships an' the *hell* with getting home to see Emma and the kids more often.

'Yessah, massah!' he yells back, tugging an imaginary forelock.

'If we was home in Alabama,' Polly Lou, all blue rinse, bigotry and mascara screeched for backup, 'my Zach would see you whupped good even f'r comin' *neah* him!'

'Oh, yeah? Him, the rest of 'is redneck mates in their pointy white hats with the eyeholes,' Crew Mess Cook Henry Manley, normally the mildest of souls, enquired with dangerous calm, '. . . an' which *other* fucking army – mam?'

Fortunately Chief Purser Trøjborg had also stepped from his office by then, and taken in the situation with a world-weary glance. Trøjborg had been a senior purser in Danish passenger ferries for nearly as long as Captain Halvorsen, recently enjoying his coffee and status on the bridge above, had commanded Norwegian ones. There were few onboard situations new to Frank Trøjborg although, admittedly, the implied cross of the Ku Klux Klan had never cast its obscene shadow over any ship he'd stewarded either.

'Hop it, Henry,' he said mildly, jerking his head. 'We'll finish the crew stores later.'

When he turned to face Zach and Polly Lou a wall went up. A wall they both had sense enough to know they better not push agin. 'Now, sir,' the Chief Purser offered with polar-cold formality. 'Do you wish to make an official complaint on the grounds of racial prejudice . . . ?'

The incident would leave its mark on the *Thompsons*: take the edge off their day aboard the *Orion Venturer* as she ploughed steadily across the grey-hazed North Sea – though not, mind you, to anything like the extent that, in just over ten hours from now, the ro-ro ferry *Orion Venturer* is destined to take the edge off their night.

In particular, the whole distasteful episode was to leave the elderly Charlie Periera feeling sick. Sick to his stomach, frightened even more of the way things were turning sour for him his first time back at sea, and not a little shocked by the devils fat Goss had suddenly revealed within him.

But then, there'd been somethin' between him and Zach Goss he hadn't never told Margrite. Something he'd never dared mention. Not even after fifty years of slamming wide awake and sweat-starin' in the middle of most nights to lie questioning whether it had borne any relevance to what happened back there east of Samar Island.

98

Something concerning him, ex-Machinist's Mate Second Class Periera, and ex-USN MM 1/c Zachary Goss from Montgomery, Alabama . . . and which may, or may not, have concerned Engineer Lieutenant (Junior Grade) O'Kane, United States Navy – listed as Missing, believed Killed in Action from the moment when Goss had slammed and dogged down a watertight escape door in his face.

. . . like the fact that the Lieutenant, same as the chef, had been a black man?

CHAPTER THIRTEEN

The Afternoon Dog Watches
1600 to 2000 hrs

Cataclysm minus ten hours

Around four o'clock, just as the second change of sea watches was taking place, Stewart McCulloch permitted himself to ease back in his chair, stretch his arms luxuriously wide, and offer a heartfelt 'Thank Christ!' to the deckhead – an understandable irreverence brought about by having at last completed his long overdue task of allocating those crucial emr numbers to the *Orion Venturer*'s crew list.

Unfortunately the Chief Officer's self-indulgent euphoria soon faded, tempered as it was by a degree of unease. Despite managing to satisfy most of the requirements of the ferry's already radically scaled-down emergency plan, McCulloch was very much aware that, even in its revised state, his strategy wasn't ideal. It still needed specialist fine tuning.

Working in the vacuum created by his mentally exhausted Captain's ambivalence had caused McCulloch to leave queries and blank spaces against some of the more obscure – to his seaman's eye, that was – emergency duties peculiar to engineering and hotel services personnel. There was no possibility that this draft of the plan could be considered foolproof until he'd obtained final input from Chief Bracamontes and Purser Trøjborg.

On the plus side, he was confident that at least he'd produced a workable marriage of skills to the most critical duties. All crew members listed by the hiring agency as holding certificates of proficiency had been matched to an appropriate emergency muster station. Anyone with a lifecraft handling, fire fighting or first aid ticket now had a response team to report to, and a clearly defined

100

responsibility should any of several potentially hazardous events assail the *Orion Venturer*.

Key crewmen like . . . well, like Pantry Rating Filippo Lucchetti, for instance? Innocently included by McCulloch in the starboard lifeboats launch group despite his never having been afloat before, and whose professional expertise to date leans more towards the exploiting, rather than the saving, of human life. Or like E deck cabins Night Steward Pinheiro Cardoso: a first-trip waiter still trying to figure his *porto* from his *estibordo*, whose prime duty in a crisis will be to evacuate the passengers in his section while preparing them to abandon ship if necessary, but who, in reality, still gets lost every time he turns a corner in the accommodation, and is still having difficulty in fitting his *own* lifejacket securely.

. . . when, that is, he can overcome his seasickness for long enough to attempt such an unfamiliar evolution.

There's also Pinheiro's very close friend, Assistant Pastry Chef Jorge Guimães, currently preparing late afternoon cream teas down in the main galley, who fixed it for both of them to embark upon this *barco grande* adventure. Jorge's sole qualification for possessing a paper issued by the Portuguese Direcção Geral de Marinha proving he's a trained liferaft coxswain is that he's good at taking photographs from a cramped position . . . although, to be strictly fair to Jorge, it's certainly true that he also feels a close affinity with black rubber.

But then, the Mate can only work with what information he's been given. Lax interviewing and credential checks by ship managers and agents, comfortable in the knowledge that they will never be involved in actually sailing aboard the big ro-ro, means that McCulloch's plan devolves positions of grave responsibility to several counterfeit ratings with illegally acquired tickets and no more sea-wise than Lucchetti or Cardoso. No more trained and mentally equipped to cope with an ocean environment that suddenly turns on them than are the five hundred-plus passengers in their care.

Equally negligent in observing that duty of care is the Master who sails without first testing for such impostors. Boat drills and fire drills and evacuation drills aboard ships are intended to focus on the human as well as the systemic flaws which, if left uncorrected and the not-by-any-means-impossible happens, will eventually kill trusting innocents who might otherwise survive.

But then: where does that awesome responsibility begin and end? Who, in a ship, *does* draw the fine line which marks the boundary between what is an acceptable compromise, and what is a negligence too far? Which man or woman earning a living from the sea, other than those hired by companies of proven integrity who do not exploit such personal dilemmas, can afford to?

Chief Officer McCulloch himself bears some liability. *He* knows that no drills have been practised by a brand new crew of untested ability – yet he hasn't dared remonstrate with Captain Halvorsen. He's scared that it's more than his job's worth as a newly appointed executive officer. So he turns a blind eye. Goes along with it ... as do the *Orion Venturer*'s other senior officers. Her Chief Engineer, Bracamontes, who, approaching retirement, knows he'll have difficulty in finding alternative employment. And Chief Purser Trøjborg – he's in much the same boat age-wise, so to speak, as the Chief. But while both of them have laid their anxieties on the line to the Old Man in private, neither of them handed over his resignation and went to lift his gear from his cabin.

No more than have the younger officers with careers in prospect, all concerned to avoid blemishes on their discharge books. Second Mates Delucci and Pert; Third Engineers Stamper and Hellström ... Assistant Purser Everard, who's vociferously aware than the lack of a common language in an emergency could prove fatal to everyone aboard the ro-ro ... all of them know bloody well that the log's been fiddled and the ship's not right: the crew's not up to speed.

Come to that, what about Able Seaman Conroy at the other end of the scale, who's seen it all before and even has a gut feeling about this one? Conroy could have jumped ship right up to the moment before she steamed out through the breakwater – but he didn't. And Crew Mess Cook Henry Manley from Liverpool? Henry's heard the buzz on the messdeck: knows even the crowd are uneasy ... but Manley's still aboard.

Even 2/O *Sandalwell* still sails with her – Ollie Sandalwell, whose own parents fell victims to a system which allows unscrupulous owners to operate an unsafe ship within the law – any kind of ship: even a cruise liner with well over a thousand souls aboard. So long as it's flying the right flag and stays lucky while visiting the ports of nations where graft can't temporarily blind an official eye.

But such philosophical observation is hardly the uppermost of McCulloch's preoccupations right now. The *Orion Venturer* is approaching mid-North Sea on her maiden service voyage to Gothenburg. He finally has not only a crisis strategy, but the means of putting it into effect should the need arise. Everyone from the Captain to the galley boy should now be able to discover just where they fit into it.

Or they will when they've seen it. McCulloch has to promulgate the wretched thing first . . . make sure everybody has access to it because it's the key to the already distributed emergency plan . . . before he can properly turn his attention to other, almost as pressing matters of a Mate's daily business. And quickly! The prospect of a mill of panicking sailors queuing at his office door while the ship burns or floods or lists under a catastrophic shift of vehicle cargo, all demanding sight of his one existing Key To The Emergency Plan, defies imagination.

Still, once he's had copies posted throughout the ship, and everybody's been able to grab a long enough spell from their operational duties to hoist in the details, by the time she reaches Gothenburg that apocalyptic scenario will have resolved itself.

Or it will for those of the ferry's complement who can understand English. Which means almost two-thirds of the crew will know what they're supposed to do by that stage . . .

Though whether or not even that sixty per cent will actually be able to do it, not having had any on-board practice in lowering several tonnes of loaded lifeboat or feeling their way along a still-unfamiliar maze of internal corridors while wearing a smoke helmet, or simply connecting up a fire hose to the type of hydrants fitted in the *Orion Venturer* – assuming they'll know where the bloody hydrants are in the first place . . .

This time, when Chief Officer McCulloch offers a prayer to the deckhead, it is simply to ask that the *Orion Venturer* be allowed to reach her destination tomorrow morning without let or hindrance.

Cataclysm minus nine hours

At five o'clock that afternoon the fog finally cleared, the sun came out, and Passenger Charles Smith in starboard cabin E248 died.

The sun's appearance was only fleeting, Mr Smith's expiry permanent.

Cornish cream teas were being served in the Admiral's Lounge for those wishing to pay a modest surcharge. Tickets for that most pleasant and civilized diversion could be purchased from reception on E deck with UK sterling, Swedish krona or Norwegian krone.

Mrs Smith got very upset about it. About the unexpected departure of Mr Smith from this mortal coil, that was – not because she'd dipped out on a Cornish cream tea.

Well . . . upset over Mr Smith's death, further compounded by an awareness that she wasn't Mrs Smith. Not the proper Mrs Smith. More of an improper Mrs Smith in the sense that she, Effie, was actually married to a chap called Sandringham, and that the real Mrs Smith was a long way away from the middle of the North Sea at the precise moment when her husband Charles reached his sell-by date. It could be considered a poetic irony to note that she – the real Mrs Smith – was actually partaking of a Cornish cream tea herself, in the front room of their – hers and the suddenly late Charles's – marital semi-detached in Birmingham. Entertaining her friends of the local embroidery circle, while mentioning her husband's reluctant absence abroad at his sales department's international conference.

One of their number, Effie Sandringham from round the corner to the Smiths, had sent her apologies. Seemed she'd been called away suddenly. To stay with her ailing sister for a few days . . .

It was all a bit complicated. It started to get complicated just after Effie had, well . . . sort of eased out from under Charles to reach for her dressing gown. They'd had an energetic afternoon, and the ferry's programme indicated that Cornish cream teas were about to be served in the Admiral's Lounge. For a small surcharge. It would be nice to relax: gaze out over the North Sea from a secluded corner table: converse awhile with her Huggy Bear about what else they could do together during their stolen weekend.

When she turned round she was immediately struck by how relaxed Huggy Bear already looked. He'd rolled over on his back

104

and was just staring up at the underside of the top berth with a . . . a sort of *astonished* expression.

Effie had taken it as a bit of a compliment.

At first . . .

'*Morto* . . . *Inerte*? Speaka da Inglese f'r Christ's sake, Tessa! Whadd'ya *mean* – he's *inerte*?' Assistant Purser Everard snarled into the telephone a few minutes later, after taking the call from an over-stressed Cabin Stewardess Teresa Campinos on E deck.

'Ohhhhh *shit*!' he muttered a moment later. '*That* kind of *inerte*?'

'What's inertey, Jimmy?' Purser Trøjborg queried absently, having just come out of his office in time to catch the last sentence.

'Bloke in Starboard Two Four Eight. Campino's just called up to say he's dead. In bed.'

'Ohhhhh *skid*!' the Dane growled, but even Chief Pursers can be excused for momentarily disregarding Bahamian legislation relating to the ship's official language.

A cadaver, even a fare-paying one, Trøjborg didn't need on this, their first service. Not that it took him entirely by surprise. Passengers do die *en voyage* in ferries from time to time, especially on the long-haul ro-ros. It's inevitable. Lump up to a thousand people of all ages, and from all walks of life, together overnight in a floating steel box and you encapsulate a fairly average cross-section of the population. By definition, on each trip the passenger list will reflect the structure of that society.

Chief Purser Trøjborg, in his long career, had come to accept with weary resignation that, every time his charge sails, she will carry aboard a representative selection of saints and sinners. Most will be ordinary citizens but there will be a small percentage who – as encountered in any city high street – are thieves and opportunists, aggressive drunks, professional smugglers, potential suicides, drug addicts, plain nutters . . .

There will also be the fit and the less fit. Heart attacks are not unknown, particularly among elderly male passengers who don't, or won't, recognize their limitations. Purser Trøjborg had a theory to explain that. The way he saw it, take the added stress brought about by any form of travel; add a few more duty-free drinks than usual in the bars, or an over-indulgence in rich food; stir it with the euphoria generated in many at the prospect of sailing to foreign parts; keep 'em up long past their normal bedtime and then, at two o'clock in the morning, stick them on the disco floor to compete with the gyrating young and encourage them to work up a good, artery-pounding sweat . . .

Trøjborg frowned. Trouble with that theory was, this one appeared to have popped his clogs before five-whatever in the afternoon. What the hell did a married man find to over-indulge in, that might have brought about an artery-pounding sweat before dinner time?

'The Swedish police will want to investigate. I'll go down and check him out. See the wife's looked after . . . get both passports from her. Meanwhile you'd better advise the Captain, Jimmy, then arrange for an additional cabin to be made available.'

Everard looked a bit uncertain. 'Inside economy or outside de luxe?'

The Chief Purser fixed his protégé with a jaundiced eye. 'I really don't think, young Everard, that even this company would expect us to charge extra. Plus a single supplement?'

'It's a question of organizing a berth with or without a window view,' Assistant Purser Everard picked his words very carefully. 'I was just wondering, Chief, whether you plan to leave the deceased *in situ* and relocate the lady. Or . . . ?'

. . . but it *did* call for a bit of innovative thinking.

It promises to call for even more innovative thinking when Mrs Sandringham finally reports back to Mr Sandringham. To say nothing of when she bumps into one particular member of her embroidery circle down the local Safeways. A recently widowed lady who lives just around the corner . . .

Always assuming, of course, that Effie should be so lucky – get the chance to explain the fine mess her Huggy Bear got her into.

. . . because, by now only eight hours and seventeen minutes are left before the sudden death of an *Orion Venturer* passenger ceases to qualify as a unique event.

Cataclysm minus eight hours
Six in the evening marks the end of what used to be called the First Dog Watch at sea. The Second Dog Watch continues from six to eight p.m.

Ask Able Seaman Conroy about the origins of the dog watches and, being Conroy, he'll tell you they don't work the dogs no more on present-day ships, thank Gawd . . . not unless they're flagged out to really iffy Third World countries where sailors still gets paid in bowls of rice an' you'd be lucky to find an octogenarian Sudanese Old Man, a fourteen-year-young Chince Mate an' the ship's cat able to keep bridge lookout.

. . . if the crowd from the foc'sle hasn't already ate the cat, that is.

Other than that, he'll tell you the dog watches wus a throwback to the times, not all that long ago, when crews used to turn-to watch and watch about – four on, four off. That the expression 'dog' is a corruption of *dodge* . . . the short 'dodge' watch intended to dodge, or vary, a routine whereby otherwise the same handful of men would finish up always standing the worst hours.

At least that way, all the sailors wus – *were!* – kept happy. Unless, of course, each and every one of them happened to be like AB Conroy. In that case, none of them would have been happy, but by golly, they wouldn't have run short of prejudices to pass the time complaining to each other about, during their dog watches below.

Chances are, having been denied much schooling, that Able Seaman Conroy will be unable to add much more to that particular aspect of sea-lore, whereas Second Officer Delucci – currently dozing fitfully in his cabin in preparation for being up most of the night, between standing the graveyard watch and then more or less going straight on to stand by for entering Gothenburg . . . now Mike Delucci, who's had a good pre-sea education being an officer holding an American ticket, would be able to trace the dog watch even further back in time for you. Even quote you its origins in Latin and everything.

Inter canem et lupum. Translates as *Between dog and wolf.* Atween daylight and dark. Unless – and much to Conroy's disgust, who 'asn't no time f'r continentals – you happen to be a Frenchie. In that case it's going to sound more like *Entre chien et loup.*

Known otherwise as the blind man's holiday. According to Conroy.

. . . but then, the whole business of maintaining watch aboard ship imposes a grave responsibility on all who do. Take Delucci again as an example. He will arrive topside five full minutes before midnight to take over from the eight-to-twelve man, 2/O Sandalwell. It will never occur to Delucci to be late, for prompt relief is a disciplinary etiquette demanded at sea: possibly more so than in any other working environment other than the military.

The *Orion Venturer*'s middle watch bridge officer is acutely aware that, in such a closed society as a ship's crew, failure to observe what is much more than a simple courtesy can create tensions out of all proportion to the gravity of the offence. Even a delay of two or three minutes can provoke an explosion of simmering grievance – most particularly when passaging mid-ocean without a lot to see or do other than pace in growing resentment while glowering fixedly at a clock which appears to have stopped.

In those circumstances, even one extra minute spent awaiting an opposite number's tardy arrival can drag past like hours. You learn *never* to be late in relieving – not if you value life outside a psychological freezer. Prompt time-keeping is bred into you from the day you join your first ship, whether it be as a deck apprentice, galley hand or boy seaman; mess steward or junior motorman.

Mike Delucci had learned the hard way. On his very first day at sea he'd been two whole minutes late in appearing on the bridge to relieve a fellow cadet. It had been four in the morning – traditionally the Mate's watch on cargo ships – with the American Lines freighter corkscrewing and slow-rolling through thirty degrees and great, black, luminous-crested Atlantic rollers bearing down on her before a whole gale blowing fit to snatch the wings clear off a flying fish.

'You are late, young man,' the Mate, a dry-humoured old shellback from New England had remonstrated above the shriek of the storm. 'And as a consequence, it is my sentence that you pull watch and watch about – meaning you shall work four hours on and four hours off, if you are still unfamiliar with the term – for the next seven days, to help you combat such a poor sense of timing.'

'Sorry, sir,' the ashen-faced seaboy Delucci had gasped between dry-retching heaves. 'My cap, sir . . . it, well, kind of blew overboard on my way up here . . . Sir!'

'Ah.' His mentor had nodded gravely and with enormous sympathy for the sea-sick, home-sick, terror-sick lonely child swaying weakly before him. 'Then in *that* case, Mister Delucci, I guess I am left with little option but to reconsider. You are hereby detailed to *two* weeks of double watches. The second for coming improperly dressed to my bridge!'

Mike Delucci had never, ever been late in relieving since.

He'd never, ever hated anyone quite so intently as that old Mate who'd proved the scourge of his first trip, either, although by God the man had taught him to be a seaman.

Several years later a small package had been awaiting him, a third officer himself by then, on his return home from a voyage. When he'd opened it, frowning at the unfamiliar postmark, two items came to light. The first was a letter from a Boston lawyer informing him that he had inherited a small legacy from a recently deceased client – a former seafaring gentleman. A Captain Ezra Dobbling.

. . . the second item had been a battered, but obviously much loved and regularly consulted, silver pocket watch.

Cataclysm minus seven hours
The row which had been brewing between Grace and Michael Miles finally exploded at seven o'clock that evening.

It was, of course, over the children. And it was, of course, brought to a head by Michael despite everything Grace had done to keep them from aggravating him.

He'd had his sleep. They'd had their sleep. Teddy had had *his* sleep, assuming teddy bears can sleep suspended by one leg from a showerhead to drip dry . . . Grace hadn't slept at all. Or only briefly: nodding off uncomfortably when she'd taken them along to the compact little cinema on the main deck to see the afternoon's Disney performance. Steer them out of Daddy's way so he could get a bit of peace: sprawl in the Admiral's Lounge with a coffee and bury himself in a paperback. Well, he was supposed to be on holiday, wasn't he? Needed a break from being a child-minder, he'd claimed. Must have spent all of half an hour exploring the ferry with William before getting bored, while Grace looked after

Lucy, tidied up the cabin which her family had already turned into a shambles, and sorted their things out for the night.

'It's seven o'clock, Michael,' she'd pointed out anxiously. 'The children's supper sitting in the cafeteria's going to be over soon.'

'Couldn't you take them along yourself? I wanted to grab a shave, freshen up before dinner.'

She frowned. 'But we'll have to eat with them.'

'Worms time, Pest,' William tormented Lucy. 'You'll have to knock your biscuits on the side of your plate until they fall out, all wriggly.'

'No I won't. Teddy and me'll jus' have ice cream,' the indefatigable Lucy countered. 'Ice cream's too *cold* for worms to live in.'

'Shut *up* for two minutes and stop annoying her, William,' Michael snapped before eyeing Grace. 'What d'you mean – eat *with* them?'

'They'll have to be got ready for bed after. Even now, by the time Lucy goes down it'll be very late for her. William can always read for a bit.'

'So . . . ? Last orders for dinner in the restaurant aren't till ten.'

Grace looked at him uncertainly. 'But we can't leave them alone once they're down.'

Michael shrugged 'Why not? Where are they going to go even if they do wake up?'

'That's hardly the point, Michael.'

'No? Then what *is* the point, Grace? Come to that, what's the point of us *coming* on holiday in the first place? If we'd wanted to baby-sit for a fortnight we could've done that cheaper at home. Like we do the other fifty weeks of the bloody year!'

'Can I get . . .' William interrupted.

'Be *quiet* when I'm talking to your mother!' Michael rounded on him.

'. . . past you to the toilet please, Daddy?'

'*Jesus!*'

Grace felt her cheeks begin to burn. 'You don't need to take it out on them.'

'Good grief, of course not.' Michael resorted to heavy irony then. 'No way. No . . . I mean, if anyone in this family's expected to suffer it's me, isn't it?'

Lucy had pulled herself back until she was sitting squashed in a corner of one lower berth hugging the bear. Her lip trembled apprehensively. 'Mummy, is Daddy angry 'bout Teddy getting juice all over him?'

'Of course he's not, darling. He's just being a little bit stupid.'

The moment she said it she wished she hadn't. She knew any hint of criticism was like a red rag to a bull with Michael when he was in one of his resentful moods.

'Not as stupid as I was four years and a few months ago, Grace.' He nodded meaningfully at Lucy, knowing how much he was going to hurt her, then at William. '*Or* seven, for that matter?'

Grace stared at her husband disbelievingly, the anger welling inside her until she felt herself sway. She couldn't believe he'd just said what he had. That he could be so calculatingly cruel. And with such childish petulance.

'Haven't you forgotten your biggest mistake of all?' she heard herself retorting. 'The one you made *twelve* years ago, Michael? When you asked me to marry you?'

Michael chewed his lip uneasily, suddenly placed on the defensive. He knew he'd gone too far although everybody says things they regret later . . . but he was still smarting. She must have *known* he hadn't meant it. You could almost argue that she was the one being unnecessarily confrontational on this occasion: telling Lucy her father was stupid. Usually she had the sense to let things go over her head, didn't turn them into issues.

He decided to play safe. Point out how over-reactive she was being, then say he was sorry. But it didn't quite come out like that.

'You said it,' he shrugged. 'Not me, Gra . . . !'

He couldn't understand why she threw herself at him, hammering his chest with both fists. 'Get *out*!' Grace sobbed, snatching the cabin door handle and pushing him unresistingly into the corridor. 'Get *out*, you . . . you selfish pig, and leave us alone. Go and *have* dinner! Go and . . . go and book yourself another cabin so's you don't have to sit and be bored by US all night!'

. . . which Michael Miles wouldn't have been called upon to do anyway, as it happened.

It was nearly eight bells in the dogs. The last full watch ever to be mounted aboard the *Orion Venturer* was preparing to go on duty.

CHAPTER FOURTEEN

The Evening Watch
2000 hrs to Midnight

Cataclysm minus six hours

The mood aboard the ro-ro changed perceptibly for her crew when the evening watch came on.

For the deck and engineering departments the eight o'clock handover heralded a clear transition to overnight routine. For a start, many of those who should have secured from day work earlier but hadn't been permitted to, were finally stood down.

Able Seaman Conroy was, as ever, to prove the exception in that he sort of . . . well . . . stood *up*, having been idling discreetly in his berth for the last hour or two: keeping his head below the bulwarks so to speak, in case Bosun Pascal got any extra-contractual ideas for his deployment ahead of going on overnight watch.

Not that Conroy wasn't a stickler for routine himself. He could pace his preparations for turning-to to the last tick of a ship's chronometer. It was precisely a quarter to eight – fifteen minutes beforehand – when the contrary AB levered himself to his feet and lit a last duty-free from the butt of the one he'd just finished.

No one shared the double cabin amidships on B deck with Conroy. By popular demand. There were plenty of spare crew berths, and forcing anyone else to live in the lethal miasma exuded by its sole occupant wasn't worth inciting a mutiny over. Apocryphal it may have been, but rumour had it that, on Conroy's previous ferry, one deckie from Marseilles who'd smoked sixty Gitanes a day himself had jumped ship without picking up his back wages, rather than coexist a moment longer with the health hazard that was Conroy.

. . . come ten to eight Conroy slowly and deliberately shrugged into the navy blue woolly pully he was expected to wear as ship's patrolman, what with him going to be in the public eye and everything as he stalked the slumbering corridors constantly alert, more or less, to the perils of unwanted flame and flood.

At seven minutes to eight, Conroy nipped the end of his cigarette between leather-annealed forefinger and thumb, stowed the precious remnant carefully back in its packet, and left his cabin with a sense of timing honed by years of never having gone over the top punctuality-wise in the fine etiquette of reporting on watch.

Six minutes and thirty seconds to go found the veteran seaman locking his door, then checking the handle with gloomy resignation. 'E'd seen the day when a bloke didn't have to lock 'is door . . . not on *British* ships, 'e di'nt, when they 'adn't got no foreign fellers aboard who'd steal the brass stud out o' an honest sailorman's wallet.

. . . which actually owed rather more to nostalgia than to accurate recall on Conroy's part, seeing how, when he'd joined his first red duster tramp near on forty years before, he hadn't even *had* a cabin door to gloom about. Just a personal locker in her foc'sle, built of necessity like an armoured battleship to preserve what few worldly goods he possessed from the thirty other honest British seamen he'd found himself berthed alongside.

At precisely forty-five seconds before eight on that first and last evening, Able Seaman Conroy arrived at the head of the internal stairway leading to the bridge deck and punched in the code of the anti-terrorist security key pad allowing him privileged entry to the *Orion Venturer's* fast darkening command centre.

Had there been a bell on the ferry with which to strike the traditional hours, then the very first of four double strokes would have marked the precise, maximum-economy second when Able Seaman Conroy announced to the relieving watch officer, who'd been up for the past six minutes: 'AB Conroy reportin' as nightwatchman, Mister Sandalwell . . . Sir!'

It might strike those observers who've been there themselves that Conroy, what with his being a British seaman and everything, had overlooked the equally traditional ceremony of rousing early enough to fortify himself with a draught of tea during his meticulous countdown to zero hour. But that would be to diminish

Conroy's sense of responsibility. In his capacity as roving ship's trouble-shooter, the very first compartment Able Seaman Conroy considers it his duty to visit in order to confirm it free of threat is planned to be his shipmate Henry Manley's Formica fiefdom down in the bowels of A deck.

The fact that it just 'appens to be the crew mess, Conroy will swear to you so sincere you'll almost believe him, is naught but pure coincidence. 'S'welp me Gawd, Sir!'

. . . notwithstanding that an illicit mug of char, partaken of in the owners' time instead of your own, tastes so much sweeter.

But there *is* a sense of new order in the big ro-ro by the start of that last complete watch, even though the brief sunlight has long departed in company with the soul of Passenger Smith. The very environment into which she steams is changing. Now the dusk is claiming the North Sea. The *haar* has given way to a line of black rain clouds ahead, overshadowing the low-lying coast of Denmark far below the horizon, still a hundred miles or so off the starboard bow.

The wind's freshening too, as the last weatherfax predicted. Backing to the nor'east and occasionally gusting to Beaufort six is the forecast, while the sea's become more irritable in the past hour, more restless, with waves a good three metres high now: white crests seen through the gathering gloom fragmenting and spattering astern as if snatched by invisible hands.

Nothing unusual at all for springtime in the North Sea. She's even beginning to porpoise a little, with a perceptible cyclic roll developing to make you feel that the ship's alive. It's a good feeling for a sailor.

Not quite such a good feeling, perhaps, for those among the catering and restaurant staff who aren't. Those ratings who, as Chief Officer McCulloch has discovered to the detriment of his emergency plan, have never actually been in a ship before. But even the majority of them feel, in between waves of nausea, that they are at least beginning to shake down into some form of routine, albeit an arduous one. For most a twelve, even a fourteen hour day while in transit will be the expected norm. During this first operational leg the main galley personnel in particular, although nominally divided into shifts geared around meal times, have worked almost continuously from the early hours, and will be required to carry on doing so until around midnight when the kitchens are finally cleaned and secured.

Under the purse-lipped supervision of Belgian Head Chef Monsieur Henri-François de Saeger labours a galley staff comprising of the ferry's Italian Provision Master, Roberto Uguccioni; an assistant provision master; three sous-chefs; one firmly heterosexual pastry cook from Milan and an assistant pastry cook of more flexible persuasion called Jorge who hails from Lisbon; two bakers, three porters, two peelers and three dishwashers – including a certain under-age Neapolitan, Filippo Lucchetti.

Three speak good English, three have a poor knowledge of English and the rest virtually none. M. de Saeger doesn't have a problem communicating with his chefs – the language of *haute cuisine*, punctuated by a fearsome temperament, is international – but it does mean he has to call upon Provision Master Uguccioni on the few occasions when he deigns to impart information to the lower forms of sweat-plastered life in his kitchen. Generally when he does, expressions along the lines of 'Tell 'im ze end of zees treep 'e ees *finito*, *révoquer*, *terminar* or blotty well *FIRED*!' figure prominently in such decrees.

Meanwhile the two overnight cabin stewardesses and two stewards, one of whom only two weeks ago was the waiter Pinheiro Cardoso, take up their duty stations fore and aft in the domestic cuddies on E deck. At least, on this first leg, they won't have to service the single rows of cabins lower in the ship – those located just above the *Orion Venturer*'s waterline on either side of her vehicle hangar.

The staff-stretched Purser Trøjborg has decided that, because D deck only carries twelve passengers berthed aft on its starboard side, and because they're travelling economy anyway, he can't spare a dedicated steward down there. Cardoso, posted immediately above on E, can keep an eye out for any problems . . . while the lowest blocks of fare-earning cabins – those along both sides of the actual freeboard deck, C deck – won't present any staffing problems at all tonight, as they're still being refurbished.

115

... those deserted and untidy cabins which had provided Swedish roadster Sven Carlsson, public hero-elect, with such food for thought as he'd walked past them on boarding?

The four cabin monitors will remain on call to cover any passenger demands until the ferry docks early tomorrow. The one safety measure they *have* been told to observe is to ensure that the flame-retarding doors – those dividing the ship longitudinally into three, hopefully self-containing, fire zones – remain firmly closed throughout the night. That shouldn't present a problem, even for the inexperienced Cardoso. The spring-loaded doors themselves are self-closing anyway. The circuit controlling the magnetic catches which hold them open during day routine has already been inerted from the console in the wheelhouse, in dutiful observance of bridge standing orders, by Second Officer Pert before his relief by 2/O Sandalwell.

But, other than staying alert, the night stewards are hardly likely be over-stretched once the majority of their charges have retired. There is no cabin call system operating in the *Orion Venturer*. If as a passenger you need steward assistance, you'll either stick your head out of your cabin and hope you see one; trail along to reception where you can expect to find a duty purser attentive to your concerns; or decide to leave whatever it was you wanted until you hear the cheerful rattle of crockery as morning coffee or tea is placed outside your door ready for the scheduled five-thirty a.m. pre-breakfast call.

If you're travel-wise you'll retrieve your tray expeditiously. Air-conditioned cabins do tend to leave their occupants with parched throats by morning, and not every fellow passenger is provident enough to order in advance or, for that matter, overly constrained by virtue. Unattended tea trays left sitting enticingly in ferry corridors must, one day, be recognized as presenting a phenomenon worthy of scientific investigation. They have been known to develop legs: scuttle mysteriously from bleary-eyed, groping arm's length to disappear forever from human ken.

But that is to anticipate an irritation which is not going to overly incommode anybody on this particular voyage ...

*   *   *

116

The supernumeraries – the not-quite-crew members employed by those who have negotiated franchises for services offered aboard the *Orion Venturer* – are also preparing to change pace by this time of evening.

Only two of the three Scandinavian female shop assistants will remain at the tills of their glazed emporia until they finally pull the shutters down at ten p.m. Business is expected to drop off now the restaurant has opened for dinner. They will open again at six in the morning for last minute duty-free purchases.

. . . or that's their intention.

Disc Jockey Rod O'Steele, born twenty-three years ago in Wigan, not surprisingly under a completely different name, has already begun to tweak his equipment and fire up the laser display in the blue-lit Ocean Runner Night Club in preparation for raising the decibel level on the boat deck. This job offers Rod his first chance to climb the ladder to the big time, maybe even break into commercial radio if the right talent spotter is aboard. Please God, make this session really *really* hot. A gig the kids are gonna remember . . . ?

Fijian Nancy Toganivalu and Jenny Shih-cheng from Taiwan, both employed by a US gaming syndicate not entirely distanced from the *Orion Venturer*'s ostensibly Indonesian owners, are about to remove the green baize covers from the roulette and pontoon tables in readiness for the evening's flutter. The Golden Casino will remain open until everybody who can't resist temptation has either lost their holiday money or learned sense. Both croupiers are extremely competent, to say nothing of designer-provocative in their evening dresses. Both will prove themselves highly adept at deflecting advances from young, and not so young, punters.

Back-up bar stewards are restocking the counters of the Admiral's Lounge bar on F deck and Ye Olde English Tavern abaft the boat deck night club, in anticipation of the evening's post-prandial blitz.

The Singing Viennese, Willi Tische – who is actually from Frankfurt only *The Singing Frankfurter* doesn't look so good on the bill – is applying the last touches of hair dye to his temples before moving up to *his* sea-watch station, manning the keyboard of the ship's piano in the Admiral's Lounge.

Unfortunately Willi, a last-minute replacement for the originally booked ship's entertainer run over by a bus outside a pub two days ago, is to singing and piano playing what Able Seaman Jerónimo Madariaga is to the art of flamenco dancing. Even more unfortunately, Willi – again in common with the *Orion Venturer*'s resident Torquemada look-alike who so loves to dance despite nursing a blind spot for his limitations – just loves to sing. So much so that, once he's started, it's very hard to stop him. Even if everybody enjoys his performance so much that they all go to bed early, he'll carry on singing and playing to a deserted lounge through the small hours.

Conroy had heard him practising earlier. According to Conroy, who can't stand either Germans or singers . . . most especially German singers . . . some sailorman with twice the talent of Willi Tische could well 'ave bin the key to solvin' the mystery of why everybody jumped overboard 'alf way through eatin' their dinners on the *Mary Celeste*.

Still, the Singing Whatever gets ten out of ten for Teutonic tenacity. Assuming his captive audience don't lynch him first, and that Willi Tische further survives the initial impact of what's shortly going to happen to the *Orion Venturer* . . . and if grand pianos can float . . . then Willi's jolly set-piece nautical medley, rendered from six inches above sea level, could well afford a whole new dimension to 'A Life on the Ocean Wave'.

. . . just before nine o'clock on that first and last evening Bosun Pascal, having finished his evening meal at leisure, collects the lists of Chief Officer McCulloch's all-critical emr numbers from the photocopier in the Purser's office, and begins to distribute them throughout the crew spaces in the ro-ro.

Bosun Pascal doesn't hurry. He's Spanish. The word *mañana* comes to mind. He sees no desperate urgency. Nothing's going to happen overnight. And anyway, he's a pragmatist. He knows full well that few of the euphemistically titled day workers capable of interpreting, or even appreciating the significance of, the lists will attempt to do so before the ship docks tomorrow.

Most, when they finally come off watch, won't spare time to tally their name against a number against a task they wouldn't know how to attempt anyway. They'll only want to collapse on their bunks and snatch the few hours' sleep available before turning-to again.

Commencing with those who – having drawn the short straw among the galley staff – are due to be called at four in the morning to start preparing five hundred-plus breakfasts.

Cataclysm minus five hours

The atmosphere aboard the *Orion Venturer* changes for many of her passengers too, once the black velvet drapes of the North Sea night close around her. Admittedly the moon's in its first quarter, and what there is of it is rendered impotent by the overcast, but the ro-ro carries the generating capacity of a small industrial complex. She moves in a pool of her own light, creates a pleasurably cosy ambience within her steel-plate carapace. There is a feeling of intimacy abroad in the ship: almost a sense of togetherness, of all being in the same boat while safely distanced from an alien world virtually indiscernible beyond the yellow cast of the upper deck floodlights.

In fact everything looks spick and span and hyper-efficient, particularly below decks. Feel assured that at least the crew's time, which might otherwise have been frittered away in practising boat and ship evacuation drills, was put to good use.

By nine the restaurant is filled almost to capacity with those cheerfully prepared to pay the modest extra premium to dine around freshly cut flowers and crisp white tablecloths from a five-course menu. It's not mandatory, of course, but why not dress for the occasion, ladies? Feel beautiful, and look it. Put on a tie, gentlemen – a jacket even, if you have one to hand, because we are talking eminently civilized travel here. She's not exactly a P&O cruise ship, and there are no sartorial rules for ro-ros, but undoubtedly Head Chef de Saeger and his harassed *brigade de cuisine* will appreciate any effort you put into making tonight, their first night on service, just a little bit special. A little bit like the way things once were, before jeans and trainers were invented.

Your choice of starter will be brought to your table by your steward or stewardess. Try the Norwegian *dronning suppe* ... ohhhh, the *dronning suppe* as prepared under the instruction of Monsieur Henri François! Queen soup, created with reverence out of fear from egg yolks, cream, sherry ... chicken forcemeat ...

119

honest to goodness, it's worth putting a tie on just to experience the *dronning suppe* alone.

The wine steward will have consulted you long before now if laser-eyed Restaurant Manager António e Cunha has anything to do with it. Fine wines and spirits, a choice of beers from eighteen continental breweries . . . Champagne? Why not! Tax exempt, it won't burn a hole in your pocket and by the time you drive off the stern ramp, some twelve hours from now, only the pleasant glow of recall will course through your veins.

Time to wander in growing anticipation to any of the three serveries constantly being replenished by amiable men in tall white hats. Do, please, inspect the carvery first if you've a mind to. It offers, under its infra-red lamps, succulent joints of English spring lamb, Danish pork, supreme quality Scotch beef – you'd be mad not to try it. Dear Lord, they're all crispy round the edges, all those prime cuts, while surrounded by a garden of vegetables, a treasure trove of roast potatoes, by individual Yorkshire puddings and apple sauce and mint sauce and horseradish sauce and great simmering vats of rich gravy . . . if your secret vice is gravy you could mainline on it here. You could float your dinner in it. Bathe in it. Launch ships in it . . . !

But stay! Mull awhile. There's absolutely no hurry.

Especially when, stretching to starboard and paraded to meet your inspection is the salad bar, the cold collation: the epicurean triumph of the Norwegian and Swedish *smörgåsbord*. Those pâtés, the pickled salmon, the herrings in sauce, the smoked eel and the hard-boiled eggs and the liver sausage. While in support lie battalions of Danish *smørrebrød* . . . finger-lickin' irresistible open sandwiches. Crisp rashers of bacon crowned with apple and onion rings. Scrambled egg and anchovy fillets on thin rings of salami. Lettuce hiding under blue cheese, topped with potato salad and chives and chopped gherkin . . . a sister lettuce leaf, this time bearing rollmop herring garnished with red cabbage, slivers of onion? You can get a lot on one plate, and you can always go back for more . . .

No, *no*! Do delay once again . . . *please*? Just a moment or two longer? Don't commit yourself to a command decision quite yet. It really is worth forcing yourself the extra few steps to investigate the hot servery's wares, for truly Monsieur de Saeger's talents have achieved the ultimate in ethnic harmony here. Indian *hara mirch*: stuffed peppers curry seeking a bedmate of saffron-yellow rice. Swedish *plommonspäckad fläskkarre* in which tender strips of pork loin mingle provocatively with prunes, anxious to make the acquaintance of a companion helping of *brynt potatis*. Hungarian *kobaszos rantocotta* . . . an exquisite union of scrambled eggs, peppers, green bacon and smoked *Wurst* . . .

Or, of course, there are always the Anglo-Saxon staples. Sausage, egg and chips; steak-'n'-ale pie ditto . . . deep fried North Sea haddock in high cholesterol batter?

. . . but only if you fancy *proper* grub.

Either way, you simply must leave room for the sweets and puddings to follow. Like the *Applekaka med vaniljsas* – apple cake with vanilla sauce? Oh dear, oh dear, oh *dear* . . . and the Puffs of Wind – *Windbeutel* the Germans call them. Choux pastry so light and floaty it has to be anchored to its salver by a cargo of fruit purée . . . and there's American lemon chiffon pie . . . and *torta Genovese* . . . *crême brulée* . . . *apfelstrudel* . . .

With cheese board and tea or coffee to finish. And *what* cheeses. And what coffee! Rich, dark Brazilian brewed in the Norwegian style by a Portuguese under the direction of a Belgian in a Bahamian ship . . .

For anyone loth, or unable, to go the full shilling, such as those youngsters sailing to backpack around Scandinavia on a limited budget – or those returning home having just backpacked around the UK on a limited budget – there is an alternative selection of economical pub snacks available in Ye Olde English Tavern on G deck, one above. Everything from a ploughman's lunch, albeit that it happens to be dinner time, to a steaming bowl of chilli or corned beef hash for the seriously voracious, to varieties of the ubiquitous toasted sandwich constructed to appeal to the most fastidious travelling gastronome.

Everyone aboard is catered for. Even those beginning to feel just a little too queasy to face the challenge of food at all by now, as the ferry slow-rolls with metronomic precision through the increasing night swell. For them there is always sympathy and mineral water available.

So *bon appétit*. Eat well if you've a mind to. And heartily.
In case breakfast is a little late.

Cataclysm minus four hours

An epicurean must or no, Michael Miles was destined to miss out on the potentially romantic *dîner à deux* which had created such a source of friction between himself and Grace.

It didn't mean he'd gone without eating following his peremptory eviction from the family bosom. While he'd kept his distance, confidently waiting for her to cool down, realize how wrong she'd been, he'd wandered into the pub on G deck to console himself.

The jumbo Cornish pasty had been very nice. Very filling. Michael had never been one to make futile gestures. Like denying himself, just to prove contrition.

At around a quarter past ten he glanced over from the top berth where he sprawled uncomfortably with his book . . . well, of course he'd gone back to the cabin eventually. And of *course* Grace had hugged him, and sniffed a bit after the first few awkward minutes of his return: a reconciliation for which he, for his part, had adopted a suitably chastened expression. And of course she'd got the children into bed: already sleeping the sleep of exhausted semi-cherubs by then although, to be fair, Michael had never intended to avoid sharing that chore. He did love them. He always enjoyed the last few quiet minutes of an evening before they went down, especially when Lucy, pink and scrubbed and smelling of soap and powder, snuggled on his knee in her pyjamas so he could tell her and Teddy a story.

Sometimes a long story, sometimes a short story. It tended to depend on when the first worthwhile television programme of the night was scheduled to start.

Anyway, Michael, having resigned himself to the latter part of their evening being one of constricted boredom and early to bed in a large sea-going cupboard, had glanced up from his paperback to catch sight of Grace grimacing into the ill-lit mirror, putting make-up on! Which seemed odd considering the kids were in the same room and . . . ?

'You're putting make-up on,' he observed, somewhat unnecessarily.

122

'And your seven o'clock shadow looks even scruffier now it's quarter-past ten,' Grace retorted. 'Hadn't you better go and shave like you intended earlier?'

'Shave?'

'The thing you do with a razor, Michael?' There was still a touch of asperity in her voice. A sense of reluctant compromise.

'Er . . . why?'

She turned. For someone who'd virtually been on the go all day and most of the previous night, she looked terrific.

'I don't suppose you've eaten for a start.'

'I . . . did nibble a few bits and pieces from the bar counter,' he volunteered cautiously.

'Well I haven't had anything at all. We'll both need a sandwich or something. You can have a Cornish pasty if you fancy one. I saw they'd got them on the bar menu earlier.'

'What about leaving the kids?' he said hurriedly.

She smiled, though there wasn't a lot of humour in it. 'Isn't that my line, Michael?'

'Seriously, love. What if they wake up?'

'I explained to them before they went to sleep that we might just pop along the corridor. William wasn't bothered anyway, and he's old enough not to do anything silly. Lucy's happy so long as she's got Teddy . . . I told them we won't be far away and we'll keep coming back to look in on them.'

Michael climbed down from the berth and stood behind her, his hands on her hips. His eyes met hers in the mirror. 'I'm sorry,' he murmured. 'I do love you, you know.'

'I know,' she said. She turned and kissed him. 'And I know it's your holiday. But we mustn't stay away too long.'

Grace could have added that it was her holiday as well, but she didn't bother. Treading the fine line between two . . . well, three masters, even discounting Teddy's regular washing demands, was hard enough without allowing self to get in the way.

She didn't mention that she wasn't really hungry, either. Or that there was nothing she'd actually like to do more than just climb into her berth and sleep until the morning coffee arrived. She just wanted them all to be happy, and experience had taught her that meant making Michael happy first and foremost.

123

Except that was a pretty unrewarding task in itself. No matter how much she gave, he always seemed to push for a little bit more.

'I'll be back and forward like a ping pong ball to make sure they're okay,' Michael assured her. He hesitated. 'You're, ah . . . planning to keep your jeans on, I suppose?'

Grace knew that hesitation, but was damned if she would make it too easy for him. 'I've re-done my make-up and I *can* eat a sandwich with jeans on, Michael.'

''Course you can. I just, well, sort of wondered . . . ?'

'If?'

'If you might like to slip into your little black dress, darling? I dunno . . . I thought maybe we might just take a quick look in the disco later. Assuming the kids are still sleeping, of course . . . ?'

Cataclysm minus three hours

Quite a few places were still occupied in the restaurant as eleven p.m. came around. One of the larger parties overstaying their leave, much to the mute disapproval of those stewards still hovering to clear and lay up the last tables for breakfast, was the group-discounted Welsh choir bound for their Gothenburg concert debut.

But then, the earlier atmosphere of Ye Olde Tavern topside had been amiably conducive to digging in. Simply getting his wandering minstrels synchronized to finish their drinks at the same time, then marshalled for the corporate move to their reserved tables, had taken all of choirmaster Dyfed Lewellyn's powers of persuasion. Not that anyone had complained once they'd hoisted in the spread before them.

Morgan Evans – the baritone married to Gwynneth who'd stayed home to look after the girls? – had enjoyed his dinner as much as any, an endorsement which, considering the former soldier's initial reluctance to sail on the *Orion Venturer* after his Falklands experience, was as generous as the most egotistical of chefs could seek.

Not that Monsieur de Saeger had exactly been faced with stiff competition, considering the last meal Evans consumed aboard ship had been a British Army ration pack some fifteen years previously. And in somewhat less opulent circumstances, Morgan found himself reflecting involuntarily. Just after ten in the morning it had been on that occasion – at much the same time, the post-battle analysis had revealed, as the three Skyhawks of *Dogo* division of the Argentine V Air Brigade were taking off from their field at Rio Gallegos, over four hundred miles from where his company of the Welsh Guards still awaited transfer ashore from the *Sir Galahad* to join the rest of the battalion at Bluff Cove.

It was ironic that an experience which, for most, would represent an unqualified pleasure – the simple act of enjoying a meal – engendered such discomfiting associations for Morgan Evans. It was precisely the reaction he'd dreaded might be triggered by once again being transported by ship . . . though had such apprehension been justified? He had to concede that, so far, he hadn't actually broken into one of those panicky, day-mare sweats which used to overpower him at the first hint of recall. All in all, this ferry trip was proving less stressful than he'd anticipated, notwithstanding that, perhaps triggered by a sea-sound or a smell or even a vibration through the deck, Morgan still hadn't quite been able to prevent his good hand from occasionally straying to his empty sleeve. But, discounting such minor anxiety attacks, could it be that the comparative equanimity he felt towards spending the coming night aboard the *Orion Venturer* represented a watershed? The final stage of his rehabilitation? The confronting, and the conquering, of his last great fear?

If it was, then he had earned his right to peace of mind. Evans, now a local authority housing officer, had fought hard both physically and psychologically for a decade and a half to overcome the hurt inflicted on him without allowing himself to be further crippled by bitterness. He'd been strong enough to realize that such futile railing against fate would eventually have destroyed him.

Anyway who, come to that, should he have directed his resentment against? The loss of his limb had not resulted from any personal vendetta. It had simply come about through a combination of disputed sovereignty, political expediency, Sod's Military Law and, above all, the uniform he'd happened to be wearing at the time, of which he'd been very proud.

Because Morgan had been a career soldier, all said and done. Had enlisted voluntarily with the intention of making the army his life. Nineteen years old, he'd gone willingly, a little apprehensively maybe, to the other side of the world to do with trained deliberation unto his country's enemies what, in his case, they had succeeded in doing unto him first. Even after the generals had awarded him his Falklands Campaign medal to demonstrate the nation's abiding gratitude, then discharged him, any resentment he'd felt was for the fickleness of his short-lived warrior's luck.

The bottom line for ex-Guardsman Evans was they'd all been professionals doing a job – him, Primer Teniente Cachon, and the Argentine's two wingmen. Destiny had decreed that his war was to hinge around a bomb with a patriot at each end. With him finishing up on the wrong end . . .

'You look as if you're half a world away, boyo. Whatever are you thinking of?'

Morgan blinked, withdrew finger and thumb from his sleeve. The lads around him were finally rising in ones and twos now, and beginning to drift from the restaurant, not one of them able to eat another mouthful judging by the way they stretched so pleasurably. He looked up at choirmaster Lewellyn feeling very much at ease.

'I am thinking there is a continental gentleman singing his heart out in the lounge down aft, but not very well, Dyfed. And that perhaps he's in need of a little help, eh?'

Lewellyn's face wrinkled in a mock-rueful smile. 'A conspiracy is it, Morgan Evans?'

Morgan grinned. 'A mutiny surely, Choirmaster? What with us being on a ship and everything.'

A brown walnut of a face, Dyfed had, with grey, sparkling eyes. A coastal farmer's face wrinkled by the winter Atlantic winds that can scream across Cardigan Bay . . . a face roughened by the elements, yet one that masked a feel for music, for the songs of Wales as tender as the zephyr breezes of summer.

'A few too many of you have said the same thing for me to insist on all of you going straight to bed . . . let me go and wet my boots then, and I'll be there to see you don't hit any wrong notes.'

It seemed a particularly cruel irony that former Guardsman Evans, having found peace through confronting his fear, should, as he made his way from the restaurant, pass a fair-haired young Swede lounging not five feet from him at a corner table, who was

126

destined to have just as traumatic an impact on the singer's life as did those South Atlantic pilots who had once flown four hundred miles to take off his arm.

Not that it will be personal this time, either. Certainly not aimed at Morgan Evans. The very last intention aspiring executive Sven Carlsson harbours is to actually harm anybody. Which makes the unfairness of it doubly cruel in Morgan's case. To think that a youth incapable of true achievement – one who is neither professional nor gallant nor motivated by duty, and who, though possibly qualified to drive an army truck, would never, *ever* be entrusted with a 500lb bomb – to say nothing of a Skyhawk A-4B strike aircraft in even the most desperate of wars – will nevertheless prove inept enough to create more appalling havoc among his fellow human beings than any . . . ?

But again, that is to anticipate. No one can anticipate the actions of a psychotic. If it had been possible to foresee Carlsson's plunge into unreasoning irresponsibility and so take preventive steps – somehow to halt, even delay the trucker's plan for another few hours – then Morgan Evans would simply have gone on to sing his resolute heart out in Sweden as scheduled, without ever realizing that the clock had begun to run against him for the second time in his life.

Although, isn't that to pursue the logic of negativity to illogical extremes? Doesn't it argue that, if Sven Carlsson *could* have been diverted from his suicidal course, then nothing extraordinary at all was likely to happen overnight to anybody – therefore all of those aboard the combined passenger and vehicle ro-ro ferry *Orion Venturer* would otherwise have been spared to do things tomorrow which, because he *was* mad, they were already fated not to do?

Take the case of the elderly Belgian spinster Antoinette Chaubert for instance, and hypothesize what would happen if . . . well, if nothing *had* happened? Which is silly, and very confusing, because it presupposes a non-event which cannot now take place. It's saying that, because a truck driver's fantasy world *is* about to implode, she will *not* complete her North Sea tour before happily returning to Liège still cherishing the illusion that the greatest risk she ran was of the discovery of her contraband pussycat Jozef.

No more than will the good Pastor Lütgendorf take up his new ministry without having his already crumbling faith further challenged by learning, in the most dreadful manner, that avoiding travel by aeroplane doesn't necessarily bind God to underwriting your journey.

Pregnant Heikki Niskanen will not be given chilling cause to conclude that what she's preparing to do to her surrogate plastic baby following the witching hour of midnight will, shortly thereafter, prove to have been a little over the top even by voodoo standards.

And the children from the Østfold junior school, theoretically in bed already but in practice still skylarking in their block of four-berth cabins down on E deck, much to the frustration, both mental and physical, of Frøken Evensen and Teacher Trygve . . . ? If what is soon to happen to the *Orion Venturer* doesn't occur, then they too will merely be returned home to their mothers having never been placed in the hands of a murderer with a penchant for lacy things, in the most terrible and bizarre circumstances.

Honeymooning twenty-year-olds Gertrud and Lennart Gustafsson, having made love to the point of exhaustion in their economy cabin down on D deck for most of the afternoon, and currently gazing moon-eyed at each other across a table in the Tavern while replenishing their energy levels for the coming night with that well-known aphrodisiac the British toasted cheese sandwich – they will still disembark in the morning as planned. Take up residence in a pretty little canal-bank house in Söderköping without ever having had the true extent of their love for each other tested to destruction.

Edinburgh couple Bill and Jean Somerville from the posh forward end of E deck, also on honeymoon albeit second time around in their case, who, having enjoyed a quite excellent dinner, are just moving through to the Admiral's Lounge for a drink in celebration of the joyful reunion with their daughter tomorrow . . . the future span of *their* lives together won't be placed in jeopardy either. No more than will the statistical prospect for longevity currently anticipated by colourful Malawi salesman, Mr Kumbwezi . . . Kombwasa . . . Kumb . . . well, by Fred Munyenwhatever?

The Japanese executive party, who throughout the day have demonstrated a closer affinity with Pentax and Canon zoom lenses than with motor cars, will not be provided with a rather more dramatic photo opportunity than they'd bargained for, and would otherwise carry on to fulfil their series of Volvo meetings in total ignorance, persuaded that having sailed aboard the *Orion Venturer* had been a good idea. A nice change from the stressful business of flying all over Europe.

Mrs Effie Smith, alias Sandringham – who's given up enjoying the voyage already on account of her lover's climactic pegging out . . . ? If truck driver Carlsson *were* to be prevailed upon not to put his idiotic plan into operation, then Effie will never discover that returning home to face the funeral music does not necessarily represent the most terrible fate that could await her!

As for Effie's bit on the side, Passenger Charles Smith – who hasn't budged since he was left neatly arranged, ship-shape and Bristol fashion by Purser Trøjborg, on his berth in starboard cabin E 248 with the curtains discreetly drawn despite not an extra penny being charged for single occupancy . . . ? Well, it's fair to say Charlie doesn't care any more either way.

If Sven Carlsson's lunacy *could* be neutralized, then it's most unlikely that Ex-USN M/m 2/C Periera would otherwise meet a shipmate who'd died half a century ago. While Grace Miles, who so dearly loves her children, *and* her self-indulgent husband for all his faults if the truth be told . . . Grace will never be given such nightmare cause to . . . ?

But no! No, that *is* to jump far too far ahead in time, and to presuppose, even then, that an event already preordained by a collapse of reason can, in some miraculous way, be prevented.

Which it can't.

So, suffice for the moment to observe that, at the midpoint of that first and last evening, Sven Carlsson is simply passing time until he judges it opportune to put his master strategy into effect. It's too early yet. There are still too many people moving in the public areas. And they'll be changing the watch personnel shortly, anyway. He doesn't know the routine, but it seems likely there could be crewmen moving through any part of the accommodation during that period.

Sven decides to linger over a third cup of coffee before he leaves the restaurant – deliberately test the patience of the waiting stewards as part of his executive observer-designate's strategy, then take a final stroll before . . . ?

He won't venture on deck this time, though. It's dark out there. A bit frightening. Even gazing through the big windows of the restaurant, out across the black sea from which, every so often, a wave larger and more ebullient than its fellows rears to stare at him, malevolent white eyes reflecting the outboard loom of the deck lights before subsiding back into itself, is enough to make Sven hastily avert his gaze.

No, he'll just check out the night life awhile: see if he can't build on his already pretty perceptive list of proposals for improving the ferry's image, then return to his cabin around midnight, shave, and change for the cameras.

Sven Carlsson is approaching his most dangerous phase now.

He's also a little piqued. The meal was disappointing. The ship's cook, whoever he was, had been *right* out of order! Carlsson hadn't been able to fault it.

I mean – how's a critic supposed to make his mark as a critic when he can't find a single thing to criticize?

THE MIDDLE WATCH CREW

Midnight to . . . ?

At midnight, with the majority of crew members already sleeping or thankfully preparing to get their heads down for the all-too-short respite before stand-by is called for approaching Gothenburg, the final departmental handovers begin.

Not that those involved recognize the finality, of course. That they are participating in a unique ceremony: the last change of watch ever to take place aboard the Orion Venturer *after her nearly three decades of being a living ship. No more than any of them realize they have been selected by fate to officiate over the beginning of the end of a roll-on roll-off ferry.*

No. As far as they're concerned, the eight bells marking a new day simply herald what is, on the face of it, an unremarkable event in any mariner's calendar.

CHAPTER FIFTEEN

Oh, pilot! 'tis a fearful night,
There's danger on the deep.
                    T.H. BAYLY (1797–1839)

Cataclysm minus two hours

Neither Second Officer Delucci nor the pony-tailed Quartermaster Madariaga considered it at all remarkable to find themselves stepping momentarily into a world without substance or dimension when they returned to the *Orion Venturer*'s bridge to take over the midnight watch.

They were both used to the experience: well aware that it takes a few minutes for a relief's vision to fully adjust to the dark. And it *is* dark on a ship's bridge during the small hours. It's deliberately kept that way to minimize reflection and so facilitate the lookout because, despite all the electronic aids that exist in a modern ferry, the human eye is still the primary sensor of what is out there, the most reliable means of observing what is taking place between the watchkeeper and the horizon.

The down side, particularly on a moon-deprived night like tonight, is that you become stricken temporarily blind the instant you first enter the wheelhouse from brightly lit accommodation. So that it's prudent to wait just inside the door a moment for your vision to adapt.

You won't need to hesitate for long. Soon your eyes will begin to make out form and shape. Almost immediately you'll become aware of an array, a plethora . . . a positive cattery of green or red or white eyes either blinking or glowing or twinkling at you from all four quarters. A few seconds later you can probably see enough to head cautiously for the chart space without risking tripping over anything or anyone. That's it just beside you to the right – that

132

partitioned refuge at the after end of the wheelhouse emitting a warm red ambience, with its broad mahogany plotting table and low-wattage anglepoise; its racks of books and nautical publications: its suite of navaids, its weatherfax and computers; its omnipresent clock . . . its control and alarm systems constantly monitoring fire and watertight integrity.

Don't rail against your temporary visual disadvantage. Use this precious time while your eyes are adjusting to maximum efficiency to philosophize. There's lots of things to see, and mull over . . . the radio fit next to the chart space, for instance? Reflect on how radios are just another part of bridge operations nowadays, while their operators – the traditional Sparks who used to preside over dedicated wireless rooms surrounded by a twittering, hissing background of Morse code – they've mostly gone now from the surface of the oceans: ceased to exist other than on the big cruise ships with their added demands for public telecom facilities.

Think on their going as being the end of yet another era, and feel a little sad that the steady old Sparks are largely becoming as redundant as the once-upon-a-time foretopmen and lamp-trimmers and stokers and donkeymen and greasers . . . as redundant as the Merchant Navy itself, come to that, in the form that countless previous generations knew it.

Feel a little threatened in your own situation, too, if you're a Mike Delucci or an Oliver Sandalwell still clinging to your ever-narrowing pyramid of command. Concern yourself over how the industry is moving inexorably towards dual manning. Two seagoers for the price of one. Captains with chief engineer's tickets; chiefs adept with dividers and parallel rules . . . and you too, Señor Madariaga – you worry for your future while you work hard at becoming a dancer. The way things are going there'll be jobs only for deckhands who can double as motormen, spanners in one fist and marlin spikes in the other . . . except half the new lads coming up won't know what a marlin spike is. Or was. And even if someone with a good memory tells 'em it was a tool for, among other things, splicing ropes and wires with, they won't be that impressed because they won't know what a splice used to be either.

Until, eventually, there won't be anybody signed aboard to tell them anything. There'll *be* no more Able Seamen Conroys left in ships, with their wealth of sea lore and their bloody-minded dedication to a dying way of life, and their unique skills known as seamanship. The ones who follow will all be called general duties or dual purpose ratings or just marine something-or-others, and will probably be much smarter, much more technically proficient. But make no mistake, without them – without the Conroys – going to sea will never be quite the same again.

Eck-teck Ed represents the flexible sailorman of the future. Australian Edward Talbot, the ferry's Electronics Technical Officer . . . ? It's ETO Talbot who also doubles as the *Orion Venturer*'s radio operator, although it's not his fault that the old Sparks had become a dinosaur and his Morse key a museum relic. Come to that, Ed's not indispensable himself. Communicating nowadays, whether it be ship-to-ship or ship-to-shore, is largely by voice transmission. Most bridge personnel are capable of working both operational and emergency traffic. No special skills needed other than a basic knowledge of the common maritime language of English.

Of course, if they don't have that – if they're one of the increasing numbers of Third-World-certificated officers linguistically incapable of understanding what's being addressed to them over the ether . . . ? Then just hope to God it's not one of them frowning blankly at your desperate Mayday, Mister, should you happen to be the next sailor feeling your ship beginning to slip from under you and there's no proper Sparks monitoring the emergency frequencies within a thousand miles.

. . . but enough talk of distress and disaster. There's still a good two hours to go before they become fashionable topics of conversation aboard the *Orion Venturer*.

Until then, as relieving watchkeeper, survey the bridge in preparation for making it yours for the coming four hours now your eyes have adjusted sufficiently to make out what's going on around you. The twin radars just ahead of you will be pulsing like a fortune-teller's crystal: PPIs constantly displaying the rotating flare of their individual scanners. If you're at all fanciful, and your opposite number's engrossed in one or other screen at the instant you arrive up top, you'd be excused for thinking you're relieving the very Devil himself, the way his – or her – features seem to hover in the darkness, sinister in the cathodic uplighting.

134

While, talking levitation, above and forward of the helmsman's grating you'll mark the illuminated ribbon of the steering gyro repeater. That too appears to float in the blackness. Stretch the imagination a little and you can pretend it's the disembodied grin of the Cheshire Cat in *Alice*, just hanging there like that over the point where the green-shaded overspill of the compass binnacle catches the brass-tipped midships spoke of the wheel . . . now there's a nice touch to warm the traditionalist. Enough, perhaps, to generate a little frisson of nostalgia simply to realize the *Orion Venturer* is old enough and stylish enough still to boast a compass in a proper binnacle. Who knows – look carefully in the flag locker or the bridge box and you might even find a little tin of Brasso still hidden away as well. Wrapped in a strip of greyish-powder-marked bunting along with a soft polishing cloth.

It's even nice to know she's got a proper wheel, for that matter, instead of a joystick thing you waggle while feeling faintly out of character: more like a jumbo jet aviator than a real ship's helmsman. Mind you, considering your twelve-thousand-ton charge is more than likely to be steaming on automatic pilot in any but the most confined of waters throughout its voyage anyway, perhaps you should count yourself lucky even to *have* a helmsman to keep you company for the coming four hours, Mister Second Mate.

. . . although on second thoughts, maybe you should count *yourself* lucky to be aboard. Because one day in the not-too-distant future, you won't be. None of you unprofitable space, food and wages-consuming add ons called crew. They're working on it – on making sailors redundant to the process of sailing ships. The technology already exists to have huge unmanned steel boxes, crammed with cargo, transport themselves without the touch of a human hand from Yokohama to Yucatán, or Delhi to Durban . . . to self-select the most favourable routes to avoid storms; to exploit the most fuel-advantageous ocean currents . . . even to tie themselves up nice and snug to wherever it is they're going once they've got there.

But don't worry *too* deeply about your impending redundancy, Second Officer Delucci – no more than should you, for that matter, Able Seaman Madariaga. Such massive technological upheaval is hardly going to overtake the long-haul ro-ro ferry industry during the next two hours and seventeen minutes.

After that, gentlemen of the middle bridge watch, it's highly unlikely that any threat of losing your berth to a robot will be the concern uppermost in either of your minds.

Third Engineer Stamper – also back on watch from midnight but, in his case, presiding over the thundering artificial glare of the engine room – would have been absolutely delighted if someone decided to replace Chief Braca-bloody-montes with a robot. In Stamper's view anyone who wished to was as good as halfway there. The man already functioned adequately without a heart.

But that's only because Bert was in a bad mood: tired and generally brassed off with the prospect of being a sailor for the rest of his life. He'd found it impossible to unwind in the period since six that evening when the Chief had finally permitted him to go and get cleaned up. By then he'd already worked a twelve-hour day, even discounting his extra-curricular struggle to coach Motorman Garilao in the finer principles of engineering. Like how to use a spanner.

The sleep he so desperately needed had evaded him. Following a hastily snatched evening meal he'd gone back to his cabin to put his feet up and try for it, but the attempt had proved a frustrating experience. His body clock was all out of kilter for a start. The outcome had been that he'd lain staring fixedly at the deckhead, willing himself to drift off . . . or he had until fifteen minutes or so before he was due to rouse, of course, whereupon his eyes had become leaden all of a sudden and sleep had converted to the most desirable commodity ever and he'd literally had to force himself to ease off his berth and shrug back into his white overalls.

It would be fair to say, then, that when Third Engineer Bert Stamper took over the *Orion Venturer*'s last engine room watch from 3/E Hellström, he was already in a thoroughly bolshie mood. So much so that he'd simply glanced through the notes and job sheets left for his attention, then deliberately disregarded them. Mostly planned maintenance items already overdue, according to Hellström, which Bert and Garilao were expected to continue with overnight. 'No way,' Stamper thought ill-humouredly. 'No *way* am

I goin' to flog my guts out for this ship all night as well as all bloody day!'

So Stamper chucked the clipboard on the console without reading through it properly. He was more concerned with getting his priorities right once Hellström had gratefully disappeared topside, heading for his bunk.

'The middle watch sannies,' he muttered anxiously to Garilao. 'You see a sannie box lying around?'

'Sah-nees, Engine-ear Temper?' the Filipino frowned doubtfully.

'Not *Temper*! My name's . . .' Stamper gave up. 'Jesus!'

'You name is *Jesus*, Turd?' Garilao goggled, impressed.

'Sand-which-*is*!' Bert stuck doggedly to the point at issue. 'There should be sannies . . . sand-wich-es . . . left out f'r the middle watchkeepers – you and me. Savvy?'

Garilao didn't look as though he did, so Bert fell back on pidgin for the first time since he'd been on the China coast as junior fourth on a Hong Kong-crewed, Turkish-flagged cruise liner. And he remembered thinking at the time that they'd had language problems on that ship.

'Makee lookee findee plastic sannee boxee . . .'

'This one, Turd?'

'Spot on,' Stamper confirmed in relief.

Assistant Crew Mess Cook Manley had done 'em proud first night out. Chicken *and* ham. He'd wait until four bells – two a.m. – before broaching them. Give 'em something to look forward to.

'I'll keep them here, under my wing,' Bert said, placing the box on the clipboard of job sheets beside him.

The sandwich box now concealed, among memos of rather lesser significance, an instruction from Dana, the Second, regarding action to be taken by the night watch in respect of certain engine room safety equipment.

3/E Hellström had read the watch orders but, being a lazy sod, hadn't bothered to do anything about it before Bert Stamper and Motorman Teofisto Garilao came down.

Stamper, not having read the watch orders at all, didn't even realize he was supposed to.

*   *   *

137

When Marianne Nørgaard took up her middle watch duty station at the reception desk on E deck, she was surprised to find Assistant Purser Everard still working, still finishing off his paperwork: balancing his foreign exchange vouchers for the day.

'Shouldn't be much happening from now on,' Jimmy yawned, leaning back in his chair and stretching. 'Look, seeing it's your first night I'll take a walk round before I go and get my head down. Check the cabin staff don't have problems.'

'I'll manage,' she assured him a little defensively.

The reception foyer was deserted and a bit untidy, she thought disapprovingly, but then it was the middle of the night and the cleaning staff wouldn't come on again until morning. The big ashtrays with litter cut-outs under them were overflowing. Someone had left an empty beer glass lying under one of the settees, clinking back and forward, timing the sullen roll of the ro-ro.

As she recovered it her attention became distracted by the ship sounds. Despite being located two decks above, the beat from the night club – well, the disco really – could still be heard faintly over the hum of the ventilators. And there was singing filtering downstairs from the direction of the Admiral's Lounge. Beautiful singing. Welsh it was, and with feeling.

'Still enjoying themselves,' Jimmy said. 'This is what it's all about, love – being a purser? Helping people to enjoy themselves.'

She began to see him in a more sympathetic light. Didn't seem so brash and pushy in the quiet of the night, and he certainly pulled his weight. 'Doesn't sound very Viennese,' she hazarded.

'The lads from the valleys,' Everard confirmed in a lilting parody which didn't mean much to Marianne, her being a Dane and everything. 'First night out our entertainer gets hijacked.'

'Maybe he's lucky that's all that's happened to him.' She couldn't resist smiling back. 'I heard him rehearse this morning.'

'Don't underestimate the pulling power of Herr Willi. Earlier in the evening, when the old dears were still lively, he had 'em in the palm of his hand. Everythin' from the Birdie Dance to the Conga. Now he's hamming it up night shift with the taffies. You're goin' to have to shoot him to get the bar closed.'

A young fair-haired man, probably Scandinavian, descended the stairway from F deck and crossed the reception lobby heading for the corridor leading to the port side forward cabins where most of the commercial drivers not booked into D deck were berthed. Marianne smiled automatically as he passed the desk and he nodded shyly back. Quite pleasant looking, she reflected absently. And polite. In her experience truckers were usually professional: seldom risked more than the odd glass of beer. They tended to keep a low profile, seldom gave trouble.

'Good night, sir,' she called after him.

Sven Carlsson studiously pretended not to hear. He could hardly explain he wasn't actually going to bed so much as going to get smartened up in preparation for making the first move to become her . . . well, her boss, he supposed. Boy, would *she* get a surprise when she recognized him in his new role . . . Good girl, though. Smart and polite. He'd make a point of remembering her. Just the kind the Company needed to project an image . . .

'Top priority, start making up the morning call sheets against orders for tea an' coffee – those are the vouchers over there.' Second Purser Everard lifted his jacket from the back of the chair while opening the reception kiosk door. 'Someone'll come up for them when the early shift turns to in the galley.'

He hesitated, obviously reluctant to leave her to cope alone. 'Other than that, take it easy. Minor problems, give me a call in my cabin: extension five one. Medical – better call me *and* the Chief Purser. Major stuff . . . emergencies? Call whoever you think fit, though ideally let the bridge know what's happening first. All the numbers are in the ship's telephone direc . . .'

'I *have* been in a ferry before, Mister Everard,' she said solemnly. 'Jimmy.'

'Go to *bed* – Jimmy!'

When he'd gone Marianne slipped off her new brass-buttoned reefer and hung it carefully on a coat hanger behind the door before adjusting her so-precious officer's epaulettes to sit square on her shoulders, then turned to survey her temporary empire with pride and, despite her brave assurances to Jimmy Everard, not a little trepidation.

What if something untoward *did* occur on her deck during the coming small hours? The four overnight cabin stewards were pretty thinly spread over a large area. From what she'd seen of them so far it was uncertain whether or not they would prove competent or even supportive in a crisis – and anyway, she was the officer in charge. It would almost certainly fall upon her to implement the initial, perhaps the all-critical response. Was she really qualified to handle a major crisis? Would, for that matter, anyone even be able to find and inform her of any emergency until it was too late to take effective counter-action?

Because twenty-four-year-old Junior Purser Nørgaard was uncomfortably aware that, from her post in reception three levels above the waterline and situated roughly amidships, she over-looked the point of convergence of three separate longitudinal corridors – port, centre and starboard – running both forward and aft from her location. Those corridors, also linked by cross passages at intervals along the length of the ferry, served the 144 cabins making up the main sleeping accommodation deck of the *Orion Venturer*. Effectively it meant that she sat at the hub of a labyrinth of passageways within which, to someone unfamiliar with the complex layout of E deck, it was all too easy to get lost.

A comparative newcomer to the ship herself, the sea-wise Mari-anne had made a point of familiarizing herself with its internal geography. She knew, however, that many of the ferry's less experienced crew – never mind her passengers – hadn't. No har-bour drills had been carried out to practise the emergency plan only distributed earlier that evening; no instruction given, so far as she was aware, regarding even basic evacuation routine, despite its being common knowledge that orientation still presented a problem to all too many of those potentially concerned with directing passengers to areas of safety during a crisis.

Even during the hours immediately before sailing she'd come across hotel staff, ostensibly posted to escort new boarders to their cabins, hesitating doubtfully with wrinkled brows themselves, simply trying to work out which way to turn to take them forward or aft – and *that* had been under the brightly lit conditions which normally prevailed below decks.

If you then complicate that disorientation further by throwing in the other major safety problem already evident aboard the ro-ro – of trying to communicate urgent directions in a crisis to key personnel separated by up to nine different languages . . . ?

Marianne preferred not to dwell on the situation that could arise during the rest of her watch should some event, even one not immediately life-threatening in itself, occur. Should the main generators fail for instance, and the ferry be plunged into a darkness broken only by the glimmer of emergency lighting? An unlikely situation, admittedly, but one in which practised reassurance from a duty staff familiar with the ship could well defuse an otherwise potentially dangerous panic.

Instead, she reached for the tray vouchers and immersed herself in tackling those priorities which the *Orion Venturer's* owners and managers did consider vital to the commercial survival of a new, fare-cutting long-haul ro-ro service in a highly competitive market. Priorities reluctantly endorsed by the ferry's pressured and morally compromised senior officers.

Junior Assistant Purser Nørgaard began to list which occupants of which cabins required tea, coffee or fruit juice with their morning call . . .

On the bulkhead behind her the hands of the reception desk clock jerked to seventeen minutes past midnight, Scandinavian time.

Her industry, while commendable, would prove of little long-term value. In exactly two hours the *Orion Venturer's* middle watch Duty Purser's labours were to become strictly academic.

Besides the steaming crew there were others of the ro-ro's complement, particularly among the hotel staff assigned to the restaurant, who should have completed their duties long before midnight but who – because that department was as under-manned as any other, and the task of cleaning, restocking the serveries, and laying up tables for breakfast had fallen behind – hadn't yet been permitted to stand down.

The stewards protested. It escalated into an unpleasant and highly voluble incident accompanied by much waving of arms, in the course of which the protesters had been summarily dismissed by Restaurant Manager António e Cunha and coldly informed they would be put ashore in Gothenburg.

Those who immediately recanted, mostly older men with

families in Portugal and a realistic appreciation of the prospects of achieving another sea-going berth for a steward branded with an unsatisfactory discharge, were re-hired on new, shorter-term contracts at even lower rates of pay. With an FOC vessel in thrall to no national seamen's union, the industrial relations philosophy pursued by the *Orion Venturer*'s owners could afford to be ruthless, cost-effective, and to apply to her complement across the board, irrespective of rank.

As her senior officers themselves had already discovered.

Sixteen, although supposedly nineteen-year-old Pantry Rating Lucchetti was another who found himself drawing an equally short straw around midnight, unpaid overtime-wise.

Having acquired his sea legs only at the cost of three trays of shattered crockery and the beetle-browed disapproval of Provision Master Uguccioni, Filippo had been sentenced to continue working, alone and sweating, in the rancid-smelling utilities galley while the watch changed in other parts of ship and the remainder of the catering crew gratefully retired below.

And, judging by the stack of food-encrusted catering utensils that had accumulated owing to a nervous breakdown of the already ancient heavy-duty washing machine's conveyor belt, and which still awaited Filippo's ministrations with wire-wool scourer and pot brush, his punishment could well keep him busy there throughout the *next* change of bloody watch!

Nevertheless, despite seasickness and feeling bone-achingly wearied by his unaccustomed manual labours, Filippo managed to keep his resentment – as well as the boning knife he was scrubbing at the time – in check. The once-wannabe *mafioso* was mongrel-cunning enough to recognize he was hardly in any position to invite scrutiny from Swedish immigration by joining the dissidents from the restaurant, having signed on ship's articles using the discharge book and safety certificates acquired from a dead man. At least he wasn't in jail. Even better, he wasn't planted in the Cimitero Monumentale. *And* he still retained all his vital parts.

Former *Picciotto di Onore* Lucchetti busied himself, up to his elbows in soapsuds, while consoling himself with the thought that this was the penance one must expect to suffer for being an official good guy now. A redeemed sinner who had cast aside all thoughts of pursuing vendettas against his fellow human beings.

. . . apart from which, if things didn't get better, he could always afford himself the opportunity of lapsing just once more an' sticking it good on that bastard Uguccioni who'd dumped him with this duty, should their paths cross ashore. Preferably in the kind of dark alley in which the born-again street urchin felt rather more at home.

Pantry Rating Lucchetti never gave a thought to the fact that, below the waterline in the fore part of the ship on B deck, where the utilities compartment was kept supplied with dirty dishes by a crockery lift from the main galley four decks above, he was working in what promised, in catastrophic circumstances, to turn into another form of prison cell.

One from which his only way of escape had to be through a series of steel-encased alleys of the kind with which he, sea-wise only on paper, was not at all familiar.

Also forming a crucial part of the steaming watch as the ferry rounded the north-western coast of Denmark were the four stewards still tending the various bars until they closed. In addition there were those crew members assigned to all-night duties, who'd been working for four hours already and were slated to continue in their posts for the remainder of the passage.

Night-watchman Conroy was one. Portuguese Cabins Steward Pinheiro Cardoso, one of the four hotel services staff looking after the passenger accommodation on E deck – in his case the starboard after section – was another.

Admittedly little Pinheiro hadn't actually *worked* so much as spent most of his first evening as a sailor either still trying to figure out how to tie his lifejacket so it didn't keep slipping to his ankles, or attempting to find his way around the seeming maze of corridors criss-crossing his domain without actually having to ask a passenger for directions. That, and retreating as much as possible from public view to his little service cuddy where he hugged his plastic bucket even more appreciatively than he'd ever embraced his very good friend and pastry-cheffing shipmate, Jorge Guimãres.

143

In a nutshell, the former hotel waiter – inadequate even on dry land, before he'd set sail in his *barco grande* – represented a classic example of all that concerned Junior Purser Nørgaard.

As the clocks moved to mark the new day, and having rinsed out his bucket for perhaps the fifth time since he'd come on watch, Pinny sagged weakly to the deck in one corner of his private hell and prayed to the Blessed Virgin Mary that the ship might sink soon because he couldn't stand it any longer. He really wasn't cut out for this sort of thi . . .

The ship jolted slightly as a rogue sea took her amidships, and E deck Cabins Night Steward Cardoso lunged yet again for his constant companion.

. . . if it's at all possible, and not *too* much trouble, Our Lady – can you make it *very* soon?

Por favor?

Not, of course, imagining seriously for one moment that, for the first and only time in his miserable, penurious life, Someone Up There might just have been keeping the Middle Watch as well?

CHAPTER SIXTEEN

The Night-watchman's Trail

When constabulary duty's to be done,
The policeman's lot is not a happy one.
S<small>IR</small> W.S. G<small>ILBERT</small> (1836–1911)

Able Seaman Conroy didn't 'ave no time for religion and prayin' an' stuff.

Well . . . he wouldn't have for a little while longer. Conroy's abrupt conversion wasn't due for a couple of hours yet, give or take a few minutes.

Until then he would continue to look upon the Master of whatever ship he wus in at the time, as being God. On its Mate as being the Right Hand o' God. On its Bosun as the Archangel Ruined. On engineers, stewards an' pursers collectively as the Unholy Trinity, and upon hisself as a sort of maritime Moses: particularly appropriate to his duties aboard the *Orion Venturer*, where his Ten Commandments were writ in Night Patrol Standing Orders and his personal Wilderness was represented by the ro-ro's several hundred metres of corridor which he was expected to wander.

Religiously.

Admittedly the analogy foundered somewhat when it came to the question of Faith between God and His Watchman. For a start, Moses hadn't been expected to clock in at forty-two way stations on 'is tour up the Mountain just to prove he'd *been* there, had 'e . . . ?

Just after midnight Conroy stirred at his unofficial office desk – the starboard crew mess table next to the tea urn on A deck down

145

the bottom of the ship – brushed the cigarette ash from the front of his woolly pully, crammed his white uniform cap at a jaunty angle on his head, picked up his torch and walkie-talkie, and reluctantly embarked upon his second patrol of the night throughout the length and breadth of the ferry.

This time he started at the top. Took the lift straight up to the navigating officers' accommodation on the funnel deck, Deck H. There he made a special point of being heard to check the now-locked Mate's office beside the Captain's quarters starboard side below the bridge itself, before stepping out over the low coaming into an increasingly gusting headwind.

Hunched with back against the driving rain, Conroy walked sharpish aft through pools of deck lights on a level with the rippling canvas covers of starboard lifeboats numbers one, three, five, seven an' nine, then down the aft ladder to G deck – the boat, or embarkation, deck itself – to nip indoors again at the entrance to the dance hall . . . the dance 'all, would yer believe? A dance hall, of all daft fripperies to put inna ship coming, as it did in Conroy's sardonic merchant service opinion, a close third in order of sea-going uselessness only after a ten-rung step-ladder and a Royal Navy officer.

Didn't even call the sweat box by a proper name. Disk-oh-teck they called it. They'd signed about every bloody nationality there is aboard except a Frenchy, yet they still 'ad to copy the language du Frog to be fashionable. Not even a band: jus' a gramophone played by some ponce of a bloke needed a good 'air cut, and the kind of flashing coloured lights you'd only expec' to see otherwise if you come off worst in a pub brawl or dropped a match in the pyrotechnics locker.

Further aft Ye Olde English Tavern wus . . . *was!* . . . fairly quiet. Its duty bar steward had already started to pull down the roller shutters on one half of the plastic oak counter. Now only a few stalwarts remained to make desultory conversation around mock-Tudor tables under artfully hung three-month-old antique swords and gaily coloured nylon heraldic flags. Shortly those drinkers who wished to continue pushing their tax-free intake to the limit would be urged to move forrard to the Ocean Runner Night Club bar – guaranteed to stay open till the last dancer dropped, which was the only sensible thing about the place – or retire below to the Admiral's Lounge while they could still walk.

Conroy nodded almost approvingly to the barman as he glanced wistfully inside. But then: havin' a decent British pub aboard, serving best bitter an' real ale . . . ?

Now that *wus* a good idea!

It would take the best part of an hour for Night-watchman Conroy to work his way down through the *Orion Venturer*, layered as she was like a sort of ocean-going wedding cake – and lookin' a bit like one too, by the AB's reckoning, who didn't consider ro-ro ferries, not even long-haul ones, as bein' real ships – from the beat, beat, beat of the boat deck down the wide central staircase amidships to Main Deck F, still four decks above the sea, where the sheltered emergency muster areas in the restaurant, lounge and both sides of the duty-free shopping and cinema foyer were efficiently indicated by shiny new tri-lingual, colour-coded signs bearing stylized lifeboats.

Their sudden appearance, just before the pre-sailing inspection by the Marine Safety Agency inspector, had invited derisive comment from the old hands.

'Next trip the company'll get round ter issuing the boardin' cards they shoulda provided to match 'em,' Conroy reflected sardonically. 'Then the passengers might even work out which muster station they gotter go *to*!'

After experimentally rattling the locked grilles of the gift grotto, Conroy first turned forward to glance inside the children's soft playroom – noisy, grubby creatures them – before trailing morosely through an almost deserted restaurant where a few stewards still laid up tables with hardly a resentful glance as he passed.

'So what 'ave *they* got to be so pissed off about?' he, not having been privy to the earlier mutiny, reflected irritably. 'Not that it's more than you'd expect inna FOC tub. Well, I mean . . . Portugees an' Eyeties? Not proper sailormen. Oughter be bloody grateful jus' to 'ave a berth while there's quality British seafarers on the beach . . .'

But then, Conroy couldn't stand blokes, especially foreign blokes, 'oo wasn't prepared to go about their duties with cheerful enthusiasm.

The discreetly lit Admiral's Lounge was still surprisingly busy at half-midnight. It appeared the attraction focused on a number of the taffy passengers having settled in around the piano beside the little dance floor in the lounge, singing what even Conroy conceded wus tol'rable ditties.

Pity about the presence of that German so-called entertainer feller, Willy Whatever, who wus bangin' away at the ivories with all the finesse of a Panzer division on the rampage. But then, Able Seaman Conroy di'n't 'ave no time f'r . . .

Humming a snatch or two himself, he threaded his way through the tables heading for the open recreation deck aft where the ferry's swimming pool was located. A key attraction in sunnier Florida climes, on this deployment it now lay drained, boarded over and rain-swept, on the basis that there's little call for swimming facilities on the North Sea at night.

Swimming *in* it, maybe . . . ? Now that *is* a possibility that shouldn't be lightly dismissed. In fact events are already shaping to make North Sea bathing a distinct possibility for inclusion in the voyage programme . . . but certainly not *on* it. Not four comforting levels above the Plimsoll line, with a reclining deck chair handy and a glass of something fortifying.

A few minutes later and the *Orion Venturer's* policeman had descended the midship staircase to the reception lobby on E deck, the main passenger cabins deck, to find a junior female purser holding the fort alone.

'Just a kid,' Conroy said gloomily. Although it may seem hard to credit, he didn't approve of women goin' to sea. 'Jus' a baby 'ardly out of nappies, yet she's wearing *officer's* stripes already!'

Shaking his head at the very idea of it, at the way every prejudice he'd ever held dear was being eroded, Able Seaman Conroy passed through the wide lobby to begin his tour of the byways of passenger country in his self-regulated search for any hint of fire, flood or other oceanic awfulness.

Having been so disparaging regarding female crew members it was ironic that, precisely because the seaman *was* a veteran, having long mastered the facility to sense his way around a ship no matter what the circumstances, he'd become insensitized to the potential for panic recognized earlier by the less experienced Junior Purser Nørgaard.

For a start, Conroy lacked imagination. Completely at one with his environment, he couldn't visualize the disorientation which could afflict the very old or the very young – or simply the ordinary traveller in an emergency, suddenly finding themselves called from their cabin into a corridor identical to all the other corridors on that deck, whereupon they could well be faced with a multi-directional choice between what could well prove life or death.

But why criticize Conroy exclusively for such dangerous myopia? He was only hired to man the ships, not design 'em. Come to that, what of the legions of masters and officers who'd sailed in the *Orion Venturer* on countless previous deployments without anticipating the dangers inherent in her construction? Wasn't theirs precisely the same lack of foresight which, even more reprehensibly, had afflicted the naval architects and the maritime safety inspectors when the plans for the big ro-ro's passenger accommodation had first been approved nearly thirty years before?

Had blinded them to, among other lethal flaws soon to be revealed, the clear threat to life arising from the fact that several runs of corridor on that main sleeping deck of the ferry actually continued past adjoining emergency exit routes to create . . . well . . .

. To create dead ends?

And give Night-watchman Conroy his due, he was doin' the job he was paid to do. Policing the ship while conscientiously clocking in at every single key statio . . . oh, all right – perhaps not conscientiously so much as prudently, then.

Largely on account of the fact that he hadn't yet worked out a foolproof system to avoid being caught if he didn't cover the whole route, and someone checked his print-out.

*   *   *

The next stage of Conroy's descent into the wedding cake took him down through deck D to its mirror image of C deck running just above the *Orion Venturer*'s waterline. Those decks didn't contain so many byways to patrol, both levels being largely taken up by the ro-ro's stern-loading vehicle hangar rising two tiers high throughout her length. Only single rows of compartments ran either side of the hangar on each deck, sandwiched between its steel walls and the hull plating.

Conroy wasn't aware of it at the time, of course – had no reason to suspect what was to come – but outside the starboard wall of the lower car deck lay the line of nine vacant cabins which had provided Carlsson, the mentally volatile trucker, with such food for thought when he first boarded. Those economy class cabins, awaiting refurbishment, only occupied the after end of the ferry. For the remaining two-thirds of her length, C deck's starboard corridor, in addition to providing access to the vehicles, continued through to the bows while serving various utility spaces including the laundry, the ship's cells, the chef's refrigerated and cold stores, and the cabin-master's linen rooms.

Four enclosed stairwells, located at regular intervals along that seemingly endless alleyway, allowed passage to the decks above and below.

After checking her forward compartments, Able Seaman Conroy's route ultimately brought him back through the ferry to the aft-most car deck door in way of those deserted cabins. It had been a long and wearisome spiral, effectively requiring him to circumnavigate the ship twice to cover both decks.

'If I'd wanted to plod round lookin' for trouble f'r a living, I'd a joined the bloody police force,' he glowered as, breathing a bit heavily by then, he grasped the chipped handle of the self-closing steel door marked CREW ONLY, and slid it wide.

The draught sucking through the echoing vehicle space struck chill on his leather-tanned face as he entered. Not that it bothered Conroy. Virtually weatherproofed by years at sea, he was immune to the sudden drop in temperature from the comfortably heated accommodation. More to the point, secure at last from official eyes, the reluctant ship's policeman waited for the door to roll shut behind him, then flashed up a duty-free under the nearest RÖKING

FÖRBJUDEN/NO SMOKING warning – help 'im get over his breath-lessness.

Inhaling luxuriously, he began to ease between the lines of cars and trailers and trucks, slowing every so often to shine his torch on a suspect fuel cap or test the tension of a lashing by probing critically with the sole of his deck boot.

Conroy didn't think anything of being in that awesome place alone although, to anyone less laid back than a hardened seafarer, the car deck of a ro-ro under way might well present a menacing, even an alarming atmosphere.

For a start it's dominated by hard-to-identify sounds, with over-head exhaust fans emitting a constant disembodied roar and the echoing clank of chain stoppers tugging at ringbolts as vehicles move fractionally in their lashings, suspensions giving to the motion of the ship. Down there the rise-and-fall throb of the main engines below invites fanciful comparison to a giant, pulsating heart while – because you are just above the waterline – you can hear . . . sense . . . *feel* the monstrous protest of the sea at being disturbed. Rumbling and grumbling and parting resentfully before the sub-surface onslaught of the ferry's bulbous bow, reverberating hollowly through the vast, slowly porpoising steel cavern.

It took Conroy fourteen minutes to complete his clockwise cir-cuit of the car deck before returning, satisfied all was well, to the door by which he'd entered. It was only after passing through to the corridor again that he hesitated, frowning. It hadn't registered with him earlier, what with him bein' anxious to get in an' grab a fly smoko, but the padlock for which he, as night-watchman, carried a master key, and which should have been secured to prevent unauthorized entry to the vehicles, was missing.

The AB glowered. Them *soddin'* Spanish deckies. Probably finished securin' the motors before sailing, then just pissed off out of it down the mess to grab a tortilla an' a glass of sangria or whatever it is they scoff, afore they was called to stand by for leaving port. So whatever 'appened to old-fashioned responsibility, eh? Course, *mañana*'s their watchword, ain't it? Couldn't even be bothered to report a padlock missin', could they . . . ?

Conroy decided he couldn't be bothered to report the padlock missing. Not until later. Not while the tea urn beckoned, reinforced by the prospect of putting his feet up in the mess awhile before his next rounds come unavoidably due. Still muttering about the iniquities of FOC crews, he turned to head for the nearest stairway leading down through B deck and back to his office.

It was, of course, unfair of Conroy to blame his fellow crewmen for the deliberate action of a passenger on the grounds of ethnic prejudice. Especially considering that, when the Bosun's loading team did finally evacuate the car deck, they hadn't even left through that door.

They'd departed by a door lying much further forward on the *port* side, not the starboard . . . and it was the mode they'd left *that* one in that Conroy should've been complaining about.

Because, located roughly amidships, car deck access door number 4P Port still lay wide open – never mind just being short of a padlock! – on account of its heavy-duty runners having jammed solid through lack of maintenance. And somehow, while the deckies had *meant* to report its failure to the engineers, they'd kind of overlooked doing so, what with all the pre-sailing bustle going on . . . while Conroy himself hadn't later discovered the potentially hazardous oversight because, in all fairness to him, a night-watchman can't cover every inch of a ship as big as the *Orion Venturer* on every patrol, way station clocks or no.

Next round he would do port side C deck . . .

It was just as he was heading off that he happened to glance through the half-open door of one of the side cabins under refit . . . it really wasn't turning out to be his night for doors . . . whereupon the old reprobate ground to a disconcerted halt yet again.

Because even the normally phlegmatic Conroy found himself a bit disturbed by the sight of what lay in starboard cabin number C313.

Just after two bells in the middle watch, or one o'clock in the morning by a landsman's timepiece, AB Conroy – though unaware of the saga which had preceded the ro-ro's sailing on account of his keeping 'is head below the parapet at the time – had chanced upon the out-of-sight, out-of-mind repository selected by his

Hispanic shipmate Madriaga for the stuff abandoned by the ship-fitters on the car deck.

Remember it?

That heavy equipment the *Orion Venturer*'s stressed-out Captain Halvorsen had icily instructed the Mate to have removed before promptly withdrawing back into his self-imposed purdah while assuming – not unreasonably in his case, considering he *was* supposed to be the Master – that His Will would be Done?

The same equipment that Chief Officer McCulloch, under intense pressure to complete his emergency plan, had been too preoccupied to oversee being re-stowed properly himself, and so had assigned an equally harassed junior mate to the task?

The equipment that Second Officer Delucci, involved at the time in loading vehicles, had – in *his* turn told the Bosun to get shifted pronto, and had meant to question his quartermaster about later, during the afternoon watch, but had been diverted by a curiously timely bank of North Sea *haar* from so doing?

The very same equipment which Bosun Pascal, last in a line of delegators, had so unfeelingly ordered an uninterested wished-he-was-a-dancer-instead-of-a-sailor to makee disappear *rápido* chop bloody chop afore sailing – then promptly vanished himself?

Remember it . . . ?

Because if you do, then it's more than anyone holding any position of responsibility aboard the ferry had managed to, never mind go so far as to enquire about what *did* eventually happen to the unwanted gear in question.

That potentially lethal excess baggage which the *Orion Venturer*'s pass the buck chain of command had landed its Torquemada look-alike with hiding from the safety inspector's sight? Without even cursory supervision or follow-up by a qualified officer?

The four heavy acetylene welding gas bottles, each containing the explosive force of a small bomb under certain uncontrolled conditions, had been stowed upright against the metal frame of a top berth: admittedly lashed securely in place in what even Conroy conceded was a seamanlike manner, with strong manila rope.

Two more pressure bottles marked OXYGEN lay wedged along

the side of cabin C313's lower bunk. It was easy to miss them at first glance. They'd been partly stacked over with 10-litre tins of marine quality oil paint and half a dozen plastic containers of painter's white spirit.

They should *never* have been left there. The regulations for stowage of hazardous substances aboard ships, particularly aboard car ferries, are rigorous. Conroy didn't know 'em chapter and verse like an officer would, but he was tolerably sure they di'n't recognize shoving potential bombs in outboard passenger cabins at sea level as being safe industrial practice. He was also pretty certain none of the mates would've sanctioned such a flagrant breach of safety.

Them bloody useless *mañana* bananas agin!

More to the point – this time they'd gone an' landed Conroy himself in something of a quandary. Despite his jaded view of his shipmates, he'd never willingly rat on them. On the other hand he *did* have a duty to report anything amiss, what with him bein' watchman and everything . . . while there's no denyin' that making your mark as a conscientious hand at the start of a trip never comes amiss if, sometime later, you does get caught out skiving.

Reaching for the walkie-talkie clipped to his belt, he hesitated yet again as a further complication struck him. He also happened to be the only deck rating on duty immediately available to shift 'em. Or he was apart from that dancer feller quartermasterin' on the bridge anyway, who didn't look like he was capable o' liftin' a bottle o' Chinee Tiger beer, never mind a pressurized steel bottle of gas weighing . . . well, weighing a bloody sight more than *he* proposed to trolley-dolly about the ship on his tod in the middle of the night!

While all said and done, he could easy have walked straight past, couldn't he . . . ? There must be thirty separate compartments from stern to bow running this side of C deck alone. He wus hardly expected to look in every single one of 'em, was he? Apart from which, the day men would be turned-to again in another hour or two, an' nothin' dodgy was likely to happen before then . . .

The *Orion Venturer*'s graveyard watch was one hour and seventeen minutes old when the AB replaced the walkie-talkie in his belt

154

clip before part closing the door of starboard cabin C313, leaving it ajar just enough to allow him to feel for, and engage, the internal cabin hook. No way was he irresponsible or anything. All that paint and stuff . . . ? Better to leave it vented rather than totally enclosed.

Night-watchman Conroy had precisely sixty more minutes left to relish the contraband comforts of his office before he would receive a rather odd call from Second Officer Delucci on the bridge.

THE MIDDLE WATCH

One a.m. to . . . ?

An hour past midnight and 160-odd passengers still remain awake and active, concentrated largely in either the Admiral's Lounge, where ex-soldier Morgan Evans and his fellow choristers are putting on their impromptu concert in collaboration with the indefatigable Willi Tische, or gyrating to the more frenetic beat of the Ocean Runner Night Club high on the boat deck.

There are exceptions. A few seek solitude, a few simply the company of another to savour the generally enervating experience of being in a ship at sea. A very few seek seclusion to pursue less commendable agendas.

The balance of the ferry's passenger complement, some 350 souls including most of the elderly, the seasick, the unfit and the children – those least fitted, by definition, to help themselves – have by now retired to their cabins on E deck.

A few will lie awake listening to the unfamiliar noises of the ship. A number are dozing fitfully: either excited by the prospect of landfall in a few hours or simply disturbed by their continually oscillating environment. Many are asleep.

None will be provided with complimentary tea or coffee when next they are aroused.

Some of the really sound sleepers will not awaken at all.

CHAPTER SEVENTEEN

Lusisti satis, edisti satis atque bibisti. Tempus abire tibi
  est . . .
You have played enough, you have eaten and drunk
  enough. Now it is time for you to depart . . .
HORACE (65–8 BC)

Cataclysm minus one hour

Charlie Periera just couldn't push himself into sleep.

Yeah, sure he wus tired – he was seventy-odd years young
weren't he and, apart from a short siesta late afternoon, he'd been
up and about since only the Lord knew what time yesterday . . .
yes'day morning, was it? And yeah, he knew it was long past
midnight – past one a.m. f'r that matter – and that in a few hours
the *Thompsons* would be roused to give up their cabins . . . de
luxe outers, mind? *With* windows . . . and drag themselves wearily
aboard that goddamn back-achin' tour coach down on the car deck
yet again to hit Gotham Cit . . . nope – *Gothenburg* City was it?
Gothenburg, Sweden, Europe, this time?

Charlie lay a few minutes longer feeling the ship roll under him,
as restless as he himself. It felt alien now, fifty years on – the
movement. Not that it still didn't jog a few too many memories.
Especially with the imagination concentrated by its being dark in
the cabin, which it pretty well was. Only a crack of light showed
below the door, underspilling from the alleyway running forward
to reception . . . or was reception aft? Damned if he could figure
which way wus bow and which was stern in this floating condo-
minium. All he knew for sure was they were located somewhere
in the after end of the ferry on E deck . . . E deck, starboard side.
Three decks above sea level, he thought.

The gap under the door let sound in, too, over and above the subterranean throb of the engines and the steady hiss of the air conditioning. Mostly the sounds of people occasionally passing on their way back to their own shacks. Noisy, some of them – talkin' at the tops of their voices, giggling sometimes and slamming cabin doors and generally showin' little care for them already tryin' to get their heads down.

'You're gettin' old and ornery, Charlie Periera,' Charlie thought, blinking rheumily up at the unseen overhead. 'Crusty and picky and too damn intolerant.'

Intolerant made him think again of Zach Goss and his harridan Polly Lou and the black chef business earlier on. He hadn't spoke two words to Zach since then: no more'n had most of the others. Not one of them had come out clear in favour of Zach's behaviour, although Charlie hadn't helped but notice how a few of the guys – some of the wives, too – had kep' a pretty low profile when it come to evincing open disapproval.

All in all the incident had left a sour taste; so much so it had kind of created a division within the group for the first time since they'd all met up at Kennedy ready for shipping out. Even their special celebratory dinner that evening had fallen flat. Oh, the food had been pretty fair considerin' it was foreign and mostly over-rich, but most had eaten as though concentrating one hundred per cent on their plates. Awkward it had been, with the conversation desultory and each couple in the party avoiding the others' eyes, and only the defiantly unrepentant Zach and Polly Lou seemingly unaffected. Still loud: makin' out there weren't nothin' amiss.

Charlie lay there feeling almost relieved that Engineer Lootenant O'Kane hadn't been around to share in their embarrassment after all. Had been spared learning the depth of resentment secretly held f'r him by some of the young kids he'd looked after so good . . . which took Charlie on to speculating again on things no man should have to question. About whether or not M/M 1/c Zachary Goss, USN, *had* slammed that watertight door in the face of a shipmate with grit and a bleeding stump of an arm because he really had bin terrified witless – or deliberate, because the man he snatched the last hope of life from had been black . . . ?

The ship lifted to a wave bigger'n most and Margrite's toiletry bag fell off of the de luxe mirror shelf. 'You're losin' the place,

158

Periera,' Charlie gloomed, gettin' more an' more stressed out. 'Now you ain't even capable of securing proper for sea, you old fool.'

'*Honey* . . . ? You there, honey?'

Her whisper carried anxious through the dark of the cabin. Charlie Periera abandoned any ideas of sleeping, eased his bad leg over the edge of the berth and drew himself stiffly erect, fumbling f'r his undershorts and socks.

'No sweat, sweetheart. She just took a sea. Seventh wave of a seventh wave, the ol' shellbacks used t'say – one a mite bigger'n its fellows? You go on back to sleep there.'

She switched her bedhead light on, struggling to come to, screwing her eyes uncertainly as she saw him balancing awkwardly to pull on his sports slacks. The glow created a halo around Margrite's head, her silver hair tinged with gold.

'Have we been called to rise, Charlie? What time is it?'

'Past one. Cain't sleep. Going topside to get me a lemonade or a chocolate malt or somethin' . . . won't be long. I'll take the key – let myself back in. You dowse that light and go on back to sleep, hon.'

'I can come with you. Keep you company if you want, Charlie?'

He hauled a sweatshirt over his head, shucked on his loafers, slipped some change into his pocket along with the cabin key on its plastic number tag, and leaned over to switch her light off himself. He could smell her perfume still sweet on the pillow and his heart surged a little with the joy her femininity brung him at the most unexpected times.

'No need. No more'n you got need to fuss over me, woman.'

She reached up and squeezed his hand. He tried not to think how weak and frail her fingers felt. 'Don't be long, Charlie,' she said.

When he opened the door the fluorescents of the alleyway allowed a sliver of light to fall across the berth like a moonbeam. It framed her still propped up on one elbow, watching him. The way she looked: the way her nightdress had slipped off one shoulder momentarily caused ex-US Navy Machinist's Mate Second Class Periera, Charles, to shed thirty years of declining virility.

He would never quite figure what compelled him to do it. He hadn't never bin much of a demonstrative husband. But, on sheer

159

impulse, Charlie stepped back into the cabin there and then and kissed her full on her surprise-parted lips.

'You close your pretty eyes and sleep awhile, Margrite Periera, or you won't never entice all them blond young Swede bucks to come flockin' to follow your wake around Gotham City.'

'Love you, Charlie.'

'I ain't fooled, woman,' Charlie said fiercely. 'I bet you say that to every ol' seadog you sleep with.'

When he closed the door she was still gazing after him. Still looking beautiful as the day he first met her.

He checked the door handle, made sure the self-locking mechanism had engaged – didn't want no intruders stumbling in on Margrite by error or worse, and she could always open it from the inside if the unlikely need arose, then, for a few moments, hesitated in the corridor, uncertain. To right and to left of him there was door after door after identical cabin door, all closed, running both sides of the alleyway and stretching away into what seemed like infinity.

He frowned at the number on his own – *E326*. Three two four wus the brass tally on the next one facing to his left . . . and he already knew they was berthed starboard side aft in the ferry . . . feeling good at having worked things out like a shipwise bluejacket should, Charlie turned and began to walk towards where he figured the bows had to be. It felt unfamiliar, the way the alleyway slow-leaned one way then the other in the seaway, but nevertheless, after staggering a bit for the first few steps Charlie felt hisself giving to it: anticipating the roll as if fifty years hadn't never passed since last he was in a ship.

A pert young lady sat working behind the reception desk in the spacious lobby extending across the whole seventy-odd foot beam of the ship. She wore some kind of ensign's shoulder straps on her white shirt and looked up with an attentive smile as he approached.

'Your momma shoul'n't let you up so late, young woman,' Charlie, in a real good mood now, joshed tongue in cheek.

The purserette laughed. 'Being all alone in the middle of the night. It's the price a girl pays for running away to sea, sir . . . can I help you?'

Seemed she wasn't a Brit. Had a slight European accent, Charlie could tell that much. But leastways she could speak American, not like most of the crewmen and stewards he'd had occasion to overhear . . . while, talking of overhearing, there was the mellow sounds of voices raised in song – real harmonious, too – filtering down from somewheres topside.

'Woke up parched as a rattlesnake's fork. You might care to point me to where I can get me a drink, miss?'

'The bar's still open in the Admiral's Lounge on F deck, sir – take that central stairway behind you. Up one level: turn aft past the duty free and gift shops and . . .'

'If'n that's where the entertainment's comin' from,' Charlie grunted dryly, 'then it seems a blind man wouldn't have no trouble finding it.'

'We have a choir travelling with us to Göteborg.' The girl looked a bit apologetic. 'I gather they're refusing all appeals from their party leader to go to bed.'

Neither Passenger Periera nor Junior Purser Nørgaard noticed a freshly shaved young man – the pleasant one Marianne had bid a good night to earlier – appear briefly from the starboard forward service corridor before walking quickly aft across the otherwise deserted lobby. Still unnoticed, Carlsson slipped furtively down the stairway leading to the ro-ro's lower decks.

Which was odd. Why would a chap apparently berthed forward on level E find cause to visit the sparsely occupied public after accommodation on D deck? While, presumably, he could have no reason at all to venture even further down in the ship to the completely deserted C deck, still undergoing its refit . . . ?

And there'd be no point in his trying to get into the car deck, which was locked.

Night-watchman Conroy would've made sure of that when he'd patrolled it only minutes previously, before heading back to his office.

Heikki had been forced to wait ages for her mother to nod off, even with the help of the sleeping pill, before daring to ease with bated breath from their cabin shortly after one in the morning. Now, already chilled and soaking wet she huddled in the shelter of a lifejacket locker high on the *Orion Venturer*'s understandably deserted boat deck. Extended before her she held the doll baby stolen from the gift shop earlier.

Although apprehensive, she couldn't help feeling a certain euphoria. She'd taken a risk worthy of the most plucky of those literary heroines she so identified with by sneaking up here, virtually to the top of the ship, to where the constant, rumbling headwind battered at fraying canvas boat covers and drove gusting rain to spiral in frantic whorls across the streaming deck while, towering over all, the awesome bulk of the ferry's illuminated funnel scribed slow, eccentric arcs against a black, cloud-fractured night sky. It was a frightening, lonely place: enough to test the mettle even of an adult unused to the way of the sea, but Heikki just gritted her teeth bravely, sustained by the knowledge that you had to expect any truly melodramatic event to take place in the most atmospheric of locations.

And at least there was no lightning, which would really have scared her, although the absence of such reliably Gothic phenomena did cause her some small anxiety too. According to most stories, lightning almost always preceded a happy ending . . . a blood-freezing stroboscopic dazzle – its accompanying sound of ripping cloth – coming as the precursor to a mind-numbing peal of thunder, whereupon threshing silhouettes of trees on menacing skylines reached to embrace you with jagged, claw-like branches . . .

. . . poor distraught Heikki. Poor deluded, pregnant, utterly desperate Heikki.

The ship moved ponderously, and the North Sea reared spitefully, and Heikki frowned resentfully at the pink squashy replica. The plastic cherub stared back at Heikki through wide unblinking eyes, moulded lips parted ever so slightly in barely concealed derision . . . no wonder she had cause to feel resentful. *She* sat in cold shadow, didn't she? Whereas the counterfeit humanoid which had imposed itself upon her was bathed in the warmth of the deck lights out-thrust, as it willed her to hold it, clear of the shadow cast by the locker: a tangible and constant reminder of the growing life-force which, for months now, had caused her such unhappiness.

Happily the plastic wasn't smart. Was too stupid to realize Heikki had done her homework. That it had selected the wrong girl to challenge to a battle of wills.

'I have a surprise for you that's going to wipe that smile off your baby face, Doll,' Nicole whispere ... *No* – she wasn't Nicole! She was fifteen-year-old Heikki Niskanen from Finland, and Nicole wasn't *really* real ... not that such a trifle precluded the fictional beauty from affording the perfect role model for Heikki who, more pressured than ever, had by now convinced herself she was a kindred spirit, a would-be rebel who might easily have experienced the same exciting adventures as Nicole if *her* father had been a romantic French colonial planter in Haiti instead of a stuffy old bank manager in Jyväskylä ...

Anyway she – *Heikki* – had seized the opportunity to leaf back through the book after dinner while waiting for Mum to go to sleep. She'd picked out a lot of jolly powerful voodoo spell-words – *voudon*, the book called them – which promised to come in handy, although the actual detail of those rituals performed in order to draw the dead souls from their tombs and use them as *victimes du sacrifice* had, on close examination, proved disappointingly vague. In particular the crucial passages describing the *voudon* arts practised by the *Baron Cimetière* – the evil *Loa* of the Cemetery of the Zombies to where Nicole had been spirited by the werewolves known as the *loups garous* before the incredibly daring Tug Rockingham came racing to snatch his beloved from the jaws of an almost unimaginable Fate Worse Than DEATH ... ! Gosh – *they'd* been really confusing.

Still, Heikki had gathered enough to reassure her that it *is* possible to enslave the malevolent *baka* which gather about the dead, and redirect them to carry out your own bidding ... something to do with capturing the *ti-bon-ange* before it flees the corpse, she recalled vaguely. That part of the soul most vulnerable to sorcery which, if not harnessed within nine days and nine nights, will return to the high solar regions from where it first drew its cosmic energy.

... or was that the *gros*-bon-ange? Either way, presumably the doll, being extruded plastic and not flesh and bone, could reasonably substitute for a proper *corps cadavre*, couldn't it? Well ... it was hardly alive, was it? And it was certainly malevolent – a

163

counterfeit baby which had already betrayed itself as evil when it urged her to discard the unborn which Heikki carried in order to supplant it in her affections, hadn't it?

It just hadn't figured on itself being a crucial part of the discarding process. That was all.

Venturing to her feet to face the full blast of the wind, Heikki drew a serrated steak knife from her jeans pocket. She'd felt really guilty about stealing it from the restaurant, her second venture into international crime that day; she would have felt a little easier had she been aware that the piece she'd sneaked into her pocket had only been one among several items of cutlery 'liberated' by other enterprising passengers, despite the eagle eye of Restaurant Manager António e Cunha, as souvenirs of that first, last, and appropriately splendid dinner aboard the *Orion Venturer*.

. . . not that those responsible were likely to find a souvenir necessary, as it happened. To remind them in future years, should they prove so lucky as to have some to look forward to, of that particular North Sea crossing.

Anyway . . . carefully Heikki placed the knife point, cutting edge upwards, against the plastiformed navel of the child-object, then tremulously cleared her throat while presenting the doll to the tearful sky.

'Oh Great Ginen, Thou cosmic community of Ancestral Spirits, hear my plea. By the power of the Cochon Gris and the Voudon . . . by the gland secretions of the Bouga Toad – by the poisons of the tarantula and the millipede and . . . an' . . .'

Her voice faltered as the wind suddenly curved inboard, curled round the locker, snatched at her long hair, plastering it wetly across her half-closed eyes . . . scourging her already numbed cheeks. Above her, cradled in its davits, the canvas cover of number five starboard lifeboat exploded in an undulating frenzy, snatched at its lashings, crackled like gunshots . . . ever so deliberately Heikki began to increase the pressure on the knife.

'. . . and the puffer fish and the odour of sulphur an' the . . . the Luminous Trail of *Ouanga*, I offer this zombi astral as a *sacrifice* . . .'

The knife wouldn't go in! It wouldn't pierce the resilient plastic forming the mock child! Heikki thrust harder. Began to sob in desperation.

'. . . and implore Thee to command That Which Grows Within Me to . . . to *be* no more!'

Horror of horrors . . . ! As the trembling knife point increasingly depressed the hollow doll, the pink figurine began to deform. To double forward in Heikki's hand while its baby-winsome head arched in grotesque appeal, Cupid eyes now staring shocked into Heikki's.

'Please, Doll?' Heikki found herself crying. 'Pleeeeese die . . . ?' Which marked the moment when the most terrible incident of all happened.

Because the doll opened its rosebud mouth and *screamed*! Contorted those sweet, prettily pouting lips into a gaping parody of agony and *screamed* as loud, as piercingly, as any tormented soul being dragged into the pit,

. . . or at least as piercingly as a distraught youngster already prone to unquestioning acceptance of the fantasies conjured in her mind, might well imagine a damned soul would scream.

Rather more plausibly, of course, is that the unearthly sibilance simply resulted from the wind gusting through taut steel wire lifeboat falls; while the fact that the screaming ceased in the precise instant when Heikki's knife finally penetrated the plastic tummy of her surrogate *corps cadavre* could only have been pure coincidence.

Much the same sort of coincidence, presumably, as that which occurred when the North Sea *haar* – also a perfectly natural phenomenon vested, quite illogically, with cabalistic powers by certain ancient races – had chosen the precise moment of Captain Halversen's ringing for *Full Ahead* on clearing harbour to embrace the already vulnerable *Orion Venturer* in its clammy miasma.

Gagging uncontrollably now, Heikki continued to saw with the inverted blade. 'I'm sorry, Doll,' she kept whispering. 'I'm so *sorry*.'

She felt a bit lost regarding what to do next after she'd completed the dissection. *Nicole of the Plantation* had got a bit woolly at that part, and anyway, she was beginning to feel really cold while, suddenly, the doll didn't seem anything more than a . . . well, than a cheap plastic doll.

Just to be certain the *gros-bon-ange* . . . or was it the *ti-bon-ange* she meant? . . . had been truly harnessed, Nicole . . . No! Heikki Niskanen from Jyväskylä . . . hacked off the hands and feet of the doll, then its head, then gathered the bits together and, crawling ever so nervously to the edge of the cliff, threw them overboard into the darkness.

She vaguely remembered the *Baron Cimetière* had cast three pennies and some rum on the zombie's grave in order to prepare it for Nicole, and had been engaged in the final ritual of beating it with a calabash stick just before Tug had leapt from hiding and, pursued by the slavering *loup garou*, had raced desperately for the cemetery gates clutching his beloved in his muscular sun-tanned arms . . .

But you can't beat the North Sea from the height of a ferry's boat deck even if you do have a calabash stick handy. And she was tired now. Really tired. And wet and cold. In fact she couldn't stop shivering uncontrollably . . .

Fifteen-year-old Heikki Niskanen regained the inadequate shelter of the lifejacket locker with an enormous effort, and allowed her eyes to close. She was the very first person aboard the *Orion Venturer* to feel the effects of exposure that night.

She hoped it wouldn't be too long before the voodoo began to work so she could . . . well, discard her worries and be happy again, and go back down to the cosy cabin she shared with Mum.

It was ten minutes to two in the morning.

Nicole . . . no – *Heikki*! . . . would only have to wait another twenty-seven minutes for something to happen.

In contrast to the boat deck outside, where the spring North Sea air temperature of five degrees Celsius was further reduced by a high wind-chill factor, it was far too hot in the Ocean Runner Night Club.

Not only that but, encouraged by Michael, Grace Miles had sipped one gin and tonic too many. Not enough to make her dizzy: just enough to relax her and stop her glancing uneasily at her watch every five minutes, worrying if the children were still all right on their own, or whether Lucy had wakened up wanting to go to the bathroom . . . or had wakened up claiming Teddy wanted to go to the bathroom?

As it happened, William had stirred briefly as she and Michael were easing out of the cabin. He hadn't protested at all when they'd kissed him goodnight . . . had that really been three hours ago? . . . and told him again that Mummy and Daddy would only be just along the corridor, and would keep coming back to look in on them.

'I'll stand the middle watch. Make sure the hands don't mutiny while you go an' reef the foretops'l,' William had reassured them bravely while casting a stern seaman's eye over his sleeping sister and Able Sea Bear Teddy, cuddled in the opposite lower berth . . . then promptly followed the crew back into dreamland again: exhausted by the day's excitement.

Grace had felt exhausted too, particularly after the row with Michael. It hadn't helped to realize they'd have to go rather further than just the end of the E deck corridor where the children were, before they could get something to eat. Having said that, she'd started to liven up a bit by the time they'd climbed two flights to the Olde English Tavern at the top of the ferry, and ordered. She even found herself looking forward to her bowl of chilli when it finally came, while it reassured her to note that Michael was obviously as concerned as she about leaving William and Lucy alone . . . so much so that he'd just picked at his Cornish pasty without any great enthusiasm – even left half of it, rather than wait too long before dashing back downstairs to check on them.

'Top it off with a g and t?' he'd urged a little later, watching her finish her lager.

'Better not. Better get back down.'

'You're on your holidays too, you know? Spoil yourself . . . or better still, let me spoil you.'

Michael could be so solicitous when he wanted to. Mind you, her looking and feeling good wearing her little black dress hadn't harmed in that respect. They hardly ever got dressed up to go out on their own at home: neither of them had other family living nearby, and Grace had never been able to bring herself to trust a paid baby-sitter. Not while Lucy was still so young.

She'd hesitated, watching the other passengers in the bar talking animatedly between themselves, just enjoying the experience. It was another world. The atmosphere at night aboard the ferry was quite exciting: the way it seemed so solid yet rolled with a not unpleasant motion which only helped to heighten her sense of adventure. Certainly all those apprehensions she'd felt previously about sea travel, particularly those conjured by the dreadful TV images of the capsized *Herald of Free Enterprise*, had long been calmed.

'What about the . . . ?'

'S'okay – I'll nip down again.' He'd already jumped up with alacrity. 'You wait here and relax, darling.'

He'd returned ten minutes later, weaving his way carefully through the still-crowded floating hostelry holding two glasses high.

'Duty free. Got you a double.'

'*Michael!*'

'They're fine. Honestly. Sleeping like tops. Need an earthquake to waken them, and there's not many of *those* in the North Sea.' He leaned across and took her hand. 'Stop worrying . . . and – here's to us?'

. . . that had been around eleven o'clock. With ever-fainter protest she'd been pressed to another three . . . or had it been four? . . . gins before the bar steward started to pull down the shutters well after midnight.

As he was doing so a weather-beaten man, wearing a white cap and dark blue jersey with a walkie-talkie clipped to his belt, stepped in and scanned the bar area critically. He looked stolid and reassuring: obviously some sort of ship's policeman. It helped her relax even more to feel they were obviously in capable hands.

She'd got up and the ferry must have hit a bigger wave than normal because she staggered a little, then giggled. 'Oooops!'

'Drunk again.' Michael grinned.

'Just . . . happier,' Grace smiled back, something she wouldn't have thought possible an hour or two ago. 'That's been nice, darling. A really nice break.'

'We don't have to end it here. Not unless you're very tired? The night club's still open next door, and . . .' He squinted, not a little unsteady himself, at his watch. 'And it's still only a quarter to two?'

Suddenly Grace Miles wanted to dance. To feel Michael's arms around her, even if only in the somewhat less than romantic

168

environment of a disco. Closing the gulf which threatened more and more to separate them *was* important – much more important than getting an extra hour's sleep. On top of which, they'd have few opportunities otherwise to be alone during the rest of the holiday. And certainly not while secure in the knowledge that the children were safely asleep with someone to look out for them – like that nice little Portuguese cabin steward, for example. And anyway, William was old enough and sensible enough now to realize they'd be back soon, even if he or Lucy did wake up.

. . . surely just half an hour longer couldn't harm?

'All right. A few minutes next door. But nothing more to drink.'

She took Michael's willing hand and led him on a slightly erratic course – only because of the ro-ro's movement, needless to say – from Ye Olde English Tavern.

Nearly two in the morning and she didn't care if she never went to bed. She felt quite reckless. Wickedly liberated, in fact.

'Though I warn you, darling – we'll be *dead* by morning,' Grace prophesied.

CHAPTER EIGHTEEN

Free from all meaning, whether good or bad,
And in one word, heroically mad.

JOHN DRYDEN (1631–1700)

Cataclysm minus seventeen minutes

Two a.m. and Carlsson was only minutes from becoming a hero.

At least, that was the way Sven had intended things to turn out. He really did believe that, very soon, he would achieve his ambition. Take his rightful place as the focus of the world's media, modestly acknowledging the eternal gratitude of many and the admiration of millions.

In fact he was only minutes from dying. Horribly. And in infinitely better company than he deserved although, naturally, he never imagined for one moment that the event he was about to initiate could lead to such a terrible outcome. Oh, come *on* . . . he wasn't *that* crazy!

Or at least, he didn't realize he was.

Which was why, in the middle of the night in the middle of the middle watch in the middle of the Skaggerak, truck driver Carlsson – instead of doing what any sensible madman would have done and thinking again: withdrawing from the deserted C deck to give himself time to come up with a rather less reckless form of lunacy – was still busying himself with preparations to set fire to the *Orion Venturer*.

Obviously he'd anticipated there could be some small risk involved. Of course he had! And because of that – because he wasn't no dummy – he'd taken good care to build a more than adequate

170

margin of safety into his blueprint for achieving recognition. Heck, not only that: he'd also worked out his subsequent moves down to the last detail. Had rehearsed over and over in his head how, in the days to come, he was going to handle the public relations aspect of his new-found celebrity status. Even down to having invested quality time in peering critically into the mirror – not, he'd been forced to concede, without a certain self-satisfaction – to decide which was his most photogenic profile: his best side to present to the cameras. Fortunately he was privileged to possess a talent for meticulous planning. It was a quality he fully intended to carry with him into the Company's executive suite. Nothing, but nothing, had been left to chance.

Admittedly, he *had* forgotten to take the disposable lighter with him first time – the one he'd bought earlier, specifically for this great adventure. Frustrating because it meant he'd been forced to trail all the way back to his cabin to retrieve it just as he was keyed up to sneak past reception before descending to these cordoned-off lower decks . . . but that had been an understandable oversight. Really successful entrepreneurs didn't lick their own stamps, did they? Generals didn't count bullets. Pop idols didn't write all their own songs . . . Jeeze, you got to understand he was a strategist: one of the organ grinders, not the monkeys. Anyway, soon he'd have a personal assistant to take care of the nitty gritty. Female, he reckoned he might go for. Blonde. Good looking, of course. With long legs . . . ?

Though right now his primary concern had to be for safety. Safety for everybody aboard the ferry. His integrity demanded that much. Safety first and safety foremost.

. . . so much so that the very first thing Strategist Carlsson did when he arrived at the empty after cabins just above the *Venturer*'s waterline was to confirm the location of the nearest fire alarm button. There it was: a glass-fronted smash-box, miniature red-painted anvil hammer chained beside it on the bulkhead between the first empty cabin, C312, and the stairwell leading up to D and E decks just abaft the corridor fire door.

Safety first, see? Leave absolutely no room for error . . . ? Like next he'd organize the fire extinguisher he'd need. One down the other end of the alleyway there. Again secured in a recessed cabinet also incorporating a fire axe and a red hose reel ready connected to a gunmetal hydrant valve . . . least they'd got *that* right!

He hurried aft, opened the glass door, yanked the heavy water-filled extinguisher from its mounting and carried it back to place it ready by the alarm. He even removed the pin from the striker before half-turning it into the ready position. All it would require to trigger the variable spray was a blow with the palm of his hand . . .

Safety first, see? *Heroes don't take risks* . . . Carlsson grinned, pleased with himself for coming up with that gem. Not if they're smart as him, they don't!

Nearly there. All he had to do now was find something to set alight.

With, of course, absolute safety.

The bedding store between outside cabins C313 and 314 of the *Orion Venturer* offered a further sign of God's approval to Sven Carlsson. Having first arranged for the deck to be deserted, He'd now provided everything an aspiring arsonist could pray for in terms of safely inflammable material. Stuff which should slow burn without getting out of hand too quickly. Racks and racks of it. Crisply laundered sheets, pillow cases, towels . . .

The ferry fell into a head sea and sort of hesitated, shaking herself. The barely perceptible shudder which ran through her startled Carlsson. All of a sudden the blood began to pound in his head while the first butterflies of unease stirred: worms wriggled nervously in his stomach. Get a move on, man! Someone could surprise him at any moment . . . there was a watchman patrolling somewhere. He'd seen him up on the boat deck earlier: a mean looking sailor with a bruiser's nose and a walkie-talkie.

Hurriedly he fumbled in his jeans back pocket for the lighter and produced it, thumb hovering uncertainly over the milled wheel. He couldn't help but notice how his hand was shaking. Understand-able. I mean, this was a tense moment, all said an' done . . . No gain without pain, pal. A guy had to be pretty heroic just to create the circumstance in which he could *be* a hero.

Carlsson still hesitated for a few seconds. He wasn't a brave young man, nor was he at all reckless in his more lucid moments.

So far he'd been pretty damn cautious even in his crazy ones . . . Maybe he should go for extra safe, huh? Maybe he should hit the alarm first, *then* light the fire . . . ? It would take time for the crew to respond. Couldn't risk . . . ?

But how *much* time? His throat began to dry as he figured the options. Say they . . . say they were a lot more organized than they seemed? Got down here too quick after the whistle blew? Say they put the lousy fire out before he even got the chance to make his mark with the extinguisher . . . ?

Hastily he rumpled up several linen bed sheets, half a dozen pillow cases from the lower rack, then bundled them into the corridor. Didn't want the fire to spread back into *that* lot! His thumb felt nerveless as he fumbled to spin the lighter wheel . . . Oh God – it wouldn't light! Bloody rotten *bloody* manufactu . . . !

It lit! Ohhh, why was it shaking so? Get a grip, Sven lad . . . ! Hero! Remember *hero* . . . ? The executive suite? That Bahamian beach, an' your very own personal assistant they'll offer you . . . the ravishing blonde with the long legs . . . ?

He had to steady his wrist with his other hand before he could bring himself to touch the lighter to the edge of the bed sheet; forcing the shuddering gas flame to run along its white hem. Slowly, almost reluctantly, the linen ignited, curling and drooping as the heat built up, little sub-flames spreading and twinkling to disappear under, and into, the rumpled pile of material. A moment later smoke, vaporous tendrils of grey smoke, started to seep from the folds of Carlsson's passport to privilege . . .

He stood up slowly, backed away from his handiwork while staring hypnotically at the living entity he'd created, beginning to feel more bullish now he'd committed himself . . . nearly over – the strain of anticipation. Even got a little cocky . . . more confident. Let the fire get a bit more of a hold . . . no *way* was it going to run out of control.

The baby flames dipped, then fought resolutely back. Crept further into the pile while at the same time giving an impression of uncertainty as to their mission: strangely reluctant, it seemed, to fulfil their sole function in life which was to grow into big adult flames. Sven forgot all about his nervousness then, and started to get impatient.

Come *on*, dammit – *burn*! Never mind *me* gettin' a grip, Fire: you get a grip.

The doubts began to surface. Maybe the linen's got some kind of fireproofing finish? Maybe it's damp: maybe returned to store too quick from the laundry . . . ?

The half-hearted, never-wannabe-grown-up flames rallied, gave a last flaring splurge . . . then went out!

Carlsson kicked the extinguisher in childish frustration: the guilty punishing the inanimate innocent.

On the ro-ro's bridge, five decks above the young man who was trying to kill her, the hands of the chart room clock advanced one further, inevitable segment.

It was now eleven minutes past two in Second Officer Delucci's so far uneventful middle watch.

One of the few advantages of being mentally unstable is that, by definition, bad moods and sad moods and even hopping mad moods never last.

Unfortunately the good ones don't either but, as Sven Carlsson's mood at that moment was a very bad one indeed, what with him having unexpectedly found himself threatened with a non-event despite all the trouble he'd taken to torch the ship in which he was travelling . . . well, it had to mean his next mercurial change of temperament would incline towards being an improvement.

And so it was. As soon as he'd conquered the pain of a foot injured by a fire extinguisher Sven began to look again on the bright side. Failure, in his case, was merely to prove a step towards happiness. Strategy, see? Meticulous planning? That was what bein' a mover an' shaker was all about. Belt and braces thinking. Making advance provision for the unexpected.

Which included being foresighted enough to carry a few litres of petrol – what firemen euphemistically call an 'accelerant' – in the cab of your rig. Just in case Plan A didn't work. In case it back-*fired*, so to speak?

Not only that, but the sliding door to the car deck was hardly ten steps away. That steel door that didn't have a padlock on it? Because someone smarter than average had removed it when he'd first boarded and, as predicted, no one else had since bothered to replace it . . . ? Oh, what a clever chap Sven Carlsson was.

Mind you, he didn't feel clever so much as outright apprehensive once he did venture into the car deck. The clanking and the rattling – all those sinister echoes? The chill of the place. The starkly revealing glare of overhead deck lights stretching far ahead as if to infinity: glinting evilly on metallic lines of crouching, menacing vehicles. The loneliness of an individual surrounded by – no: *submerged* in! – the continuous rumble of dividing water . . .

Nervous . . . ? Sven was practically hyper-ventilating by the time he'd snatched the five-litre plastic can from his Scania's cab and hurried back to the linen store.

He was really panicking over the delays now. Picking his way to the reefer and back had taken a good five minutes. The patrolman, someone from the crew, *must* come down here again soon – and even if he managed to avoid being caught himself it would mark the end of his grand design. They couldn't fail to notice the extinguisher standing ready, the rumple of charred linen outside the store room . . .

Urgently Carlsson unscrewed the cap from the petrol container while trying desperately to regroup his thoughts. A splash . . . just a *tiny* splash to help ignition but not enough to leave traces for any future fire investigators to pick up on. He wasn't born yesterday. He'd seen on TV how they could tell whether a fire was started deliberate or not. That's where he'd picked up the term 'accelerant'.

What about the alarm? Yeah – this time he *would* trigger the alarm beforehand . . . take no chances on its running out of control. Safety, see? Safety first! Remember the cardinal rule, Sven lad?

He closed his eyes briefly, willing the pounding in his temples to ease off. Think, dammit – *think*! Maybe he should allow time for one last quick run through the drill . . . check the extinguisher's to hand . . . cap already off the can . . . lighter ready . . . hit the alarm then . . .

Oh, jus' *do* it, for Christ's sake . . . !

Truck driver Carlsson shattered the glass protecting the red alarm button with the special hammer provided, and then pressed it firmly. Instantly he felt better: in control again. The sign of pure executive material. When the going gets tough, pal, the tough get going.

Even as the circuit completed – silent on C deck but revealing itself as a blinking red light backed by an audible alert on the *Orion Venturer*'s bridge fire warning console – Carlsson was already moving towards the pile of bedding with Plan B held angled before him.

Throughout the ferry the clocks ticked remorselessly to two-seventeen a.m.

His initial, tentative dressing of petrol proved far too timid.

Carlsson watched the amber liquid soak instantly into the linen sheet and disappear from sight. It was awkward: not easy to control the flow holding a plastic can in one hand and a lighter ready in the other . . . hurriedly he replaced the lighter in his back pocket then gripped the can, tipping it with both hands. A little more should do it, he reckoned. With tongue-protruding concentration he allowed about a cupful to dribble over the pile of material. Frowned irresolutely. Added another splash, just to make cert . . . ?

Awwww Jesus – is that *smoke*? Please . . . not *smoke*? Barely perceptible? Hardly even a wisp curling out from below the folds of the . . . ?

Carlsson's eyes were still widening with abruptly dawning realization when the baby flames sprang out to surprise him. He'd hardly begun to draw back: to try to avert the petrol container before they flashed excitedly, maliciously, up its still-drizzling stream – flames which, apparently, *did* wannabe big grown-up flames after all. Had fully intended so to be all along but had proved a lot smarter than he by waiting in ambush: twinkling Judas embers hiding beneath the seemingly inert, charred surface of the sheet.

When the plastic can in Sven's hands exploded he wasn't even afforded the mercy of time to avert his face from the still liquid-cored fireball expanding from chest height. You can't do a lot to protect yourself – not even scream, come to that – in the last micro-second of your being a whole person.

You can always try running, of course . . . or stumbling, really.

You might just have time to lunge, shrieking, for the fire alarm

176

button and punch it again in a last futile bid for help as Carlsson – suddenly, agonizingly finding himself restored to superheating reality – did.

You might even have time to reach the next one, closer to the stairway . . . always assuming, that is, that your locomotive systems haven't been shocked into paralysis by then . . . and trigger *that* in the desperate hope that doubling your appeal may call down some miracle twice as quickly to take the pain and fear away . . .

But simply pressing an alarm – a hundred alarms! – won't help you survive a moment longer in the end . . . not even if a whole fire brigade of rescuers miraculously arrive in the instant. Because by now you're beyond help, human or divine: flailing blindly through an airless, searing void of blazing high octane in suspension even as your clothing ignites and your skin begins to peel and your once-fair hair becomes a copy-cat fireball, and your lips and eyelids begin to droop like melting candle wax . . .

While, even if you do escape to wherever you're trying to go – to yet another manual alarm position, for instance – you'll only discover that that's already started to burn too, by now. Particularly if it's as combustible as the wipe-clean, laminated plastic panelling with which the builders had lined the *Orion Venturer*'s corridors nearly thirty years befo . . . !

. . . but that, again, is to digress far too prematurely into technicalities hardly pressing in the heat of the moment.

Suffice to say that Sven Carlsson lived, if such an inadequate euphemism can be employed to describe the last agonies of a melting man, for quite a long time after his own body fats had ignited without giving a single passing thought to such important considerations as calorific values and smoke gas velocities, or the flame spread characteristics of the various materials used in ship construction during the sixties and early seventies.

He didn't even reflect, however belatedly, on the flashpoints of the more hazardous petrochemical products.

Although he *might*, had he been given time to realize it, have afforded one despairing moment to rage against the exquisitely cruel irony of his never having had to die at all . . . not if he'd only thought to lift the retaining hook of the cabin door adjacent to the linen cupboard.

In there – in Cabin C313 – he would have discovered a much safer, much more docile accelerant left conveniently ready to hand. The sixty-odd litres of painters' white spirit stored in there would have proved ideal for his purpose.

But then again, had Carlsson looked he could hardly have failed to register that there were other, considerably less docile accelerants hidden in there, too, negligently abandoned in the belly of the ship. Their clearly lethal potential, apparent even to someone as divorced from reality as he, might just have shocked Sven into recognizing just how close to triggering a major disaster his fantasizing had brought him. Might even have persuaded him to abandon his plan altogether, in favour of living long enough to disembark in Gothenburg.

Those inflammable drums of paint. The oxygen-filled welding bottles? Topped by the four pressurized cylinders of dissolved acetylene gas . . . ?

Carlsson was still alive, still trying to escape, still reeling and flailing from side to side of the fire tunnel which was forming around him when, ahead, he saw – no, it was more that he sensed, because he had little true vision left by then – the self-closing door which separated the *Orion Venturer's* fire containment zone 2 amidships from fire zone 1 aft, push open to reveal the heat-shimmering silhouette of his very first rescuer transfixed in frozen disbelief.

Somewhere deep down inside him, Sven became conscious of an overwhelming sense of gratitude. Of self-vindication. So he wasn't a failure after all. He had finally achieved his desire to become the focus of attention . . .

Opening his arms wide he lurched forward, a human fiery cross, to embrace Able Seaman Conroy.

CHAPTER NINETEEN

For every time she shouted 'Fire!'
They only answered 'Little liar!'
HILAIRE BELLOC (1870–1953)

For several vital minutes nobody believed there was fire in the *Orion Venturer*.

Other than Sven Carlsson, of course.

And Able Seaman Conroy. Who had just begun to.

But apart from those two, not even Second Officer Delucci or Quartermaster Madariaga, both of whom could actually see and hear the second series of alarms being activated from C deck, really accepted the ro-ro could be on fire. Not like . . . well, like on *fire*? On proper fire, as in *burning*?

Theirs was an understandable incredulity. The bridge watch-keepers, being situated far forward in her superstructure, were high and remote from any incident taking place in the lower stern section of what was a fairly large ship. It's a bit like expecting the residents of an eighth-floor penthouse to climb unquestioningly out to their window ledge purely on the strength of a call suggesting a blaze has started in some third-storey apartment at the opposite end of the building – a call which promises to prove malicious in the end, anyway.

Delucci's dilemma was further compounded by the riddle posed by the time lag between the fire board's present twin-light configuration, and the original alert which he'd cancelled out. Why wait some minutes before triggering the later alarms if there really was an emergency situation down there? And why, come to that, only activate two alarms when there were other manual locations further forward?

Unless the night-watchman had done so on his arrival at the

scene? But in that case, why wasn't Conroy using his walkie-talkie to call for backup?

It all added to Delucci's suspicion that – while there was undoubtedly something strange happening down there – whatever that something was it didn't . . . well – didn't add up?

. . . other than by reason of a short-circuiting circuit: still the logical solution. Or by their having shipped a lunatic aboard. Which was crazy . . .

The young American's reluctance to concede the unthinkable was supported by the normality of the sea world around him. He'd just completed his hasty visual appraisal from the wing. Those other ships passing through the Skaggerak in company – the cruising love boat or sister ro-ro hull-down in a halo of light to the north; the fishermen astern; the white stern light showing a small vessel four miles or so ahead of the port bow and leading on a similar course . . . ? Okay, so that was illogical too, but their comforting presence did tend to reinforce his illusory sense of security.

He'd also scrutinized the floodlit length of the *Orion Venturer* herself, searching for sign of anything amiss. At that stage she'd shown every indication of situation normal – even to the fact that it had deteriorated into the kind of bloody awful night you can expect from the North Sea in spring: what with the increasingly irritable sea state and the rain now driven by a blustery headwind to spatter, whirling dervish frenzied, across her deserted upper decks.

In addition, the beat of Oasis over-spilling from the night club to compete with the haunting strains of 'Myfanwy' rising in lusty choral rendition from the Admiral's Lounge one deck lower, had more than supported his impression of all being well aboard.

So, although Second Officer Delucci's scepticism was fast giving way to grave anxiety as the seconds ticked by, he still inclined towards the probability of an electrical fault and continued to draw back from initiating a general alarm throughout the ferry. Not without the sanction of a senior officer. Certainly not in the absence of confirmation from the night-watchman . . . from anyone below decks . . . that there was indeed a crisis spawning.

Such tentative optimism didn't prevent his finger from trembling perceptibly though, as he grabbed for the telephone, stabbing in the Master's cabin extension number.

Third Engineer Stamper, on the other hand, didn't have a problem determining whether or not the ship was on fire because, where *he* was at that moment, deep down in the bottom of her, nothing had so far happened to tell him she was supposed to be – the duplicate fire warning board in the engine control room having been disconnected to await a replacement. But only *after* the man from the UK Marine Safety Agency had completed his inspections.

In fact Bert's greatest dilemma since he'd opened the box at four bells in the watch had been whether to go for chicken or ham. Following a close-run mull over such gastronomic choice while waiting for the kettle to boil, he decided on chicken. With lettuce and mayonnaise, no less.

Virtuously he left the York ham with English mustard sandwich pack untouched in its clingfilm and waved it enticingly at Motorman Garilao through the control room window. Teofisto brightened visibly as he looked up from the one job 2/E Stamper had finally decided the little Filipino's ticket eminently qualified him for – which was washing down the bulkhead behind the starboard harbour service de-aerator – and conscientiously began to clear away his cleaning gear.

By the time his diminutive watch assistant entered the control room, Bert was burping discreetly. He shoved the remaining sandwich pack towards Teofisto while ladling four spoonfuls of sugar into a mug.

'Get yer gnashers into them, mate,' he invited hospitably in fluent British merchant seaman's Esperanto. 'Put some lead in yer pencil.'

. . . then Bert remembered the ate – eight! – Garilao bebbies in the photo, and wondered whether such an exercise was necessary, or even prudent?

'Tank you much very, Engine-ear Jesus.'

It was only when he'd undressed his two o'clock in the morning elevenses that the man from Manila's expression changed from hungry anticipation to plain crestfallen.

181

'*Pig*, Turd,' Garilao accused.

'Steady on, pal – no need to be like that,' Bert defended, a bit taken aback. It was his engine room, after all. No point in bein' the bloody officer if you couldn't claim first choice from the watchkeepers' sandwich box.

'No – they is pig sah-nees, Mista Temper. Yes?'

'Ham,' Stamper qualified encouragingly. 'With mustard.'

'But is *haram*.'

'No, Garilao – ham. *Ham!* Haitch . . . aye . . . emmm . . . ?'

'No – *haram*, Turd. The Prophet Muhammad say *haram* food contain *hajis* – dirty tings? Not like *halal* food which is good. We do not eat the pig. Or the dog.'

Bert wasn't too sure about dog himself, with or without mustard, but he still brightened visibly. Chicken, he was beginning to cotton on, had proved a more inspired choice than he'd first anticipated.

'You sayin' you're a *Muslim*, Garilao?'

'Yes, Engine-ear Jesus.'

'An', religion-wise, you definitely aren't allowed to eat them pig sannies I left f'r you?'

The little man shook his head dolefully.

'Now that,' Third Engineer Stamper commiserated while selecting the first of the eight neatly cut triangles to save wasting food, 'really is what I call a crying shame . . .'

'C'mon, Cap'n. Come *on*, come *on* . . . !'

Second Officer Delucci detected the silhouette of Madariaga hovering nervously in the darkness, eyes reflecting devil-red pinpoints from the fire panel, and jerked his chin while impatiently cradling the phone.

'Knock her off auto-pilot, Quartermaster . . . *finito automático?* Go to manual steering; same headi . . .'

'*Ja? Hva er det . . . ?*' Halvorsen surfaced, fully awake, at the other end of the line and converted to English. 'What is it?'

'Bridge, sir. Delucci. Sorry to distur . . .' then the tension got to him and he thought *bugger the politenesses* and ended up blurting, 'I have a fire warning aft. C deck cabins service alleyway!'

There came a silence. Followed by a sort of sigh. The sigh didn't make Delucci feel better. It could have been the reaction of a man anticipating his worst fears being realized – or preparing to get bloody irritated if they weren't.

'Did you clear it?'

'Them, sir. I got two more flashing up soon after. Same location.'

'And you've sent someone down to investigate?'

'The night patrolman's on his way.'

'I'm coming up. Call the Chief Engineer and Mister McCulloch.'

'Any further action you want me to ta . . . ?'

'Do you know for certain that we have a fire, Mister Delucci?'

'No, sir.'

'Then do nothing more before I arrive. I do not wish the passengers to be given cause for concern at this stage.'

The phone cut off abruptly, leaving Delucci with the uneasy feeling he'd just peaked out in his career. For a moment he almost hoped there *would* prove to be a fire aboard . . . but only a very small one, please God? A one-extinguisher blaze, jus' big enough to get me off the hook?

Bracamontes sounded plain dubious, growling, 'Chances are it's the goddamn electrics. I'll shake the ETO. You see any smoke from where you are, Delucci?'

'Christ, no,' Delucci said. *If I was lookin' at smoke this high up in the ship, Chief, you wouldn't need no phone to hear me*, he reflected earnestly.

He alerted Stew McCulloch, the Chief Officer, then hurried out to the starboard wing again, ignoring the rain tattooing the back of his reefer, to scrutinize the after decks even more assiduously. Still nothing. No smoke although, unless it was pretty dense, any emerging into the open would immediately be shredded and dissipated anyway by this goddamn wind . . . but definitely no sign of fire, and surely he'd detect flame against the blackness astern if any existed?

The only change from before was that Oasis had given way to Fugees, although 'Myfanwy' continued to rise with exquisite clarity to the wind-torn sky.

Marginally reassured, Delucci moved back inside to the chart space and began to take off the *Orion Venturer*'s position. Just in case. While doing so he debated whether to call Stamper, the engine room watchkeeper, despite the Old Man's stricture. Advise Bert to go to emergency stand-by: suggest he ran up the fire pumps and charged the mains. Come to that, shouldn't he at least be alerting E deck reception? Warning the duty Purser – wasn't it that pretty Danish kid, Marianne, standing the pusser's middle tonight? Anyway, warning whoever promised to draw a very short straw down there in the event of an evacuation becoming necessary, to begin marshalling the night stewards . . . ?

There was also the question of selectively shutting down ventilation from the bridge console to reduce draught through the possibly affected areas. Simultaneously Delucci felt he should be triggering the release of the secondary automatic fire doors – certainly those located in the after sleeping sections of D and E decks directly above the alleged incident . . . ? Maybe he should even go so far as to rouse the Bosun? Have him cobble together some semblance of a fire party, particularly in the absence of any kind of proper emergency plan, and get them moving down aft . . . ?

Trouble is, where does one draw the line in the face of a direct instruction to do nothing . . . apart from by doing nothing?

Halvorsen's order had been uncompromising and left no room for interpretation. And to be fair, the Old Man probably was justified in refusing to act in haste, without firm intelligence. It was a tough call for any passenger ship master to make. The Captain could no more afford to overreact than hesitate too long, with people aboard who were elderly, possibly disabled, some maybe not too well, out of their element and vulnerable even to falsely perceived anxieties. Apprehension can quickly spread in a ship. It's like seeing uneasy expressions on the faces of an airliner crew. Cause one crewman to run when he should be walking – worse, arm a whole gang of Spanish sailors with fire extinguishers and send them into the passenger areas – and you've good as sown the seeds of panic.

A cynic less charitable than Delucci might have recognized Captain Halvorsen, already under pressure from his owners, as finding himself also hostage to a rather more commercial consideration. Peace and tranquillity *en voyage* sells repeat bookings. Upset passengers unnecessarily by even hinting at possible problems aboard – they take another operator's ferry next time across!

Whereupon the crew replacements start from the top down.

Second Officer Delucci decided to do nothing. Take no unilateral action which might subsequently be judged hysterical or premature. Not even though a snippet of long-forgotten college Shakespeare kept surfacing to disturb his uneasy musings as he waited.

Henry VI, Part Three, was it? Or *Two*?

A little fire is quickly trodden out.
Which, being suffered, rivers cannot quench.

Shakespeare was smart. By the time her Captain arrived on the bridge at 0228 hours to take decisions, eleven minutes of the combined passenger and vehicle ferry *Orion Venturer*'s disaster response period, starting from Carlsson's triggering of his first alarm from the deserted C deck, had been squandered in irresolution.

By then the blaze raging in that level's starboard aft corridor had achieved a critical effect of 200 kilowatts – hot enough to ignite the actual structure of the ro-ro – and was spreading remorselessly towards the nearest stairwell leading up to her cabin accommodation.

Where, despite the fact that not a single lick of flame had yet reached them, the first of her remaining 515 passengers had already begun to die.

CATACLYSM

The disaster fire probably began shortly after 0200 hours in the corridor adjoining the entrance to stairway 2S on the starboard side of deck 3 (C deck). There is little doubt that the fire was ignited with a naked flame, about the size of a match or lighter flame [and] assumed to have been started in bedclothes deliberately placed on the floor of the corridor.

Within a very few minutes the fire had reached such a strength that it set the whole cross-section of the corridor alight. From this point on, the fire developed extremely rapidly. From the flashover of the whole corridor, the fire entered the stairway on the starboard side, continued up to deck 5 (passenger cabins deck), crossed straight over to the port side and down the stairway there to the car deck, deck 3 (C deck), while part of it continued up the stairway to deck 6 (main deck) and the bar area there.

Large quantities of dense smoke were rapidly produced and spread along the corridors on deck 4 and deck 5 (passenger cabins deck) in the after part of the ship . . .

Norwegian Official Report, NOR 1991: 1E
The *Scandinavian Star* Disaster of 7 April 1990

CHAPTER TWENTY

All things, oh priests, are on fire . . . the eye is on fire; forms are on fire; eye-consciousness is on fire; impressions received by the eye are on fire.

BUDDHA (5th Century BC)

Able Seaman Conroy hadn't recognized the thing weaving and flailing blindly before him as being a burning man.

Not right away. Not in the instant which marked his becoming the first crewman aboard the *Orion Venturer* to establish beyond doubt . . . beyond all doubt! . . . that the ferry was indeed on fire.

In fact Conroy's initial impression, having resentfully shoved part-way through the after C deck stair-lock door only to halt, utterly transfixed by the scene which awaited him, was that he must've been struck dead somewhere betwixt the tea urn on A deck and this starb'd aft alleyway, an' that here wus him about to be signed on as junior coal trimmer in Lucifer's stoke-'old!

. . . because everything was burning! Hardly more'n a boat's length ahead of him the corridor shimmered through an arch of flame. The bulkheads was burning; the cabin doors was burning; the deckhead was burning – even the deck *itself* wus burning . . . even the very air he tried to breathe seemed to catch fire the instant it sucked past his ears through the part-open door, drawn from the foreparts of the ship to further fuel the holocaust he'd chanced upon.

And then there was the smoke. Funeral black smoke. Great turmoiling billows of smoke: acrid and catching at his throat already – even *his*, a fifty-ciggies a day man. Smoke bobbing and curtseying at the whim of the rising, heat-frantic air currents. Smoke trapped high up against the ceiling panels, all red-tinted and flickering and sort o' curling and whirling an' squirlin' back

187

into itself like it was trying to roll its way along the corridor to freedom . . .

Now AB Conroy was a hard man and fire-fighting trained. Been there, seen it, done all the courses, 'ad all the susstificates; knew as much about shipboard fires as most blokes at sea – but this . . . ? Jesus – *this* wasn't no ordinary fire: this wus like . . . well, almos' like facing up to a living, breathing, constantly expanding creatu . . . !

Because, *awwwww* Christ, *it was alive – the fire*? Deep inside of it something was moving: dragging itself from the heart of the blaze . . . blundering towards him, reeling an' banging agin plastic-coated corridor walls which, every time the Creature touched them, seemed to feed off its caress – become smeared with little fires which fizzled an' sizzled tentatively in turn before suddenly bursting into life themselves . . .

Conroy was still standing froz . . . or perhaps frozen isn't the most appropriate description, seeing how his eyebrows had already begun to singe before the heat while the little fuzzly bobbles on his woolly pully had started to fuse . . . more like he was stood standing *welded* to the spot? – when the Fire Creature, which had by then taken on much the same blunted form as a snowman, only its carapace was flame instead of crystal and it was uttering whimpering, animal sounds whereas snowmen don't generally make any noise at all . . . when it opened its arms wide, not hardly a decent spit from the appalled night-watchman before advancing a further stumbling lurch with the clear intention of embracing him. Warmly.

For one terrible moment the Fireman and the Fire Man stood almost toe to toe, face to face. And then the Fire Man opened his eyes, glittering black inside his superheated mask, and they looked straight into Able Seaman Conroy's with such supplication: such awful appeal. Whereupon the melted lips parted too, and an unearthly rattle escaped them.

And wasn't even that accompanied by a little puff of *smoke* . . . ?

Well, that was when Conroy completely lost his bottle. Just plain panicked.

Because, as Sven Carlsson finally sank to his knees before curling up and gratefully dying at too-long last, the fire tunnel which had regurgitated him gave out a great celebratory sigh, appreciating, no doubt, the top-up oxygen of life bestowed upon it by the open door – and immediately began to flash and roll and grumble and expand along the remaining length of corridor towards Conroy!

The so far un-Able Seaman, whose own exposed skin had begun to blister by then, uttered an even more heartfelt 'Jesus *Christ*!', devout enough this time, it seemed, to be rewarded by having locomotive power abruptly restored to his legs ... whereupon he promptly swivelled hard to port without so much as an *excuse me* to his briefly met companion, and promptly hurled himself from the path of the closing fireball to race helter-skelter up the adjacent stairway as if all the imps of Satan wus hard on his heels.

Which they more or less were. Because instead of behaving like any reasonable flash-over might have been expected to, and simply continuing straight along the corridor via the door still jammed part-open by the melting Carlsson, the fireball also negotiated a *whoooooshing* right-angle turn before continuing aloft in hot ... *very* hot pursuit of the *Orion Venturer*'s fleeing Night Patrol.

That eccentric route taken by both fireman and fireball led upwards to the after section of D, and then on to Deck E where, at twenty-four minutes past two in the morning, the majority of the ro-ro's passengers were either sleeping, or at least dozing fitfully behind closed cabin doors.

The fireball would itself die at that point. Exhaust the energy and impetus given to it by exploding petroleum vapours. It would never succeed in reaching the open decks, or do more than scorch the stairway walls as it passed, and inflict much the same surface damage to Able Seaman Conroy while scaring him half to death in the process.

But then, neither the fireball, nor even its parent fire, were to prove the most malign force to be released when a mentally disturbed nobody succeeded in burning up both himself and the vessel he travelled in. Not in terms of human life. Because, by then, the smoke was preparing to follow in the wake of the fireman and the fireball.

It was that smoke which would carry Carlsson's most lethal legacy.

*   *   *

189

All smoke is a killer. How quickly it kills depends on the volume and chemical composition of the smoke inhaled.

The form of smoke released into the *Orion Venturer* was produced very quickly, in vast quantities, and was particularly toxic. That lethal combination had begun to be produced from the moment the gasoline-fuelled bedding fire raised by Carlsson attained 200° Centigrade: hot enough to ignite the surfaces of C deck's corridor walls and ceilings.

They caught fire at that comparatively modest temperature because nearly thirty years previously, after having constructed the cores of the ro-ro's bulkheads, walls and deckheads with non-combustible materials, mainly steel, the builders had then proceeded to surface them with 1.6 millimetre-thick, low-maintenance, wipe-clean laminated-plastic panels which were not only flammable but possessed high flame spread characteristics – as did the majority of surfaces throughout the *Orion Venturer*'s interior.

Successive owners had never felt compelled to replace those lethal panels because, although fire prevention legislation in respect of more recently built vessels has been considerably tightened it is not, in general, retroactively enforceable. No more than are the international regulations applying to materials used in the construction of ships, which still don't stipulate toxicity limits for smoke produced by their catching fire anyway.

It was perfectly legal, therefore, for the smoke given off by the burning plastic linings in the *Orion Venturer* to contain fatal concentrations of carbon monoxide and hydrogen cyanide – vaporized prussic acid – as well as lung and airways irritants such as nitrogen oxides, isocyanates and formaldehyde.

In addition, the smoke carried carcinogenic substances in the group known as polycyclic aromatic hydrocarbons. Those most significant cancer-producing agents would ensure that, if it didn't succeed in killing *en voyage*, it still harboured some prospect ten, even twenty years down the line, of claiming, as deferred victims, those who inhaled it in any significant volume during that last middle watch of the *Orion Venturer*.

But then, smoke seldom is in a hurry. It has a placid disposition. From the instant of its spawning, Carlsson's Bequest pursued a more leisurely agenda. Took a little bit longer than the fireball – and Able Seaman Conroy – to depart from the seat of the fire in search of space and lungs to occupy. Allowed itself to amass volume and density in C deck corridor before permitting the superheating air currents, ably reinforced by the ferry's own ventilation systems, to draw it effortlessly to its prospective killing grounds.

Smoke is also more inclined to thoroughness: to methodically entering and exploring corners which fire tends to overlook in its first excitement of being. It isn't extroverted and brash like flame. It's more subtle; more insidious in its approach. It stalks silently ahead of its parent conflagration: a black velvet assassin in the night. Instead of consuming and crackling and warning of its coming, smoke tends to steal in mute billowing search of its prey, find nooks and crannies the fire hasn't even got round to thinking about yet.

Ask Conroy about smoke. He's got all the susstificates. Admittedly he's no chemist – he wouldn't recognize a reactive isocyanate molecule if it jumped up and bit 'im – but he knows how lethal smoke can be. Especially in the confines of a ship.

Go on – *ask* him!

If, that is, he's got time enough at the moment to stop for a crack wi' you.

. . . doin' a bloody good imitation of Road Runner as he passes.

CHAPTER TWENTY-ONE

And he smiled a kind of sickly smile, and curled up on
   the floor,
And the subsequent proceedings interested him no more.
                        FRANCIS BRETT HARTE (1836–1902)

At two twenty-seven a.m., just as Captain Halvorsen was leaving his cabin to hasten with mounting apprehension to the bridge and 3/E Stamper was poised to enjoy a fortuitously acquired extra York ham sandwich, African businessman Kumbweza Munyenyembe awakened abruptly in his single-occupancy cabin in D deck's starboard corridor.

It was hard to define precisely what had aroused him. Some distant noise? A half-uttered cry? The muffled sound of . . . footsteps, had it been. Running? Up the stairway not far from his door . . . ?

For a moment Mr Munyenyembe blinked uncomprehendingly in the darkness, trying to recall where he was. Then remembered he was aboard the ferry heading for Gothenburg: his starting-point for the final leg of a sales tour of UK and Scandinavian importers of the African tribal art dealers he represented.

He also recalled somewhat ruefully that, in the big lounge after dinner, he had partaken of rather too many Danish lagers in company with several most companionable British singing gentlemen whose accents he hadn't quite understood, but whose collective voice had been that of angels . . . and as a consequence his bladder, now he'd awakened, had begun to insist it wasn't as tolerant as it used to be, and that he required to make most urgent passage to the gentlemen's rest room.

Unfortunately, exchange rates being what they are in Africa, the expenses provided by Kumbwez . . . by Fred's employers back in

192

Mzuzu hadn't been generous enough to cover the surcharge for an en-suite cabin: a minor inconvenience which would necessitate his journeying to D deck's common washroom facility, happily situated not too far along the corridor from his cabin.

The Malawian lay for a few precious seconds longer, vainly resisting the call of nature while, at the same time, frowning slightly. He was frowning partly because his head still spun from the alcohol he'd over-imbibed, and partly because, as he recollected it, there had been rather more light filtering through the gap below his cabin door than there now appeared to be. Yet one would have thought they might have maintained *some* illumination in the corridor if only for their passengers' convenience?

Reluctantly he fumbled for the switch of the bunk light above his head before uncoiling his too-long legs from the too short berth, then hesitated again. He thought he could just detect a smell – a faint smell of . . . *cooking*, was it? Or simply of other unfamiliar European shipboard odours? He smiled to himself, and dismissed the silly thought. You want to smell a ship, boss, sail African on some of our coastal routes. Try a Zambezi ferry. Book economy class, you lucky if you don't have a piglet, or chickens alive in a basket, stuffed under the wooden spar bed next to yours.

After shrugging into his long caftan to ensure propriety should a nocturnal confrontation with some simultaneously disadvantaged fellow traveller occur, Fred unsnibbed his door and – still half asleep – stepped unsteadily into what seemed, quite disgracefully, a virtually blacked-out corridor after all . . .

Colourful Kumbweza Munyenyembe was about to become the first innocent to die on that maiden UK–Scandinavia service of the *Orion Venturer*.

Or the second actually, if you count Passenger Charles Smith who had preceded him by some nine hours. At around the time when Cornish cream afternoon teas were being served in the Admiral's Lounge for a modest surcharge.

But then, Mr Smith had passed away in the arms of Effie, while in the pursuit of love. Mr Munyenyembe . . . Fred . . . would die alone and in pursuit of an even more pressing form of relief.

Charles Smith died because his heart had proved less durable than his sexual proclivities.

Kumbweza Munyenyembe would die because he was too tall. And because he yawned at the wrong moment.

Disregarding the phenomenon of the short-lived, incandescent gas ball which flashed into and up the stairwell following Carlsson's fatal blunder – a hard thing to ignore, admittedly, if you happened to be Able Seaman Conroy at the time – the first indication of anything amiss on the level immediately above the seat of the fire was when the smoke arrived on D deck . . . Fred Munyenyembe's deck . . . some two minutes later.

There it split its forces. While the main body of the smoke column continued to be drawn upwards to the next level, E deck, a still-considerable volume overspilled from the stairway landing, attracted by the ventilation currents in that part of ship, and began to explore the *Orion Venturer*'s after end.

That break-away smoke still hadn't had the opportunity to establish a sound beachhead in the lower levels of the ro-ro by the time the strapping African reluctantly surrendered to the call of nature: no more than had the high-temperature gases which intermingled with it during its silent invasion.

For that reason, and because smoke stays high, smothers the defences of breathable air from the ceiling down, it had only managed to penetrate part-way along the length of the corridor: still drifting aft like a wedge, leading end uppermost against the deck-head, as Passenger Munyenyembe stepped unwittingly from his cabin into the Judas-dim corridor.

As he did so he yawned, closing his eyes involuntarily. A great, luxurious yawn which drew a considerable draught of the corridor's surprisingly warm atmosphere into his lungs . . .

Had Fred only drunk a couple of Danish lagers fewer, so that his perception of danger had remained unimpaired . . . If he'd only realized that the lighting in the corridor *was* quite bright, but masked by the smoke already creeping shoulder high past his door . . . If he hadn't been so tall that, as he yawned, his nose and mouth inevitably penetrated that upper, denser mix of carbon monoxide and gaseous cyanide . . .

But he hadn't, and he didn't . . . and he was.

Kumbweza Munyenyembe, who'd travelled safely all the way from Malawi to meet his destiny in a cold northern sea, felt his world spin briefly as the receptors to his brain shut down under the monstrous toxic assault.

He didn't suffer. In fact he was probably unconscious even before he'd finished sagging – eyes wide, confused, and unseeing, back propped against the cost-effective wipe-clean plastic surface of the corridor wall – to a sitting position.

He was certainly dead within three minutes of the smoke ceiling having descended to envelop him completely.

Gertrud was so happy.

She didn't mind that it was nearly half past two in the morning, and that they'd both be tired when they finally arrived to take up residence in their new house in Söderköping, with its white-painted windows and postage stamp garden overlooking the Göta Canal. She was simply content to lie clasped in Lennart's arms, as she'd been content to do for most of the past two weeks since she'd become Mrs Gustafsson, even though it was proving a bit cramped tonight on the lower berth of their economy class cabin on D deck.

Mind you, it was only meant for one. They just hadn't been able to bring themselves to sleep apart, which was why they'd folded the upper bunk against the wall as soon as they'd boarded, and sacrificed comfort for togetherness. Otherwise the cabin was perfectly adequate. Spotlessly clean. So recently decorated that it still smelled faintly of varnish and sanitized plastic.

And it had been their decision to honeymoon as cheaply as possible, preferring to save what they could to spend on the house which, considering the extra low inaugural fares offered by this new North Sea ferry service, had meant they were returning to Sweden very cheaply indeed – at a fraction of the cost of flying over to the UK two weeks before.

Apart from which, you don't *need* a wide bed when you're both twenty, newly married, and the world is your oyster. And they really were very much in love, the young Gustafssons. Undeniably theirs was the greatest love the world had ever seen. They'd known it since they were at school. From the moment they'd first laid eyes on one another as fourteen-year-olds, they'd realized they were preordained to spend the rest of their lives together. That had been six years ago and now, at last, the fairy tale had come true.

Gertrud lay with heavy-lidded eyes, just drifting and thinking back over the honeymoon and ahead to tomorrow when the first thing – well, maybe the *second* thing she intended to do, because Gertrud's libido had joyously proved to be even more unquenchable than that of Lennart – was to choose material to make curtains for her kitche . . . !

Abruptly she opened her eyes fully, blinking uncertainly. It was odd, but she could've sworn . . . ? Hadn't the comforting glow filtering below their cabin door suddenly dimmed? Reduced the depth of contrast in the shadows previously spiralling gently across the cabin ceiling as the ferry rolled . . . ?

Probably the crew cut down the lighting during the quiet hours. Perhaps to save electricity . . . ?

Distracted, and now fully awake, she began to feel uncomfortable: still sticky hot and in desperate need of a shower. They'd made strenuous love yet again since they'd returned from their toasted sandwich supper *à deux* in the upper deck bar just after midnight and, while she didn't exactly relish the prospect of having to use the clinically impersonal bathroom facility down the hall at this time of night, she knew that, if she didn't force herself to make the effort, she wouldn't sleep soundly even for the few hours left of the voyage.

Reluctantly, ever so gently, she slipped from Lennart's embrace to feel in near-darkness for their unisex bathrobe before picking up her towel and toiletry bag. He stirred, uttered a little grunt, and she hesitated, concerned not to disturb him: sensuously aware of the cool airstream from the ventilation blower above the door exploring her still-perspiration-damp hair.

She'd just grasped the handle when his sleepy voice called, 'Love you, precious. *Ever* so much.'

The most lucky wife there ever was smiled to herself, all warm and happy inside, and looked down on her dimly seen Adonis before stooping to nuzzle the precious curls behind his

196

ear. 'Love you too. Lots and *lots* . . . Won't be long, sweetheart: promise.'

Quietly Gertrud eased through the door, withdrawing backwards into the darkened corridor, unwilling to take her eyes off her beloved for one second longer than necessary.

It was only as she pulled it to, and felt the latch engage, that she realized too late she'd forgotten to take the key needed to effect re-entry without Lennart's co-operation.

Barely a second later the brand new Mrs Gustafsson sensed the first wreaths of smoke descending around her from the corridor deckhead. Swivelling in mystified apprehension she stole one alarmed glance forward – registered a billowing, eerily undulating fog advancing upon her . . . watched blankly while it crept sinuously around . . . then *over* . . . then *swallowed* the stiffly outstretched legs of a black man who, quite bizarrely and despite his brightly coloured gown being all rumpled up around his waist, appeared to be sitting without any concession to modesty at all on the floor outside a cabin two doors from her own . . . ?

Having finally become persuaded that what she thought was happening, really *was* happening, Gertrud began to beat hysterically upon the door she'd just locked against herself, and to cry aloud for Lennart.

One deck above the distraught honeymooner, Able Seaman Conroy and the fireball reached the top of the second flight of stairs at much the same moment. More or less achieving a dead heat, you might say.

There they'd both collapsed – the fireball in a haze of carbonized petrochemical fumes with a sort of *phut* like a wearily deflating child's balloon, Conroy with a strangled 'Fuckin' *hell* . . . !' as he tripped on the last riser to enter E deck head-first, horizontal and still travelling fast – *bloody* fast in fact for Conroy who, before that moment, had proved undisputed ship's champion at turning lethargy into an art form.

It was there, after skidding helplessly across the non-skid corridor deck, that the *Orion Venturer*'s night-watchman struck his heat-frizzled skull with considerable force against the opposite bulkhead.

Although only partly conscious, the desperately shocked seaman still realized that, having forgotten to lift his walkie-talkie when leaving the crew mess on his ill-humoured quest for a false alarm, he was no longer equipped to warn the bridge: *still* denied vital intelligence on whether or not the ship really was on fire, of the absolute certainty that the false alarm bloody well wasn't . . . an' that she – the ship – bloody well *was*!

Despite the excruciating pain of his flash burns, Conroy hauled himself erect with grim resolution to sway, trying to focus his seared eyes; desperately scanning the interminably long, bright-lit alleyway for some sign of life . . . a steward . . . passenger . . . ? Anyone, please God . . . ?

But there was none. On either side of him E deck's starboard passenger service corridor stretched endlessly between lines of closed and locked cabin doors. Deserted. Just inclining gently; first to port . . . then to starboard. Unhelpfully obeying the motion of the ferry.

. . . of the burning ferry.

Conroy tried to shout *FIIIIIRE!* like a proper night-watchman should, but only a pitiful croak escaped his peeling lips. With a half-sob, half-curse he began to stagger and stumble forrard towards the nearest manual alarm point . . . smashed the thin glass uncaringly with one red-raw, soot-black fist: triggered the button – forced hisself on to the next one forward: hit that . . . then vaguely recalled the hose reel stowage in this part of ship lay aft of where he wus . . . thought dully, '*Got to put a spray wall up across that fuckin' stairhead, mate – gotter hold back the smoke till they cobbles a fire party o' some kind together . . . !*'

Able Seaman Conroy had only made it part-way back – had just driven himself to return to the point where number two starboard stairway had now begun to funnel increasingly dense clouds of toxic gas up to the *Orion Venturer*'s main passenger deck – when his already addled senses failed him completely.

Helplessly, almost appreciatively, he collapsed insensible before the path of the smoke.

*   *   *

Of nine remaining passengers by then sleeping soundly in the starboard outer row of car deck cabins occupied by the Gustafssons and the already stricken Munyenyembe, only one awoke to hear a young woman scream, followed immediately by the tattoo of fists drumming frantically upon some nearby door.

The uncharitably disturbed traveller was a fifty-year-old Dublin trucker called Garret Ó'Leary, a driver every bit as professionally adept at rolling his articulated juggernaut on and off inter-European ferries as ever Sven Carlsson was ... had been!

Already Ó'Leary had hauled his valuable Stockholm-bound load of whiskey across the short Irish Sea freight ferry route to Liverpool, then on across the UK overnight to join the *Orion Venturer* ... and bejasus wasn't he wearied from foightin' the temptation extended by all dem lovely glass bottles of potential amber bliss following not a leprechaun's skip behind his cab?

... which went some way, at least, to explain why Ó'Leary listened unsympathetically to the girl's hysterical shrieks for a few disenchanted seconds: thought grumpily: '*Sure enough, if Oi'd been fortunate enough to bring a harpy of a drunken wumman loike that aboard wi' me, Oi'd have throwed her out meself afterwards, so Oi would.*'

... then promptly went back to sleep.

But he, like AB Conroy, had long accepted that you come across all kinds o' people in a ro-ro ferry and, if you're naturally gregarious but are obliged by your trade to ensure an alcohol-free crossing, generally have as little to do with them as possible.

Had the Irishman been a little less cynical, or even a little more chivalrous as befitted a true Knight of the Road, he would surely have stirred himself into investigating ... and might well have survived the voyage as a result.

But then, so might many more of those aboard the *Orion Venturer* during that interrupted middle watch who, instead of responding immediately to unusual and often outright alarming noises outside their cabin doors, would elect instead to stay uneasily put, and either hope such untimely nocturnal disturbance would go away or that a trained member of the crew would soon arrive to give them instructions.

Which explained why – the next time trucker Garret Ó'Leary from Dublin woke up – it would be to foind himself dead.

... as he might very well have put it himself.

Three economy cabin lengths from Ó'Leary, twenty-year-old Lennart propelled himself from under the covers, galvanized into shocked wakefulness the instant he registered Gertrud's appeal, followed by her frantic pounding on their door.

The fear crystallized within him even as he scrabbled desperately in near darkness to locate the handle ... snatch the inward-opening door wide to find himself staring, straight ahead at first into a drifting pall of smoke, and then *down* ... stunned, disbelievingly *down*! ... into the tumble of wet-golden hair that marked where Gertrud had already subsided to her knees.

She was choking. Even as she summoned the effort to arch her head and gaze up at him with such trust, such child-like certainty that he, her Lothario would save her, her suffused features contorted in a paroxysm of coughing. Ever so weakly she extended one arm towards him, urged him to take her hand and make everything better.

'*Help* me, darling ... ?' Not so much a plea as a retch of utter bewilderment.

... but then the smoke billowed mischievously, stirred by the ventilation currents from the cabin, and made a spiralling feint for the open door; and Lennart caught the first wisping promise of his own imminent death in the air ... whereupon the fear already in him escalated to absolute terror.

With a strangled sob he slammed the door against the most precious thing he'd ever gained. The one person whose life he cherished almost as dearly as his own.

Lennart Gustafsson, bare minutes from becoming a widower after only two weeks of joy, was crying as he scrambled on hands and knees in near darkness to find their complimentary tartan travel rug before packing it tightly to seal what little gap remained between Gertrud and the bottom of the cabin door.

Retreating as far as the confined space would permit, he sank to crouch against the furthermost end of the berth, shoulders forced hard back against the ship's side, eyes riveted, wide and blank with shock, on the tenuous barrier which separated them.

The hysterically renewed pounding became weaker: Gertrud's disbelieving appeals more and more laboured.

Very soon they ceased altogether.

CHAPTER TWENTY-TWO

Be sober, be vigilant: because your adversary the devil,
as a roaring lion, walketh about, seeking whom he may
devour.

New Testament: 1 Peter, 5:8

The smoke began to increase its speed of advance as the fire, still
spreading towards Stairway 2S reached, and exceeded, a core temperature of 400° Centigrade to produce an ever-increasing concentration of lethal gases.

The first accelerating streamers climbed two levels to arrive at
E deck ninety seconds behind Conroy. Because the stairwell did
not extend further upwards into the ship at that point, it was there,
directly above the comatose night-watchman, that the toxic cloud
next began to mass, trapped against the deckhead.

Finding itself temporarily frustrated by having nowhere higher
to go, that smoke was left with little alternative but to find another
way of escape. It still had a wide choice of routes open to it. Any
one of the labyrinthine network of alleyways forming the rear
section of the ro-ro's main passenger cabins deck in the area contained by fire zone one, for a start.

It should not have been allowed to explore further afield. That
was the whole point of vertically sub-dividing a ship into incident
containment zones. It should have been prevented, or at least
delayed, from travelling towards the fore parts of the ferry by a
flame-retarding corridor door immediately forward of the stairway,
one of many located throughout the ship to inhibit the spread of
fire and smoke in just such an emergency.

That particular door, having been closed remotely from the
bridge the previous evening by Second Officer Pert in dutiful

observance of night standing orders, should, and indeed would, have fulfilled its vital function of gaining time most efficiently.

. . . or would have done if first-trip Night Steward Cardoso, sea sick and permanently attached to his bucket, hadn't hit upon his clever wheeze.

Shortly after Conroy had completed his previous patrol round – in part intended to combat such daft and dangerous practices – Cardoso had come up with the labour-saving device of overriding the fire door's release mechanism by jamming it wide open again. He'd shoved a compacted bath towel under it, so that, simply by sticking his head out of his service cuddy occasionally, he could keep an eye open down the full stretch of the corridor without actually having to stagger down its swaying length and thus precipitate further nausea.

He'd done so out of stupidity, and in all innocence. When Assistant Purser Everard, making a special point of enunciating in simple English to leave no room open for misinterpretation, had briefed his cabin staff prior to sailing on the *dos* and *don'ts* of their night monitor watch duties – including, particularly, the *whys* and *why nots* of ensuring fire doors were kept firmly closed – the linguistically challenged Portuguese had nodded vigorous assent in amiable determination to please . . . despite not having understood a bloody word Everard had uttered. And, just as the strength of a chain lies in its weakest link, so the efficiency of any safety measure depends on its strict application.

. . . which was why, if smoke could celebrate, it would have thrown a party at that moment. For instead of being contained at least temporarily in E deck's aftmost fire zone, large enough to precipitate devastating tragedy in itself, it could now seek to occupy a further third of the *Orion Venturer*'s length by moving through to midships fire zone two, which embraced all cabins located as far forward as the reception lobby.

It had been presented with draught-induced access to an even more fertile killing ground.

Both zones combined, spreading six cabins wide across the *Orion Venturer*, were served by three corridors running fore and aft and linked, themselves, by no fewer than five transverse corridors. Altogether, thanks to the thoughtless action of an untrained and sea-inexperienced hotel waiter, the smoke was now afforded unrestricted access to a mix of nearly eighty twin or four-berth cabins located within a multiplication of right-angle turns and by-ways which offered, between them, the only escape routes for nearly three hundred persons.

And although, by virtue of the jolly mood which prevailed on that first service, many of the more hardy of E deck's occupants were still disporting themselves in the ro-ro's upper public spaces at five bells in that blustery early morning, the vast majority of their fellow voyagers had prudently seen fit to retire below long beforehand.

Well over two hundred of them, in fact.

Not counting the twelve who had already begun to die one level below them.

Among those passengers who had retreated behind closed doors even before Carlsson had finished debating which was his best profile for the cameras, then cheerfully gone off to commit involuntary suicide and murder, was American tourist Charlie Periera's ailing wife Margrite. And most of his wartime buddies from the valiant USS *Thompson* come to that, along with their partners.

Not far from Mrs Periera snuggled the Miles children, William and Lucy: sleeping like exhausted angels while Mummy and Daddy were aloft trying hard to save their marriage.

There were the eleven-year-olds from the junior school in Norway's Østfold region – all fourteen of them – who hadn't so much retreated behind their cabin doors as been told firmly to stay put by Miss Evensen. That was before she'd also disappeared topside to let her hair down with Trygve for the last time that trip.

Then there's Herr Neugebauer, berthed just down the corridor from those so vulnerable kids, who firmly believes that early to bed, early to rise allows you plenty of time to select your coming day's underwear.

And Heikki's mum in E334, sleeping off her sleeping pill unaware that her rapidly chilling daughter is slipping into the second stage of terminal exposure two decks above after experimenting with hopefully abortive black magic . . . then there is the spiritually insecure Pastor Lütgendorf contemplating the opposite end of the divinity spectrum; already prey to considerable doubt regarding the existence of such a thing as God's Infinite Mercy . . . and doughty Belgian octogenarian Antoinette Chabert who, while she would have been more than happy to sink a few nightcap beers in the lounge herself, doesn't think it fair to keep her cat up too late awaiting her return.

. . . and the 230-something other souls relaxing in their plastic-lined boxes three levels above the big ro-ro's waterline.

One might have thought, considering the presence of such a large and diverse group of people on the after passenger deck that, statistically, the odds would have been in favour of the fire being discovered before it could prove Shakespeare right? That one or more of them would, if for no other reason, have felt the need to respond to a middle-of-the-night call of nature, just as Fred Munyenyembe had moments before, only in their case with a greater prospect of surviving the experience before the smoke grew from an oxygen-diluted irritant to a dense, poison-laden suffocator.

Indeed, the saddest irony lay in the likelihood that some of those on the very brink of hazard may well have done so – yet had still been denied the opportunity to influence the course of events. For the facilities provided on the *Orion Venturer*'s E deck were such that, even if they *had* embarked on a pilgrimage to the nearest toilet, they still wouldn't have been spurred to initiate a shock-wave of alarm throughout the ship compelling enough to persuade the irresolute young officer on her bridge that he really was presid-ing over a major emergency.

Conroy would have been able to tell you why. Or would if he'd been stood standin' upright an' fully compost mentis, anyroad.

AB Conroy could have explained, in his usual forthright manner, why, irrespective of statisticals, or whether or not anyone *had* felt the need to crawl out o' their de luxe berth to take themselves to the heads during that crucial period when the smoke come prowlin' . . . why few of 'em even then were likely to have ven-tured into the starboard corridor to register an eerily coiling miasma beginning to form above Stairway 2S.

. . . *to say nothin'*, Conroy would have found it irresistible to add petulantly, *of above the unconscious form of some poor hard-working bloody seaman flat out, sportin' a half-melted woolly pully an' flash burns to his face and skull!*

Why . . . ?

Because the majority of cabins on that level had their own self-contained mini-bathrooms, di'n't they . . . ? Which meant their surcharge-paying occupants didn't have to step out into no public alleyways to pump bilges like the economy class punters, in common with the proper sailors down below the waterline on A an' B decks, was expected to do.

That wus bloody why!

CHAPTER TWENTY-THREE

Action is transitory, a step, a blow.
The motion of a muscle, this way or that –
'Tis done, and in the after-vacancy
We wonder at ourselves like men betrayed.
                        WILLIAM WORDSWORTH (1770–1850)

Halvorsen was first to arrive on the bridge.

Despite the alacrity with which he appeared, the Captain managed to turn up in full square rig with cap set firmly above his brow. Second Officer Delucci couldn't figure how the Old Man had achieved such a sartorial feat in the short time that had elapsed since his rude awakening. Not unless he'd been resting already part-dressed . . . almost as if he'd been half-anticipating – or dreading? – a summons.

Which seemed highly unlikely. It implied the behaviour of a man under considerable strain, whereas the last emotion Delucci would have attributed to the dour Norwegian was anxiety.

More pertinently, it reminded the OOW that the Master had made it plain on several previous occasions that, in his view, full uniform for passenger ferry officers included wearing caps when on duty.

Delucci thought '*Shit!*' . . . found and crammed *his* flat-aback on his head, automatically noted the Old Man's time of arrival in the log – *Captain to bridge: 0226 hrs* – then hurried from the chart area to meet him.

'Morning, sir.'

He pitched the greeting carefully low key. Concerned but competent seemed about right.

'Mister Delucci.'

It was hard to tell whether Halvorsen was simply acknowledging the stilted formality, demanding an immediate sitrep or, momentarily night blind, just trying to identify who the hell he was talking to in the darkness.

'No further warnings flashing up, sir. Not since the second series from C deck starboard aft. No report from the watchman as yet. No visual indications of fire from the wing . . . Quartermaster's just taken us off auto-pilot.'

Precise, comprehensive and succinct. In control.

'Where are we now?'

'Well into the Sleeve. Approximately eighteen miles off . . .'

'Approximately, Mister Delucci?'

The already tight-wound young Second Mate blinked, a bit taken aback. Shouldn't getting precious over navigating to a couple of decimal points – identifying *precisely* where they were in the Skaggerak – come second . . . fourth, fifth – even *tenth* down the List Of Vital Things For A Master To Do when his ship might well be on fire? Particularly as, at their current rate of progress, she could be several miles further down track before, God forbid, any need arose to broadcast their position anyway?

Unless, of course, Halvorsen didn't intend to wait for proof of a worst-case scenario? Order an immediate reduction in revolutions and the hell with causing unease among their more nervous passengers? Doing so would achieve the added safeguard of diminishing the forced draught of passage entering the ferry through her ventilators and open forward dampers.

Either way the 2/O failed to prevent a smidgen of resentment from tingeing his defence.

'I entered my fix on the chart three, four minutes ago, sir. Since then we *have* been making good twenty knots.' Delucci's very temporary rebellion fizzled out and he qualified pacifically: '. . . or nineteen point eight, actually.'

The Captain didn't order a reduction in speed. Instead he walked over to the bridge fire-warning console and frowned at the schematic showing the general arrangement of the *Orion Venturer*'s nine decks as if willing the two red lights to go away. Precisely the response Delucci himself had made some twelve minutes beforehand, when it all began.

The audible alarm was still squalling. Pensively Halvorsen

reached out and cancelled *audio*, then re-set it. The lights stayed on while comparative silence descended over the wide bridge deck, broken only by the ro-ro's butting into a trough before a spatter of sea spray, skied by the wind, curled back over the foc's'le to rattle the windows before them. Horizontally acting wiper blades cleared the water instantly.

'*Do* something, Cap'n!' the Second Mate urged silently.

The Captain did. He tapped the glass in the area of the red lights with his knuckle.

Delucci changed his mind about the Captain's doing things.

'Jesus, don't go out on me *now*, lights,' the young OOW prayed. 'Not right *now* – not after one little tap from the Old Man?'

The lights – Carlsson's lights triggered even as he was burning, though they didn't know it topside – remained obdurately loyal to the enigma they posed: refusing to extinguish despite the four gold rings on the cuff that commanded them. Delucci couldn't decide whether to feel relieved, or more apprehensive.

A fluorescent sliver slashed across the wheelhouse as Bracamontes and the Mate barged through the security door together. McCulloch, last to be alerted, hadn't bothered with cap or tie and was still hurriedly buttoning his reefer. The ferry's portly Chief Engineer hadn't bothered to court anyone's sartorial approval: hadn't even bothered to button his multi-coloured Hawaiian shirt. He'd shoved bare feet into Shanghai flip-flops which contrasted oddly with navy trousers dragged over pyjama bottoms: the only concession he'd made to uniform.

. . . apart from the cap. He *was* wearing his cap.

First thing the *Orion Venturer*'s senior engineering officer did was thump the console with a technically qualified palm. The lights stayed on.

'Could still be the lousy electrics, Captain,' Bracamontes grunted, sounding unconvinced. 'These the first to come up, Delucci?'

'Second, Chief. Only one showed initially. Same location – C deck.'

'Who've you sent down to investigate, Mike?' from McCulloch.

'Conroy, sir.'

It was the Chief Officer's turn to mutter, 'Shit.'

'How long ago?' Tightly, from the Captain.

Delucci eyeballed the chartroom clock equally anxiously. The fluorescent hands jumped as he watched. Jesus – two twenty-*nine*? Seemed as if time itself had begun to accelerate.

''Bout eight . . . nine minutes now, sir. But he had to get up there from A deck.'

'And he carried a walkie-talkie?'

'That's what I called him on. Yeah.'

'Tried him since?'

Delucci realized his oversight too late, and blanched. 'No, sir.'

'Call him again, Mister Delucci. Now!'

'Aye, aye, sir.'

The Second Mate hastened to lift the handset from the chart table and thumbed its pressel switch. 'Conroy – Bridge! Fire patrol, do you read . . . ?'

Above the continuous hiss of the unanswered walkie-talkie he couldn't help listening appreciatively to the opening bars of a Spice Girls number carrying faintly into the wheelhouse from the Ocean Runner Night Club . . .

'If Conroy's set is u/s, he'd need to make his way up to the reception phone to report all clear,' McCulloch reasoned positively. 'That could account for the delay.'

'So would the guys being too goddamn preoccupied with first-aiding the fire to make courtesy calls,' Bracamontes growled.

'Conroy's an old hand. And not exactly excitable. He'd've punched every alarm within range first.'

The Chief pointed to the two red lights. 'Exactly.'

Halvorsen chewed his lip, gazing unseeingly ahead through the big windows. The stress pains had begun to concentrate to a knot in his chest. Eight or nine minutes was a long time – yet by the same token it seemed inconceivable, if fire *did* exist, that no one else lower in the ship would have sensed anything amiss by now. Trouble was, at five bells in the midnight watch very few people had cause to be abroad in those lower levels.

'Please make your way down to C deck without delay, Mister McCulloch. Collect any crew you run into on the way. But discree . . . !'

. . . the previously reset alarm began to clamour as a brand new light flashed up – this time on E deck – closely followed by a second.

They indicated someone had just triggering manual warnings: not one, but *two* decks above the orig . . . ?

'Guess you c'n forget discreet, Mate!' Bracamontes supplemented shakily.

But Chief Officer McCulloch didn't hear him.

He'd snatched up a spare radio and was already running for the internal stairway.

To the fifth and somewhat rank-eclipsed sailor at the wheel, who'd so far stood silent and ignored by that braid-encrusted assembly, it was disturbing to observe that none of those remaining on the *Orion Venturer*'s bridge deck seemed to know quite what to do next.

But then, neither did Quartermaster Madariaga.

Like . . . well, like whether or not this was quite the best time to mention the high-pressure gas bottles he, Atienza and Valverde had stowed in starboard cabin C313?

Pantry Rating Lucchetti was probably the first crew person after Conroy to become physically aware of fire in the ro-ro, even though he actually worked some distance from the seat of the blaze. One deck lower in fact, on B deck, and half the ship's length forward of the incident

Maybe it was just Filippo's innate capacity for survival, a facility honed to perfection through working the Neapolitan street corners, that compelled the frustrated *camorristo* hopeful to pause halfway through scouring one of the, thankfully last, food-encrusted symbols of his penance.

He simply sensed something was wrong. He didn't know what; he didn't know where . . . but he could feel it. An unease about the ship.

Frowning, Lucchetti crossed to the door of his soapsuds fiefdom: bundling his soiled apron to dry hands now swollen white and puffy as bleached prunes from his labours, while stepping into the short corridor to peer both ways.

Nothing. No sign of life, and certainly not of impending death, existed down there in that part of ship below the waterline at 0229 hours. The only sounds he could identify were the steady throb of her engines and the muffled sigh of the sea passing along her starboard hull plates. An unsecured cabin or compartment door was banging somewhere further forward where, as far as he knew, several crew cabins were located . . . or, he thought it was forward anyway. Filippo, who shared a claustrophobic cabin even further down, on A deck with one of the other messboys, still hadn't quite worked out direction, or even levels, during the short time he'd spent aboard.

Other, that was, than to keep taking mental bearings of where the nearest stairway *up* lay – a natural extension to the counterfeit rating's sense of self-preservation which, in one so unversed in the sometimes capricious ways of the sea, displayed a remarkably perceptive grasp of priorities.

. . . he decided aft meant turning left. The route took him past the dry stores room, which stirred Lucchetti to again reflect darkly on the medium-term future of that pig-faced Provisions Master Uguccioni, then further aft down the bleak, steel-encased alleyway until he came to a solid bulkhead behind which, though he wasn't aware of it, lay the pump and compressor room situated forward of the main engine room itself.

His sense of direction was proved right. A stairway did lead both downwards and aloft at that point. The crudely stencilled vertical red arrow on the once-upon-a-time buff painted egress bore the legend: EMERGENCY EXIT – SALIDA DE EMERGENCIA – 3S.

There the youngster hesitated, unsure of where it might take him. His clumsy inexperience had already landed him in trouble once, while those officers who made up what would, in the Sicilian heartland of the Cosa Nostra, be described as the ferry's *sistema del potere* – its system of power – were unlikely to look kindly upon some grubby galley youth, especially one clad in apron and sweat-stained singlet, appearing like a jack-in-the-box upon any deck where passengers consorted.

For a moment Lucchetti debated whether to forget the whole thing: mind his own business and return to complete his punishment. Another ten, fifteen minutes should see him clear and free to head gratefully for his bunk for the less than four precious hours left during which, hopefully, his seasickness and dog-weariness could repair in sleep.

But the niggling unease persisted. He heaved a philosophical shrug. Having come this far he might as well nip up to the next level and check that out too. Discreetly.

On breasting the upper landing of the stairwell, Filippo found a padlocked sliding steel door facing him from the opposite side of a long corridor running both ways: obviously the main car deck, meaning he was just above the waterline. That corridor was plastic-lined rather than painted steel, and generally boasted a rather better quality of finishings. Dust sheets and a couple of folded painters' trestles suggested the whole area was being revamped. The cynic in him surmised that if he wasn't actually in passenger country he was getting very near it.

So this had to be C deck, then? The young rating felt pleased with himself: already he was becoming a real *marinero*, huh?

Cautiously he poked his head into the alleyway. A pleasantly cool current of air instantly disturbed his tousled hair. More'n a current: almost a wind in fact, the way the draught was being sucked past him from . . . forward, it would be? Yeah, from *forward*, seeing he now stood with his back to the ferry's right-hand – *starboard* – side . . . anyway, he registered what appeared to be a line of ship's offices and more store rooms running opposite the hangar deck wall until his line of sight was blocked by a closed fire door several metres distant.

When Pantry Rating Luchetti looked to his left – meaning aft? – he observed yet another door, held partly ajar this time, past which he could just detect . . .

. . . he could detec . . . ?

Santa Maria . . . !

Another member of the catering department who should have been sleeping but found himself unable to, was Assistant Crew Mess Cook Manley.

It had been his run-in with that Yank passenger that done it. Got Henry so wound up he'd found it impossible to dock in the Land of Nod. The sheer venom of Zach Goss's attack had stirred a resentment in the black chef that he thought he'd long ceased to give a damn about. He'd come within an inch of banjoing the old geezer – probably would've done if it hadn't been for Frank Trøjborg's intervention – and the whole unpleasant incident had left Henry shaken and simmering.

Which accounted for why, instead of being snuggled up forrard at twenty-nine minutes past two on that cold morning in the Skaggerak, the insomniac Liverpudlian had eventually wandered along to his own mess, which doubled as Able Seaman Conroy's office – or was it the other way round? Anyroad – had wandered down the bottom of the *Orion Venturer* where he'd finished up lounging alongside Conroy nursing a large mug of tea and an even larger grievance.

Oh, it wasn't as if Henry had never met prejudice before . . .'*course* he had. He was a Trinidad Manley, resident in the UK, wasn't he? Hell, there was a few of their honky neighbours back in the Pool, even in the tower block where he and Emma – where three *generations* of Manleys had lived for over fifty bloody years, f'r that matter! – who still weren't above making their antipathy plain. Them he could handle . . . had grown up with it.

But on board ship? He'd never had no problems during his sea time in freighters. Not even on those FOC vessels you might expect to be hotbeds of disharmony, where multi-racial, multi-language, multi-religion crews are thrown together to develop strains potentially far more divisive than just the colour of a bloke's skin . . . yet even aboard them, most manage to get by without startin' an ethnic bloody war.

Mind you, as Conroy pointed out with an uncharacteristic flash of commiseration for someone else's resentments – the baldy guy wus only a passenger. An' it was well known among passenger ship men, Conroy had assured him, that passengers had little to commend them as a species to blokes like us, mate, wot unstintingly serves their every whim.

But then, learning that Conroy didn't like passengers very much hadn't exactly come as a surprise to Henry. In fact it was hard not to link prejudice and Able Seaman Conroy in the same thought process. They sort of went together like Samson and Delilah, eggs and bacon . . . like gloom an' despondency.

Having said that, the chef had grown to harbour a soft spot for the crusty old seaman despite his regularly declared aversion to

. . . well, to *most* things when it come down to it. Manley even began to feel a bit better about the afternoon's confrontation since he'd talked it over with Conroy – or rather, since Conroy had talked it over to him, which tended to be the way conversations with Conroy usually went. Certainly, listening to Conroy detailing his prejudices had been an education. Taught Henry there wus things to be bigoted about that he hadn't even *thought* of . . . things that made even that Klansman feller sound like a liberal.

. . . it was then that Manley noticed the walkie-talkie: still lying where the night-watchman had forgotten it beside his overflowing watchkeeper's official ashtray.

He frowned up at the clock above the servery – around eight, nine minutes it must've been now, since the AB had trailed off in search of disaster mutterin' dark observations on the general quality of second mates an' ships' electrics, an' how he couldn't *stand* bloody . . . ?

Went up to C deck, didn't he? Where Mister Delucci's false alarm was supposed to have originated – because, like Conroy, Henry had never given serious credence to the alarm maybe being for real. He'd better follow and find the old misery. Take him his radio before turning in.

Apart from which, Henry Manley, as he left his mess on A deck at around five bells in the graveyard watch to head unwittingly for the seat of the fire, simply had to settle a mystery which, if left unresolved, he just knew would keep him awake and worrying for the rest of the night. A question that had been forming on the tip of his tongue at the very moment when the call came from the bridge, and which had bothered him on and off even before the ship sailed.

Assistant Crew Mess Cook Manley just had to find out, this time, why Conroy was so biased against *rabbits*?

Marianne Nørgaard was making herself a cup of coffee at the kettle in the Purser's Office when she thought she heard a muffled shout – Conroy's as it happened, before he collapsed without quite making it back to the hose point.

Frowning, she stepped out to the reception desk which, being

215

aft-facing, overlooked the long central corridor serving the passenger cabins in the rear section of the ferry. Not so much because she felt cause for concern but because, at two-thirty in the morning, the last thing passengers who've retired appreciate is horseplay from late revellers returning noisily to their cabins.

She registered nothing amiss. There was no one to be seen, either in the reception area or skylarking in the long central corridor. She did notice that the smoke containment door some distance down its length was closed, as she would expect it to be under night running routine.

Had Junior Purser Nørgaard pursued the matter – left her reception kiosk and crossed to the starboard side of the wide embarkation lobby to look down *that* corridor – then at least some lives may have been saved: an alarm given while the smoke from C deck was still a half-formed infant cloud above stairway 2S . . . but she didn't. Instead she hesitated, listening to the choir faintly heard from the Admiral's Lounge above. They were singing 'Men of Harlech' now: full-throated and lusty and unutterably stirring. The Welshmen would be finishing very soon, she suspected. Tired and happy and fulfilled . . .

As, indeed, was the newly promoted Marianne herself, unaware that two . . . no, *three* of her middle watch charges – because Gertrud Gustafsson had stopped banging or even scraping weakly at Lennart's sealed door by then – already lay dead on C and D decks below her.

She returned to the office, carefully applied a dab of fresh lipstick, proudly checked the set of her officers' epaulettes before the mirror once more, then finished making her well-earned cup of coffee.

While, less than half a minute's walk from her along that starboard after side of E deck, a black shadow continued to spread, all the time gaining in density and toxicity, to infill the narrow void separating twin lines of closed cabin doors.

Cabins Night Steward Cardoso vomited at half past two precisely.

Again!

Jeeeze, you wouldn't believe anyone could be so sea-sick!

He didn't see the smoke creeping down the corridor towards his cuddy either. Not with him being more preoccupied with examining the bottom of his bucket to see if, this time, any anxiety-provoking bits of his internals had finished up in there. Not even when it had been his idea to jam open the door that would otherwise have prevented the smoke from reaching his personal hell.

But then: Hell is a subjective vision conjured by the minds of individuals. Everybody's idea of what constitutes Hell is different.

Pinheiro Cardoso was about to discover that what *he'd* come to think of as hell during the preceding twenty-odd hours really wasn't like hell at all.

Give him another two minutes and there's one thing for sure. He's going to discover it's got nothing to do with plastic buckets.

Pantry Rating Lucchetti had already come face to face with *his* concept of hell.

Yet, despite the scene that met him, Filippo managed to stay cool. Scared, yeah. Still incredulous enough to make him question whether he was dreaming – or more like experiencing a nightmare? – but nevertheless in control.

It seemed the smoke along the corridor, boiling black against the ceiling in the immediate area of the part-open containment door, had so far been prevented from drifting further forward by the wind born of the fire's own hunger for oxygen . . . but, clearly, it wouldn't stay frustrated for long. The youth could make out flame licking and flickering through the smoke-head: already curling around the part-open door to bypass its temporary irritation: beginning to ripple across the plastic surfaces in his part of ship . . . flames evidently much more resolute in their progress than was the insubstantial by-product of their combustion.

Which made it even more commendable that the former wannabe big-time mobster, having survived a few too many sticky moments in his short but violent life only by thinking smart and moving fast, didn't panic. Instead he drew breath a moment, let the mongrel factor kick in: weighed the odds.

It seemed his current situation was not good, what with him finding himself placed roughly amidships and barely above the waterline of a long steel box which was, apparently, in the process of turning itself into a giant floating oven. In fact, considering his presence aboard had merely been intended as an alternative to ending up as several disconnected parts in the Cimitero Monumentale down the Via Santa Maria del Riposo, he could reasonably assume he'd opted for a career change which made even his former prospects seem long term.

The way Filippo figured it, he had just come face to face with his moment of truth, and he had two choices.

Either he started running. Very, very quickly. And climbing. And at least make it to the open decks where presumably, being in possession of a certificate issued by the Ministero della Marina Mercantile which proved he was capable of commanding a lifeboat, he would virtually be guaranteed the opportunity of getting into one . . . though what he did with it then was somethin' he'd have to work on while it was being lowered on those wire rope things?

. . . or he could give thought to others for the first time in his flawed young life. Stay, and truly earn the accolade of *Picciotto di Onore*.

Meaning he had to close that door fully to stop, at least delay, the fire from racing forward through the whole ship . . . ?

There was an alarm position nearby. And an extinguisher point just past it. Lucchetti had never used an extinguisher, but what the hell – it couldn't be *that* hard. He elbowed the fragile glass of the alarm, hit the button . . . grabbed the heavy extinguisher, then started to run, keeping low as he could, for the fire break.

It was then that even Lucchetti's resilience faltered when he realized that the door was being jammed open by . . . *Mamma mia!* . . . by a *body*, was it?

Sprawled in the corridor?

. . . an' that the body itself was on fire!

The corpse – male . . . female? – either way barely recognizable as human – was virtually encased in a suit of flame. Just a shrivelled, black-peeling monkey-thing lying on its back, forearms obscenely crooked to point claw-rigid hands to the blazing deckhead . . . arms that still *moved* feebly nevertheless, as the tendons of the cadaver continued to shrivel under the grill fuelled by its own body fats.

Which heralded the moment when the most terrible event of all took place . . .

For, even as Filippo Lucchetti gazed with revulsion on the disintegrating ebony head, hairless and black-shiny as a Tar-Baby's, it *jerked* and began to *search* for him . . . ! Adjusted itself with articulated precision to critically observe his approach . . . and then bared its teeth to exhibit a pearl-white, rictal yawn into which tiny, sizzling flames immediately began to curl, and to explore.

Gagging, dearly wishing to God he *had* opted for a sharp exit to the boats, Lucchetti hit the striker of the extinguisher without knowing – without bloody *caring* whether it was set to spray or jet – whereupon instantly, mercifully, the burning corpse became hidden by a discreet shroud of vapour.

He continued to play the water on and around the edge of the door and its surrounding plastic lining until the extinguisher was exhausted, by which time acrid fumes from the steam had swirled around, and caused him to retch convulsively. He could feel his own hair beginning to shrivel – the heat radiating through the gap had grown in intensity even since he'd arrived. All he could see on the other side was a furnace of flame beginning to spread into, and climb what appeared to be a further stairwell to the upper decks, dear Jesus . . .

Rasping for breath now, and nearing the limit of his endurance, the young rating gave it one last shot. Bundling his apron carelessly to protect his face he threw himself prone, legs extended, to kick and push and pummel at the door-stop cadaver in a final desperate attempt to force it clear and so permit the door to close freely

The cadaver – obviously a non-conformist corpse, having, only three hours previously, been contrary enough to evince displeasure because its dinner was too *excellent* to criticize! – resisted to the end: only sliding free in stiff resentment just as Filippo Lucchetti was about to give up and start running.

. . . but then, the living soul it once was always had been a bit self-serving, a bit jealous of others' successes.

So perhaps it was understandable that, even in death, Sven Carlsson should feel quite put out by the realization that he himself was providing the focus for some other impostor becoming a hero.

CATACLYSM

Phase Two

Although only a handful of crew members knew of, or suspected, an incident had occurred on C deck by two-thirty in the morning, several passengers still abroad on the upper levels had begun to complain that it really was becoming far too hot for comfort in the ro-ro's public spaces.

Ironically, the steadily rising temperatures in the Admiral's Lounge – and more particularly, in the Ocean Runner Night Club where the disco set were still perspiring to the amplified turn-tablings of DJ Rod O'Steele – owed nothing whatsoever to the fact that the vessel was on fire below them.

It was simply that one section of the ageing ventilation system, which should have provided a constant supply of fresh air to those after parts of ship located high on F and G decks, had broken down during the previous evening, and the concerted efforts of the Orion Venturer's *already over-stretched engineering staff had proved inadequate to repair it until a spare part could be flown out to await the ferry's docking in Gothenburg.*

The failure of that particular piece of auxiliary machinery, causing discomfort at most rather any diminution of the ship's safety regime, was nevertheless about to prove significant over the course of the next few minutes.

Disastrously significant.

CHAPTER TWENTY-FOUR

Awake, arise, or be forever fall'n.
JOHN MILTON (1608–1674)

Up in the ship's lounge Charlie Periera was one passenger gittin' hot under his collar, with or without no ventilating systems workin'!

Zach Goss was the cause of Charlie's irritation. Seemed Charlie couldn't go nowheres in the ship without finding the Alabama Turbo-tongue around to loud mouth and attract attention – 'specially this time of the morning, when everyone else seemed happy to sit and nurse their nightcaps and listen in appreciative silence while the Limey crowd, along with that German Willy feller with the dyed hair at the piano, come to the end of their impromptu choral concert.

The real annoyance was that Periera had only left his worryingly frail Margrite to sleep, build up her strength, because he'd felt he was disturbin' her with his tossing and turning. Had needed to get himself a drink, hopefully calm his own anxieties . . . only to find the main cause of them danged anxieties already sitting there: wavin' him over like they was old buddies from way back.

Which they weren't. Far as Charlie was concerned, him and Zach only ever had the one thing in common – and he was bones, trapped f'r an eternity of shattered ambitions in a crab-infested hulk under the blue Pacific somewheres east of Samar Island.

Or that's the way he'd seen things before yes'day afternoon. Since then, after taking into account Goss's immoderate behaviour to the young black chef, old Charlie had begun to question how close even that tenuous bonding had been justified. Hadn't been able to rid himself of the suspicion that Goss had been motivated into slamming that door on the Lootenant least as much by the

221

colour of the officer's skin as by the former MM 1/c's own desire to survive.

Wouldn't never know now. Whether Zach, like himself, had simply been a young sailor scared out his wits in the bottom of a dying warship: doin' all the right things – the hard things the Navy trained 'em to do once *Abandon Ship* had been piped – in order to maintain watertight integrity in the riddled destroyer long as possible an' so gain a millisecond's edge over Death . . . or whether Goss, as senior rate, hadn't gone a mite further than simply performing his duty. Betrayed hisself to be a guy so eaten with racial hatred, it transcended even his terror?

. . . it seemed Zach had been settled in the lounge for quite some time before Charlie found his way up there, judging by the alcoholic flush making the burn on the already florid face stand out red as a rooster's comb. Didn't look like he'd been to bed at all since they come aboard, not even to grab an hour's sack-time yes'day afternoon.

Over an hour later, and Zach had sunk a few more beers until now he jus' slumped skew in his chair with a glaze to his eyes – yet *still* running off at the mouth loud enough f'r everyone around to take note of how he, ex-Petty Officer Goss, US Navee, had bin some war hero, you-all hear? A guy that'd been sunk . . . wus it two more times since the *Thompson*, Zach claimed, or three? Yet, accordin' to Zach, he'd *still* got himself posted back to the Fleet each time at his own request. Fought his way clear from Midway thru to Tokyo . . . showed them goddam Japs what True American Grit really meant, huh?

President Truman – Mister Winston Churchill . . . they must both have bin mighty grateful to the Lord for sendin' them Zachary Goss in their time of desperate need.

Charlie ran out of grouchy humour and shifted uncomfortably instead; stole an embarrassed peek at the group of four Japanese men sitting impassive around their drinks less'n earshot away before, feeling concerned 'bout Margrite, screwing up his eyes to make out his watch . . . Lord above – two thirty?

He hadn't meant to stay topside so long, but Zach being drunk like he was had placed him in kind of a quandary. Couldn't leave him up here on his own: the man weren't capable of findin' his way back to his de luxe cabin . . . and they *had* been shipmates once. You didn't leave a shipmate to fend f'r hisself. Not even one who wus a pain in the butt . . . Not unless his skin weren't the right colo . . . ?

'Time to go down, Zach,' Periera urged, ridding his mind of those terrible thoughts while placing his hand on the fat man's shoulder.

They began to sing 'Men of Harlech', the Brits. Triumphant. Emotive. A song of war long past, but stirring enough to make the blood course in the veins of even a old has-been like Charlie Periera.

Men of Harlech in the hollow . . . Do you hear like rushing
   billow
Wave on wave that surging follow . . . Battle's distant
   sound . . . ?

'Ain't *goin'* down,' Goss slurred, shrugging Periera's hand away.

'You got to go down. Mary Lou, she'll be worryin' over you.'

'Leave me be, you hear . . . ? I ain't goin' down to no lower deck this side of docking . . .' Old Zach seemed to sag then: kind of crumple where he sat while his eyes took on a rheumy, panicky aspect. 'I . . . I cain't, Periera.'

Onward, 'tis our country needs us, he is bravest, he who
   leads us
Honour's self now proudly heeds us – Freedom, God,
   and Right!

'Course you can. Now you're talkin' foolish, Zach. Take more'n a few beers to knock an ol' war hero like you off'n his sea legs . . . ?'

Charlie broke off sudden then, just starin' at Zach Goss. There was somethin' . . . something different about the previously pushy, over-loud Zach. Somethin' about the way beads of sweat had begun to form around where burning fuel oil had destroyed the facial tissue fifty-odd years before. And they weren't nothing to do with the ventilation bein' down.

Hurl the reeling horsemen over, let the earth dead
    foemen cover
Fate of friend, or wife, or lover . . . Trembles on a blow . . . !

'You're *scared* to go below, aren't you, Zach?' Charlie said, feeling disbelief.

'I ain't scared of *nothin'*, Periera,' Goss cried, with that hunted look starin' from his eyes now. 'You got no *right* to say that! No right at all.'

Men of Harlech young or hoary, would you win a name in
    story . . . ?

'You never *did* go back to the Fleet, did you? You ain't never *been* in a ship since the *Thompson*!'

'Sure ah have! You keep your poky nose out of mah business, old man! You keep your goddam accusa . . .'

'What draft *did* you talk them into givin' you after survivor's leave, mister? Sailin' a desk in Seattle Navy Yard engineer stores, wus it, Zach . . . ? Along with your citation f'r bravery an' your Purple goddam Heart and your PO rate?'

The Japanese – even the Brits – wus staring discomfited over at the two grizzled veterans by then, but Charlie Periera was hopping mad hisself now. Here he'd been plagued for fifty years an' more by feelin' shame that Zach Goss must've possessed ten – *twenty* times more moral fibre than him 'cause, despite them both sharing the same horrifying experience, Charlie knew he, himself, couldn't never have gone back into no fighting ship agin: not even if'n his crippled leg hadn't seed him invalided out. He'd've gone AWOL: done time in the stockade rather than . . .

'Did you tell 'em how you tried so hard to save the Lootenant, Zach? Wus that why they give you your cushy number an' your goddam *medal*?'

Strike for home, for life, for glory . . . Freedom, God,
    and Right!

Zach Goss began to cry through the drink. Tears, oozing like plasma from a corpse, trickling to varnish the scarlet destruction of his face.

'O'Kane wus a nigra, Periera! They di'n't have no right to make a *nigra* an officer over white men like you an' me . . . !'

Old Charlie Periera closes his eyes a moment, feels the nausea rising. The deck of the ferry tilting under him . . . he c'n see the eviscerated part-corpse of birthday boy MM 2/c Marcora, who jus' won eighteen bucks shootin' craps, now driftin' away, spread-eagled an' face down in the burning water . . . see Engineer Lieutenant Junior Grade O'Kane, US Navy, wading thigh deep, grit-eyed determined towards him while the spume whirlpools to drag him back, khaki shirt shrapnel-ribboned – one hand supporting a bloodied, tattered stump where his other used to be . . .

'Shut the door, dog it *down*! We ain't gonna make it topside elsewhys!' Goss is bellowing . . .

Charlie Periera frowns.

. . . because what he hears ain't Machinist's Mate First Class Zachary Goss hollerin' over half a century back – seems it's some foolish woman screaming. And anyways, this isn't no Fleet escort destroyer dying in war. She's a ro-ro ferry on a routine European service . . . !

When he opens his eyes it's only to gape. The screaming woman's in a party over near the starb'd aft staircase up frum the lower decks. While around her a whole group of people have risen in panic: begun to scatter . . . ?

Charlie's vision isn't what it used to be, but even to his ailing sight the smoke seeping up the stairway is dense enough to make out plain beneath the overhead.

Unlike most of the passengers still awake at that time, Heikki hadn't become over-warm following the breakdown of the ventilating system for the lounge and night club. But then, out on the exposed upper deck with the headwind still biting and battering at the canvas boat covers, it was irrelevant to the schoolgirl huddled in the scant lee of a lifejacket locker how hot or cold the ship felt inside.

. . . not strictly true, of course. It was bound to affect Heikki as much as anyone else aboard that, in one part of the ferry – down on C deck – the temperature was nearing *five* hundred degrees Centigrade by now, and the doors of those vacant outer cabins lining the starboard corridor had begun to burn through ... in fact, that fire has already entered some cabins that had been care-lessly left open – or with doors simply hooked back as, for instance, AB Conroy had left the door of C313 when he'd compromised between safety and hassle. Made sure the space was properly venti-lated on account o' all the inflammable stuff like white spirits and acetylene an' bottled oxygen that should, more properly, have been instantly removed from there.

Certainly Heikki Niskanen didn't feel as chilled as she had after she'd killed her baby ... well, her *doll* baby. So far, anyway. Until the power of the *voudon* worked ... in fact she felt sort of cosy now, snuggled down beside Nicole: the two of them proper tomboys like all the heroines of all the books Heikki had ever read.

Nicole smiled, and touched Heikki to attract her attention. Heikke blinked up and saw one of the ferry's ventilators towering above her. There was smoke, quite a lot of grey-black smoke coming out of it, which was odd because Heikki had always thought that's what ship's *funnels* were for ... ?

She'd stopped shivering now, despite her thin anorak being soaked through. Her pulse and respiratory rate had slowed, her skin felt cold and dry to the touch. Her body temperature had fallen some way below 35° C. And she had begun to die.

Heikki didn't know she was dying, of course. And even if she had suspected it, she wouldn't have minded, or even been fright-ened. Soon the sun would come out, and she'd be warm again, because now she wasn't on a nearly thirty-year-old North Sea ferry: she was on a graceful private yacht and sailing with Nicole to her father's plantation in beautiful, romantic Haiti. And she was *so* looking forward to meeting Tug Rockingham ...

But then, another symptom of advancing hypothermia is irrational thought.

Jozef was being difficult. And there's simply no reasoning with a cat that's being difficult.

Mme Chabert in Starboard E327 hadn't met any problems at all in catering for Jozef's natural functions going over on the Zeebrugge ferry. She'd bought a roll of heavy-duty aluminium foil before leaving Liège, which – when turned up around the edges and sprinkled liberally with cat litter, then laid on the cabin floor as a sort of disposable feline porta-potty – her contraband travelling companion had taken to using like a proper treat.

But not homeward bound he hadn't. Jozef had prowled around the narrow cabin incessantly, most uneasily, since shortly after midnight ... done everything but cross his furry little legs, yet never once squatted to permit a surge of ecstatic relief to briefly animate his almond-shaped, inscrutable green eyes.

By half-past two in the morning the sodding cat – Mme Chabert may have been eighty-two years old and outwardly a bit posh, but she still believed in calling a spade a bloody spade! – had begun to *meowl* and claw at their cabin door.

The Belgian spinster felt somewhat disconcerted, having believed she'd successfully weaned Jozef off flower beds and got him into aluminium, which now seemed not to be the case. Although where he expected her to find a flower bed in the middle of the North Sea in the middle of the ... ?

But she dearly loved Jozef, and the cat was becoming quite distressed. She simply had to allow him some space. Crooning tolerantly, the elderly lady slipped a warm dressing gown over her nightdress, slipped her feet into fur-lined boots and, gathering her umbrella in case it proved inclement out on deck, opened the door a crack ... which would have been all right had she only thought to clip Jozef's cat lead to his diamanté-studded flea collar first.

Jozef let out a blood-curdling *myeowl!* Scrabbled, paws blurring on the polished deck until they built up full-ahead traction, then bulleted through the narrow gap like a black and white torpedo! Almost as if he knew something his mistress didn't, regarding not hanging around in enclosed spaces at the wrong time on the wrong ship?

Rats are said to develop much the same awareness of incipient danger.

Much upset, Mme Chabert hastened to follow: caught a concerned glimpse of her darling moggie vanishing down the deserted corridor, heading towards reception under the overcast, and . . .

. . . the overcast?

Alarmed, she turned urgently to look the other way. It wasn't difficult: the fire door along the corridor which, she recollected, had previously been closed now stood wide open . . . smoke was billowing out of a stairwell some distance from her towards the rear of the ship and, even without her spectacles, she thought she could see someone sprawled beneath the massing cloud: probably *un pompier courageux* directing an *extincteur* or something . . . ?

Well, Antoinette Chabert hadn't lived for eighty-two years without coming to appreciate the need for priorities. On the other hand, she *did* question the ability of the ferry's officers to do the same. It was just possible, if indeed the vessel *was* on fire and its sailors liable to be preoccupied with putting it out, as the man in the corridor obviously was, that they might well be loth to allocate adequate resources for a simultaneous search and rescue operation to recover her *petit* Precious.

Gathering her dressing gown about her, she began to call most insistently for a steward. As she went she drummed peremptorily with the handle of her umbrella on each cabin door. In the considered view of the eccentric Madame Antoinette Chabert, the situation aboard the *Orion Venturer* was rapidly developing into a *crise extraordinaire*. The time for half measures was past.

The more people she could arouse to take part in her mission, the greater the prospect of finding Jozef before he shot clean over the side to continue his voyage to Sweden independently, thinking he was a rat . . .

So, while all nine lives of a highly perceptive Belgian cat might well have hung in the balance at half past two on that dreadful morning, the animal did at least achieve, albeit by brolly-assisted remote control, the saving of the more singular ones of several startled passengers who otherwise might never have heard a knock upon their door until it was too late.

If, indeed, any such knock had ever come at all.

Surely even Michael was about ready to abandon the high life and call it a day – or a night in this case?

Grace Miles couldn't help succumbing to the teeniest surge of malicious satisfaction to see her husband running with perspiration as the Spice Girls finished and he staggered off the dance floor with her to flop at their table.

'Jesus, it's hot,' he panted. 'You'd think they'd've fixed the damn ventilation by now.'

'They don't seem to be too hot,' Grace said, pointing to the crowd, mostly youngsters, waiting in close embrace for Rod O'Steele to spin his next disco delight.

'They're all a hundred years younger than us,' Michael muttered. 'Except that big Scandinavian blonde with the long hair. Mind you, she looks classy. Like she could go on for ever.'

'Oh, thank you *very* much, Michael!' Grace snapped in gin and tonic induced resentment. She always got a bit over-sensitive when she'd had a few too many. Tugging at the shoulder straps of the little black dress she'd felt really good in until now, she snatched her handbag and began to rise.

'Where are you going?'

'To bed! Where *old* people *should* be at . . .' She squinted hazily at her watch in the dim blue light and got a shock. 'D'you realize it's half past two in the morning, Michael?'

'And d'*you* realize I'm on holiday, Grace?' His retort was a little slurred as well. They'd both had too much to drink. 'An' that some wives wouldn't nag their husband f'r staying up an hour or two later on his bloody holiday?'

Grace Miles knew then that it had all been wasted. Her special dress; the care she'd taken with her make-up – bringing herself to overlook his hurtful petulance earlier last evening . . . That Michael, true to form, was about to push to stay just a little while longer. Knowing that even then, when they *did* eventually go down, the implication would still be left hanging that it had been she who'd cut short his enjoyment.

Her. And the children.

It must be well over an hour now since either of them had returned to the cabin to look in on William and Lucy.

'Well, I'm going. You can stay if you wan . . . !'

Grace cut off in mid-sentence and stood there sniffing uncertainly.

'Oh Lord, she's not going to start *crying*, is she?' Michael muttered disbelievingly to no one in particular. 'Look Grace, if you feel *that* . . .'

'Be *quiet*, Michael!' Grace blurted, desperately alarmed. 'Can't you *smell* it, for God's sake . . . ?'

The smoke appeared at the head of the starboard stairway leading up from the Admiral's Lounge . . . sort of sucked back in on itself – then *belched* in a great blue, ultra-violet-tinged cloud which continued to expand and revolve until quite bizarrely, at the whim of invisible air currents, it seemed to gather pace yet again before snaking clear across the deckhead of the night club to plunge, an amorphously twirling serpent, sharply downwards into the port stairwell . . . !

Someone choked in terror, 'Fire! There's *fire* somewhe . . . !'

The Portuguese steward behind the club bar leapt over its counter and began pushing kids towards the starboard door leading to the deck. '*Incêndio, incêndio!* Every bodies . . . get *out*!'

Grace began to scream hysterically. '*The children, Michael!* My *babies* . . . !'

Michael Miles didn't hear her. Ignoring the breakaway smoke already spreading through the cramped disco, he'd slumped to cover his face with his hands while sobbing, 'I'm sorry. Oh dear *God*. I'm so *sorry*, Grace . . .'

Four decks below his parents, William opened his eyes and blinked in alarm. He couldn't think where he was . . . ? Then he looked over at Lucy, still fast asleep and cuddling Teddy in the lower berth opposite, and remembered with a surge of excitement that they were on The Great Voyage.

For a moment he visualized the Captain standing straddle-legged at the wheel above him: waist deep in seas that crashed and foamed around the poop deck, with the sailors clinging desperately to the rigging crying to him to save them, while the storm *ripped* the sails to pieces an' plucked at the brave Captain's oilskins an' the white frost clung to his beard . . .

. . ., an' then William realized the boat wasn't *really* pitching and rolling very much at all, an' felt a bit disappointed because, as well as not having any sails to rip, it seemed they weren't even likely to be shipwrecked now or anything exciting like that . . .

Mummy and Daddy hadn't come back from helping the Captain yet. Di'n't bother William. Even better, it still left him in charge of the Crew. He rubbed the sleep from his eyes and climbed out of bed. They'd left one of the upper berth lights on, and some light was coming through under the cabin door so he could see quite easily . . .

. . . but then, just as he went to check on the Watch Below, and tuck the cover in around the pest . . .'round Able Sea Person Lucy! . . . the light under the door dimmed – and seemed to go out.

William frowned. He was smart enough to know they wouldn't switch the lights off in the boat. Not before Mummy and Daddy came back. Curiosity got the better of him. He slipped into his rabbit slippers and was standing on tip-toe, struggling to un-snib the door latch, when Lucy woke up.

'Where's Mummy?'

'Go back to sleep.'

First Mates didn't have to say 'please'. Not to Crew.

The least fluffy member of the Crew mutinied.

'Won't! 'Cause I want my mummy. *An'* my daddy!'

'Well tough, 'cause they're not . . .'

William got the door open and became very frightened when he saw the smoke drifting past. It must be that which had blanked out the corridor light. He shut it quickly.

'What's wrong?' Lucy's eyes widened: fascinated. 'Did you see a sea monster, William . . . a . . . an *octlepuss*?'

'Octopus, stupid! An' shut up. I want to think . . .'

He knew he would have to go and find Daddy: tell him 'bout the fire. But he didn't dare take Lucy . . . even in supermarkets she could vanish from Mummy's side within seconds. If he lost his sister in all that smoke he'd never find her again an' he'd get into the mos' *awful* trouble . . .

'You stay here. I won't lock the door but you *mustn't* go out into the corridor. Promise?'

'No.'

'You *got* to.'

'Won't stay on my own, so there.'

231

'You're not on your own – Teddy'll stay with you. An' it's really *dark* out there.' William played his ace. 'There could be ghosts outside, see? An' Horrible Things . . .'

Lucy hesitated.

'*Please*, Lucy?' the Mate conceded with gritted teeth.

'Teddy says you have to leave him some sweeties first, William.'

William rummaged in Mummy's squashy bag and found a tattered packet of mints. 'Hard tack. Now shut up an' be good.'

'Bet you get into trouble f'r going out of the room.'

'Bet you get an Indian burn if *you* do!' William forecast darkly.

Acting on an impulse he went over to the berth and kissed her.

'*Yugh!*' Lucy grimaced, wiping her cheek.

''Bye. Won't be long.'

The last time William saw his little sister she was sitting up in the berth sharing Teddy's hard tack. She hardly glanced at him as he prudently pulled on his yellow sou'wester, took a deep breath, then slipped out into the corridor, pulling the unlocked door to behind him.

He was very brave. Like the Captain was, in the book Mummy had bought him. He never cried although he soon found, to his distress, that he couldn't really see anything in the dense smoke. He even tried walking on tip-toe to try an' see over it . . .

He got an awful fright when he stumbled over something big and soft on the floor – he didn't realize it was Able Seaman Conroy prone at the top of the stairwell from D deck . . . he didn't even realize it was a person – but the shock made William draw breath sharply.

His lungs were only seven years old. They hadn't had the opportunity to develop any tolerance at all to withstand the assault of so many toxic gases combined.

Still wearing his pyjamas and rabbit slippers, William managed to stagger a few yards further, feeling *so* tired and dizzy. An' a bit sick.

He sank down to wait for Mummy and Daddy to come for him and make his cough better.

And, very soon it seemed, they did.

William was smiling happily, peacefully in their loving arms, when even the dream died.

CHAPTER TWENTY-FIVE

The noble Duke of York,
He had ten thousand men,
He marched them up to the top of the hill,
And he marched them down again.
                    Anonymous Nursery Rhyme, 18th Century

At two-thirty in the morning the fire again increased in ferocity.

So far it had fed on draught created by the ferry's continuing twenty-knot passage against a brisk easterly headwind. Even some two minutes after the blaze had found an escape route up Stairway 2 Starboard, open ducts in the forward face of the superstructure were still scooping night air into the hull and along its lower alley-ways. Aided by the fact that no secondary fire doors had yet been closed from the bridge while other first-line doors stood open, this self-sustaining air flow had been largely responsible for driving smoke – its natural inclination being to rise anyway – upwards from C deck where it had begun to permeate the whole after part of the passenger accommodation.

But now a further, and quite unforeseen, phenomenon began to influence both the spread and speed of advance of the fire.

The ventilation system in the *Orion Venturer* was based on creating an over-pressure in her living and public spaces, maintained by blowing cool air into them, and under-pressure, or suction, in the car deck, from which powerful extractor fans drew exhaust and other fumes before expelling them high above the ro-ro.

But due to the failure during the previous evening of the mechanical air blowers servicing the Admiral's Lounge – and the night club located even higher on G deck, nearly at the top of the ferry – that balance had been disturbed. The pressure within those areas had also dropped below that in the main body of the ship.

. . . and smoke is attracted to areas of low pressure.

Certainly the nearest low-pressure area to the seat of the blaze was the two-storey vehicle hangar on the same deck – but Carlsson's terrible legacy had initially been prevented from being sucked into that space by its starboard access corridor's steel sliding doors, which were all closed. The fire didn't mind. It was becoming adult by then: had developed a mind of its own, whereupon the buoyancy of its super-heating air currents began to generate a momentum of their own.

While the combustion gases had been climbing two levels into D and E decks they'd also steadily increased in temperature. As soon as that temperature reached the critical 200°C required to ignite the plastic panels lining the route, the stairwells themselves burst into flame, That *further* raised the temperature . . .

A self-perpetuating chimney effect had been created which, attracted by the unexpected bonus of low pressure from above, accelerated the smoke's progress even faster up through the ship, clear into the Admiral's Lounge and immediately onwards up into the night club on G deck.

. . . where, upon its precipitate arrival, the smoke was confronted by yet another influence. A bit of a quandary in fact, because smoke only knows how to conform to simple rules of physics, and isn't in itself very smart.

After having laboriously reached the top of the hill by the starboard route, it then sensed the low-pressure suction beckoning it from the opposite side of the ferry. Suction created this time by the *Orion Venturer*'s part-open car deck door five levels below on her port side . . . which explained why the startled occupants of the disco had seen it spiral over – and then dive *downwards* . . . back into the depths of the ferry!

. . . and where the smoke went, the flames would inevitably follow.

Very quickly now.

Yet still no one on the ro-ro's bridge was receiving hard information on where the fire was located.

Or even absolute confirmation that a fire existed at all.

234

CHAPTER TWENTY-SIX

Taken together, the actions of the crew during the fire present a picture of a lack of co-ordination and leadership at all stages. The operational command never functioned as laid down in the emergency plan ... this meant that the members of the crew acted most of the time on an individual basis, and that they never conducted them-selves as an organization ... [however] it must be emphasised that the fire developed and the smoke spread extremely rapidly from the moment the fire was dis-covered.

Norwegian Official report, NOR 1991: 1E

The *Scandinavian Star* Disaster of 7 April 1990

Thirty seconds after Chief Officer McCulloch's hasty departure from the bridge, the Captain reduced the ship's speed to zero by means of her starboard combinator, which regulated both engine revolutions and propeller pitches. Even that action he took with reluctance, conscious that many passengers would be startled by the sudden decrease in vibration. But while Halvorsen was being increasingly forced to recognize the possibility that his ship could be in hazard, he was still not persuaded that she was.

He did not apply astern power to take draught-inducing way off the ship as quickly as possible. The *Orion Venturer* would coast for a further eight minutes before she came to rest. Nor did he immediately move to follow the perceived wisdom urged – albeit silently – by Second Officer Delucci regarding shutting down all forced ventilation in the suspected areas of fire. Torn by the con-flicting demands on him as a responsible shipmaster, and loth to declare a full emergency without further confirmation, the Captain did not even consider it justifiable at that moment to broadcast a preliminary PAN PAN Urgency Signal – a possible risk situation developing – to alert the shore network of Maritime Rescue Co-ordination Centres, in addition to placing all vessels in the immediate area on listening watch.

Nevertheless a momentary silence fell over the darkened bridge. All were conscious that on the veracity of a cluster of red lights hung the prospect of their participating in an event dreaded by all mariners during the course of their sea-going life. How significant that event was about to prove they did not – *could* not! – have anticipated even in their worst nightmares.

'Call the engine room, Mister Delucci,' Halvorsen said quietly. 'Advise them why we've stopped, and that I intend to retain man-oeuvring control from up here. Have them run up the fire pumps and stand by for further orders.'

'Guess I better get down there, Cap'n,' Bracamontes muttered. He didn't sound enthusiastic.

Better you than me, Chief, Delucci thought as he reached for the E/R phone. He hated the claustrophobic heat and noise of any engine room at the best of times – and with the ship maybe about to burn above the heads of whoever was down there, this was definitely not one of the better times.

'Control room – Third Engineer?' Bert's almost instant response sounded tight. But then Stamper, still grasping his last bonus quarter round of pig sandwich nine decks below, was trying to figure why the bridge had abruptly cut his main engines back to tick-over revs. *Approaching imminent collision* was the phrase his suddenly hyperactive imagination kept latching on to.

'We got a situation here,' Delucci said. 'No confirmation yet, but we could have fire starboard side aft – C deck up through E. The Mate's on his way down there.'

'You want me to switch to engine room manoeuvring?'

The Third sounded almost relieved. Perversely so, yeah – but maybe when you're the man in the white boiler suit far below the waterline, fire seems to offer a little less immediate threat of extinction than the picture of several thousand tons of another ship's bow about to plough through, and over, the point where you might very well be standing . . .

'Negative. Captain proposes to control from the bridge combinator. Jus' run up the pumps for now: prime the fire lines and stand by.'

The telephone began to crackle and Delucci frowned. Never been a problem before.

'What condition are we in?' Bert asked uncertainly.

The Second Mate hesitated. He was tempted to say 'Bloody worried!' but knew what Stamper meant. There were five stages in the emergency plan, each calling for escalating levels of response from individual crew members. Or at least, from those crew members who had the slightest idea of what the *Orion Venturer's* emergency plan required of them. Even the bridge copy lay unopened on the chart table beside the emr numbers list where Bosun Pascal had left it late last night, still smelling of photocopier chemicals.

But the first degree of response, Condition White, covered the phase they, by Delucci's reckoning, were in at the moment. Essentially, Command and Control planning to combat unquantified disaster out of total bloody ignorance!

Green and Blue each jerked the required responses up a notch depending on the location and type of emergency, while Red . . .

Tonight, aboard this particular ship, Condition Red – the penultimate horror – must inevitably involve public alarms and lifeboats and rafts being readied amid the smell of panic, with maybe people already dying . . . to say nothing of five hundred-plus souls, many of them frail, inebriated or inadequately dressed requiring directions in some seventeen languages – from a crew who themselves required direction in roughly nine – converging on the embarkation stations – *if*, that assumed, they knew where those emergency assembly points were . . . And Second Officer Delucci wasn't thinking exclusively of the ro-ro's passengers in his last observation!

While Condition *Black* . . . Delucci didn't want to even *think* about Condition Black right then. Apart from to reflect that its colour coding had been bloody aptly chosen.

'I'll keep you posted, Bert. Soon as the situation becomes clea . . .'

The telephone connection to the engine room splurged, then cut.

Dead!

The young 2/O swore and tried the call button again. Still nothing! Not a crackle of life from the all-vital communications link between the ferry's bridge and her engine room.

Unaware, Halvorsen called, 'Also tell the watch engineer to start the bow thrust motors while . . .'

'The phone's down, Captain,' Delucci responded numbly. 'The fucking *phone's* gone . . .'

'Try the lines through the automatic exchange. Try reception! Request a status report on the conditions on E deck.'

Delucci grabbed for the internal network phone: had just begun to key in the extension numbe . . .

'*Muchas alarmas, Señor Capitán!*'

The cry from AB Madariaga caused a shiver of *déjà vu* to assail Second Officer Delucci. He didn't need his undivided attention drawn to the new alarms beginning to trill like a treeful of hysterical sparrows through the blacked-out wheelhouse. He could already see the series of little red lights beginning to spread across the fire warning panel representing the ro-ro's gridded maze of corridors . . . climbing and multiplying and expanding now to embrace virtually every deck in the ferry's after section.

The ship continued to coast under her own momentum. Rain spattered across wheelhouse windows. There was a feeling of . . . *sadness*, could it have been, despite the major concerns of the moment? Of the great initiative of the new service being over before it had properly begun . . . ? From the wing outside a signal halyard, abraded by the wind, emitted a keening lament.

Above the chart table the clock jerked to 0231 hours Scandinavian time as, in the ship below them, more cabins became overshadowed by an ever-expanding toxic cloud.

Seen dimly through the middle-night gloom, lit only by flickering radar impulses and the green glow from the binnacle and from bank upon bank of dials and switches, the *Orion Venturer*'s Master appeared to shrink in Second Officer Delucci's eyes: to visibly diminish in stature.

But his next order was still given clearly, without hint of the hopelessness – of the now unqualified acceptance that he'd made the wrong call – that banded tight in his chest.

238

'Sound the fire alarm, Mister Delucci,' Captain Jorgen Truls Halvorsen decreed.

By the time Crew Mess Cook Manley had climbed two flights from the bottom of the ferry up to the car deck, intent on his two-fold mission to return AB Conroy's radio and ask him about rabbits, he'd begun to simmer all over again about his previous afternoon's clash with that bloody Yank passenger. The incident really had touched a previously unsuspected raw nerve in Henry's normally genial view of his fellow men.

Which was why he got rather alarmed when, as he breasted the head of Stairway 4S on to the C deck service alleyway, he saw another black man, a young feller, running helter-skelter towards him down the corridor from aft.

The guy was obviously one of the catering crew. Manley could tell that from his blue and white check galley pants and the filthy apron . . . *bloody* filthy in Henry's opinion: surprised that Head Chef Mon-sewer de Saeger permitted such insanitary rig in his kitchens . . . I mean, Henry was damn sure he wouldn't allow no rating to turn out scruffy as that for work in his own crew galley . . .

But he was digressing. What the bloke was wearing wasn't really the point at issue right then. Henry Manley was more concerned to think that this ethnic thing might be developing into an obsession with him. Getting right out of hand. That he was beginning to conjure up mirror images of hisself all over the shop . . . because, far as Henry knew, there wasn't another black man signed as crew in any department aboard the *Orion Venturer*. He was as unique in his way as . . . well as AB Conroy was unique by being the only nineteenth-century sailor aboard a late-twentieth-century ship.

. . . which was when the penny dropped with Henry that the chap approaching on a collision course with both engines goin' full ahead wasn't a black brother at all, but a honky . . . shit, there 'e went again – was a white man. Only his face was all covered in soot and grime, with his hair singed and his . . .

Henry stepped out in front of the bloke, suddenly anxious. After all, Conroy *had* gone off grumbling topside to investigate a supposed fire.

For his part, Pantry Rating Lucchetti didn't half get a fright. A mirror image of what he figured *he* must look like after wrestling with a burning corpse, suddenly materializing from nowhere? *Mamma mia!* – surely there couldn't be *two* fires aboard . . . ?

'Steady kiddo,' Henry snapped. 'What's your problem?'

The imitation Henry gasped something about *Il ponte di comando* an' *Capitano* before finishing with '*Qual'è che parte si sale?*', which didn't tell Manley a lot other than it was a fair bet the kid wasn't British and, from the way he was gesturing at the deckhead, seemed to be looking for the way up to the bridge.

. . . or to the boats?

No one else seemed to be around. Apart from the two of them the car deck access corridor appeared deserted. Feeling very nervous now, Manley gazed over the youth's shoulder towards the closed fire door aft. It was too far away to make out detail, but he could see a haze around it. And black streaks . . . ?

'Jesus, you *have* come from a fire down aft.'

Lucchetti didn't understand. What little English he'd picked up from dealing with the Naples *turisti* was largely limited to phrases like *You want nice girl: ver' clean*? an' *Hash or heroin* . . . ? *Mexican Mud, Joe? Good stuff. Pure* . . .

Henry got scared for Conroy. 'You see a sailor . . . *marinero* . . . back there?'

'*Morte. Finito!*' The kid shrugged: a hard little bastard now he'd got his breath back. 'He burn.'

'Aw *Jesus*,' Manley repeated feeling sick. Then realized the fire alarms weren't sounding and put his grief for Conroy on hold while he started to run for the smash box beside the nearest hose point. When he'd triggered the alarm he turned to see the youngster frowning somewhat wryly at the object he clutched in his hand – Conroy's walkie-talkie!

'Bridge – this is C deck!' Henry snarled into the set, feeling a bit foolish. 'It's an *emergency* . . . come in, Bridge?'

A green light flickered up on the walkie-talkie. *Battery Low* the legend beneath it assured him. He threw it down and shouted, '*C'mon!*'

'Dov'è . . . ?'

'Well, we can't jus' leave it, can we?' Henry yelled reasonably.

Filippo thought they could. He'd just *closed* the fuckin' door! *'Non fare lo stupido . . .'*

Like Conroy, Assistant Crew Mess Cook Manley had done the Merchant Navy fire-fighting course: earned his susstificate, although that *had* been a fair old time ago . . . He yanked open the door of the fire point: spun the hydrant valve to charge the hose as far as its nozzle and began to struggle aft, trailing the still disappointingly flaccid canvas snake as it ran off the reel.

'Probably an air lock – go like a bar of steel when I open the nozzle valve,' Henry assured his pressed assistant. 'Take some controlling. You take a grip in behind me – an' f'r God's sake, stay low.'

Lucchetti stayed *very* low, shielding himself behind his leading fireman. He didn't understand what the *loco* cook was saying, but he *did* know what was coming . . . suddenly even the prospect offered by the Cimitero Monumentale seemed marginally more appealing.

For some reason Henry had to shove hard at the door to open it. So he *shoved* hard! The flames boosted through with a ferocious roar, immediately re-igniting the plastic lining of the corridor and radiating a blast of heat enough to take Manley's eyebrows and most of the hair on the forrard end of his scalp clean off! Henry screamed with the shock of it and, desperately if somewhat belatedly, yanked the nozzle control valve to establish a protective spray wall.

About five bucketfuls of sea water dribbled out of it, then dried up altogether. Whether you do, or don't, possess a fire-fighting certificate, it's generally best to confirm that the ship's fire pumps have been run up, rather than automatically assume your hose has pressure in it.

Pantry Rating Lucchetti, feeling more like an aid worker than a fireman, managed to close that particular door for a second time, then helped the groggy cook clear of the burning area. The youngster had begun to retch again by then, while Manley's face and arms had been badly burned. Filippo had sustained a few more himself.

241

In fact it would have been hard, even for someone as prejudiced as Passenger Zach Goss, to tell them apart as they stumbled forward together to try and warn the bridge.

They were both bloody heroes.

Just forward of amidships on E deck, Junior Purser Nørgaard cradled her cup of coffee appreciatively as she stepped from the Purser's Office.

She happened to glance at the clock while taking her first sip, noting it had just passed two-thirty. Only another hour and a half before her very first middle watch at sea as an officer ended.

Then the cat appeared.

Marianne blinked. The *what*?

Yes – definitely the cat!

The small creature materialized from the starboard after corridor travelling fast: a black and white symphony of extended forepaws propelled by graceful, rippling posterior muscle, ears flat aback and eyes focused unblinkingly on the main stairway leading to the upper sales foyer.

Then it was gone . . .

Even after it had vanished aloft Marianne was left frowning doubtfully, wondering whether or not she'd actually seen such an unlikely thing as a cat in a ship in the North Sea in the first pla . . . ?

'Jozef . . . ! *Jozef?*'

The imperious call, accompanied by a series of peremptory raps, acted as a prelude to an elderly lady appearing next on the concourse, apparently in pursuit of the cat in question. She was wearing a dressing gown trimmed with Belgian lace, furry boots, and waving an umbrella. Immediately upon sighting the young woman in the white uniform shirt and black tie, she appealed for . . . no – the formidable Mme Chabert positively *demanded* Nørgaard's urgent attention.

'*Mademoiselle? Mon beau chat . . .*'

'*Socorro! 'elp! Socorro!*'

'What *now?*' Marianne swallowed, still trying to catch up with events.

The small Portuguese night cabin steward – Pinheiro, Marianne knew him as: she couldn't remember his second name . . . came bulleting out of the starboard corridor a close third in the race. '*Socorro, Senhora*. You 'elp *passageiros* . . . ? The smock . . . *fumo*?'

'*Jozef* . . . ?'

'Smock? What's smo . . . ?'

'*Incêndio!*'

Junior Purser Nørgaard's coffee cup smashed unheeded on the deck. Abruptly galvanized by a fearful concern for her charges, she wrestled to unlock the security gate of the reception desk then raced across the foyer only to halt again in disbelieving horror.

Already the smoke stealing forward down the starboard cabins service access was less than ten metres from her. Advancing remorselessly, a rectangular pall framed by the plastic-lined corridor walls, impenetrable at ceiling level while thinning, becoming more fractured and wispy towards the deck . . .

Marianne heard someone – herself? – scream with the shock of it before training took charge. She ran back to activate the two manual smash alarms positioned in the foyer, then grabbed the ashen-faced Portuguese steward and pushed him towards the corridor where – thank God! – *some* cabin doors not yet lost in the gloom were beginning to open tentatively in startled response to Mme Chabert's earlier command.

'The passengers! *Wake the passengers* . . . !'

The steward vomited: whether from sea-sickness or fear-sickness not even Cardoso himself could be certain by then. All he knew was that he'd been startled by a rap on his cuddy door, had parted company with his bucket for long enough to peep uncertainly into the corridor . . . and seen the *smock*!

Marianne shouted at the fool in Danish – *hating* him for his ineffectiveness – and then hated herself for the dreadful look of hurt in the little man's sloe-black eyes. '*Please,*' she appealed, reverting to the ship's official language. 'Get as many out as you can. I have to warn the bridge: call for smoke diving equipment . . . we must act on our own until a fire party arrives.'

He nodded, understanding nothing but brutally aware of her meaning. '*Valha-me Deus,*' God help me, he said. The last Nørgaard saw of Night Steward Cardoso was his small form hurrying resolutely towards the advancing smoke wall, kicking on doors and shouting, '*Incêndio . . . Vamos . . .*'

She whirled – the eccentric lady had gone: presumably in single-minded search of her pet – and raced back to the desk, reaching frantically for the bridge phone. It was dead. She threw the receiver down with a sob, hovering on the verge of breakdown – she should *never* have accepted the responsibilities of an officer! – and tried desperately to think where the nearest sets of breathing apparatus were stored. But Junior Purser Nørgaard didn't know.

Since joining only five days ago – well, nearly six, now – she hadn't been afforded any introduction, any conducted tour of the ro-ro's emergency equipment. All members of Frank Trøjborg's department, from the Chief Purser himself down to the pantry ratings, had been kept too busy cleaning and preparing the ferry to receive passengers, sharpening up the hotel services operation . . . pressured into garnishing the sizzle, rather than thoroughly cooking the steak.

There was no point in breaking out an extinguisher or even running out the reception area hose line. She didn't have any idea of where the seat of the fire lay, while the sheer volume of smoke told her that she couldn't hope to fight it on her own: certainly not without a breathing set. She did recognize, however, that despite her line of sight down the central aisle being interrupted by its properly closed fire containment door, smoke must already be crossing to the port side aft by means of the transverse corridors . . .

Until an organized and properly equipped fire party arrived there was little more that twenty-three-year-old Nørgaard could think of doing other than start running down that central alleyway feeling totally helpless, banging on doors while screaming '*Fire!*'

She was *so* relieved when the *Orion Venturer*'s bell-type alarms began to clamour, presumably triggered from the bridge in response to her smash-box alert . . . thank God the Second Officer had taken an immediate decision to react without waiting for phone confirmation. Seven short rings followed by one long continuous note – surely their 80 decibels output must alert the passengers to the previously silent danger which already threatened to engulf them?

She would have been less relieved had she realized that many

244

of those unsuspecting travellers still wouldn't be disturbed. Not instantly. That some really heavy sleepers, when the alarms rang at two thirty-one a.m. in that nightmare middle watch, would never rouse at all. Like the Irish trucker Ó'Leary below on D deck, they would slumber until the toxic miasma found entry, and die peacefully without a single moment of conscious regret for what might have been. They represented, perhaps, the more fortunate of Carlsson's unintended victims, considering the terrible alternative which awaited those who did evacuate their cabins too late.

. . . but then, a Junior Purser could hardly be aware that a person in the deepest phase of sleep is unlikely to be immediately awakened by any sound level of less than 15 decibels above background noise. On E deck of the *Orion Venturer* the external sea wash and the inboard hum generated by the ship's engines and auxiliary equipment maintained a fairly constant sixty. It meant that, to be effective, the alarms required to transmit a minimum sound output of at least 75 dB to each bedside.

In all too many instances, that didn't happen.

The volume of the emergency bells – positioned only in the central corridor – was sharply reduced by the damping effect created by intervening blocks of accommodation, and also by the fact that most cabin doors were firmly closed. The result within the confines of many sleeping spaces, particularly those located along the sides of the ship and so some distance from the alarms, was that the all-crucial warning initiated by the bridge barely penetrated their walls. Even those occupants who were only dozing would hardly be aware of the muffled ringing. In some cabins the alarms simply couldn't be heard.

On being informed that the company had refused to extend the system's coverage, Electronics Technical Officer Talbot had even pointed out the problem with antipodean directness to Captain Halvorsen before the vessel sailed.

'Suit yourself, Cap'n,' he'd shrugged. 'But up around E deck the panic bells wouldn't wake a dozing pussy cat.'

Although ETO Talbot would have been first to concede his dark prediction had already proved over-pessimistic in one respect.

He'd been wrong about the cat.

*　　*　　*

245

As soon as he'd been cut off so disconcertingly from 2/O Delucci on the bridge, Third Engineer Stamper tried the direct line to the Chief's cabin. Nothing! Not even an unanswered ring. It remained as inert as the main ship's telephone system did when, next, he keyed in the Second Engineer's cabin extension before snarling 'Shit!' and finally trying reception – again to no avail.

Motorman Garilao tumbled into the control room looking almost as apprehensive as Bert felt. It isn't just the passengers get nervous when main engines are stopped for no apparent reason.

'Go to the fire locker an' break out the BA sets. Bring two in here: I want to check 'em out,' Bert snapped, wondering what the hell he should do now they were virtually isolated communications-wise.

'Bee Yaye, Turd?' the Filipino queried predictably.

'Breathin' apparatus, dammit!' Stamper got a grip. 'Bridge say we maybe got fire topside aft, Garilao. Fire makee smoke, yeah? Smoke makee cough cough . . . YES?'

Garilao may not have been too smart at sandwiches but he was bloody good on fire. 'We gotta *fire*, Turd?' he yelled without the slightest need for clarification.

'Nothing to worry about,' Bert lied. 'Now, piss off *jaldi* an' bring the smoke diving kit in here.'

Garilao, looking like he knew the Turd was lying, hurried off.

From the control room console, Stamper flashed up the four fire pumps situated in the various compartments, entered his action in the engine room log, then checked their readings on his dials. While doing so it occurred to Bert that, considering each pump was capable of delivering ninety cubic metres of sea water per hour into the ship's mains, if they lost their heads topside and cracked all the hydrants at the same time, then the drainage from the upper levels of the ship might not cope.

He hoped the fire parties knew what they were doing. Tackling any shipboard fire puts you somewhere between a rock and a hard place. In his view, continuously discharging tons of North Sea into the attic of a ro-ro ferry wasn't a good idea: particularly if a lot of it eventually collects on the car deck where it would tend to create a free surface effect – a mass of water swilling from side to side and running serious risk of de-stabilizing the ship. He ran up the general service pump for good measure, in the hope that most of that water would find its way to the bilges and require pumping out again.

Bert Stamper fervently hoped he wouldn't still be in the engine room if events proved his reservation well-founded.

It never occurred to the Third to start the motors of the bow thrusters in case a need arose to manoeuvre the ship while at rest. In that respect he wasn't as farsighted as the Captain. It represented yet another crucial omission out of many which, even then, were allowing an already grave situation to escalate to full-scale disaster.

3/E Stamper ran out of initiative then, and bit absently into his last quarter round of sanny while trying to visualize the likely situation topside. It was a time for steady nerves. Stuck down here without contact with the outside world, he had no way of assessing how bad the fire was, or even if one existed at all.

He debated momentarily on whether to abandon the engine room to be on the safe side, as there seemed little more he and his motorman could do. All engine and propeller controls were duplicated on both wings of the bridge, while they'd made it clear they didn't propose to revert to old-fashioned telegraph orders when the Old Man again required the main engines, currently idling at a steady throb. The ventilation systems and smoke and watertight doors could equally be shut down or closed at the flick of a switch up top. Even the fire pumps could have been started remotely from the wheelhouse, and Bert couldn't help wondering why no one had thought to . . . ?

Third Engineer Stamper dismissed the idea of abandoning of his own volition. Obviously Command didn't consider the situation life-threatening yet: not even grave enough to sound the fire alarm, which would have been repeated down here in the ER. The rest of the engineers would be turning out as he chewed, while the Chief was bound to arrive any moment and might not be too chuffed to find the factory deserted – might, in fact, be inclined to voice a certain degree of displeasure when he finally did track down his Engineer of the Watch. Sitting in a lifeboat. Waiting f'r a non-existent fire to start!

Taking that brief time out for reflection made Stamper feel a little easier. Okay, so the still inexplicable and seemingly catastrophic failure of the telephone system was inconvenient, but . . .

Little Garilao came barging back into the control room shaking like a leaf and waving a breathing set complete with twenty-minute duration compressed air cylinder. The black neoprene face piece dangled limply on its air line: strangely forlorn, like a redundant juju mask.

'No – *two* sets, Garilao. Wun – two . . . uno, duo?' Bert growled, sticking two fingers up at the Filipino: not without a surge of malicious satisfaction unworthy of an officer. 'You an' me, we ain't married, see? So we don't share a bed together – an' we don't share a one-man bloody breathing set *either*! An' stop panicking f'r Christ's sake! Nothing's likely to happen.'

'One Bee Yaye is *all*, Turd Jesus. On'y *find* uno wono . . .'

'Don't be bloody ridicul . . .'

Something sparked in Bert's memory then. He snatched for the watch orders attached to the clipboard now providing a handy teapot stand, and began to thumb through their pages desperately. When he eventually found it, the memo from Second Engineer Dana had been quite specific . . . that instruction which Bert's preceding watchkeeper, Third Engineer Hellström, hadn't bothered to do anything about. And that Stamper himself had merely glanced at before ignoring it in a fit of weary disillusionment.

Seemed the Second had taken all but one stand-by breathing set from the engine room BA locker yesterday afternoon, to recharge and test them. The compressor required for that function was situated in the CO_2 inerting systems control room at the top of the ship on H deck – along with, it now transpired, the engine room's other three escape sets which *should* have been uplifted and returned below to ensure their availability in the – okay, admittedly unlikely – event of an emergency occurring overnight . . .

Give him his due, Bert didn't panic like his watch assistant seemed set on doing.

Not simply by virtue of a largely administrative oversight.

He wasn't allowed time to. Because it was then that Garilao's already frightened eyes opened wide as the bottom of a Tiger Beer bottle, and the little Filipino began to wave speechlessly, frantically, at something above Bert's head.

When Stamper swung to look up, suddenly gripped by a surge of unreasoning fear the like of which he'd thought never to experience, he saw an apparently solid jet of smoke discharging from a ventilation blower into the control room where they stood.

When he eventually whirled back to gaze in foreboding through the window overlooking the main engine room, he heard somebody explode, 'Awww, Jesus Christ!' and guessed the half-prayer must've come from himself, considering it was hardly the first expression one would expect to trip off the tongue of a Muslim as devout as Motorman Teofisto Garilao.

Bert stared in growing horror as his engine room grew darker by the second. Watched the invading smoke drift to dim the brilliance of the overhead lights: a seemingly suspended dark grey veil, undulating at its base while spreading steadily to mask the white-painted deckheads, already sealing off the watchkeepers' escape route with suffocating efficiency. Stamper didn't know whether it was the suction from the engines drawing gases from somewhere higher in the ship, overcoming the marginally greater air pressure in the engine room, or smoke being pulled down through the ventilation system itself . . .

The Klaxon-type alarms went off suddenly, terrifyingly! Drowning even the rumble of the engines and the high-revving roar from the GSP and the fire pumps.

Garilao began to sob.

'So *now* you fuckin' tell us!' Third Engineer Stamper raged, directing his resentment up past the smoke to the upper deck world of useless seaman officers and comparative safety and fresh air, and of stars in the sky above.

But that was only because he realized that the time for him to act as a man of initiative had passed. Now he had to become a magician.

It was the only way he could think of to get the two of them up through maybe several decks full of suffocating gas – maybe even super-heating gas, which would call for a *bloody* fast transit through the hot spots before their clothes ignited or their eyeballs cooked or . . .

An' *that* merely summarized the easy part.

Deciding which one of them should be afforded the privilege of breathing on the way promised to be more difficult.

*   *   *

249

Another crew member fully preoccupied with retaining the useful ability to breathe at 0231 hours in the middle watch was Able Seaman Conroy.

So far the *Orion Venturer*'s night-watchman had only survived the unsurvivable atmosphere by then existing at the top of Stairway 2S because, for most of his hard life, he'd been a heavy smoker. In fact AB Conroy was proving the very antithesis of the warning on the packet. His lungs and bloodstream were so used to absorbing, as a matter of course, many of the noxious and potentially lethal compounds common both to tobacco smoke and to those given off by the burning plastic, that he didn't suffer quite the same degree of instantly immobilizing toxic shock suffered by the fire's more health-conscious victims.

. . . that, and the fact that, while in his concussed state, Conroy had collapsed prone and face down. One scorched cheek was pressed hard against the deck where some breathable air still existed, for a depth of a few inches, even in sections of corridor where the concentrations of carbon monoxide and hydrogen cyanide were at their highest.

Maybe it was the pain of his flash burns; maybe it was the distant clamour of the alarm bells that finally roused him. Or maybe it was the swelling chorus of people retching and coughing as they turned out, most of them half-asleep and few of them realizing what was happening, into the poisonous miasma which had enveloped the after end of E deck starboard side within fourteen minutes of the fire's developing from a spark trapped inside a bed sheet.

Whatever it was, Conroy came round to find hisself not knowing *where* he wus, with a singing in his ears an' a splitting headache worse than any 'e'd had since the las' time he got throwed out o' Bangalore Pete's bar in . . . ?

'Gawd!'

He remembered then!

The AB could hear the flames now roaring out of the stairwell almost directly above him: *feel* the heat grilling the back of what was left of his woolly pully. Cautiously opening one eye he saw . . . well, perhaps *didn't* see wus more accurate . . . that the visibility around him was less than the length of his extended arm. He knew he only had to lift his head a fraction and he'd immediately trigger

the countdown to his own death, so he'd better 'ave a plan afore
he went for it – a bloody good plan!

Conroy couldn't think of one.

So he took a long, tentative breath . . . felt the acrid smoke draw
down to the deck an' catch the back of his throat any-bloody-way,
instantly precipitating a bout of convulsive hacking worse than he
regularly experienced on lighting up first thing in the morning.

Clawing to his feet, capitalizing on his natural seaman's faculty
for sensing direction in the ship, Conroy forced himself to stumble
forrard blindly towards reception, feeling along the corridor wall
as he went. Around him – not far from him – he could hear the
nightmare sounds of people dying even above the muted ringing
of the alarms . . . his foot caught in something soft and Conroy fell
to his knees with a sob – there was a body under him. A very
small body . . .

'Aw Jesus! Jus' a kid, it 'ad to be . . . ?'

The AB tried to pick up William Miles, but couldn't. He was
starting to pass out again, the gases beginning to block the supply
of oxygen to his brain . . . he made one last futile attempt to grab
hold of the child's dressing gown an' drag the tiny feller but by
then Conroy couldn't muster the strength to even . . .

A terrible rage – a contempt for all owners, ship managers, all
officers . . . all useless bloody FOC ships' crews wot di'n't know
their port sides from their soddin' midships, suffused Conroy. He
wusn't frightened of dyin' but by *God* he couldn't *stand* . . .

Where's the Mate . . . ? Where's the fuckin' fire party?

. . . the cabin door swung inwards soon as his feebly extended
arm brushed the handle. He sort of half-fell, half collapsed through
it before, with superhuman effort, contriving to push it closed
again behind him.

Conroy did wish he'd had enough strength left to haul the little
feller in with him, even though it wouldn't have done no good.
He knew he hadn't gained more than an extra few minutes of life
for hisself f'r that matter, but all of a sudden them few minutes
seemed enormously precious.

Odd, really. Proper contrary. For a bloke who'd spent most of
his fifty-odd previous years complainin' about its vicissitudes.

Once Conroy had got back some of what little breath he'd been able to muster even before the fire, and rubbed some o' the sting from his streaming eyes, he discovered he was flopped with his shoulders against the door of an inside four-berth passenger cabin. One of the bunk lights was switched on an' he could see it had already been abandoned, thank God. Whoever formerly occupied this one hadn't hung around. Had 'ad the sense to take it on their toes . . . ?

He knuckled his eyes again – this time savagely, and with a terrible fear dawning within him for what he thought he'd seen.

The little girl in the pink dressing gown, sitting with her knees drawn up and hugging a dilapidated teddy bear, was watching him silently through big, brown, utterly trusting eyes.

Now, normally, if there wus one thing Conroy couldn't *stand* it wus kids . . . an' especially kids aboard ships.

. . . except this wusn't normal. And anyway, she wasn't hardly a ship no more, with the fire consuming her guts. And the child didn't look like a monster: she looked more like a . . . well, like an angel. A beautiful, delicate angel.

Just f'r a moment Conroy began to wonder if 'e hadn't died out there in that smoke, an' gone up to heaven? Then reflected sadly, bitterly, that, considerin' the circumstances, only the most exquisitely cruel contrivance of all the demons in hell could burden a man with as much pain: such anguish as he felt for that sweet infant who gazed down upon him so reliantly.

'Hello,' the angel said.

''Allo, little girl,' Able Seaman Conroy croaked. 'Wot . . . what's your name then?'

'Lucy. Lucy Miles. And he's Teddy Miles.'

She waggled the stuffed bear and one of his eyes fell out.

'. . . but sometimes my daddy calls him Nelson.'

''Allo, Teddy,' Conroy managed faintly, trying to believe this wasn't happening. Not now. Not the way things were turning out. Not with only minutes to go before the smoke inevitably found it way into the cabin.

Or worse – *much* worse . . . the flames.

CATACLYSM

Phase Three

Had it been humanly feasible for Captain Halvorsen to obtain a full report on the status of his command at that moment, it would have made for bleak digestion.

It would have indicated that even then, within sixteen minutes of her being stricken by one of her own passengers, it was unlikely that he or any other shipmaster would be able to do anything to forestall the Orion Venturer's inevitable destruction.

On decks A and B below her waterline, smoke had begun to permeate the foreparts of the now gradually slowing ferry, forced down companionways by the headwind still driving into open ventilating ducts.

That smoke was thin: drifting in barely detectable concentrations through her living and service spaces while, even in alleyways, only serving to accelerate those crew members – mostly catering staff – berthed down there who suddenly found themselves awakened by the clamouring of totally unfamiliar alarms. Enough to scare the daylights out of anyone abruptly roused to the smell of it, but insufficient to cause them to do more than either get dressed sharpish and evacuate or, in rather too many cases, just evacuate an' the hell with propriety.

No crew persons on A and B decks would find themselves in immediate danger. Adequate escape routes to the upper decks existed in the fore sections of the vessel. All they had to do was find them.

. . . other than in the engine room, into which vast quantities of smoke were still being drawn by a voracious demand for air to

253

feed the ferry's powerful twin engines and auxiliaries, and where Third Engineer Stamper and Motorman Garilao were currently confronted by the decision as to which of them should continue to breathe in it.

One level higher in Conroy's wedding cake, on C deck just above the waterline, the temperature at the seat of the blaze had reached 700 degrees Centigrade by twenty-eight minutes to three in the morning.

Virtually every combustible surface was burning, including the face of the fire door left closed by Manley and Lucchetti. Fire had entered all unoccupied cabins along that starboard corridor aft of the door.

The hottest spot in the *Orion Venturer* was now the interior of Cabin C313, where plastic containers of painter's spirit instantly melted, permitting their contents to further fuel the fire. Cans of oil paint had also begun to explode, adding to the holocaust.

On the deck itself, almost submerged in a sea of roaring liquid flame, lay two pressurized bottles of welding oxygen. In the midst of that highly efficient crematory were stowed a further four acetylene gas cylinders, propped vertically against the ship's side and originally secured in place by Able Seaman Madariaga with stout manila rope. The rope no longer existed, although the heavy cylinders still remained vertical, tenuously defying the movement of the ship.

As the acetylene cylinders heated, so their dissolved gas contents expanded and became thermodynamically unstable. They would autoignite once the temperature inside the bottles touched 325°C. Already they had become ultra-sensitive to shock and pressure.

Each bottle was only part full . . . their most volatile and dangerous condition of all.

The fire had, by then, also overwhelmed and eaten into the starboard after compartments on D deck immediately above. One of those compartments housed the ship's automatic telephone exchange. Its incineration explained why Third Engineer Stamper had been so mysteriously disconnected from Second Officer Delucci, and why no one else could tell anyone else what was – or more crucially, wasn't – happening.

All twelve passengers berthed on that level were far beyond aid even before the fire alarms had gone off at 2.31 a.m. They'd included the pyromaniacal Carlssen's first victim, African salesman Kumbweza Munyenyembe, and Irish driver Garret Ó'Leary who had slipped into oblivion after going back to sleep thinking wistfully on of the amber liquid bounty which had been entrusted to his care. Nine other truckers had died in much the same manner as he: a company he would have approved of, because Ó'Leary had been nothing if not a sociable man when unfettered by the professional need for sobriety on the morrow.

Poor recently wedded Gertrud Gustafsson had been afforded no such companionship: no one to hold and comfort her in her final uncomprehending moments. Such unselfish commitment to their so joyously consummated marriage by her young husband wouldn't have prevented her dying, but it might have made it a little less distressing, a little more bearable if Lennart had elected to stay with Gertrud instead of abandoning her as he did.

As it happened, reacting instantly to the tug of love and trying to help her evacuate the corridor – a perfectly feasible response from Lennart at the time had he kept his head and stayed low – would ultimately have proved the kinder option for him too, even had he failed in such gallant endeavour.

Because all his faint heart achieved in the end was to condemn him to die, equally alone but in infinitely greater agony and terror when the fire eventually breached his cabin to consume him as cruelly as it had consumed Carlsson. Before the concentration of toxic substances in Lennart Gustafsson's blood, frustrated from entering in advance of the flames by the rug he'd crammed under the door, had been afforded time to despatch him into merciful unconsciousness.

... but then, many of the *Orion Venturer*'s passengers on that night would recoil instinctively on sighting the smoke: retreat instantly to the illusory sanctuary of their cabins and so forfeit their only chance for survival. Every professional fire-fighter is aware that, while people will run even through flame if they believe a chance for escape beckons from the other side, all too often they cannot bring themselves to breach the psychological barrier of thick smoke.

The proof of the fact was being enacted throughout E deck and, to a lesser extent, throughout all the upper levels of the burning ro-ro even while Captain Halvorsen, remote on his bridge and with all communication links severed at the most crucial moment, still awaited absolute confirmation that his ship was on fire.

Even before Chief Officer McCulloch arrived pell-mell at the bottom of the main staircase leading from the retail area on F deck, he already knew more than his Captain. As he'd passed the duty-free shop he'd been confronted by people running from the Admiral's Lounge shouting 'Fire!' or *'Feuer!'* or *'Brand!'* or *'Incendie!'*

A shocked appraisal through the double doors revealed others evacuating onto the open recreation deck aft, where the swimming pool was located. Quickly registering that the smoke, congregating thickest on the starboard side of the lounge, was originating from further down in the ship, McCulloch bellowed 'Everybody get out on deck . . . !' only to find his advice somewhat unnecessary as he was carried bodily astern for a few paces by a surging mass of escapees.

The Mate tried to lift his walkie-talkie to his mouth but it was struck from his hand almost immediately to disappear under the crowding feet. *If I try an' pick it up*, he thought desperately, *I'm going to cause one hell of a pile-up, with me underneath . . .*

Fighting clear of the press he found himself the only one heading below, once more stemming a mass of passengers intent on reaching the upper decks. McCulloch wasn't aware of it then, but they were almost all from the forward sleeping sections: those – perhaps the more nervous – who'd reacted instantly to the alarms. Some hadn't even delayed to prepare for the bitter cold of the upper decks. Many were in varying stages of undress . . . one young woman apparently wore only a pair of flimsy briefs supplemented by a man's coat thrown over her shoulders. Another, older, man had gone so far as to meticulously knot a tie around his neck before slipping into a tweed jacket – but had overlooked the usefulness of trousers in his haste . . . panic hung in the air, tangible as the smell of smoke now becoming ever more acrid in the Mate's nostrils as he descended to the reception area.

He came upon a crewman dressed in the maroon waistcoat of a duty bar steward, urging passengers upwards from the half-landing: a hardly neccessary function in the circumstances. The man looked scared but at least he wasn't leading the stampede.

McCulloch shouted above the alarms, 'Run up to the bridge – tell the Captain we probably have fire starboard side aft, at least as far down as D deck. Get him to shut down all ventilation in those sect . . .'

'*Perdão, Senhor?*'

'*Jesus!*' McCulloch yelled. 'Il Capitano bloody *pronto* laddie! Incendio . . . ! Ventilaçao makee kaput – ventilaçao arrow, ul?'

'*Sim, Senhor* . . . I go *com pressa*. I hurry.'

'Good man.' The Mate forced a smile of reassurance he most certainly didn't feel, then descended the last flight to reception at a run – only to halt again in utter horror.

Across the width of the ferry, black smoke was now billowing from all three longitudinal corridors serving the after sleeping sections of E deck, dense and filling from the starboard alley, becoming less prolific from centre and port. A thickening haze was already drifting across the foyer; eight or nine passengers in night attire coughed convulsively by the Purser's desk . . . another, seemingly a youth, lay inert under the smoke pouring from E starboard.

Even as McCulloch stared uncomprehendingly, thinking over and over again *This can't be happening: this CAN'T be happ* . . . more escapees: three men – a young girl . . . a woman clasping a baby with a wet towel wrapped around its tiny head – stumbled retching from the port alleyway: blundering and reeling with tight-closed, tear-streaming eyes . . .

. . . but where the hell were the rest of the passengers who'd been berthed back there? Where the hell, f'r that matter, was the crew . . . ?

Chief Officer McCulloch, having done his best to plan for a crisis despite being denied time and support to complete the task efficiently, now found himself participating in a runaway nightmare. He didn't *know* how many travellers still remained fearful in their cabins awaiting rescue from that suffocating fog . . .

A thickening shadow in the smoke of the central corridor and one of the Junior Pursers emerged, half-supporting, part-dragging an elderly woman. McCulloch ran to help and between them they assisted her clear. The purser, a girl – McCulloch hardly knew any of the recently joined hotel services staff – was panting and severely distressed herself. She stared at him through shock-dilated eyes, her uniform shirt grimed and dishevelled although McCulloch noted, absently, that her lipstick was immaculate.

'How many still back there?' the Mate shouted, dreading her response.

'Hundred, sir . . . hundred and fifty . . . ?' Marianne answered simply, in a very controlled voice. Then began to sob.

The alarms continued to clamour. More escapees began to emerge, largely from the central and port side corridors, many with coats or wet towels wrapped around their faces. McCulloch realized with a glimmer of hope that only two or three minutes had actually passed since the alarms first sounded – that people were still able to move back there; that others might be finding their way aloft through the after escape routes leading to the mooring and recreation decks.

'I'm going for BA sets. Don't go back in there – direct anyone who can make it up the main staircase.'

He ran forward to the fire room on the port side and grabbed two breathing sets from their stowage. On returning to the foyer he felt inordinately grateful to see Frank Trøjborg and Second Purser Jimmy Everard arriving at the run along with one of the Danish engineer officers – Hellström? All evinced the same initial reaction as he when they first ground to a halt . . . they simply couldn't comprehend the speed with which the smoke had built up.

'I need a volunteer,' McCulloch said, pointedly handing one set to Hellström. The engineer grinned wryly, shakily, and began to shrug into the shoulder harness.

'What the hell was Cardoso doin' – an' where *is* he?' Everard, still in shock, snarled at Nørgaard. She shook her head weakly, indicating the starboard corridor into which she'd last seen the little night cabins steward disappearing, then walked away abruptly

258

to kneel beside the casualty on the deck. She saw from the suffused features that he was dead even before she felt for a pulse. One of her tears landed on the young man's already waxen cheek. It was the only apology she could offer.

'Doesn't matter now. C'mon, Jimmie,' the Purser said calmly. 'Start kicking on doors. Many as we can . . .'

McCulloch hurriedly tested the low-pressure alert whistle on his own BA, then shrugged into it with Hellström, ready suited, manoeuvring the air cylinder cradle onto his back. Neither of them realized the bottle was only part-full. He'd unscrewed the valve and was holding the face mask with both hands, ready to slip over his head, already breathing in the plastic smell of silicone and bottled air, when two more crewmen arrived on the scene, this time from *below*. Stumbling up the central stairway from D deck. They were both black – Mess Cook Henry Manley and Pantry Rating Lucchetti.

There was no need to enquire where they'd come from.

'How bad?' the Mate asked.

'Bad, sir,' Manley said. 'Everythin's burning from Two C aft along the starboard quarter.'

'Any chance of a fire party getting down there?'

'We *was* the fuckin' fire party!' Henry Manley winced, picking tentatively at the skin peeling from his forearms.

'Get up to the bridge. Report on the situation. Tell 'em only God knows how far the fire's spread below, but one thing's f'r sure – we're well into Condition Red!'

The Mate slipped the mask on and listened to his own harsh breathing. He nodded grimly to Hellström and together they moved cumbersomely towards the poisoned cloud filling the starboard corridor. Without trained support, without a plan, without cohesion or direction there seemed little more he could do.

Chief Officer McCulloch knew then that the ship, and his career, were already finished.

One minute later, and four decks above, the *Orion Venturer*'s Master finally received the first confirmation, other than by electronic means, that his command was indeed in grave hazard.

As soon as the alarms had begun to sound he'd moved quickly to the open starboard wing to observe the ferry's after decks for himself. Almost immediately he had observed smoke pouring from both big ventilators aft on the funnel deck – unmistakable as such now even against the darkness: turbulent grey-black clouds whirling astern, under-lit by the halogen deck lights before being snatched and then obliterated by the wind.

As Halvorsen, sick at heart, ran back into the wheelhouse he found it filling with anxious crew members, some still temporarily night-blind, all seeking the information he could not offer them. The two watch-below Second Mates, Sandalwell and Pert; Second Engineer Dana – who, for that matter, might have been better employed in finding his way down to his emergency station in the engine room . . . Five or six stewards or seamen: two already wearing lifejackets, hovering nervously in the background . . . Quartermaster Madariaga at the wheel, holding the slowly coasting ferry to her original heading – but *why* did the pony-tailed AB look so damned uneasy? He was in the safest place aboard, wasn't he, assuming such a description could apply to any part of a burning ship . . .

The Captain felt inordinately relieved when he made out ETO Talbot standing calmly by the radio fit – no need for a technical expert now to interrogate the veracity of the warning lights still bleeping urgently on the fire board . . . and too late for the refinement of a PAN pre-warning.

'We do have fire aft, Mister Talbot! Initiate a full distress – our position's on your clipboard.'

'Aye, aye, Cap'n,' Talbot said, cool as if he'd been acknowledging an instruction to change a light bulb. He triggered GMDSS transmission over the International Safety and Calling frequency and began to enunciate carefully, in measured tones that belied the gravity of the message's import.

'*Mayday – Mayday – Mayday! This is Passenger Ferry Orion Venturer, Orion Venturer, Orion Venturer: call sign . . .*'

Meanwhile 2/O Delucci had been pinned, swearing in angry frustration, at the emergency console during the minutes since the fire board indicators had gone mad. Incredibly the *Orion Venturer's* alarm could only be operated by continuous manual pressure on the button – there was no simple switching system incorporated to enable even the bloody fire bells to sound automatically!

Seven short periods – one long . . . seven short: one long . . . seven short fuckin' stabs – one long . . . !

A key officer rendered impotent for want of a fingertip. In the climate of inaction that still existed on the bridge no one thought to take over the mundane task from him. The Captain never thought to order it so – not immediately . . . not even Delucci himself thought to delegate, even though there were plenty of adequately qualified and otherwise unoccupied fingers available to relieve him for more – should that have been *less*? – pressing duties.

Yet it isn't a complex element of crew training, really – holding down a button. It doesn't require fluency in nine languages to do it. Pressing buttons isn't listed as a necessary examination skill to acquire a certificate of competence in sea survival under *Chapter VI, Regulation VI/1 of the STCW Convention* . . . doesn't even rate a mention in the *Convention on the Safety of Life at Sea (SOLAS) Chapter II, Regulation 10, subsections Three and Four* . . . .

. . . but *utterly* vital to any passenger still asleep anywhere on the ferry's E deck at twenty-five minutes to three on that terrible morning, while the majority of her officers and crew milled around in various parts of ship wondering what to do next, and which of them would do it.

'. . . on fire aft. Approximately five hundred passengers – I say again, five hundred . . . figures fife zero zero passenger – and one hundred crew on board. Request immediate assistan . . .'

A steward in a maroon waistcoat appeared from somewhere, shouldering unhappily through the gathering silhouettes.

'Capitão, Capitão! Incendio feroz – D deck *estibordo . . . Senhor* Mack-Kullock he say *ventilação* you sweetch off *rapido, sim . . . ?'*

'Hvor er . . . where is Mister McCulloch now?'

'E deck, *Senhor. Muito fumo –* much smoke. *Passageiros* they . . .'

The steward ran out of vocabulary and drew an extended index finger across his throat in a chilling mime which needed no translation.

Halvorsen whirled. 'Mister Sandalwell?'

'Sir?'

'Start shutting down the ventilation on the starboard side of ship. Close all secondary fire doors . . .'

A terrible contempt for his own weakness overwhelmed Jorgen Truls Halvorsen. A shame for his lack of resolution: of courage. Above all, of his pre-sailing willingness to place expediency before honour. To permit commercial pressures to blind him to his responsibilities as a shipmaster to those who were in his charge.

Mayday Orion Venturer, Orion Venturer, Orion Venturer – this is Tjøme Radio, Tjøme Radio, Tjøme Radio. Received Mayday . . . Rescue Co-ordination Centre Sola is appointed to handle your emergency . . . All Ships – All Ships – All Ships stand by for distress traffic . . .

The Captain heard himself calling as if from a distance: 'Mister Delucci – have someone else do that, for *God's* sake! Take Second Officer Pert with you. Collect as many hands as you can without drawing them from evacuation or fire limitation duties below, and begin lowering the boats to embarkation level. Ensure all liferafts are clear to launch . . .'

He felt the pains – unbearable pains – again in his chest.

'Prepare to abandon when ordered to.'

CHAPTER TWENTY-SEVEN

Most of those who managed to escape from the interior of the ship did so without help. There is no doubt that a large number of the people on decks 4 and 5 were completely dependent on physical help or directions in order to get out. It was difficult to find one's way. Closed fire doors made it even more difficult, and so did the signs, which were deficient and in some cases misleading. Exit routes led into blind ends if turns were missed . . . a considerable number of bodies were [later] found in areas of corridor that showed that they had lost their way.

> Norwegian Official Report, NOR 1991: 1E
> The *Scandinavian Star* Disaster of 7 April 1990

The always slender window of escape effectively closed for anyone who hadn't already evacuated the after sections of E deck within eight minutes of the first smoke reaching the top of Stairway 2S.

Nearly half the occupants of those cabins – over a hundred persons in all – had made no attempt to leave in that period. Some because they hadn't heard the alarms; others, sadly, because they were unable to move without assistance; all too many more choosing to await specific guidance from the ferry's crew, a response which was already proving fatal.

The lesson being demonstrated was both simple and cruel. Unless instructions to the contrary are given over the public address system, it is never prudent to remain below in a ship once the audible alarms have sounded, although, in doing so, those who did elect to stay put aboard the *Orion Venturer* simply duplicated the reactions shown by forty-six per cent of passengers in other, similar, shipboard emergencies.

Ironically, Captain Halvorsen's reluctance to endorse Second

Officer Delucci's shutting down the ventilation throughout the ro-ro before making his own assessment of the situation did, despite flying in the face of recommended fire limitation practice, actually succeed in saving several lives, although the Captain would never become aware of that totally inadequate consolation.

For, while the blowers forcing fresh air into cabins had been left to function, they continued to maintain an over-pressure within. That over-pressure prevented smoke from seeping unsuspected below doors into spaces where occupants had not instantly been roused by the alert. Some were afforded vital extra seconds in which to surface from sleep and – if they were numbered among the statistical 54% of passengers who *did* make the right decision – depart.

But then, statistics are only statistics. They are not an absolute guarantee of safe passage. Not even assuming the atmosphere welcoming the more tardy escapees turning out into the corridors was still capable, by then, of sustaining life.

Because sometimes, as Chief Officer McCulloch had already been given cause to reflect earlier in the voyage, *The best laid schemes o' mice an' men gang aft a'gley.*

. . . which must surely prove that Robert Burns, as well as William Shakespeare, knew all about ship fires.

Take the case of Herr Neugebauer, for instance.

When Herr Neugebauer awoke to the subdued ringing of alarms, he most certainly didn't delay. He slipped instantly from his berth, donned his steel-rimmed spectacles, and crossed quickly to the cabin door to investigate.

There was a lot of smoke in the central corridor. Neugebauer closed the door pretty *schnell* and frowned. He had not found himself in such a personal pickle as this since he had been faced with the problem of how to engineer the interment of his dearest Trudi so that nobody would notice he had first strangled her then cut her quite exquisite throat.

Remembering his previous morning's constitutional in the teeth of the German Ocean wind, Herr Neugebauer debated briefly on whether to change from his negli . . . well, from his somewhat unconventional gentleman's sleepwear into something less diaphanous: some cladding more appropriate to face both the inclement conditions and the ribald sailory he anticipated one might encounter on the upper decks. He decided against wasting time, preferring to survive rather than pander to the crude prejudices of those with inflexibly conformist standards, and settled for slipping his Harris tweed coat with its suede trim over his head and shoulders before kneeling on all fours, drawing a measured breath, and reaching up to open the door.

Already the visibility in the upper strata of the starboard corridor had reduced to considerably less than one metre – an internationally accepted critical value for orientation, the knowledgeable Neugebauer reflected dispassionately as he crawled, which virtually denied any assistance from overhead lighting – but happily less dense at floor level where he sensibly remained.

He was making quite excellent headway in the direction of the reception area, lowering his face to the deck every few moments to inhale just enough breathable air to sustain him in such endeavour while resolutely closing his ears to the most distressing chorus arising behind him – reminiscent in some ways of the sounds poor Trudi had emitted while he'd applied the flex of her favourite bedside lamp – when suddenly he became aware of a cabin door opening a tentative crack beside him.

'*Feuer! Räumen* . . . evacuate – *schnell!*' Neugebauer urged involuntarily before beginning to cough. It was the first mistake he'd made in his so far meticulously planned life: showing concern for others.

'*Vær* . . . Pleese? *Hvordan kommer man opp på dekket?*'

Well, it so happened that Herr Neugebauer was pretty fluent in Norwegian, working as he did as a hydraulics consultant for many Scandinavian enterprises – although his familiarity with children was rather more sketchy. He and Frau Neugebauer had never been blessed with little ones. Hardly ever tried for them, in fact, after their first few weeks together.

Just as well, perhaps. Considering . . . ?

But the frightened voice above his head, pleading for directions to the deck, was undoubtedly that of a child. He immediately recalled the party of junior school pupils from Norway. The ones

265

with the formidable blonde schoolmistress and the young man . . .

Neugebauer knew then that he couldn't abandon them. That all the calculating and planning in the world would not permit him to. To do such a callous thing would prey for ever more on his conscience . . . and if there was one thing Herr Neugebauer had always been able to pride himself on possessing, it was a crystal clear conscience.

'Quickly, boy. Open the door!' Naturally he slipped faultlessly into their language. The smoke followed him into the cabin, underlining the need for haste as he entered breathing heavily – *not* part of his original plan – and with his spectacles awry. He felt mildly irritated about the spectacles. Made him look eccentric. No wonder the four already understandably scared youngsters were staring at him so strangely.

'How many of you altogether?'

'Fourteen, *Frøk* . . . sir!'

'*Gut*. Then the rest of your friends must also live in the three cabins next door, *ja*?'

The four little boys nodded dumbly.

'And your teachers?'

The four little boys shook their heads uncertainly. During their English holiday they had become used to Miss Evenson and Mr Valle disappearing immediately after lights out to do grown-up things.

'So be it. *Gut!*' Herr Neugebauer rubbed his hands briskly. This was indeed a psychological and logistical challenge worthy of his meticulous mind. 'Then now,' he said, 've will play what I shall call the Snakes *und die* Ping-Pong balls, *ja*? We will pretend there is a forest fire, and that each of you is a wriggly snake, and that you have a little ball you like very much. But because you are a snake you have no hands, you understand? So you must push *der* ball from the forest *mit* your noses. You cannot . . . you *must* not! – lift your noses from the floor, *ja* . . . ? *Und* then you will slither, slither one behind the other, pushing your ball and keeping close to the snake in front until you see the brave firemen. And on *der* vay I will collect your friends from their cabins *und* explain to them also about this game we are playing . . .'

When more than a dozen eleven-year-old boys and girls

appeared in reception from under the smoke, crawling in a line and claiming that they were snakes pushing table tennis balls, Purser Trøjborg could hardly credit that miracles could happen even in Hell.

No more than he believed that a Chief Snake – some of the little ones said he'd been a gentleman clown; others swore she was a small fat lady with a moustache – had ever really existed other than in the collective imaginations of the luckiest children alive.

But that was because Herr Neugebauer delayed just a little too long in making his own escape. Had unwittingly permitted the poisons he'd inhaled continuously and subtly while ensuring – meticulously, of course – that all his little snakes had been evacuated from their cabins, to accumulate to incapacitating proportions before attempting, too late, to follow in their tracks.

... so no adult of either persuasion ever appeared from the smoke to disprove Purser Trøjborg's much more likely theory that some miraculous mass hallucination, probably brought about by a surfeit of anthropomorphic Disney films, had inspired the children from the Østfold to save themselves.

Although having taken a sleeping pill earlier had delayed her awakening and left her with a dry mouth and a fuzzy mind, Mrs Niskanen from Jyväskylä in Finland was another who evacuated her cabin as soon as the clamour of fire alarms penetrated her subconscious. Not, in her case, because she was ship-wise enough to be aware that her statistical prospects for survival were negligible if she didn't, so much as because she discovered, on fumbling for the berth light, that her daughter had already left.

She didn't know what was happening. All she could think of was that Heikki had seemingly been cruel enough – *indifferent* enough! – to run away without even attempting to rouse her first. How could she do such a terrible thing as to abandon her mother to . . . well, to whatever it was the ferry's officers were ringing the alarms for?

But then, Heikki had changed so much during the past few months from being a loving, if sometimes over-fanciful, child to a brooding introvert harbouring what both Mr and Mrs Niskanen considered an unhealthy absorption in luridly pseudo-romantic novels. None of the obviously difficult teenage phase she was undergoing made sense to either of them. They'd begun to fear for their daughter's health: watched apprehensively for her to evince signs of fatigue or weight loss or whatever . . . but to their enormous relief she hadn't. Quite the reverse. She'd pleasantly surprised them in recent weeks by becoming more plump and rosy-cheeked than ever . . .

Panicking as much over her daughter's disappearance as the possible reason for sounding the alarms in the first place, Mrs Niskanen became very upset while casting about for her shoes and top coat – was already sobbing, drawing great convulsive breaths of maternal distress even before she opened the door to run unheedingly into a dark, incredibly hot corridor.

The point where Heikki's mother left her cabin was close by Stairway 2S. It was in that area that the smoke had been afforded time to amass its highest concentrations of hydrogen cyanide and carbon monoxide. In addition, the burning plastic had begun to produce significant quantities of carbon dioxide by then. And carbon dioxide triggers a tendency to hyperventilate. And hyperventilating induces a more rapid intake of other gases which, in turn, ensures that a fatal dose is reached more quickly . . .

The fire had also consumed vast quantities of oxygen, sucking that most essential life-sustaining element from exit routes even as far forward in the ship as reception. And, as Chief Snake Neugebauer discovered rather too late, a lack of oxygen even further accelerates the speed of the body's uptake of toxic substances . . .

The manner of Mrs Niskanen's dying was typical of the *Orion Venturer* fire. The end came quickly and mercifully. She wasn't even given time to become aware, in the half minute before all awareness ceased, that twenty-three other souls within anguished earshot had already collapsed in the starboard corridor of E deck – eleven of those, including a four-month-old infant clasped in his father's arms, all piled together in a literal dead end which, having never been recognized as a potential hazard since it was first prescribed on a designer's drawing board nearly thirty years before, continued a full three metres past a right-angled escape route all too easily missed by terror-fumbling hands attempting to feel their way in almost total darkness.

But at least she didn't have to worry about Heikki any more.

Although Heikki, still huddled, semi-comatose, in the lee of the lifejacket locker on the boat deck, was still conscious enough to sense that the *voudon* magic had finally begun to work. She could feel a growing discomfort within her such as she'd never imagined before. Hard to explain for a fifteen-year-old . . . the movements in her abdomen. That really *weird* sensation of periodic contraction and expansion . . . ?

It never occurred to Heikki that they were actually physiological, rather than demonological, symptoms she was experiencing. Symptoms that someone more familiar with such things would have recognized right away for the – admittedly very special – magic they heralded.

Someone like . . . well, someone like a midwife, for instance?

It must have been coincidence that Pastor Oskar Lütgendorf, who had only taken passage in the *Orion Venturer* because he'd considered travel by aeroplane too tempting of the divine providence he no longer believed in, was also about to experience a magical event.

. . . or that was the way the Pastor was content to interpret what happened, anyway.

Feeling somewhat drowsy he'd left the Admiral's Lounge just after midnight. Reluctantly so, because he'd been enjoying the impromptu concert given by the Welshmen to the accompaniment of Herr Tische at the grand piano, although he *had* harboured reservations regarding the Singing Viennese's claim to being a compatriot of his. Secretly Lütgendorf suspected that Willi's execrable pseudo-Austrian baritone smacked more of downtown Frankfurt than up-market Vienna.

But then, being a tolerant man by vocation, to say nothing of possessing a wry sense of humour by nature, he fully appreciated the entertainer's reticence to bill himself as *Die Singwurst*.

He might just as well have stayed to see the concert out. Listened entranced, as Morgan Evans and his fellow choristers added their own touch of vocal magic to 'Myfanwy' and 'Men of Harlech' because, ultimately, he'd only lain wide awake and questioning the loss of his faith anyway, as he'd done on so many anguished nights before. Simply wrestling with the insoluble conundrum of whether God had abandoned him, or had he abandoned God?

Yet was the insoluble really so unsolvable . . . ?

Perhaps the troubled Pastor Lütgendorf came a little closer to the truth – to learning who had actually deserted who – in the terrifying moment when the fire alarms went off . . . ? Perhaps, for that matter, he really *did* experience divine intervention at precisely 0231 hours in the Middle Watch in the middle of the North Sea? Perhaps he *was* pre-positioned by some greater Power in order that he could minister to those who already slept under the path of the advancing Shadow of the Valley of Death . . . ?

Even though he didn't immediately recognize the eighty-decibel clarion call as such . . . ?

Certainly it would be impossible for even the most sceptical to deny that – unlike the majority of those who had retired to their cabins on E deck in advance of Carlsson's turning the *Orion Venturer* into an all-too-realistic approximation of Hell – only the constant presence of God in the thoughts of Pastor Lütgendorf had kept him alert and thus instantly able to react on comprehending that something grave had occurred.

It inspired him to be the first passenger to emerge into the central corridor aft of the properly closed fire door. Even then the smoke had begun its remorseless spread through the cross-alleyways from starboard Stairway 2S to crawl and undulate and swallow those cabins located towards the ro-ro's stern. Unquestionably, if it hadn't been for Lütgendorf's having been charged by *some* benign influence to run forward, hammering on doors and shouting '*Raus!* Get *out* . . . *Feuer*! Hurry! *Beeilung* . . . leave your cabin . . . !' then twenty, thirty more souls might well have perished under the poisonous miasma.

When he himself reached reception, coughing and pushing and chivvying his still-dazed flock, he was confronted by a scene of utter confusion. In that wide space the bells were deafening. Smoke was now vomiting from the starboard corridor: a rolling pall creeping across the ceiling, beginning to diffuse even the bright lights of the foyer. Passengers were still leaving the forward part of ship, many resolute and controlled, others stare-eyed and verging on panic as they emerged to be harried up the central stairway to F deck by a male and a female night steward who, themselves, cast apprehensive glances towards the source of the fire.

Oskar Lütgendorf caught a brief glimpse of two ship's officers wearing breathing apparatus moving awkwardly, unfamiliarly, into the pall that hung at the entrance to the starboard after corridor ... another two men he recognized as pursers assisting hunched, distraught escapees from the smoke now coming from even the *port* corridor, dear God! And a young woman – another officer: only a girl with her blonde hair in tangles and the epaulettes awry on her grimed, once-white shirt kneeling, desperately attempting to revive people – whether living or dead the Pastor could not tell – lying black-faced and inert where they had collapsed ...

Where were the rest of the ferry's *crew*?

No hoses – no fire teams! No organized attempt to ... ?

Lütgendorf raced to help Everard with a boy – thirteen, fourteen years old? – the Assistant Purser had dragged clear of the smoke. The youngster emitted a ghastly, croaking rattle and stopped breathing even as the two of them bent over him. 'Aw Jesus, *Jesus, Jesus* ... !' the young officer kept repeating until the fumes got to him and he turned away to vomit.

With trembling fingers Oskar Lütgendorf tilted the casualty's head backwards to clear his airway then, pinching the already bluing nostrils while sealing his mouth around the boy's, administered two inflations before feeling quickly inside the relaxed mouth. It seemed clear of obstruction ... the child still wasn't breathing ... the Pastor administered fifteen – he thought ... *hoped* it was fifteen as his training had taught him? – chest compressions, then cupped the boy's lips again ...

'I got him,' Everard said, spitting then continuing with the chest. '*Wun* and ... TWO, an' ... *thuree* and ... FOUR an' ...'

Our Father which art in heaven ...

... thirteen ... fourteen ... FIFTEEN breaths! Or should that have been five ... ?

Hallowed be Thy name ...

Chief Purser Trøjborg staggered over looking bleak. He wore his uniform jacket over pyjamas. 'We're going to have to withdraw soon . . .'

'He's breathin',' Jimmy Everard suddenly echoed in a surprised voice. 'He's fuckin' well *breathing* . . . !'

'Thy will be *done*, Lord!' Pastor Lütgendorf cried gratefully aloud through his tears, knowing then, beyond any doubt at all, that he could only have been placed aboard that ship for a purpose.

There were bizarre moments.

For instance, the last person to continue searching the lethal maze of the *Orion Venturer*'s ill-fated E deck without the aid of breathing apparatus was Portuguese Cabins Night Steward Cardoso.

But if anyone had been determined to make amends for his previous inadequacies it was little Pinheiro. Alone in the semi-darkness, constantly retching and blundering through an atmosphere that was killing people around him, he must have been responsible for alerting several of those who would otherwise have perished.

One cabin's occupant *wouldn't* respond to his frantic knocking. Fumbling for his master key, the first – and last – trip steward eventually inserted it in the door and fell across the threshold . . . *Graças a Deus!* His persistence had been rewarded – there was an unconscious form still prone in the lower berth within the dark space.

Without even switching on the light Cardoso summoned the last of his strength to manhandle the inert body to the deck before dragging it into the corridor, then, gathering the passenger's weight . . . it was a man . . . staggered in a state of near collapse himself to the blessed, if only comparative, safety of the reception foyer where he sagged in the arms of no less than the Comandante Comissário de Bordo himself.

'Bloody hell!' the Comandante said when he recognized Cardoso's stiffly unco-operative burden.

'Bloody *hell*!' Second Purser Everard echoed faintly as the smoke swirled round and the alarms still clamoured and people still streamed up the central staircase behind them. 'He's saved Mister *Smith.*'

'You knows heem?' Pinheiro summoned weakly.

'Not well,' Trøjborg conceded. 'Not really. Not considerin' he died yesterday.'

CATACLYSM

Phase Four

Mayday Relay, Mayday Relay, Mayday Relay – This is Tjøme Radio, Tjøme Radio, Tjøme Radio – Mayday . . . Ro-ro Ferry Orion Venturer on fire. Approximately six hundred persons on board. Requires immediate assistance . . .

Distress traffic over VHF Channel 16, frequency 156.8 MHz, is call-queuing in the Skaggerak by O236 GMT.

Mayday – Orion Venturer, Orion Venturer, Orion Venturer – this is German Warship Vorderst. Vorderst . . . We are proceeding full speed. Our passage time fifty-seven minutes. Figures fife sayven – fünf sieben – minuten . . .

'This is *Venturer* – Roger. Out.'

Brief. Professional. Unemotional. Another station comes up with a hiss. 'Thank God,' the Captain thinks, 'for ETO Talbot's calm handling.'

Mayday – Venturer, Ferry Orion Venturer – American Cruise Ship Sea Maiden . . . hers must be the lights hull down to the north? Good morning, Sir. Our speed twenty-eight knots. We see your loom and are making for you. ETA zero thuree four zero. Over.

'Roger – Out!'

Mayday – Orion Venturer . . . All Ships: this is Rescue Co-ordination Centre Sola, RCC Sola . . . German Warship Vorderst will assume responsibilities of On Scene Commander on arrival the casualty. OSC to co-ordinate evacuation if required. Søværnets Operative Kommando – Danish naval operational command – advise Super Puma rescue helicopter 278 scrambled. Two Norwegian Sea Kings with medical teams from Torp air base also en route. MRCC Göteborg will despatch smoke diving personnel by helo soonest . . .

Such reassurance from the ether is already too late for many who, only some eighteen hours previously, had taken passage in the Roll-on Roll-off Combined Vehicle and Passenger Ferry *Orion Venturer*.

CHAPTER TWENTY-EIGHT

The Captain received no information about whether the various emergency plan groups had been mobilized, nor did he ask for any . . . No attempt was made at any time to obtain information in an organized way. No crew members made use of walkie-talkies [although] there were a number on board, some on the bridge, others in crew cabins.

Norwegian Official Report, NOR 1991: 1E
The *Scandinavian Star* Disaster of 7 April 1990

When the *Orion Venturer's* momentum finally diminished to a gentle slide through the water, she immediately became prey to the wind and began to weathercock. With her high bow profile and forward top-hamper acting as a vast headsail, the ferry's stem blew away to port as, ever so slowly at first, she started to pivot through one hundred and eighty degrees to present her stern to the brisk easterly blowing straight down the Sleeve from Sweden.

Quartermaster Madariaga, temporarily shelving his secret anxiety over what lay in Cabin C313, tried to meet her – applied full starboard wheel. She continued to veer off course as the gyro repeater above him ticked off the ship's changing heading.

'*Perdido gobierno, Capitán* . . . I lose steerage way,' he called urgently with the spokes hard over, the rudder indicator brought up against its stop without effect.

'Thank you, Quartermaster.'

Halvorsen delayed a moment on the open wing where he'd been reduced to pacing in frustration while bleakly observing the desperate activity on the boat deck. It seemed that, second by second, more and more escapees – some already gratefully bulky in orange lifejackets, others shrugging uncertainly into more now

276

being produced from deck lockers – were arriving to swell an already aimlessly milling crowd.

Clearly little attempt had been made to muster passengers at the designated emergency stations within the shelter of the accommodation, although the Captain suspected those areas must be untenable by now anyway. He could see smoke spilling through the open doors of the night club and, in even greater volume, from the after end of the Admiral's Lounge, spreading and twirling in wind-fretted clouds above the open recreation deck around the decommissioned swimming pool.

He had hesitated because he'd just recognized the formidable bulk of Bosun Pascal, accompanied by Christofides, the *Venturer's* Greek Cypriot carpenter, pushing through the press of bodies to where Second Officer Delucci, the only seaman officer on the starboard side, directed preparations for abandoning: grimly chivvying a group of plainly uncomprehending hands into lowering number one lifeboat to the level of the rails.

That arrival topside of two of the ro-ro's senior petty officers – both supposedly emergency group leaders – was a further indicator of a rapidly deteriorating situation. It suggested few, if any, measures were still being taken to fight, or even limit the spread of the blaze . . . he could only assume the Mate had sent them up – which McCulloch hadn't. As with the majority of the crew, the Bosun and Carpenter's presence on the upper deck had been spurred partly by the two men's disinclination to be anywhere else in the ship, but largely by their ignorance of the whereabouts of their reporting stations under the emergency plan. Neither of them had been given time to read it; the monolingual Chippie wouldn't have been able to interpret it even if he had.

But then Halvorsen, effectively rendered impotent to either monitor or shape events by the complete breakdown of on-board communications, was unaware that only three fire hoses had been half-heartedly deployed throughout the rest of the ship by individual crew members – and even those soon forced to retreat in the face of the smoke – while the one determined attempt that had been made to form even an ad hoc fire party had come about only through an accidental alliance between a mess cook and a first trip galley rating.

On the other hand, the Captain sensed with sinking heart that a decision to abandon his ship was becoming increasingly inevitable. In that case his priorities had to change: meaning that Pascal and Christofides were in the right place. Second Officers Delucci and Pert would need all the experienced help they could muster to ready the lifecraft for evacuation . . . and that created yet another problem – deciding not only if, but when he, as Master, should issue such a final order. The nearest rescue ships were an hour distant. In such brutal weather conditions it was vital to minimize his passengers' exposure time in the open boats . . .

The Captain turned wearily to the wheelhouse, rain running from his white cap cover, diamond-twinkling drops reflecting the floodlights, to trickle unheeded inside the collar of his reefer and soak the back of his uniform shirt. There was one action he *could* take without relying on others.

'Mister Sandalwell?'

'*Sir?*'

'Put her dead slow ahead to bring us back on track, Mister Sandalwell. We must keep the smoke downwind.'

'Dead slow ahead. Aye, aye, sir,' Sandalwell answered as he moved to the combinator, calm as if they'd been docking in light airs.

Jorgen Halvorsen had always set great store by the courtesies, considering them fundamental to any shipmaster's ability to remain at a distance from his crew. Discipline and informality, in his view, made poor bedfellows in the pursuit of safe navigation. The cruellest irony was that his demeanour had itself been a cause of that high aspiration turning to dust . . . he would have been horrified to learn that his key officers had misinterpreted such aloofness – further aggravated by the barriers he'd erected to conceal his lack of resolve to stand against the owners – as criticism of their own performances to date.

Had Jorgen Truls Halvorsen been seen to be a little more approachable, then perhaps the intolerably harassed Chief Officer McCulloch, instead of being made to feel his career was on the line in preparing the ferry to sail on schedule, might have felt more ready to turn to his captain for help in preparing the emergency plan. Might even have risked pressing more forcefully for time to be allocated to resolving the on-board problems they were now suffering from. To establishing proper chains of command and communication: to crew training and familiarization with the ship – above all, to rehearsing full-scale fire and evacuation drills.

Perhaps Chief Engineer Bracamontes – of whom nothing more had been heard, and who may or may not have made it to his engine room after leaving the bridge earlier – would, instead of harrying the engineering department into working flat out on last-minute make do and mend tasks, have felt able to brief his watchkeepers more fully on what emergency actions to take without awaiting orders.

Perhaps, then, the system wouldn't have degenerated into the kind of slackness that encouraged a Second Engineer to leave potentially vital breathing sets in the wrong place when he knocked off. And caused his juniors to be so disillusioned they hadn't even bothered to carry out his orders to collect them, even then . . . ?

Perhaps, for that matter, Officer of the Watch Delucci, as the focal point for initiating a confident response at the moment when a passenger finally went mad, might have been less reluctant to take immediate measures to counter the first electronic warnings before seeking his Captain's approval.

Perhaps . . . ?

The unknown steward in the maroon waistcoat was still doggedly continuing to ring the alarms. It struck Halvorsen then that a lowly crewman, whose name he didn't even know, had so far proved of more practical value in the emergency than he himself. But: *Surely to God*, he reflected, still cushioned by his remote ignorance from the full scale of the horror of what was happening below his feet, *everyone aboard must be aware we have a problem by now?*

'Leave it, steward. I'd be obliged if you would go down and help with the boats.'

When the bells stopped, it seemed a hush fell over the ship until the ears adjusted to realizing there wasn't a silence at all. There still remained the sigh of the wind and the steady spatter of rain; the restrained murmur of voices from the upper decks broken occasionally by a sharp order; the continuing putter of idling engines from the funnel high above . . . the bang and clatter of items moving sullenly as the ferry's roll became more acute under the action of the seas already breaking obliquely on her bow . . .

The VHF crackled into life yet again.

Ferry Orion Venturer, Orion Venturer – this is Dansk skib Søløv, Søløv, Søløv . . . I am vier meile – four mile – ahead of you and am coming quick, but my radar not so well. Please you fire rocket to identify yourself . . .

Talbot's terse reply. 'Danish ship Solov, Solov – Orion Venturer. Wait one . . .' The ETO stuck his head through the door. 'I guess it makes him favourite to get here quickest, Cap'n?'

Halvorsen instinctively recoiled from the prospect. To send distress rockets into the night sky *à la Titanic* might just prove the ultimate trigger of panic among both passengers and crew. For the Captain no longer harboured any illusions regarding the quality of many of those he so tenuously commanded. On the other hand, the Dane – the *Sealion* – was indeed the closest vessel to them and Halvorsen could tell from her distant steaming lights and her echo on his own radar that she was only a small vessel, probably a coastal trader. Her Master was obviously concerned not to steam off, probably at all of twelve knots, to stand by the wrong ship.

Say twenty minutes to get here . . . ?

'Make it so, Mister Talbot.' Halvorsen's feet dragged like lead as he moved to the pyrotechnics locker.

The Australian nodded, not being much of a one for the courtesies, and went back inside. '*Solov, Solov – Orion Venturer . . . Affirmative rockets. Three reds to come. I say again – figures thuree reds. All ships copy. Out!*'

The first star rocket soared from the Captain's outstretched arm with a *whooooosh* to explode high above the ro-ro where it hung in transient appeal before floating seawards: a slowly fading red orb . . . blood red – *fire* red? . . . illuminating the strained, upturned faces on the after decks. A sigh rose from the crowd . . . somewhere a woman screamed from the shock of it.

Halvorsen released a second rocket . . . *whooosh – bang!*

When the aerial echoes died he could hear a baby crying and, just for a brief moment, closed his eyes.

A *very* brief moment . . .

Because Second Officer Sandalwell came to him then and said

in a shocked voice, 'I'm sorry. I can't get the combinator to respond. We can't regain steerage way.'

'Dammit, Sandalwell – then go to engine room manoeuvering!'

Halvorsen cut himself short. They *couldn't*! They'd already lost communication with the engine room, and now, even *more* disastrously, it seemed that either the steering signals from the bridge had been affected by the fire, or the hydraulic pumps delivering pressure to the propeller pitch controls had failed. The end result was the same – they'd lost propulsion to bring the ship head to wind again.

'Bow thrusters?'

Sandalwell shook his head. 'Negative, sir. According to the rev counters the ER watchkeeper hasn't started the Kamewa motors – and as you know, we can only operate them from up here. We can't activate them remotely.'

Already, as the ship had fallen further off the wind, so the smoke had begun to lead at an ever increasing angle from the port quarter instead of directly astern: a black pall now visible even beyond the cast of the deck lights. Very soon, once she'd completed her inexorable pirouette and her counter came upwind, that smoke would be drifting from aft straight down the length of the ro-ro to make conditions on the boat deck – and the bridge itself – intolerable.

Even then there were still options open to the ailing Jorgen Truls Halvorsen to have countered the wind's effect and regained at least *some* directional control over his drifting ship . . . or were there?

He had already been shocked to observe how slow his un-drilled crew were actually proving in lowering the boats – an inadequacy made even more acute by the language difficulties his officers were experiencing in making even their most simple orders understood. Even had he thought to, could he have risked further delaying the preparations to evacuate by taking some of those key, and already hard-pressed, deck staff to go forward and let go the anchors – which would, even had they not reached bottom, at least have acted as sea anchors to hold her to the wind? While the prospect of identifying enough experienced hands capable – even in normal conditions – of working in the darkness of the foc'sle head to pay out heavy, barely manageable hawsers to form a drag loop around the bows . . .

The Captain truly was, as Delucci had wryly reflected earlier, experiencing a shipmaster's version of being caught between a rock and a hard place. Worse: the more he tried desperately to think of a solution, the more his already over-stressed mind shut down under the intolerable pressure.

'I apologize for my outburst, Mister Sandalwell!' was all he could think to say as, with an increasing sense of foreboding, he fumbled to strip the ignition tape from the final distress rocket.

Or at least, it was all he was allowed time to say.

. . . before a muffled, rolling detonation from somewhere far below literally *shook* the ship. Caused her ten-thousand-ton bulk to shudder even as the after observation windows of the Admiral's Lounge blew out across the exposed recreation deck: a fan of plate glass shards carried on an expanding, rolling ball of flaming gas.

Halvorsen's view of that area was largely obscured by the after superstructure although he knew – could *hear*, dear God, even from where he stood with hands gripping the teak capping of the wing, rigid and trembling white, that there were . . . *had been* . . . people out there.

But he *could* make out the line of the starboard rail which bordered a deck space once occupied, during the veteran ferry's previous incarnation, by smart-coated stewards carrying trays of deliciously clinking glasses, and by dozers in recliners and by lithe – and not so lithe – sun-bronzed leisure seekers.

Mercifully for Jorgen Truls Halvorsen the flailing figure aft was too far distant to be distinguished as anything more than a matchstick man . . . or matchstick woman? . . . as it was propelled on the blast wave: a flaming brand arcing outwards over the rail before curving downwards to be swallowed and instantly extinguished by the black sea.

. . . just as Second Officer Sandalwell, who'd run to lean right out to gape from the wing in shocked disbelief called numbly, 'Our hull seams have opened down to the waterline – an' the plates are *red hot*, sir! They're bloody *glowing* in the dark!'

282

CATACLYSM

Emergency Condition Black

When industrial cylinders containing dissolved acetylene are treated with respect – are properly handled and stored – they are safe.

If they are not properly handled and stored they become less safe.

To what extent they become less safe depends on how improperly they are handled. Or stored.

If they are handled so improperly that they suffer undue shock, they can become unstable. If excessive heat is applied to them, they become more unstable, although even then there are safety measures built into them which will permit any over-pressure to bleed off: hopefully before they become so unstable as to explode.

But if, like Able Seaman Madariaga, you first place them in a steel box and surround them with volatile materials and then, like Sven Carlsson, set fire to the contents of that box . . . and if that fire attains a high enough temperature to cause steel plate to become red hot – and if it reaches that frightening temperature so quickly that the resultant increase in pressure inside each acetylene cylinder overrides the speed with which its pressure release valves can – well, can release the pressure building within it . . . ?

By then you really ought to be doing something about it. Even if you only start running.

But if, on top of all the abuse you've already subjected your cylinder to, you *then* choose that hypercritical moment to agitate the platform on which it is tenuously balanced, as happened to the *Orion Venturer* when she lost steerage way and the seas came on her bow . . .

... and if *then*, as a direct result of such destabilizing motion, the cylinder falls over with a considerable impact to strike two bottles of equally volatile oxygen literally submerged in fire? Followed domino-fashion by three *more* extremely heavy cylinders, all of them super-heated to the point where they're about to auto-ignite anyway ... ?

Even before the cylinders fell in C313, the stricken ferry had become a floating time bomb. Already a funeral pyre on C and D decks where, in parts, the fire would attain an effect nearing 1,000 kilowatts before beginning to burn itself out, the air temperatures in the corridors serving the after sections of E deck, and in the smoke-filled starboard stairways leading to the Admiral's Lounge and night club, had also risen steadily.

Within thirty-seven minutes of Second Officer Delucci's having responded to the first bridge fire warning by refusing to believe it, the heat in those escape routes had become too great to sustain life for longer than it took to draw a few tortured breaths, irrespective of the smoke's toxicity. That now lethal airflow was about to trigger a further potentially devastating phenomenon.

As the air temperatures had increased, so the various plastics and paints and fittings within the corridors had begun to exude highly flammable vapours. By 0254 hours those superheating vapours were poised to create their own explosive effect. The very air itself had become volatile. The condition is known to firemen as the 'flash-over' stage.

It can transit behind ceiling panels, inside ventilation ducts ... even through small apertures cut in bulkheads to permit the passage of electrical wires and pipework.

It can be very violent. And travel *very* fast.

With or without the aid of the explosive acceleration it was also about to benefit from. Unwittingly engineered, just before the ro-ro sailed, by welding-bottle-humpers Atienza and Valverde, working under the dubious supervision of the ship's Torquemada look-alike.

*   *   *

284

When a string of demolition charges is placed by shadowy, fleet-footed action men wearing camouflage jackets and steely expressions, they will not be triggered simultaneously. Saboteurs have long known that multiple explosions have a calculably greater destructive effect if fused to allow a micro-second delay between each detonation. In that way, the blast from the first will be incrementally reinforced by the blast from the second . . . and so on.

The technique makes a little go a long way.

. . . as it did when the improperly stowed acetylene cylinders, heated first to peak instability then brutally agitated by their fall, finally exploded against the inner hull of the *Orion Venturer*.

Triggered by both shock and sympathetic detonation, three of them went off within a fraction of a second of each other, their joint destructive power further enhanced by the steel confines of the area in which they erupted. One of the two oxygen bottles also exploded.

The frail partitions separating the line of compartments were instantly demolished as the periodic blast wave emanating from Cabin C313, already squeezed between deck and deckhead, expanded horizontally inboard until it met the steel walls of the vehicle hangar. At that point it was deflected *back* against the hull to add to the multiple strike effect.

. . . but ship's hulls are only built to withstand pressures from *outside*. Their steel plates are affixed to the outboard faces of frames which, in turn, are fashioned to resist water compression – not internal expansion. In addition, the ferry's structure had suffered the inevitable corrosion and consequent attrition of designed strength that any ship is prone to after nearly thirty years of service.

. . . and, as Second Officer Sandalwell had observed to his severe discomfiture, those plates and frames in the immediate area of the explosion had also become red hot – even *more* vulnerable to deformation.

The breach created in the ferry's hull from car deck level down to below her waterline wasn't particularly dramatic. Sprung plates; cracked welds; more a fissure than a hole, really, and nowhere near as severe as the cavity that could have been blown in the ro-ro by, say, a torpedo fired from an eighty-year-old U-boat – a silly thought dismissed, along with the prospect of meeting an iceberg in the North Sea, as being over-fanciful by Grace Miles during even her most apprehensive pre-sailing moments – and nothing like the damage that would have been inflicted upon her by the rather more modern 500lb bomb once dropped by a Argentine A-4BS Skyhawk strike aircraft on Morgan Evans, baritone and former soldier of the 1st Battalion Welsh Guards . . . and *certainly* not as devastating as the Japanese ordnance which had rained down on the gallant USS *Thompson* on the twenty-eighth day of October 1944 when a very young and very frightened MM 2/c Charles Periera found himself privy to an act of racial hatred . . .

But the end result was still much the same.

At 0254 hours GMT, the *Orion Venturer* began to sink.

CHAPTER TWENTY-NINE

Someone had blundered:
Theirs not to make reply,
Theirs not to reason why,
Theirs but to do and die.
ALFRED, LORD TENNYSON (1809–1892)

'The children, Michael! My *babies* . . . ?'

Even as the smoke accomplished its serpentine climb-to-the-top-of the-hill then all-the-way-back-down-again evolution via the night club on G deck, Grace Miles had grasped her husband's slumped shoulders and hysterically begun to shake him like a doll. Like a battered Teddy with an Able Sea-Bear rating and one and a half eyes . . . ?

'Dear God, I'm so *sorry*, Grace . . .'

'We've got to get down to them . . . Michael – *Michael*?'

He came out of his alcoholic daze and climbed erect, scattering his chair. 'Come *on*!'

The bar steward was still pushing terrified youngsters through the door to the open embarkation deck. '*Incêndio! Partir* . . . Everybodies out! *Vamos!*'

Michael snatched Grace's hand and began to haul her through the press of bodies shouting, 'We can't get down the internal stair, there's too much smoke.'

People in varying states of dress were beginning to arrive on the boat deck as they emerged into the wind: many wide-eyed with shock, some coughing and staggering . . . nearly all staring blankly, anxiously, out into the darkness beyond the halo of the ferry's lights. A grim-faced young officer in full uniform, wearing a white cap and two gold rings, slid expertly down the ladder from the bridge, supported only by his hands gripping the rails . . . he hit

287

the deck running, already calling 'Boat's crews to me! All cox'ns muster at number one boat!'

'We're *sinking*, Michael,' Grace cried. 'Oh dear *God* – William and Lucy . . . ?'

'It's okay, ma'am, it's *okay*!' the officer said hurriedly with a strong American accent. 'A containable incident. But we have to take precautions . . .'

'Please. Our children – they're down below,' Michael appealed. 'On E deck?'

'The night cabins . . . in the rear section. Starboard side.'

The officer's expression suddenly went wooden: defensive. He was in shock himself. And anyway, 2/O Delucci had six-hundred-odd people on his conscience. 'Then I guess they'll be evacuating them from that area . . .'

'What d'you mean – you *guess*? Don't you bloody well *know*?' Michael had exploded before Grace read between the lines.

'He's saying that's where the *fire* is, Michael,' she screamed. 'Down on E deck – where William and *Lucy* are!'

Michael yelled, '*Help* us. For pity's sake, man: help us find them. Please?'

Delucci flinched. 'I'm sorry, sir. I have my orders. I must go about preparing the boats.'

Grace started to pull Michael. 'We have to get to them . . .'

'Don't try to go down there, ma'am!' the young American shouted. 'You can't go dow . . .'

An elderly woman, wearing a dressing gown and carrying an umbrella, seemingly oblivious to the escalating pandemonium, pushed imperiously between them to address the ashen-faced Second Officer.

'*Attention, Monsieur le Capitaine! Avez-vous vu mon chat* . . . ? 'Ave you see *mon beau* pussycat . . . ?'

'Oh *God*,' Grace whispered, desperately praying she might wake up soon. 'Oh God, oh *God*, oh *GOD* . . . !'

. . . by the time they'd finally fought their way down the central staircase against the human tide heading for the top decks, the acrid stink of smoke was drifting up: a pall already hinting at death in the air and becoming ever more ghastly as they descended. There were others pushing with them who'd joined that counter-wave –

others who must also be seeking loved ones down on E deck . . . ?
Grace recognized the tall blonde and her young Viking companion
from the disco ahead of them: equally distraught returnees. She
tried to sympathize – had to focus on something . . . *anything!* . . .
to prevent her from breaking down herself and screaming her
anguish aloud. She simply knew she couldn't – she *daren't* give in
now. Not for the children! Not for . . . ?

The reception foyer wasn't bright and cheerful as she
remembered it when she'd passed through earlier, in her determination to try to salvage her marriage at the expense of her concern
for William and Lucy. Now it was dim and filled with smoke.
Unconscious forms – young . . . old . . . *bodies,* were they?
Corpses . . . ? Dear Lord, please, no? – lay higgledy-piggledy around
the information desk in grotesque abandonment while shadowy
figures, some in uniform and parts of uniforms, others in
sleepwear, coughed and stumbled about their grim work of trying
to revive: to help still more from the fog over-spilling the after
corridors . . .

A high-pitched continuous whistle cut across the Dantesque
scene of panic and vomit as a *monster* lurched from the smoke in
the starboard alleyway to lean weakly – an unexpected action for
a monster to take? – against the desk. The low cylinder-pressure
alarm stopped whistling as the monster removed its neoprene face
with trembling, black-sooted hands and became a ship's officer.

'Where's the Third? His BA must be running out too.'

'He's not come back.'

'Another air bottle . . .' Chief Officer McCulloch gasped. 'Rig me
another *air* bottle . . . an' the rest of you – get OUT! There's areas
back there must be approachin' flash-over.'

'Get out yourself, Mate,' someone – the Chief Purser? – advised.

'Go to hell, Frank.'

'I'm here already, Stewart,' Trøjborg snarled bitterly. 'I'm fuckin'
here already.'

'Please – our *children*?'

'Where?'

'Along THERE . . . !'

'I'm sorry,' McCulloch retched. 'Jesus, I'm *sorry*!'

The blonde Scandinavian woman began crying as one of the

rescuers spoke to her while gesturing aloft. But – tears of *joy* . . . ?

Grace watched her dully. She knew now that joy would never enter her life again . . .

'I see *William*!' Michael suddenly shouted and started running, literally hurdling corpses, towards the starboard corridor.

'*Stop* him!'

'No, Michael . . . *no* . . . !'

The smoke sucked back as wind toyed idly with the airflow round the deck ventilators high above, and then returned to the foyer, swirling and reinvigorated in an ever-swelling cloud as the wind changed its mind.

'Go, go, go! Everybody topside!' the Chief Officer bellowed, then replaced his mask as the Second Purser tapped him on the shoulder to indicate the replacement bottle was functioning, and began to move back into the cloud: this time along the port corridor where there might still remain *some* slender prospect of finding life.

Michael reeled, sucking for air, from the nightmare clutching a tiny form to his breast. The child was purple-faced: stick arms and legs flopping aimlessly, disjointedly. Even through the stygian gloom they could see it was dead.

'That isn't *William*,' Grace screamed. '*That* isn't my *baby*!'

She never spoke again. Not even to protest – not even to tell Michael how much she despised him as they pushed and harried her unresistingly towards the upper decks . . .

It would have provided Grace Miles with no comfort to realize that her four-year-old daughter was still alive then – and being happily entertained by a hoarse-voiced Able Seaman Conroy – within twenty metres distance from her as the smoke drifts.

Although it might as well have been twenty miles distant, for all the hope of rescue that Conroy reckoned they had left.

Frail Margrite Periera had already passed away peacefully in her sleep, along with a lot of others down on E deck, by the time the smoke first billowed into the Admiral's Lounge through the starboard stairwell to cause an abrupt cessation to 'Men of Harlech' as well as to ex-USN MM/2c Periera's long-brewing confrontation with Zach Goss.

The cancer within her – a cancer which, for the twelve months previous, ol' Charlie had tried so mighty hard to pretend didn't exist – had been almost grateful when Second Officer Sandalwell finally carried out his Captain's order to shut down the *Orion Venturer*'s ventilation from the bridge, and so permitted the smoke to creep, silent and undetected, under her door.

The fire was kind to Margrite. It simply allowed her to stop breathing. Drift featherdown-gentle into the tender embrace of the Lord she so devoutly trusted in . . . and in the middle of dreaming she was young again, and her skin smooth and fresh-smelling as the petals of a rosebud: and she'd been wearing that magnolia print dress that her darling Charlie admired so much, while runnin' lickety-split on them once favourite bright red, teetery high heels of hers to throw her arms clear round the neck of a handsome young sailor . . .

Course, Charlie himself didn't know none of that. Never would, because he was never to see the love of his life again. Wouldn't see hardly none of his former shipmates from the gallant *Thompson* again neither – *or* their ladies. But that was because the guys who once would have been up in the bar hard drinking along with him and Zach until the rest of the ferry's passengers wus under the tables . . . ? Well, they'd mostly gone, bone wearied, down to their de luxe berths on E deck to say 'howdy' to their bunks after chow time last evening.

Anyways, all Charlie knew at that point was that smoke had come into the lounge and people was screaming and trying to get clear of it, whereupon the Brits who'd sung so melodiously faded to an uncertain halt, while the Willy character at the piano swore *Verdammte Mist*! while cutting his accompaniment short with an even more discordant crash of the ivories than was his usual . . . which was when the little choirmaster with the walnut-brown face shouted, 'Clear out. There's a fire, boyos!' and someone else – the baritone: a youngish feller with one fin? – immediately stepped forward in front o' them like he wus familiar with what to do on a burning ship, and called, '*Steady*, lads! Steady the Welsh. No need to *rush* now, is there . . . ?'

But then, Ex-Guardsman Morgan Evans, having been brought to confront his greatest fear, was discovering that the anticipation can often be worse than the event. It may have been Morgan's disciplined background: his indomitable spirit, for that matter – or even knowing that, whatever horror awaited him in the North Sea, it could be no worse than that he'd already suffered on an island half a world away. The thought of actually *dying* never entered Evans's head. Fire wasn't instant, like an aerial bomb or a bullet. Supremely fit, he'd bloody float if he had to.

Charlie Periera was different. He and Evans may, unknown to either of them, have shared a common nightmare, but Charlie had Margrite with him this time. Trouble wus – he had fat ol' Zach Goss, too. And Zach wus still slumped there in his chair, drunker'n a cat flea in a whisky vat: wholly incapable of gittin' out the way of the smoke. And *that* put Charlie in kind of a fix because, for fifty years, he'd been tormented by the memory of how him and Zach had abandoned a shipmate to die – not that he'd known the full truth as to why Goss had done what he had done, until tonight – but that still didn't alter no principle. The one thing he'd learned from that terrible event was that you cain't be picky 'bout whether to try and help a man survive . . . just can't make it dependent on whether you takes kindly to him personally or no.

To do *that* would be as reprehensible as to leave him because of his religion. Or the colour of his skin.

'We got to get back down to our wives an' the guys,' Charlie shouted, pulling at Zach while the smoke began to swirl about them. '*C'mon*, Zach – you an' me, they *need* us!'

Goss peered dully about him, his voice still slurred, resentful from the drink. 'You ain't bin fair to me, Periera. That Lootenant O'Kane wus too uppity. Gotten way too far 'bove hisself f'r a nigra . . .'

'Margrite – I have to go make sure she's roused. An' there's . . .' Even her *name* stuck in Charlie's craw, 'There's Mary Lou, Zach. You got to get down to help Mary Lou.'

'We white men oughta stick together . . .'

Worried sick 'bout Margrite, Charlie Periera puffed up red-faced as a turkey cock at that. 'Damn me if I ain't *tryin'* to, you ol' goat . . .'

The foolish woman started screaming again over the other side the lounge. The smoke had spread so quick Charlie couldn't see people over there no more: just shapes blundering through the fog. It was then the singer feller with the deep voice and the one arm had run to them and grabbed Zach, started to haul him out of his chair. Goss peered blearily about him . . . registered the smoke f'r the first time and, despite it – or because of it! – clung like a barnacle to his seat.

'Where you *takin'* me?' he shouted.

'On deck, sir,' Morgan Evans said positively. 'You can finish your row just as easy out there, can't you?'

'He's comin' below with *me*!' Charlie yelled even more positively. 'The rest've our guys are down there. He got his lady wife to take care of . . . I got my *Margrite*! This time he's gonna be a hero if I has to *drag* him down!'

'I ain't goin' below,' Zach howled, the terror clear in his puffy eyes. 'We go below, Periera, we ain't *never* gonna make it topside again.'

. . . it was then that Charlie Periera sensed the futility of taking his anger out on Goss. Realized, deep down, that he was too old and too disabled to do anythin' to help his beloved Margrite. That only the Lord and the ferry's crew could provide for her now. And – because Charlie did still worship reg'lar despite everything that happened half a century before – he just knew the Lord would do the right thing by her . . . which, in the circumstances, some might well argue the Lord had already.

He was so glad now. That he'd kissed her before he left their cabin.

'C'mon, Zach,' he said heavily. 'Let this good gentleman take you out to the deck.'

They'd just got Goss unresisting to the after doors of the lounge facing on to the covered-over swimming pool when the strangest thing happened.

Zach suddenly froze again. Went rigid as a block of stone. Staring bug-eyed he was, with the old burn on his face suddenly gone bleach white.

'No,' he choked. 'By the Holy Mary – *NO* . . . !'

Turning, mystified, Charlie Periera saw him then, too.

The Lootenant.

Engineer Lieutenant Junior Grade *O'Kane*. United States Navy . . .

Killed in . . . no – *Murdered* in Action: October Twenty-Eight, Nineteen Forty-Four.

He was bearing down on them out of the swirling smoke on the recreation deck: his arm held out appealingly like he done all them guilt-ridden years before. And his clothes wus *still* torn and blackened from the fires in the *Thompson*'s machinery space jus' like Periera remembered . . . like Ex-MM 1/c Goss did too, it seemed, judgin' by the way Zach was trembling and beginning to whimper.

'I'm sorry, Lieutenant,' Charlie heard hisself whisper to the advancing spectre. 'As the Good Lord is my witness, sir, I'm *sorry* f'r what we done to you . . .'

'He come for us, Charlie,' Zach cried, still fuddled by the drink. 'He *come* f'r us to take us back down with him – that nigra officer . . .'

And with that, Zach Goss twisted out of the startled and utterly disbelieving one-handed grip of former Guardsman Evans to stagger, mouthing incoherently, back into the smoke beyond the reach of anyone's aid at all!

. . . which was a terrible way for an old war hero, especially one so brave as Zach claimed to have been, to die. And quite inexplicable to the other escapees watching open-mouthed. Understandably so.

Because when Charlie Periera turned with tears filling his eyes, *knowing* then that his sweet wife had been taken too, 'stead of him, to settle a half-century-old due – even *he* could see the Lieutenant was gone.

. . . almost as if he'd never been there in the first place.

But of course, Charlie knew something the others didn't.

He knew that Engineer Lieutenant O'Kane had returned to rejoin a lot of other gallant dead men in a riddled hull under the Gulf of Leyte. To rest in peace now, for the very first time since two young sailors, one obsessed by hate and the other possessed by fear, had callously slammed a door on the life and loves he might otherwise have experienced . . .

'I was only tryin' to *help* 'im, mister,' Assistant Crew Mess Cook Manley from a long line of Trinidad Manleys – who'd merely stopped by in passing, on his way to report to the bridge – protested uncomprehendingly.

Though it has to be admitted – in view of the fact that Henry had already met Zach once – without feeling *too* distressed.

There were several alternative escape routes from the engine room open to the two watchkeepers down there.

And all of them, in Third Engineer Stamper's view, unattractive.

His problem, being unable to communicate with the bridge, was that he didn't know where the seat of the fire was located. Other than that it was somewhere above their heads.

Which was pretty bloody obvious, and didn't require two engineer officer's gold rings overlaid on a purple background on his sleeve to work out, considerin' they were trapped at the *bottom* of the fuckin' ship!

It wouldn't have helped Bert's morale much to learn – even while his engine room continued to fill with ever more poisonous smoke despite his having shut down all E/R ventilation from his own console – that the *bridge* still didn't know exactly where the fire was located either. Which rather made the business of selecting an escape route – one which would prove to *be* an escape route and not an entry into a further suffocating space – a bit of a game of Russian roulette.

. . . or Bahamian roulette, in this case?

The good news, Stamper thought, trying desperately to adopt a positive attitude, was that they wouldn't both die if things should turn out that way.

They did have one set of breathing apparatus. One of them would almost certainly make it to the upper decks.

Trouble was . . .

Feeling very frightened now, Third Engineer Stamper stared at little Motorman Garilao over the incredibly desirable cylinder and mask lying on the deck while, for his part, Motorman Garilao stared back at Bert through big black limpid eyes, and with such mute appeal.

Bert, still single and fancy free without any kids back home that he knew of, remembered Teofisto's photograph: his undisguised pride in his pretty Filipino wuff and their ate bebbie . . . *eight* babies!

'I had the extra sannies, mate,' he said. 'That makes it your turn to take the BA.'

'But Turd . . . ?'

'Get it *on*, dammit!' Bert yelled, feeling himself beginning to fall apart. 'Jus' get it *on* an' piss off outa here afore I change my . . .'

'. . . I no 'ave certificate for the breathing.'

'Jesus!'

Stamper snatched up the bottle in its abrasion-resistant harness and began to fumble with the straps, slipping them over the rating's shoulders while trying to sound reassuring rather than jealous.

'Breathin's easy, Garilao. Honest. Even without a certificate. Bebbies can do it. You jus' suck air *in* through your mouth an' nose – then blow it out, see? In . . . Out . . . In . . .'

Garilao practised breathing, and looked pleased.

'P'rhaps you should wear the face mask while you're doin' it?' Bert urged gently.

'Which way I go, Turd Jesus?'

Stamper thought hard. Being able to breath was only half the battle, far as the Filipino was concerned. Finding his way in the dense smoke would make up the other half. Bert would dearly have loved to have been in a position to take him by the hand and lead him up, but he knew he'd die in the demonstration. Too much smoke had already consolidated high against the deckhead for a man without BA to make it through that barrier alone. Even the brightest lighting was dimming under its suffocating pall. Gloom was descending with increasing speed to blot out everything around them . . . while God only knew how many more smoke-filled levels might lie on the other side of the engine room's main exit door.

'Straight up, mate,' Bert advised urgently. Neither of them had much time left. 'Up that starboard ladder into the car deck: through the watertight door an' out into the accommodation. If there's more smoke up there, don't panic. You got twenty minutes before your set runs out . . .'

He realized Teofisto was still working on tryin' to interpret *straight up* and felt a bit foolish, but *Christ* he was scared! Talking seemed to help being scared . . . he gestured aloft instead. There didn't seem much point in trying to remind Garilao to *feel* any door before he opened it – make sure there wasn't too much heat the other side . . .

'Hop it,' he finished lamely. 'You'll be right, Teofisto mate. No sweat. Promise.'

The Motorman had tears in his eyes. Bert felt really embarrassed when the little guy threw his arms around him and hugged him. Blokes jus' didn't hug each other too often in Sunderland where he come from.

'You *good* man, Turd Jesus. Ver' good man,' Garilao sniffed, swallowed, then tentatively fitted the mask over his face and stuck one thumb up with eyes reflecting surprise that he *was* still breathing, before turning heavily away, sounding like a miniature steam engine, to make for the ladder.

'Give my love to the wife an' kids,' Bert called, a bit watery-eyed himself.

But then, Third Engineer Stamper couldn't have known that, for all his selfless heroism, he'd just sent Motorman Teofisto Garilao the wrong way.

. . . that the little Filipino would be dead within three minutes of their parting.

Because like Bert said: the main escape route from the control room would take him though the car deck and then, taking the most direct line, out into the corridor serving C deck cabins starboard. And the temperature in there, just where Carlsson had started his fire was – at the moment when they evacuated the engine room of the *Orion Venturer* – approaching 800 degrees Centigrade, with the acetylene coming nicely to the boil. And of course, what with the smoke, and never having done any fire drill, and being in a hurry to live and everything, little Garilao just didn't think to feel that second steel watertight door with a cautious hand before he opened it, like Bert had intended to remind him to do if they'd shared a common language.

. . . just to make sure it wasn't *too* hot on the other side.

By a bizarre twist of fate Third Engineer Stamper – who'd already won an extra sandwich that night, and should have had the odds stacked heavily against his escaping from the bottom of the ferry without a BA set – walked free and clear within minutes.

He'd left by the back door, so to speak, taking a chance that the smoke hadn't had time to work its way downwards. His route had proved a tight squeeze: couldn't have been negotiated with the bulk of an oxygen pack hampering him. Or a lifejacket. Aft through the auxiliary engine room then through a tiny watertight door into a short run of shaft tunnel . . . then back out through an even more slim-line hatchway into the sewage tank room which, while not very nice, was the aftmost compartment in the ship.

From there Bert had been able to climb a vertical ladder running up through trunking inboard of the ship's square counter, and rising six nerve-racking decks in all – until he opened the very last hatch and found himself at shoulder level with . . . *Jesus* it was a *fantastic* feeling! . . . level with the open recreation deck abaft the swimming pool on F deck.

Blinking in the harsh glare of the lights, the Third saw smoke pouring from the glazed after end of the Admiral's Lounge right away, and knew the ship was in dire hazard – that he was bloody lucky to have got out . . . People were still reeling from the interior, coughing most of them an' in a bad way . . . he hoped little Garilao had made it topside by the more dependable first-class route.

Letting the hatch fall back he eased himself from it and sat, just for a moment, with his legs dangling over the coaming, just gazing up at the sky while thinking he'd never seen such a beautiful sight before. There weren't any stars: only thick overcast . . . the rain began to soak through his once-white boiler suit right away. But Bert didn't care. Bert just tilted his sweating, soot-encrusted face to that rain, threw his arms wide with the sheer joy of living – whatever the bloody weather – an' yelled: *'Welcome back, World . . . !'*

The time of Stamper's salvation was precisely 0254 GMT.

He ceased to exist fifteen seconds later.

. . . when the acetylene finally detonated in Cabin C313, not only did the intermittent shockwave rupture the ro-ro's hull: it propelled an expanding white-hot fireball up through corridors

298

already seeping flammable vapours approaching the flash-over stage . . . which, in turn, triggered the flash-over so that everything combustible in the after sections of the *Orion Venturer* exploded into flame.

It was that doubly reinforced and superheated pressure wave which had careered upwards through E deck and up through the reception foyer to level F, where Captain Halvorsen had witnessed it eviscerating the viewing windows of the Admiral's Lounge.

. . . as well as observing the flaming matchstick that had been Third Engineer Stamper, Engineer of the Middle Watch, being blown overboard, his arms still spread wide in euphoria.

'. . . so I'm ackshully *inside* o' this ginormous whale wot swallowed me after I fell overboard,' Able Seaman Conroy said with absolute veracity, 'an' I looks to *port* o' me . . .'

'Then what?' his fascinated audience whispered.

'Then I looks ter *starboard* of me . . .'

'*Then* what?'

'. . . an' d'you know what I sees inside that great big fish's tummy?'

Lucy shook her head, hypnotized, eyes like saucers. Even Able Sea-Bear Teddy seemed impressed.

'Ships – *that's* wot!' Conroy revealed triumphantly. 'Ships frum olden days right through ter a big transatlantic liner complete wi' four stacks an' a twenty-piece orchestra still playin on 'er poop deck. There wus Roamin' galleys and a Chinee junk an' a . . . a *pirate* ship. An' a Gyppo felucca an' a couple o' East Indiamen an' an ol' red duster shelter decker . . .'

'How did they all fit *in* there?' the little girl demanded unexpectedly, because four-year-olds can be pretty smart. Especially at the wrong times.

'Well, it wus a . . . a very big whale, wusn't it?' Conroy defended uncomfortably. Then added hurriedly to change the subject, 'You, ah . . . got any o' them mints left, 'ave you?'

He eyed the bottom of the door speculatively while Lucy fiddled with the sweet wrapper. The smoke had begun to seep under when the Old Man finally switched off the ventilation, and he'd shoved a blanket along it automatically so the little girl might live a bit longer, but now he wusn't so sure he'd done the right thing. He'd thought an' *thought* of the options, but there weren't none . . . Miracles wusn't goin' to happen – not with that *mañana* crowd of Mediterranean hystericals down the foc'sle who wouldn't know a fire hose frum a towin' hawser, while he hisself wus still off 'is sea legs after that bloody smoke had got to him. He knew he coul'n't carry her more'n a few steps down the corridor before he collapsed again hisself, and dying like that would terrify the little angel more'n anything. Better, he reckoned, to sit tight an' wait . . . and pray to God that sweet child went off to sleep afore he did.

Although it was the thought of the fire getting to her before the smoke that *really* frightened the old seaman. He'd already seen what it could do to people . . . Able Seaman Conroy would never forget the whimpering, tormented Fire Man he come face to melting face wi' down on C deck. Would *never* forget their terrible confrontation as long as he liv . . . !

Then Conroy grimly recalled it di'n't exac'ly seem like *that* psychological scar was goin' to bother him f'r long . . . but the memory of it did explain why he was havin' second thoughts about holding the comparatively merciful smoke back any longer . . .

'One for you, one for Teddy – and one for *me*!' Lucy said, chewing happily. 'And that's them *all* gone until Mummy comes back wiv more.'

'You can 'ave mine as well, until she does,' Conroy refused generously, at the same time surreptitiously fumbling to ease the blanket away from under the door. He could sense the smoke curling up almost instantly. 'An' it doesn't look like Teddy's goin' to eat his either, so you can 'ave *that* too. Now why don't you jus' slide down in that nice cosy bed an' have a snooze 'til Mum arrives, eh?'

Lucy lay down and wriggled a bit, then sat up suddenly.

'How *did* you get out of the whale's tummy?'

Conroy opened his mouth, then looked blank. He hadn't thought of that. An' if there wus one thing he couldn't *stand* it wus gettin caught out by a superior intelligence.

. . . it was his second reason for being grateful for miracles when there was the sound of a boot kicking at the door – and it swung inwards with a *bang!*

The Creature stood snorting through its corrugated trunk for a moment, with the smoke swirling in around it and the eyes, hollow with fatigue, blinking through a black-sooted visor . . .

It was the very first time in Able Seaman Conroy's whole misbegotten life he'd actually been glad to see an officer.

Even a Chief Officer!

'Don't be frightened,' Conroy said – suddenly concerned about the little girl being scared – while McCulloch hurriedly closed the door again to protect them from the smoke before wearily dragging his face mask off. 'It's only another sailor, not a sea monster or nothin'.'

. . . though there'd been plenty o' times in the past when he hadn't held quite that view.

'Don' be silly. *He's* not a sailor,' Lucy argued knowledgeably and not at all frightened. But then, little girls aged four live in a dream world where every story has a happy ending and very little surprises them. 'Sailors have yellow hats an' wellingtons like William's got . . . *he's* a fireman. Firemans *save* people – I seed them save people on television.'

'Quite right, pet,' Mister McCulloch said. 'Don't you believe everything that gentleman tells you. *I* certainly don't.'

'He says he's been inside a *whale*,' Lucy announced.

'That's what I mean,' the Mate said solemnly and cocked a concerned eye at Conroy.

'Won't make it. Lost steerage way.' Conroy answered the unspoken question. 'Jus' hold you up, sir – slowest ship in convoy. An' two of us can't risk sharin' a mask, anyroad. Not with a cargo precious as that.'

'I'm sorry, Conroy.'

Conroy summoned a grin. It made the flash burns on his leathery face hurt. Suddenly he felt very tired. 'There's worse things 'appen at sea.'

Mister McCulloch felt very privileged. Nobody in the *Orion Venturer* had ever seen Conroy smile.

'The nice fireman's goin' to wrap a blanket round your 'ead so's you won't smell all smoky when 'e gives you to your Mummy.

And you got to hold your breath long as you can, see? Pretend you're a . . . a . . .'

'Fish?' Lucy suggested.

'That's *it* – a *fish*!' Conroy agreed, looking extra pleased so she'd try her hardest.

Before he put his mask back on, Chief Officer McCulloch reached his hand out to grip Conroy's shoulder, and squeezed. Held on to the old rating for quite a long time. It meant a lot to Able Seaman Conroy, that silent accolade.

The little girl looked so fragile and perfect – *so* pretty, with her big black eyes just peeping over the fluffy blanket. Conroy tucked Teddy down inside it with her and allowed his hand to brush against her golden hair ever so briefly.

'Are you coming later?' she asked. 'To finish the story 'bout the whale? Tell me how you got out of his tummy?'

'I'm goin' to 'ave a bit of a sleep first,' Conroy explained. '*Then* I'll p'raps come . . .'

He grinned again, this time deliberate at Stewart McCulloch. Not often he got to put one over on a man with three gold rings on 'is sleeve. 'But if I don't see you, the nice fireman'll finish it for me.'

Lucy wriggled in the Mate's embrace and stretched out her arms to Conroy. Wrapped them tight around his neck, and kissed him. It didn't hurt Conroy's burned cheek at all.

'Goodnight. Sleep tight,' she whispered.

After they'd gone, and the tears had dried on Conroy's face, he fumbled hopefully in his charred back pocket. He had one cigarette left, in a very battered packet. He hadn't wanted to smoke it while his Angel was in the cabin. Smoking can be extra harmful to little lungs.

The old sea-going British dinosaur eased himself painfully over to the bunk and stretched out before lighting up and inhaling luxuriously. It tasted even better when he remembered he was still officially on watch, an' that he was ackshully lazin' around in the owners' time.

When he'd smoked it down to the bitter end he carefully stubbed it out, because you can't never be too careful when it comes to fire prevention on a ship.

Then Able Seaman Conroy got up leisurely again. And hobbled across the cabin caressing his stubbled cheek ever so wistfully. Ever so tenderly.

And opened the door.

FERRY DOWN!

When stately ships are twirled and spun
Like whipping tops and help there's none
And mighty ships ten thousand ton
Go down like lumps of lead.
                    RALPH HODGSON (1871–1962)

They got all the boats loaded and away within twenty minutes of Captain Halvorsen's order to abandon ship. Quite remarkable really, in the circumstances. A tribute to the seamanship of Second Officers Pert and Delucci as well as to the discipline of the passengers themselves, who never did actually panic although, on occasions, sections of the crowd on the embarkation deck came very near to it. Especially after the *Orion Venturer* completed her turn from the wind and the smoke began to blow down her decks from stern to bow.

Most of the crew did well, too. Not as sailors, because all too many of them weren't. But they *were* extremely proficient at looking after people's comfort, and they helped calm the distress a lot by distributing lifejackets and even warm clothing brought up by volunteers from the still-habitable forward ends.

One hundred and fifty-two passengers were beyond help. Not that they'd been afforded much even before they died. Plus crew members Third Engineer Robert Stamper, Motorman Teofisto Garilao and Able Seaman Conroy.

. . . it was funny how nobody aboard had ever learned Conroy's first name? In fact, nobody knew much about Able Seaman Conroy at all, come to think of it. Apart from the fact that he smoked like a chimney and couldn't tolerate most things. Not even rabbits.

. . . not even *children*, would you believe?

Or not accordin' to Conroy, anyroad. Who'd reg'larly spoke disparagingly about such 'orrible creatures in his office down the crew mess next the tea urn.

Third Engineer Erik Hellström died too. Not a high-profile member of the crew . . . hardly anybody knew much about him either . . . but a very brave one. His low-pressure alarm went off while he was still searching cabins in the starboard corridor, and Hellström had simply lost his way back to reception in the poisonous darkness.

One life was created during the time it took for the *Orion Venturer* to die.

Pastor Lütgendorf was the first to discover the miracle, which was most appropriate for a man who, for an agonizing period of his life, had stopped believing in them. He'd come, shaken and heavy-hearted, up from the hell of the main foyer when Chief Purser Trøjborg had reluctantly been forced to order it abandoned in the face of the creeping death . . . until suddenly – just as he was passing a locker on the boat deck – he heard a baby cry.

. . . and there, *Hallelujah: Praise to the Lord*, it was! Still attached to its mother by the umbilical cord. A little boy child. The stewardesses had worked hard to save them both: especially Heikki . . . or was her name Nicole, because that was what she kept whispering, although the passenger list later proved that presumption wrong? Either way, she got better and went back home to Finland where her father welcomed her in tears: his grief at losing his dear wife at least mitigated in part by the joy of having gained a somewhat unexpected grandchild.

And Pastor Lütgendorf? Well, even had he suspected for one moment that such a wondrous coming of life in the midst of death might just have been the product of Voudon magic, he would still have dismissed the hypothesis as an unfortunate young girl's fantasy.

A man didn't abandon his Faith quite so easily as *that*.

As far as others numbered among the *Orion Venturer*'s passenger complement on that ghastly night in the North Sea were concerned: Mr and Mrs Somerville from Scotland went on to a tearful reunion with their daughter in Gothenburg, albeit a little late. They had a lot to talk about. Mr Somerville, who'd always been a bit of a Burns fan as was appropriate for an Edinburgh man, hadn't been able to resist quoting a few lines he felt appropriate to the voyage.

The best laid plans . . .

The Japanese executive party, who'd also been berthed in first-class cabins forward on E deck, went on to meet their Volvo factory opposite numbers in Gothenburg as well. And when they got there they produced the most *amazing* front-line candid snaps of disaster at sea. Quite remarkable. Much better than they'd have got travelling by plane.

One of their fellow travellers in particular would have loved to have featured prominently in them. Especially so because of his intimate involvement in the tragedy. But Sven Carlsson never did get the opportunity to present his best side for any photographer's lens to capture . . . never even got his name in the papers for that matter, other than being recorded as one among a sad and far too long – unnecessarily long – list of casualties. Certainly he never made the headlines, either as hero or villain. Because nobody ever discovered who actually caused the fire.

Jozef never even got a mention in the casualty list. But that might have been because he *was* only a cat . . . Mme Chabert spent two weeks scouring the beaches of northern Denmark for trace of him, hoping he'd possessed not only the instincts of a rat but also the floatability of one. But he either went down with the ship or found another home and mistress in Jutland, as cats are inclined to do. Preferably one who wouldn't smuggle him aboard any more bloody ferries.

Effie Sandringham, alias the clandestine Mrs Smith, arrived back in the UK to a barrage of flashbulbs, expulsion from her local embroidery circle and the commencement of divorce proceedings. Effie's over-strenuously amorous shipmate, Passenger Charles Smith, never actually made it home. Never even made it from the reception foyer to the boats for that matter, despite having been rescued so gallantly from his makeshift chapel of rest by the most seasick hero there ever was.

Singer and ex-soldier Morgan Evans returned to Gwynneth and the girls a stronger man. He sometimes thinks he would like to visit South America: maybe even try to meet the surviving pilots of the Argentine V Air Brigade who'd flown their A-4BS Skyhawks with such deadly precision on that black day for the British Army back in 1982. Doing that would allow him to confront, and again hopefully conquer, his very last fear of all.

Veteran US Navyman Charlie Periera got hisself a draft to a sunset home when he finally got shipped back to the States. He would live to a ripe and ornery old age and, after a while, would come to accept, right or wrong, that his beloved lady wife hadn't never been taken by a ghost to settle a due – that all along it was the good Lord done what was best for his sweet, suffering Margrite, and saved them both a lot of pain.

That did suggest, of course, he'd been let off easy f'r his part in what happened east of Samar Island. It may have been wishful thinking on the part of an old man, but there was no denying that after Zach Goss fell victim to his own drunken imaginings – run back into the smoke to meet what some might say wus poetic justice – the Lieutenant never *did* come back frum the depths agin, not f'r one single minute in the middle of one single night, to sit on ol' ex-Machinist's Mate Second Class Periera's shoulder and make him sweat.

And Grace and Michael Miles . . . ?

They would both grieve, following that terrible catastrophe, for the rest of their lives. But Grace would stay with Michael. Not only for the sake of Lucy, but for William too. Her boy-child would never grow up, but he would always be a part of them: a part of her so-precious family, and she knew, if she allowed that to disintegrate, then she would be letting William down every bit as much as Lucy.

And it so happened that she came to love Michael again. Slowly. But perhaps that was because he didn't try hard to be an unselfish husband and father: he simply became one.

It was a shame that neither of them did little more than notice Able Seaman Conroy glancing with approval into the bar on that terrible last morning – not that Grace would have thought much of him, even if she had spoken to him. It wouldn't have taken Conroy long to make it clear how 'e coul'n't *stand* kids in ships.

. . . which only goes to prove that angels come in the most

unlikely guises. They don't always have to be tiny, and carry one-eyed Teddy Bears.

The crew of the *Orion Venturer* met with varying fortunes after they were repatriated.

Cabins Night Steward Pinheiro Cardoso, for instance, went back to Portugal . . . by air, where you only need to clutch a paper bag and not a whole bucket . . . to live happily ever after, if sometimes a tad waspishly, with his very dear friend, Jorge the pastry chef. Neither of them ever signed aboard a *barco grande* again.

Quartermaster Jerónimo Solbes Madariaga never returned to the sea again either. He was a proud man, in the tradition of the Spanish gypsy, and would carry a burden of guilt ever more over the matter of the acetylene cylinders, although it's doubtful whether their improper stowage made any difference to the terrible outcome of that voyage. The responsibility for that lay at the doors of many individuals, stretching back over thirty years, and holding far greater sway regarding how a ship is designed and operated than any deckhand.

Madariaga's consolation is that he *is* a professional flamenco dancer now, and does receive some degree of appreciation for his set-piece 'Ferruca Andalucia': albeit usually from the more inebriated patrons of the smaller *tabernas* on the circuit. Not a lot, because he's still a pretty mediocre hoofer – but at least he's doing what he loves despite his critics. There are spiteful people who claim he only got *that* far because of the publicity he received after the *Venturer*'s loss. That . . . and the fact that he looks remarkably like Torquemada with a pony tail.

Assistant Crew Mess Cook Henry Manley from Liverpool continues to serve in ferries sailing out of the UK. The proper run ones, this time, where safety claims priority and everyone aboard knows their emr number and drills regular.

Henry still can't credit that any man, even one so demonstrably faithful to his bigotry as that Yank passenger, should have preferred a suffocating death to accepting a helping hand from him. Not that Henry Manley regards that as bein' the greatest frustration he inherited from the loss of the *Orion Venturer*.

He never did get the chance to discover – and he never will now, of course: no more than will anyone else – why Able Seaman Conroy wus so against rabbits . . .

Henry's apprentice fire-fighter and former *Picciotto di Onore*, Filippo Lucchetti, acquitted himself well both before and during the abandoning. He *did* figure what those rope things were for, and managed to successfully unhook the right ones at the right moment when his lifeboat hit the water, which is as much as any seagoers with their real names on genuine certificates can claim.

Filippo also went back to sea again. As a fully fledged galley porter next time, and not only on the personal recommendation of Head Chef *Monsieur* Henri-François de Saeger but also on that of Provision Master Uguccioni.

Still only sixteen years old, Filippo Lucchetti was stabbed to death, and for no apparent reason that the Squadra Mobile could discover, some three months after a carbonized man had suddenly sat up and stared at him.

The incident happened the very first time his new cruise ship docked in Naples.

As far as the *Orion Venturer*'s surviving officers were concerned, few of them came out of the subsequent Official Inquiry well.

Chief Purser Trøjborg retired voluntarily after being criticized by the Board for having failed to ensure proper training had been given to those members of his hotel services department involved in the abortive evacuation of F deck.

Assistant Purser Everard was never offered another seagoing appointment despite making many applications, and now works as an assistant hotel manager somewhere in South Africa.

Junior Purser Marianne Nørgaard did manage to get back to the sea she loved, but only as stewardess in an FOC cargo vessel. She consistently refuses offers of much better jobs in passenger ships.

Chief Engineer Bracamontes failed to sustain the tough guy image he'd always cultivated. He also retired in a welter of hostile press publicity after it was disclosed at the inquiry that he had never attempted to go down to his own engine room after the fire began. He had been observed on the boat deck early in the disaster, still wearing a floral Hawaiian shirt but having discreetly disposed of his uniform cap. He'd commandeered a place in the first lifeboat to leave the ship.

Australian Electronics Technical Officer Talbot – Eck-teck Ed – was commended for his professionalism and deportment in maintaining communications throughout. The plane he flew home on to Melbourne crashed in the Pacific. There were no survivors.

More passengers and crew died in that one disaster than in the *Orion Venturer*, which – Ed himself would have been the first to concede – puts marine accidents in their true perspective.

Second Officers Sandalwell and Pert were absolved of responsibility for any part of the disaster. They are both working in ferries again: Ollie Sandalwell as relief Chief Officer, which would have made his father and mother very proud.

Second Officer Michael Delucci was commended for his part in launching the boats successfully, and without causing further harm or injury. The Board then suspended his watchkeeping ticket for two years for not having responded more quickly and positively in the initial phase of the tragedy.

Mike Delucci now serves as a deckhand on a charter yacht out of Baltimore. He still carries a battered old silver watch to remind him never to be late for his relief.

Chief Officer Stewart McCulloch also lost his ticket and is currently unemployed. It is not the greatest punishment he suffered. He still holds himself largely responsible for the loss of those poor lost souls . . . *and* he had to think up an end to Conroy's story to tell little Lucy Miles.

. . . Able Seaman Conroy would've smiled a bit at that.

And Captain Jorgen Truls Halvorsen: a good man, but one who found himself confronted by a personal challenge when it came to questioning the fitness of his command to go to sea and failed to meet it?

Captain Halvorsen was neither called to give evidence before the Formal Investigation into the Loss of the Combined Passenger and Vehicle Ferry *Orion Venturer*, nor was he sanctioned as a result of it.

But that was only because, when Second Officer Sandalwell had finally managed to wedge the dying ro-ro's siren button down to sound the, this time continuous, blood-chilling bellow that was the signal to abandon ship – and run back out to the starboard bridge wing, he found his Captain slumped with back against the rail and eyes devoid of awareness: incapable of either speech or movement.

He had suffered a catastrophic stroke. Even now he sits stare-eyed in a wheelchair and nobody knows – or perhaps nobody can imagine – what horrors, what dreadful spectres of guilt, the Captain replays over and over in his locked mind.

But one thing is beyond doubt. The *Orion Venturer* killed Jorgen Truls Halvorsen in all but the actuality, just as surely as she killed his trusting charges.

The ship – or, more particularly, those who designed her, and managed her, and inspected her, and sailed her . . . and above all, her elusive tiers of corporate owners who'd placed profit before responsibility. The last so protected by their flags of convenience, hidden within their international legal maze, that it's unlikely they'll ever be brought to account.

When she finally sank on tow, some six hours after all the living were gone from her, she went quietly and without fuss. Almost as if ashamed at what she'd done. Or what she'd been forced to become.

Oh, she made a bit of a dramatic sight surrounded by ships and hopeful salvage tugs playing water onto her red hot decks, with the fresh white paint that had hidden a multitude of sins peeling from her hull, and a pall of smoke black as an undertaker's hat streaming out of her for half a mile across the Skaggerak before it blew to pieces in the wind.

Until the VHFs on a dozen-plus bridges crackled, and an urgent voice warned: *All ships – All ships – Immediate! Ferry down: ferry down! Slip tows and stand clear. We see the ferry going DOWN . . . !*

Next thing she listed a bit to starboard with the steam belching out of the crack in her . . . then, as the water built up a free surface effect on her vehicle deck – thundering and cataracting from side to side – she sort of recovered a moment with a sigh of agony . . . then rolled a good thirty degrees to port before coming back vertical again – only she didn't stop there: she kept on rolling this time, until the roll became a list and the list became a capsize, and her starboard heat-blackened slab side hit the angry sea . . .

. . . and then all the seamen on all the decks of all the ships that were hurriedly shying from her death throes heard her cry aloud as water forced air up through ventilation shafts and ducts and exhaust pipes and sounding pipes and – just for a moment of exquisite harmony – turn them all into one giant theatre organ which wailed forth the most terrible, the most emotive lament a sailorman will ever hear . . .

And then she was topsy-turvy, with the seas crashing and threshing and desperate to get a hold of her at last, while tons of water briefly trapped along her flat keel poured and rumbled outboard: white-contrasting against her scarred, once-red anti-fouling and cascading from her stilled, shiny-bronze twin pro-pellers.

She floated for a while, then, with a gentle curtsey as befits a once proud lady, albeit an indigent one now, dipped her stern in final salute . . . and her inverted bow rose up until it was pointing to the grey sky, and you could hear the *crash* and *bang* of lorries and cars and trailers tumbling monstrously, higgledy-piggledy down inside her . . . .

Whereupon the steam – a volcano-full of steam – formed a wreath on the North Sea, into which her bow began to slide. Slipping faster and faster. Gathering an awesome momentum . . .

. . . and the *Orion Venturer* was gone.